D0891620

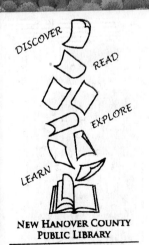

THE COLLECTED STORIES OF
DIANE WILLIAMS

ALSO BY DIANE WILLIAMS

This Is About the Body, the Mind, the Soul,
the World, Time, and Fate

Some Sexual Success Stories Plus Other Stories
in Which God Might Choose to Appear

The Stupefaction

Excitability: Selected Stories 1986–1996

Romancer Erector

It Was Like My Trying to Have a Tender-Hearted Nature

Vicky Swanky Is a Beauty

Fine, Fine, Fine, Fine, Fine

THE COLLECTED STORIES OF
DIANE WILLIAMS

SOHO

Jacket painting reproduced with permission from
The Croatian Museum of Naïve Art and Damir Rabuzin:
Ivan Rabuzin *On the Hills – Primeval Forest*, 1960, oil on canvas, 692 x 1167 mm,
Collection: The Croatian Museum of Naïve Art, Zagreb, Croatia.

Published by Soho Press, Inc.
853 Broadway New York, NY 10003

Library of Congress Cataloging-in-Publication Data

Williams, Diane.
Title: The collected stories of Diane Williams / Diane Williams ;
introduction by Ben Marcus.
I. Title.
PS3573.I44846 A6 2018 813'.54—dc23 2018027943

ISBN 978-1-61695-982-1
eISBN 978-1-61695-983-8

Interior design by Janine Agro, Soho Press, Inc.

Printed in the United States of America

10 9 8 7 6 5 4 3 2 1

CONTENTS

v

SOME SEXUAL SUCCESS STORIES PLUS
OTHER STORIES IN WHICH GOD MIGHT
CHOOSE TO APPEAR (1992)

THE STUPEFACTION (1996)

—◦—

ROMANCER ERECTOR (2001)

IT WAS LIKE MY TRYING TO HAVE A TENDER-HEARTED NATURE (2007)

———

NEW STORIES

ON DIANE WILLIAMS BY BEN MARCUS

Diane Williams has spent her long, prolific career concocting fictions of perfect strangeness, most of them no more than a page long. She's a hero of the form: the sudden fiction, the flash fiction, whatever it's being called these days. The stories are short. They defy logic. They thumb their nose at conventional sense, or even unconventional sense. But if sense is in short supply in these texts, that leaves more room for splendor and sorrow. These stories upend expectations and prize enigma and the uncanny above all else. The Williams epiphany should be patented, or bottled—on the other hand, it should also be regulated and maybe rationed, because it's severe. It's a rare feeling her stories trigger, but it's a keen and deep and welcome one, the sort of feeling that wakes us up to complication and beauty and dissonance and fragility. It's a sensation we can only get by reading (that's the only place I've ever found it), and once you've had it you want to keep having it again and again. This feeling avows the complexity of life, it does not flinch from our harder suspicions about how vulnerable and brutal our enterprise is. Such work feels—I don't know how else to say it—brave. It is difficult to encounter the world as it is experienced by Diane Williams, but this difficulty seems necessary.

So how does she do it? What is this literary approach? What is her trick?

Williams' unusual literary method reveals the thin rigging of most narrative, and then deploys that rigging to make spectacular shapes—abstract, maybe, or realistic, who can say? Every shape is abstract in the end, and every shape is familiar and intimate in the right context. Yes, she's using the tools of narrative, and her language often is plain in that it sounds spoken rather than labored-over and page bound. There's a Dick and Jane quality to the prose, if Dick and Jane had been forcibly drowned and then brought back to life, maybe starved for a while, induced with madness but warned, at pain of death, to conceal it.

The conventional narrative tools Williams uses to bring her fiction to life are disfigured here. It would seem that she's melted them down and made them into new weapons. Sharper, weirder, more brutal. They get the job done and they make a kind of bloodsport out of the domestic scenes she so often creates. We recognize this sort of fictional material—families in crisis, romantic partners at each other's throats—but there is so much that is creepily detuned, so much that is just alien and odd. These mad, unsettling texts wear the costume of short fiction but that costume has been torn up and sewn back together. A stitch-work disguise, a masquerade. Is it poetry, what she does? Is it prose, is it magic, is it biological weaponry? Is it real, is it a sham? Well, yes to all of these questions. Yes, I think so.

These are some of the most defiantly resistant texts (resistant to easy understanding, I mean) that I have read, even while they seduce and beckon. They are intimate and dark and intense, often, but they remain cryptic and removed, as if they are being told in a language we don't quite speak, or as if they are driven by a deeper code that we can't crack, a code that governs the composition of these stories and determines what they will be and how they will operate.

I've been a pusher of Diane Williams' work since her first book came out in 1990. You'd think I would have developed a slicker pitch about it by now, a quicker sell. You'd think. But woe to anyone who tries to summarize the uncanny attacks on reason that constitute this body of work. And yet it is still tempting to try to make sense of it all, not just because most of us are doomed to hunt for sense, to douse ourselves with certainties and clear points and meaning. It's that the stories themselves flirt so wickedly with sense but rarely quite build it, rarely quite commit to an entirely coherent scene or moment in narrative time. This is part of the shock to reading Diane Williams for the first time. Her stories end so soon after they've begun, and we readers are thrust back into ourselves to wonder and worry. What was that we just read? What did it mean? What happened? What was it about? Each sentence becomes a piece of evidence, designed to mislead as much as it is designed to clarify. On the one hand these stories would seem to give so little, at least in the quantitative sense. Yet how is it that they resonate so profoundly? How is it that they endure?

Well, I don't know. I just don't, and this ignorance does not really trouble me, because it does not keep me from a profound enjoyment of this work. These stories matter because they derail us from our expected feelings and belief, and in so doing put us face-to-face with our world, undisguised. These stories work the way art does: with great mystery, and, you know, why do we need to mess around with that?

It could help to say what these damn things are about. They are about people. Foolish, foolish people. In other words, all of us. The stories chart the kind of behaviors we show the world when our desires get the better of us. Desperation is on terrible display, and who is not a culprit when it comes to rash acts? These stories are comedies of manners, or tragedies of the absence of manners. They document desire gone wrong, which is to say that they document desire. In a Diane Williams story there is frequently a narrator who surprises herself, who comes to revelations as if by accident, and who encounters the world at large with awe and wonder. Wisdom is rarely handed down by a narrator. It is stumbled across, discovered accidentally, or missed entirely. Wisdom is in the next room. Innocence and confusion reign supreme, but these states are always one thought away from some kind of difficult revelation, and it is this territory that Williams stakes out as her own. The threshold before understanding.

What's often slippery and mysterious in a Diane Williams story are not the individual sentences—although these can be stunning, and indeed they traffic in sharp and unexpected syntax—but the eerie and sometimes inscrutable transitions between the sentences. This is where wild leaps take place, where logic falters and gives way to something more impressionistic and disruptive. We can't help but look for one thing to lead to another, and here one thing does lead to another, but it's such a funny another, such an unexpected one, that the result is often bracing and can be wholly, deliciously disorienting. In a Diane Williams story, we think we know something, but we certainly don't know the next sentence, and it's an uncertainty that Williams exploits to great effect.

Stories are a strange term for what Diane Williams writes. We might not read them for plot or sequence or narrative, exactly, even though those things rear up sometimes. In the earlier stories especially there is a kind of narrative continuity, an adherence to plot. But not so far into her career she tinkered with the machine, and the texts took a turn toward the cryptic. I used to think she was making prepared texts from unexpected source material: turn of the century gardening books or etiquette manuals, that sort of thing. Found texts. Now I'm not so sure. And the truth here might not matter. Even if there is found language afoot, Williams had to unearth it, and she had to put it in the order we now hold in our hands. It's been masked and cut up and proofed far beyond recognition, resulting in something that is her very own. She saw something in the language that no other writer could see.

In many of these stories, a character speaks, something happens, objects in a room are described. But Williams is so restrained and selective that we see just slivers of her world, and soon enough she brings down a kind of hammer and the story has ended. The abruptness and anticlimactic quality of some of her endings can be challenging, but it asks us to reflect in different ways, to feel resonance where we may not have initially been alert to it. It is tricky for a writer to end such short texts. One expects that there would be a temptation for revelation, a lowering of the boom, and this happens now and again in a Diane Williams story. But sometimes too these endings misbehave and chart an unsettled space that is rarely explored in fiction.

In the end maybe these stories enact the dark impossibility of true understanding. They show us how little we can know, how doomed we are when we seek absolute comprehension. Yes, they are funny and manic and unexpectedly entertaining, but beneath their antics rests a grim view of human congress, a kind of inevitable despair around life among people. However much we puzzle over these stories, Diane Williams knows perfectly well what she's doing, and that's perhaps all we can ask of a wholly original literary artist.

THE COLLECTED STORIES OF
DIANE WILLIAMS

THIS IS ABOUT
THE BODY, THE MIND,
THE SOUL, THE WORLD,
TIME, AND FATE
(1990)

LADY

She said *please*. Her face looked something more than bitter, with hair which it turned out was a hat, which came down over her ears, which was made of fake fur, which she never removed from her head. She had glasses on. Everything she wore helped me decide to let her in.

She wore flat black patent-leather shoes with pointed toes, with black stockings, wrinkled at the ankles, with silver triangles set in on top of the toes of the shoes to decorate them, and she had on a long black coat, and she was shorter than I am.

Her skin was a bleak sort of skin, and there was no beauty left in her—maybe in her body.

I felt that this lady is fast, because she was at the place where I keep my red rotary-dial phone before I was, after I said, "The phone is in here."

She said, "I know the number."

Sitting on the arm of my sofa, she dialed while her knees were knocking into and tipping back onto two legs my too-small table, which my phone sits on, and my oversized brass lamp, which sits on the table too, with the huge shade, might have crashed. The lamp was clanging, ready to go. She got it back.

She said, *"Merla!"* into the phone receiver.

I knew it—she must have known it—Merla knew it too, that Merla was only a matter of one hundred to two hundred yards from my house, because this woman I had let in, she had told me right off the house number she was looking for. She was telling Merla that it was *impossible* to get to her, that there was no way on earth, that she had kept on running into this east-west street.

"A nice picture," she said to me. She had gotten herself up. She was looking at all of those men dressed for one of the dark-age centuries, marching through foliage, trekking around a hunched-up woman at a well, with their weird insignias on their chests, that nobody I know can figure out, with their faces—version after version of the same face.

She said, "I have a"—something something—"reproduction—" I cannot remember the dates or the royal reign to which she referred, when she was toying with this miniature chair that I have, grabbing it by its arm, and swiveling it on the clubbed foot of one leg, as she was leaving, after everything had been agreed upon with Merla. She would not be getting out of her car for Merla. Merla would meet her at the corner. Merla would.

She, the lady, must have been curious or put off by the jumble of dirty things at my front door that I suppose she first noticed when she was leaving, or by the splendor of my living room just off from the jumble. She missed going inside of it to see what was going on in each of the pictures in there.

What this woman had done to me was incalculable, and she had done it all in a period of time which had lasted no more than five minutes, which so many others have done, coming in here only for the telephone, because I had waved at her while she was shouting at Merla, I had said, "Would it help you to know the number of *this* house?"

Then I had told this little person my wrong address, not because I wanted to, nor because of any need on my part to make up a lie.

I said 2-7-0 which is way off the track, except for two digits, but I had rearranged them, the 7 and the 0, but I did not know I had done that. All that I knew was that I had done something unforgivably uncivil.

It was a lapse to reckon with. I took her into my arms, so that she could never leave me, and then jammed her up into the corner with the jumble by the front door and held her in there, exhausting myself to keep her in there. I didn't care. It hurt her more than it hurt me, to be a lady.

Violence is never the problem. Love at first sight is.

THE NATURE OF THE MIRACLE

The green glass bottle rolled into, rolled out of my arms, out of my hands, and then exploded, just as it should, when it hits our bluestone floor, and spreads itself, and sparkling water, on the territory it was able to cover from our refrigerator to the back door.

The bottle used to fit tightly in my hand, easily, by the neck, and the way one thing leads to another in my mind, this means I should run away from my marriage.

I should run to the man who has told me he does not want me. He does not even like me. Except for once he took me, and my head was up almost under his arm, my neck was, and my hand went up his back and down his back, and he copied what I did to him on my back with his hand, so that I would know what it would be like, I would have an idea, and then

I could run home to my marriage afterward, which is what I did before, after we were done with each other; and the way one thing leads to another in my mind, this means I should run to the man for more of it, but the way one thing leads to another, first I will tell my husband, "I would not choose you for a friend," then I will run to the other man, so that I can hear him say the same thing to me.

This is unrequited love, which is always going around so you can catch it, and get sick with it, and stay home with it, or go out and go about your business getting anyone you have anything to do with sick, even if all that person has done is push the same shopping cart you pushed, so that she can go home, too, and have an accident, such as leaning over to put dishwasher powder into the dishwasher, so that she gets her eye stabbed by the tip of the bread knife, which is drip-drying in the dish rack. It is a tragedy to lose my eye, but this heroism of mine lasted only a matter of moments.

ORGASMS

I swear I did not have anything of hers except for my dark idea of her which I have been keeping to myself until now.

Even better than catching my own husband in the act with her, I opened my mouth, but I left her probably forever, before I made a statement.

She was presiding with her face flattened by some shadow. Her shoulders and her arms, and all across the front of her also were gray which was what made the idea of her dark.

I saw the top half of her blotted out—more than half of what was behind her—nothing more, except some of her black hair curled away up into the—the way hair will, the way hers did. What of it?

If you care, it was like, like going by her like I was this big fish swallowing a big big fish whole, but because I am bigger, and what of it?

She kept on having orgasms with my husband.

The orgasms—where do they go?—crawling up into—as if they could have—up into—dying to get in, ribbed and rosy, I saw seashells were the color mouths should be, or the nipples of breasts, or the color for a seam up inside between legs, or, for I don't care where. Since they are pretty is why I collect them.

KILLER

Past the shimmering gewgaws on the velvet shoes at N-M, I went on by them, chasing two women, especially the one in the raccoon coat, who is glamorous—Marlene—my neighbor's new third wife—he had to have—a divorcee with five children, a convert from Catholicism for him for love—I was on her side. They are all so devout.

I adore I adore I adore—she should have said, I love only you, when she took what I had to give her away from me, because the sunglasses on the counter where I had just paid for my lunch might have been hers, and they *were* hers! She said something ecstatic and I hardly had to do anything, except ride back down the escalator, past pricey purses, veering nearly into jewels, and then into the jewels, where I said no, then on out the huge doors of N-M. I needed to go along over the black pavement, stamping and looking, and, bingo, with my instinct, I would see my car. Postponing the joy of getting into it, for what I would be doing next, I stood and took in the air, and looked around at so much air.

You know how it can hug you and kiss you all over because it is all over you anyway, and inside of me, and I was out there like a smoker—not to try to smother my lungs—just to have something to do with my fingers, and with my hands, and with my mouth, pressing them up against absolutely nothing at all, or aiming to get through it, when there is not a human being I know of who wants to do it with me, my feelings are hurt, when all they would have to do is bat their eyes at me and I would consider myself half the way there.

He doesn't have to stand on his head. Who cares what he does? I think my luck will hold for me. Yesterday they picked up Squeaky Fromme—two men did, after her breakout out of jail. Her being wanted, it didn't go on overly long.

ALL AMERICAN

The woman, who is me—why pretend otherwise?—wants to love a man she cannot have. She thinks that is what she should do. She should love a man like that. He is inappropriate for some reason. He is married.

When she thinks of the man, she thinks *force*, and then whoever has the man already is her enemy—which is the man's wife.

The woman makes sure the man falls in love with her. She has fatal charm. She can force herself to have it. Then she tells the man she cannot love him in return. She says, "You are in the camp with the enemy."

Of course, the woman knew the man was sleeping with the enemy before she ever tried to love him, and the word *enemy* gives joy—the same as I get when the wrong kind of person calls me *darling*, as when my brother says, "Okay," to me, "goodbye, darling," before he hangs up the phone, after we have just made some kind of pact, which is what we should do, because I have to force myself to love the ones I am supposed to love, and then I have to force myself on the ones I am not supposed to love.

I got my first real glimpse of this kind of thing when I was still a girl trying to force myself on my sister. I didn't know what I was doing until it was obvious. We were in the back seat of the family car. The car had just been pulled into the garage. The others got out, but we didn't. I thought I was not done with something. Something was not undone yet—something like that—and I was trying to kiss my sister, and I was trying to hug my sister, and she must have thought it was inappropriate, like what did I think I was a man and she was a woman?

I must have been getting rough, because she was getting hysterical. I remember I was surprised. I remember knowing then that I was applying force and was getting away with it.

THE UNCANNY

Her silver hair ornament was awfully big. I saw a great emerald-diamond ring. I saw the platter of steak tartare leave its position near me and then dive away into the party crowd on the back lawn. Then I saw my own husband having the meat on a Ritz cracker. I saw it in his hand next to his mouth. I drank my iced drink while it was changing color from a deep gold color that had satisfied me deeply to a gold color that certainly did not.

I asked Mrs. Gordon Archibald what she would have done with all of the people if it had rained. I gave her a suggestion for an answer she could give me which was an antisocial answer. She had a different antisocial answer for me of her own.

After this, my husband and I went off to a dinner club

where there was dancing, where a woman touched my earring. She got it to move, saying, "These are buckets!"

My husband said to me while I was swooning in his arms, "Why are all the longest dances the draggiest?"

I took this to mean that he has not loved me for a very long time. Everything means something, or it does not. I have expressed an opinion. Every effect has a source that is not unfamiliar. It's all so evil.

CLAUDETTE'S HEAD

Heddy had no baby. Then we saw Heddy pluck the baby out from somebody's arms. Heddy's face when she turned to us, holding the baby, exposed the feelings any competent woman of this century could have in my opinion. I didn't think it then, but I think it now.

Heddy brought the baby to us.

The baby was curled into her arm and into her breast, and was not crying. It was not at all one of those forlorn babies.

I have seen a face on a baby just after the delivery that made me think you could dress the baby up in a business suit and it could, just as it was, go to the office and run things splendidly. Not this baby. But this baby, which belonged to Heddy's sister, with its good nature, was reassuring to me, which meant absolutely the world at the time.

That's the moment I chose to tell Heddy's sister about the stranger-than-fiction newspaper account I had read the night before, when Heddy gave the baby back to her sister for its bottle.

I said, "Tell me if this surprises you," after I told her what the story was about. Heddy's sister Claudette is an emergency-care doctor, who selected that specialty, she had said, because she likes the variety and the surprise of it.

It probably was not fear I saw in Claudette. It was probably discomfort I saw. The baby probably had been stepping on her arm, pinching her, or scratching her, or something, when I said, "It's about a woman delivering her own baby—one of *those* stories."

Claudette said, "I am trying—" and by then she had the baby in a sitting posture in her lap, and she had the nipple of the bottle stuck into its mouth.

I don't even want to go into the gory details again of the newspaper story I told Claudette, of that woman giving birth in the airplane bathroom. Suffice it to say, the woman accomplished the birth undiscovered. She traveled then, afterward, unremarkably, from Newark to San Francisco, and the baby was lying under the sink for six more hours—but was not dead.

What I did was I pressured Claudette into saying the story surprised her, because I could tell she was not surprised. But I got her to say with a laugh, *"Any—"* and then I interrupted and filled in for her the rest, until she was shaking her head gaily, yes, yes. What I said was, "There never is any follow-up." I said, "These reports of women who squat in the field, who give birth, and then who carry on in the field with their work, these reports, they never mention for how long those women carry on. These women, down through the ages, could have dropped dead within minutes. Who does the follow-up?" I asked, does she, Claudette, do any follow-up at her hospital, after she gives these patients their emergency care, because Claudette had said she had to make a fast good guess about what was wrong with people. Claudette said she had to use common sense. Claudette said, "It is such a small community." She said, "You hear, and if you really care, you call, and you find out." About her baby, she said, "He always does this. He just plays." About me, of course, she didn't say. I didn't say a word about it either, because my husband was there with us also, listening to every word.

I am terrified I will be found out.

There was a downhill sweep of burnt lawn that I could see out the window behind Claudette's head, which led the eye to the grander blue sweep of a lake with sailboats on it and to the sky, which was not too much—all of it—to take in.

THE KIND YOU KNOW FOREVER

I had just met them—the brother and the sister who had fucked each other to see what it would be like. And then they said—either he said or she said—that it was like fucking a brother or a sister, so they never did it again.

That they had fucked each other was gossip intended to warn me away from the brother at the party where I watched the sister spread her legs carelessly, so that anyone—for instance, me—could look up her skirt to see darkness when she was sitting on the sofa.

Her husband was next to her—a thick man in a suit which was too small for him or was just under strain. The suit was ripped, I could see, under the arm at the seam. He had his arm up and around his wife, the sister who had fucked her brother.

I wondered if the husband knew, if he knew everything about her or not. I wondered as I watched her legs, her knees bump together, and then spread apart, and I kept my eye on him, while we were sitting around, but I forgot about the husband altogether while we ate. It was a fine meal we had.

And after that meal, the woman who had tried to warn me away from the brother took me aside. We went together from her kitchen to her bathroom. It was her party, and she led me there, and she closed the door. She said, "Look, you be careful." She said, "He's knocked up six girls."

And I said, "What does that mean?"

Then I saw how her long dark hair moved back and forth on either side of her head while she was moving her head, while her eyes were moving around, but not looking at me, while she was figuring me out. She said, "He got them all pregnant."

And I said, "And he didn't care what happened to them?"

"Yes. That's it," she said. "Now you be careful."

She must have known then her party was almost over, because there wasn't much time left after that. She handed out little wrapped gifts in such a hurry at the door, when we were all saying goodbye—it was such a hurry—I didn't get to see where she was getting all of her gifts from. All of a sudden there was just a gift in my hand, as I was going out the door. At the end of a party, I had never gotten a gift before, not since I was a girl, and then we thought we deserved those gifts. So now, something was turned around.

The gift she gave me was a cotton jewel pouch, in a bright shade of pink, made in India, which snapped shut.

I left the party with the sister-fucker. It was logical. We were near to the same age and we were both pretty for our kind, which must have mattered. Let me not forget to add that his sister was pretty, and that her husband was handsome, and that the woman who gave the party was pretty, and that her husband was handsome too.

The sister-fucker and I had both come to the party alone, and it was his idea that we should leave together. First we stopped at a bar, where we both had some drinks. I held onto a matchbook. I turned it by its four corners while he told me everything he was in the mood to tell me about his life, so that I felt I had known him forever.

Then I told him everything I was in the mood to tell him about my life—everything that mattered. I couldn't say now what that was. Then he said, "Write your phone number on the matchbook," which I did.

I asked him, "Should I write my name too?"

And he said, "No, not your name, just your number."

We were at the door in darkness ready to leave the bar when I gave him the matchbook. He gave me a kiss. He pressed hard on my mouth for the kiss and then I was waiting to see what would happen next.

I still see him backing away covered in the shadows. Then he pushed his hands up into his hair. One of his hands was still holding the matchbook so that the whole matchbook went up into it too, sliding under. He was pushing so hard up into his hair with both hands on either side of his head, that he was pulling the skin of his face up and back. He was turning his eyes into slits. He was making his nose go flat. His mouth at the corners was going up.

I didn't know if he was playing around with me, if he was angry, or if he was trying to figure something out. I didn't ask, What does that mean? Now I think it meant he really cared, but it never made a difference. I have fucked him and fucked him and fucked him, and I have felt all that hair on his head in my hands plenty of times.

THE HERO

My aunt was telling me about them coming to get them after I brought back the second helping of fish for me and the vegetables she asked for—the kind that have barely been cooked that look so festive, even with the film of dressing that dulls them down. I didn't want her to have to get up to get her own, not since she's been sick.

My aunt was saying, "They're going to get us. Hurry! Hurry! They're going to kill us!" after I put the vegetables down for her.

She said, "Your mother was a baby in my mother's arms."

She said, "I get out of breath now when I eat. Jule says I'm not the same since I was sick. He says to me, You've changed."

"You haven't changed," I said.

She said, "They had the wagon loaded. They had the cow. You know they had to take the cow to give the children milk to drink. They were going to hide! To hide! To hide in the woods! And then Jule said, I've got to go!

"Everything was loaded. They said, Hurry! They're coming! They're going to kill us! But Jule said, I've got to go! So they said, Do it! Do it! Hurry! So then Jule said, But I need *the pot!*"

"He said that?" I said. "I never heard that story. Does my mother know that story?"

My aunt smiled, which I took then to be no. And my mother wasn't there, so I couldn't rush to her, I couldn't tell her, Do you know the story about your family? How you were going to be killed? How Uncle Jule stopped everything to go?

Uncle Jule appeared then. He was wearing a white golf hat.

My aunt said, *"You could put it in your hat."* She said that to Jule. I don't remember why she said that—*You could put it in your hat.*

He must have said something first to her about her vegetables—could he take home what she wasn't going to eat? Maybe that was it—but it doesn't matter.

Uncle Jule was blinking and smiling when she said, *You could put it in your hat.* He was blinking faster than anyone needs to blink.

Cauliflower was what my aunt left on her plate. It looked to me like some bleached-out tree.

TEN FEET FROM IT

His body shifts and gets closer to me in a shady part of our house where hardly any natural light can get to, unless a bathroom door is open fully. At no time during this is he more than two or three feet away from me, and always he keeps turning to me so I can see how he is, not to prove anything to me. He is not the kind to do that. I am.

He is my son, one of them.

My other son broke down for me later in this day, my husband the same, a few days ago, my brother later in this day. My mother said to me, "I am not with it," just after we both witnessed my brother.

I can put the sight of any of them up in front of myself again anytime I want to: my son in grief because I would not believe that he really is; my other son the same; my husband, when he told me, "That broke the ice," after what I had said to him—whatever it was; my brother, as he was telling me his life is at stake.

My mother, her grief is the most overwhelming.

She was sitting with her Old Testament which has such tissue-thin pages and she was making the pages make a noise when I found her.

The biggest, broadest window of her house was in front of her, where she was sitting with the open book. I have the same dark red leather-bound version of the text.

I said to my mother, "Let me kiss you." I was up close to her, my hands on her forearms to get closer to her, but I did not get closer. For some reason she was standing at that time, perhaps to let me try, and then she was down, sitting at the desk which had been my desk when I was a girl.

She was looking at the shake-shingled roof, at the plum tree, at the trees all pushed together beyond it, at the violent plunging-down that our land takes below that window where one of my sons killed himself, because he was trying to keep my other sons from killing themselves, just about ten feet from the plum tree. He was shouting at those boys, or he was talking softly to those boys, who were talking softly to him, so all of them had to lean so far over to hear what they had to hear, so one of them could die.

It is just a sight with the body of my mother in front of it.

I can refer to the window glass. I can refer to the sky which might as well be the sea.

I go down the stairs of my mother's house, satisfied and slowly.

I cannot get a sight up in front of me now of little boys or of grown-ups together, so that I can hear what they are saying, so that I would want to repeat what it was they were saying, so that what they have said would change everything once and for all.

DROPPING THE MASTERS

There was a clatting sound, for all this kissing, for all this copulation. My boys could get those Masters of the Universe up and onto the dresser top in one swoop up—*a kiss to the bride! a kiss to the bride!*—it was the only way they got them married, the way my youngest boy had decided they should get them married. One swoop down and then they could rock a pair and make those Masters copulate just as long as they wanted them to. Until I let my boys see me so that I saw the faces of I'm hot and I'm caught, and I saw the faces of this has got to stop—that's the way I saw them when they were stopping, when a hand was up with a Master, when a boy the height of our dog begging was up on his knees like he was handing out a bone.

I was going nowhere after I stopped them, just down the

hall toward the bathroom, just stuck almost at the end of the top of our house so that of course I didn't want to stay there where I had no business being or intention, where I felt stupid and strange almost in the bathroom. Now their door was shut so that I could hear the sound of them, but I could get no meaning. I could hear rough scrubbing and more clatting and not know anything about it at all. But I was back in front of the shut door of their room and there was nowhere else I wanted to be more than watching again or just to know what they knew—to know everything about what they knew and so that is where I stood.

So then I opened their door.

But this time the stopping was not like the stopping before, it was an altogether different kind of stopping. This was how dare you with the Masters being deeply ground down I thought maybe so they would break because these Masters break.

What I got to see then was the sluggishness of let's do another thing—the turning away and then the boys hopping the Masters and then dropping them.

These Masters weren't broken, they were only done—and my boys were walking out on me, finished.

THERE SHOULD BE
NOTHING REMARKABLE

There should be nothing remarkable about reading a lovey-dovey Hallmark card out loud to your old father, nothing, please bear with me, as bad as the hope that you are being smuggled into the United States, so that you can be a restaurant hostess, and then you end up in a brothel, as a slave, in New York, San Francisco, or Colorado—or nothing, let me go further boldly, as remarkable as the difference between announcing this notion of extreme affection with words which are not your own, and the fate of a poor girl, which might be the same, if you would indulge me wildly, as the difference between a duck! which my father asked me about when I was a girl.

Perhaps it wasn't his own question—original with him— "What's the difference between a duck?"—but I worked on it as if it were, not even hopelessly. Right away, in my mind, I'd search those webbed feet, or my eyes would rise up the white neck of the duck, ever so slowly, alert for the presto change-o, so I could be the first one to tell him what the difference was. I am sure I tried to tell him. I don't remember the words.

I have seen the photograph of this act, of my father waiting for me. The envelope is cocked, the card is on the way out, my hand is on it, and I am positively demure with my eyes cast shyly down. I think he waits the way the beauty would wait—imagining—"This way," her own elegance, "please," so correctly distant, so that those prospective eaters could worship her from any distance, before, during, or after being led off.

Speaking for myself, the worst fate I can imagine would be a restaurant job of any kind. I don't think my attitude about that will change, ever, unless I have become near dead with hunger—wasted—but in that case, I could not get a real job. You must look the part of a worker to get yourself paid, and isn't money very much to the point? or what is it which is the root of all evil—how you sign yourself away? physical beauty? *You be my slave*—you throw yourself at somebody's feet—*I am yours*—it is so cozy, what I have done. It is my idea of family.

BABY

Nobody was getting up close to me, whispering, "Do you get a lot of sex?" Nobody was making my mouth fall open by running his finger up and down my spine, or anything like that, or talking dirty about dirty pictures and did I have those or anything like those, so I could tell him what I keep— what I have been keeping for so long in my bureau drawer underneath my cable-knit pink crew—so I could tell him what I count on happening to me every time I take it out from under there. Because it was a baby party for one thing, so we had cone paper hats and blowers, so we had James Beard's mother's cake with turquoise icing, and it was all done up inside with scarlet and pea-green squiggles, and the baby got toys.

Nobody was saying, "Everybody has slept with my wife, because everybody has slept with everybody, so why don't we sleep together?" so I could say at last, "Yes, please. Thank you for thinking of me." I would be polite.

Just as it was nothing out of the ordinary when the five-year-old slugged the eleven-year-old on the back and they kept on playing, looking as if they could kill for a couple of seconds. We didn't know why. And then the baby cried in a bloodthirsty way.

My husband sat stony-faced throughout. I don't think he moved from his chair once. What the fuck was wrong with him? He left the party early, without me; he said to get a little— I don't know how he was spelling it—I'll spell it *peace.*

I spoke to a mustached man right after my husband left. He was the first man all night I had tried to speak to. I know he loves sports. I said to him, "I think sports are wonderful. There are triumphs. It is so exciting. But first, you have to know what is going on."

Then my boy was whining, "Mom, I want to go home." He was sounding unbearably tired.

The baby's aunt said she'd take us. She didn't mind. She had to back up her car on the icy drive. She said, "I don't know how we'll get out of here," when we got into the car. "The windows are all fogged up." She said, "I don't think I can do it." She opened the window and poked her head out. She said, "I don't think so."

When she closed the window, we went backward terrifically fast. I don't know how she knew when to spin us around into the street. It was like being in one of those movies I have seen the previews for. It was like watching one of those faces on those people who try to give you the willies. It was like that, watching her—while she tried to get us out.

CLOUD

How it was in the aftermath of it, was that her body was in the world, not how it had ever been in the world before, in her little room or in *their* rooms—the people who owned the rooms—or at least were managing the rooms, their hallways, or the stairwell, which was not hers either, that she went through and through and through. A man laughed at her for what she had said, and then someone had brought her to this bed.

She looked at the bed stacked high with so many coats and she decided, It all stops here.

She was clearing up to be helpful before she left, steering herself, when she saw her purse go flying and then it fell down into a corner.

She was down too, walloped by a blow, by some man, and she thought, I understand. She thought, This is easy. She thought, It's as easy as my first fuck. She had opened up so wide.

In the street, crossing to go home, her purse swung on her arm by its strap. She thought the dark air was so soft to walk through.

And for all that the girl knew there had not been a jot on her when she looked—no proof JACK WAS HERE! on her skin in red and in bright green ink, with any exclamation she could see, about them doing things, or about any one of them being of the opinion that her tits sucked.

And for the rest of her life, the girl, the woman, she never made a mark on anyone either that proved anything absolutely for certain, that she could ever see, about what she had done at any time, and this does not break her heart.

FORTY THOUSAND DOLLARS

When she said forty thousand dollars for her diamond ring, where did I go with this fact? I followed right along with her, hoping, hoping for a ring like hers for myself, because of what I believe deep down, that she is so safe because she has her ring, that she is as safe as her ring is big—and so is her entire family—her husband who gave her the ring, all of her children—and no one has ever tried to talk me out of believing this fact, because I would never speak of it, that the entire quality of her life is totally secure because of the size of that ring—that the ring is a complete uplift—that every single thing else about her is up to the standard the size of her ring sets, such as even her denim espadrilles, which I love, which she was wearing the day she was talking to me, or her gray hair pulled back, so serene, so that she is adored, so that she is everlastingly loved by her husband, and why not?—just look at her!—and she is loved by her children, and by everyone like me who has ever laid eyes on her and her ring.

She was waggling it, which I loved her to do, because I loved to see it move, to see it do anything at all, and she said, "I make my meat loaf with it." She said, "I like that about it, too," and I saw the red meat smears she was talking about, smearing up the ring the way they would do, the bread all swollen up all over it, all over the ring part and the jewel. I saw my whole recipe on that ring.

She said, "It goes along with me to take out my garbage, and I like that," and I saw what she meant, how it would take out the garbage if it were taking it out with me, how it would go down with me, down the steps and out the back door—the ring part of the ring buried in the paper of the bag—and the dumping we would do together of the bag into the sunken can, before the likelihood of a break or a tear, or maybe I'd have to step on top of a whole heap of bags that was already down in there and then stamp on the top of the heap myself, to get it all deep down, to get the lid on with the ring on.

She said, "I never knew I was going to get anything like it. All that Harry said was, 'We'll need a wheelbarrow for you *and* the ring when you get it.' A wheelbarrow!" she said. "But now don't worry," she said to me. "You'll get one someday, too. Somebody will die," she said, "then you'll get yours—" Which is exactly what happened—I never had to pay money for mine, and mine ended up to be even bigger than hers. "This much bigger—" I showed her with two fingers that I almost put together, the amount, which is probably at least another carat more, but mine is stuck inside an old setting and cannot be measured. That was the day I walked behind her, that I showed her, that I walked with her to her car when she was leaving my house.

The rings were of no account outside, when we were saying goodbye, when we were outside my house going toward the back side of her car, because we were not looking at the rings then. The heels of her denim espadrilles, which matched her long, swinging skirt, were going up and down, so was her strong ponytail, and her shoulders, and I wanted to go along with her to wherever she was going.

And then the sense I had of not being able to stay behind her—of not being able to see myself in my own clothes walking away—the sense I had that I was not where I was, that I could not possibly follow in my own footsteps, was gone.

PORNOGRAPHY

I just had a terrible experience—I'm sorry. I was yelling at my boy, "Don't you ever!" I saw this crash. I saw this little old man. The door of the car opened and I saw this little old man tottering out. Somebody said, "I saw him!" The same somebody said, "He's already hit two cars."

There was this kid. He wasn't a kid. He was about nineteen. He was screaming and screaming on a bicycle.

Then I saw him, the kid, on the stretcher.

That little old man did more for me than any sex has ever done for me. I got these shudders.

The same thing with another kid—this one tiny, the same thing, on a stretcher, absolutely quiet in a playground, and I was far enough away so that I did not know what had happened. I never found out. Same thing, shudders that I tried to make last, because I thought it would be wonderful if they would last for at least the four blocks it took me to get home and they were lasting and then I saw two more boys on their bicycles looking to get hit, not with any menace like they wanted to *do* anything to me, because I wasn't even over the white crossing line, not yet, and the only reason I saw either one of them was because I was ready to turn and I was looking at the script unlit yellow neon *l* on the cleaner's marquee which was kitty-corner to me, when just off that *l* I saw the red and the orange and my driver's leg struck up and down hard on the brake without my thinking, even though I think I was ready to go full out at that time, because where was I going, anyway? back home to my boy?

My car was rocking, the nose of it, against the T-shirts of those boys, first the red one, and then the orange one, and they each of them, they looked me in the eye.

Back home, my boy, he's only five, he's going to show me, making himself into a bicycle streak down our drive, heading, he says, for my mother's house, heading for that dangerous curve where so many horrible accidents have happened or have almost happened. What I did was yell at him DON'T YOU DO THAT! but he was already off, and then this goddamn little thing, this animal, this tiny chipmunk thing races with all its stripes right up at me, but not all the way *to* me, and then the thing, it whips around and runs away, like right now with my boy—I can't—there is no other way to put it—I *can't come.*

HERE'S ANOTHER ENDING

This time my story has a foregone conclusion.

It is true also.

After I tell the story, I say, "You could start a religion based on a story like that—couldn't you?"

The story begins with my idea of a huge dog—a Doberman—which is to me an emblem—cruel, not lovable.

The dog is a household pet in a neighborhood such as mine, with houses with backyards which abut.

The huge dog is out and about when it should not be. It should never be.

When the dog returns to its owners, it is carrying in its mouth a dirty dead rabbit.

The dog's owners exclaim—one of them does—"The neighbor's rabbit! He's killed it!" The dog's owners conclude,

"We must save our dog's reputation at all costs." They think, Our dog is in jeopardy.

The dog's owners shampoo the dead rabbit and dry it with a hair dryer. At night, they sneak the rabbit back into their neighbor's yard, into its cage.

The morning of the following day, the dog's owners hear a shriek from the rabbit owners' yard. They think, Oh! The dead rabbit has been discovered! They rush to see what's what.

One of the rabbit's owners—the father in the family—is holding the limp, white rabbit up in the air. He says to the dog's owners, "We buried her two days ago!"

The dog's owners explain nothing. They won't, but not because they are ashamed of themselves.

There is another, more obvious reason.

MY FEMALE HONOR IS OF A TYPE

I did some V last night of a kind I have not done before. I gave myself permission. I said to myself calmly in my mind—on this occasion I will give you permission to do the following— listen carefully to yourself: you are allowed to cut up your husband's money which is on his bureau top, just the single bills, there are not too many of them; cut up his business card which is in his card case, and then cut up a folded piece of paper—you do not know what it is. There, you are cutting paper.

He gave me permission when he saw me, even, even when he saw me leafing through big bills with the scissors and the card case, flipping to choose, and sorting the paper, the opportunity for cutting.

The occasion for this V which I permitted and which my husband permitted was anger of a type.

I said to her, "*You should fear for your life!*" Tonight I said, "Tell *them* you feared for it!" Whereas my husband would have left. He would have walked out mildly and back to home.

They say so, and then their head is in your vision, only their spooky eyes, or their bony nose shaking, not even their mouth is in your vision because you are too close, maybe some of this someone's platinum hairs mixed up with silver and brown and white, and pale pale yellow hairs, antiseptic hairs is what I call it, clean out of grease or refuse.

But not the hairs on *her* head, not the crisply cut card with the credentials she put for me to see, hairy letters on a hairy card, the card of someone who ran the whole show, that I could not even see the name, because of hair, nor did I want to.

"*You've got what you wanted!*" she said, so that all the hairs were not enough hairs, or the telephone in the bag she gave me, the black phone. All the hairs were not like the hairs on *her* head which she pinned up or she pulled down which she waved, which she lustered fully out. All the little rings on the black cord to put your finger in, to hold your finger, all the little rings that stretch to ringlets, all the twirlies.

We left. It was between her and her. The husband and the mild-mannered boy behind her, and the husband did not play key roles. We ran the show and when I left something did die, a little something, and later on she will know something teeny keeled. I took that teeny thing, and the fat phone in the fat bag. I took the teeny tiny pathetic, that can climb in between hairs all by itself, that can lay down their eggs to hatch.

I would not do murder for a phone. I would do it for hair.

GLASS OF FASHION

My mother touched the doctor's hair—"Your hair—" she said. I was looking at the doctor's eyes—black and as sad as any eyes I had ever looked at—doleful, mournful—but I thought she is hard-hearted too, this doctor. She must be hardhearted. Hard-hearted is part of her job. It has to be.

The doctor's hair was full and long and down, kinky and wavy and black. My mother's hair is short and white and kinky and wavy and I could see why my mother was admiring her hair. I was admiring the doctor's body in her jeans. She had what I thought was a girlish and perfect form in her jeans, an enviable form.

There were four of us backed up to the large window at the end of the hall, because I had said, "Let's go over to the window to talk"—my mother, my sister, and me, and this very young woman doctor with black hair, black eyes, and jeans on.

We were at the window at the hospital, at the end of a hall, down from what was left of my father. We were getting the report on my father, because I had said to the doctor, "Tell us."

Maybe the doctor was a little ashamed too, or belligerent, when she was telling us. Her eyes had such a film over them, so that they sparkled when she spoke of his cerebellum, about his brain stem, about the size of his cortical function. She said, "He doesn't know who he is. He does not know who he once was. He does not feel grief or frustration. He does not know who you are." What I was envying then were the doctor's legs in her jeans. "Maybe—" I said, "you know, maybe—he had such a big brain before—it is just possible," I said, "that even if his brain has been ravaged, he is still a smart enough person."

The doctor did not say anything about that. No one did.

Chrissy, one of Dad's day-shift nurses, was coming along then toward us. Her glasses are the kind my sister will not wear. She will not get glasses like that. My mother will not either. A serious person's glasses—even if Chrissy is only just a nurse, even if she cannot explain very much about the brain, because she explained to me she has been out of school for too long—I can tell she is serious, that she is serious about me too. If she were a man, I would call what we have shared romantic love—we have shared so much, so often here—talking about my father with feeling. If she were a man—even if she couldn't remember half of what she had learned about the brain—even if she had forgotten it all—no—if she had forgotten it all, totally, I don't think I'd want to spend the time of day in her presence. She would disgust me if she were a man like that. So when she called us, when she said, "Your father—" and then when I called "Dad! Dad!" from the—and it sounded even to me as if I expected he would rise up—then I was ready for what I was feeling when I touched his forehead—which was still warm. His mouth was open. The front of the lower row of his teeth was showing. The teeth had never looked, each of them, so terribly small. Some of his teeth were the last things on my father that I ever touched.

PASSAGE OF THE SOUL

———◆———

S he said, "Don't get excited," to the scar-faced man.
He was excited, more like agitated. I remembered lots of
men I have been with being like that. It was a worry. Maybe he
was someone who shouldn't have been out.

She said, "We don't have to stay," and then I saw him in
the snack line, way behind me, stuck in the heavy crowd, from
where another woman's voice scolded somebody, "You had to
pick the most popular picture of all the pictures!" Next, I found
my husband. I always can. He goes ahead without me for the
seats.

We hardly speak in theaters, waiting. I twisted myself
around to watch a girl behind us feed her boyfriend one popped
kernel of corn, and then kiss him, and I saw him touch her
breast, because we had to wait and wait, even for the previews

to begin. I decided her boyfriend was no one I would want touching from, and I didn't flinch; he did, when I watched him watch me make my decision. It was as if he couldn't believe it, that he couldn't believe it—that I would judge him with such haste.

I would have run off with the character named Tom in the movie, so that they could see once and for all, as he put it to the woman, how they would be together, away from all of *this*. She ended up unappealing. She must have had a moment of horror—the actress—when she first saw herself like that.

At one time, seven years earlier in the movie, it seemed the whole audience had heaved a huge sigh watching her—not me, I just listened—I never would want to let on what I was thinking, You are so bold and lucky, when she dropped the prophylactics into her purse before she went out, and I was eager to see what would happen.

There are so many other things to recount about that movie. I left the theater with our balled-up empty popcorn bucket in my hand, to throw it away at home: that's what I was thinking about on the way to our car, that I'd have to hold it in my hand, which I did, feeling it, the squashed-up waxy rim of the bottom of it, all the way home; that somehow I had ended up like this. I had missed, just to begin with, the opportunity to throw it away inside the theater.

When we were getting ready for bed, I got myself into sort of a state. I saw that my husband was wearing what I considered to be the trousers of my pajamas—I have only one pair—which I had planned to put on, which had belonged to him once long ago, it's true, but hadn't he given them to me?

"What do you think you're doing?" I asked him. "I don't get it. What are you doing?"

I saw him, his body, his bare chest, which is sleek and perfectly formed by my standards—he was pulling down and folding the spread of our bed, in those cotton striped trousers. My husband is so graceful, how he moved around the foot of the bed was so graceful, how he gently, carefully folded.

Oh, he gave me back the trousers; so then we slept.

I didn't know what the issue was.

When the ringing of the telephone woke us in the night, we both knew what it could mean—everybody does—or it could have been just somebody borderline, wanting to hear the sound of anyone in a fright. That's what it was that time.

More will happen.

It will be stunning.

It's what I'm waiting for.

Some people are lucky—just walking, just going around, when you look at them.

ORIGINAL BELIEF

I was thinking, Would someone else's husband—*not mine!*—would Nancy Harp's husband want the woman?

To make a judgment I thought, do I want her?

Oh, yes!

When her cutaway shirt buckled and slid, I saw the perky, side-view form of her naked breast.

Nancy Harp's husband, I thought, must be beside himself all the time with this woman—and she was straight-legged, and she intended for her face to be pretty, and it was!

The Harps' whole kitchen, where I met the woman—their Formica getting all the sun—the wood floor, when I looked down, I thought, *It must be cherry!* was driving me crazy.

Oh, I knew the woman was a do-nothing maid. Her employer, Nancy—and Nancy is my friend—told me she does not allow this maid to cook. Nancy said she told the maid, "I do that!" when the maid had said, "I could do that."

While I watched her, the maid went this way or she went that way, ever so lightly on her bare feet. She was not upset. But, she may have considered the possibilities to share with me, because neither my son, nor any member of the Harp family, was on the premises, and they should have been when I got there.

At the stairs, she called, "*Davey!*"

It could be a blessing that I was not worried, to not know what she did not understand, because there was the problem of the language problem.

She did say, "Who are you?" so I said, "The mom."

I underscored *naughty* about Davey because he should have been there at the Harps'. He said he would.

I was safe and she was safe, including Davey, with my *naughty*.

Something about cute and safe means the same thing to me. But I didn't stop there. I got myself degraded.

THE SPOILS

The girl did not know why the boys were looking for her when she was spoiling herself—what to her was a spoiling—why the boys inside from the garden party in the hall of her house were banging on the locked door to get to her. She knew who they were. They were her guests.

The girl had not yet spoiled herself—but when she was full of it—full to bursting—she broke out of there. She broke out of there to get to those boys.

Now none of them had to break in or out of anywhere because now they were meeting in the hall of her house.

With one stroke in the hall of her house, for those boys, slipping suddenly out, she left her spoils for them—neatly coiled. She looked to see.

It was the tops of their heads, the three tops of their

heads that she saw, because those boys were looking to see too.

Then the girl was going back out to more guests—to the garden, to the garden party, and she was going on, back out to where she was the smallest daughter of the host and hostess of the garden party, the party which was for every aunt and uncle and cousin and for all friends.

This garden was full of it for her. She could name the flowers in the garden. She could name the flowers that had been in the garden. She could name the flowers that would come into the garden.

Her largest uncle was scolding in the garden—her uncle with the ring of hair around his skin-topped head—like teeth biting neat bites, she thought, all the way around his skin-top. She heard him. He said *You are so spoiled* with his head hanging over his daughter, so that to the girl watching, his head was where his daughter's head should have been, and the daughter and the uncle were stuck on the stony path between the hedges that led to the steps up back into the house.

When the uncle said *You are so spoiled*, neither of them moved, and those hedges, those big green hedges were brushing them.

Then the uncle's daughter was going up the steps, leaving the uncle, because, the girl thought, because *You are so spoiled* means you must leave.

That girl will meet the boys inside there when she gets inside there, the girl watching thought.

And the girl watched the girl disappear.

INTERCOURSE

At the post office the woman finally got a good long look at the monster, a stare. She was breathing the same air, not as before, deprived.

When she had first sighted the monster, this woman had not been sure whether or not to trust her instinct.

Was it a monster?

What it was was a monstrous posture she had seen, and the hair on top of the head was heaped so that it appeared as a bulge of hair, with far too much hair coming down at the side, so as to be an abnormal amount. Otherwise, the form of the monster was spindly. It was a small-sized monster.

The eyes were pale turquoise. The facial skin was milky milky white. The nose was a short, finely shaped nose. The mouth was full-lipped, painted coral. The hair was the woman's favorite color hair—cinnamon color. The voice was girl-like when the woman heard it. The black-inked handwriting on the brown-paper-wrapped package was indecipherable from the distance it was observed from, but it was a curvaceous handwriting. The high-heeled shoes with ankle straps were made of metallic gold leather. The purse was like bronze.

Okay, the emergence of this bombshell has gone on long enough for me. Occasionally I select a man, but my preference is for women who could easily steal away my beloved husband who is not taboo.

Carnality is common in rude society. The incarnation is temporary or permanent.

SCREAMING

I thought she had grabbed her whole pearl necklace in a fist
to stop it at her throat so that we could speak, because it had
been crashing into itself, back and forth across her breast, as
she was moving toward me.

"Your dog Heather"—was all I could think to say to her—"I
still remember your story about Heather, your dog, and about
your daughter coming down the stairs in the black wig."

"That was Heidi," she said.

"Your daughter is Heidi?"

"No," she said, "that's the dog."

"Oh, and she's not living," I said as she let the pearls go and
they fell back down against her chest.

"That's right," she said. "Heather is. Heather's a better
name—that's why you remember Heather. Heather is—" and

she rolled her eyes so that I would know that I should have remembered Heather.

We did not talk about Heidi anymore that night, and I did not bring her up for conversation, because I did not have to. I spoke to her husband instead.

Still, I remembered how when the daughter was coming down the stairs in the black wig, wearing the kimono, Heidi ran away. I want to say that Heidi ran away screaming when she saw the daughter—but Heidi is the dog. She was a dog.

For the sake of conversation, when her husband and I saw a woman neither of us knew, I said, "I bet she's not afraid of a living soul." I said it because the woman had obviously done her hair all by herself for this gala—just stuck bobby pins you could see into her white hair, just worn an old, out-of-fashion cotton dress.

I told the husband I'd like to shake that woman's hand and ask her if it was true what I had guessed.

I was considering it, getting up close. I wondered would she get scared or what she would do—what I would do.

"What about that one there?" her husband asked.

That one there was a woman who was trying to get back behind my husband. The woman was wincing as if she had just done something awful.

"A gambling problem—that's what she has," I said. But that wasn't sordid enough. So then I said, "I don't have a clue."

"Now me," the husband said. "Do me."

"You," I said, "you are hardworking. You are—"

"No," he said, "*not that—*" The man looked frightened. He looked ready to hear what I would say as if I really knew.

Then someone was at my back, tugging at my hair, moving it. I felt a mouth was on the nape of my neck. It was a kiss.

I did not have the faintest idea who would want to do that to me. There was not a soul.

When I saw him, when I turned, his head was still hung down low from kissing me.

Thank God I did not know who he was.

I kept my face near his. I liked the look of him.

I was praying he would do something more to me.

Anything.

HOPE

She had the proof to prove it to me that her dying father's idiot wife, who was not her mother, was a real idiot. My friend said that this woman spelled the word *wife* W-I-L-F on the hospital information request form, so that my friend had to do everything for her father, because he said to her, "You have to help me!"

She had taken care of the funeral arrangements, and her father was not dead yet.

My father's dying was not planned for so carefully by his daughter, and it is over with. He's dead.

We had appointments—my friend and I—at the exact same time, and if it had not been for her arriving, just when she did, at the third-floor hallway of the Professional Medical Arts Building, I would have left after arriving there first, all alone, and knocking and knocking and hammering and yelling at the office door, and twisting and twisting the doorknob.

We were well along in our discussion, comforting one another about our fathers, we had even compared our teeth, when our dentist arrived, his staff, his hygienist, and so forth.

My friend had told me, by then, how awful her father was—she had proof—and so had I told her that my father wasn't that awful, but that he might as well have been—because I had hated him as much as she had hated hers by the end.

Once inside the office, while I was in the chair, the hygienist had the nerve to ask me a question after she had put a pick tool and a plastic tube into my mouth.

It was unbelievable, unbelievable that a daughter such as I am, whose father had been so loving to her all of her life, who wanted to tell me what I needed to know anytime that I needed to know, that I should deliberately ask my father a question after the doctors had rendered him positively without the power of speech, that I should ask him a question, and then act as if it were a matter of life or death that my question had no answer.

Every time I do not know what else to think, I go back to how my hands were grabbing onto my father's ankles or onto his toes. I felt so incredibly nervy. He was down in his bed. I was at the end of it. My father put his head forward toward me, crazy to tell me the most essential thing I will ever need to know.

THE DIVINE RIGHT

"What your king did—" she was saying to the Dutchman.

"King? Do you even know the country? You don't even know which country. We have no king," the Dutchman said.

"No king? Your consort—the queen's consort?" she said.

"You mean the prince?"

"Bern—Bern—what he did was terrible, taking all that money. Why did he take the money? He doesn't need the money. He's married to the richest woman in the world."

The Dutchman laughed. "The richest woman in the world? Do you think so? Well, I hope so."

"Doesn't she own most of Fifth Avenue, along with that other queen? the Queen of England?"

"Well, I don't know," the Dutchman said.

"You don't know? You don't think it was a bad thing what he did, taking that money?"

"No, none of us do," the Dutchman said. "We all like him very much. The money was offered, and he took it. It's no big deal."

"Well, here we all thought it was terrible. I thought it was. I hated him for it. I felt so sorry for the queen."

"What I can't get over," the Dutchman said, "in your country, are all those rich people's names plastered all over your museums—those plaques. Rich people in our country would never do that. They would be so embarrassed to do that."

"They would be?" she asked.

"Yes. They would never do that."

"Well, I wouldn't really do it either," she said. "Maybe a tiny tag that I had donated this or that, but not a huge plaque announcing a whole wing or anything like that. That would be embarrassing. It would be so obvious."

"What you were after?" the Dutchman laughed. "Are you very rich?"

"What?" she said.

"*You*, are you *rich*?" the Dutchman asked.

"I suppose that I am," Mrs. Osborne said. "Will you excuse me, please?"

In the mirror of her host's bathroom she saw her small oval face and her large earrings, each earring the size of one of her ears, rectangles of lapis lazuli framed in gold. She was embarrassed by the size of the earrings. She took the earrings off. She slipped them into her purse.

She was embarrassed by the size of her purse, the leather was too luxuriantly soft. She remembered the price of the purse, of the earrings.

She found Mr. Osborne in the host's kitchen, pouring himself a glass of wine. "I want to go home," she whispered.

"You tired?" Mr. Osborne asked.

"No," she answered, "I am not tired."

She held her gloved hands up in front of her as they walked to their car. She thought her gloves were a gaudy shade of green. She remembered what she'd paid for the gloves. It would not bother her never to wear them again.

Sliding inside their car, she was afraid suddenly they were being watched. In this neighborhood, for the cost of the car, they could be killed. They could be killed anywhere.

Mr. Osborne petted his wife's arm, before he turned the key to begin the drive home. He was petting the sleek seal fur of her coat. One of his hands, the glowing flesh of it, was all that she could see. She was frantic. She thought, What if I am really adored too—if it is true! She remembered.

POWER

How do they do it? She cannot bend her legs.

Here I go, I must see him propping up her legs some way onto his shoulders, or with some contraption that they have had to devise, or do they simply put a bunch of something under her hips, or does he get into her from behind when they are lying down? or something else so obvious, but I don't know. She sits in his lap in a chair? and does it hurt her, because it is awkward? or do they even bother to try, because it is never fun? Or does she do it for him some way with her mouth? How would she do it that way?

Her legs shine under the mesh nylon of her hose. I look right at her legs when she says, "Oh, these legs." I do not know these people, the husband, and the wife, or the driver of this car that we are all paying to please get us home. At least, I know I have been away.

I do not know where to begin with this injury—with the sharpness of her nose which seems to solve something, the brightness of the light shooting off from her lacquered cane, or her laughing many more times than once, so that her husband said to her, "What is the matter?" or her ever-constant soft drawing up of a breath through her nose—once, then twice, and then pause—the sense of the stupid loss of time, that for once did not matter to me.

I thought, Let us keep on at this looking for the house they are looking for. It does not matter that the driver of the car cannot find it. Once I thought that.

She said to me, "I did not mean to throw my cane at you."

The door of the car had opened, the cane had been flung by someone onto the seat toward me, then her body. She had flung her body onto the back seat the wrong way—flat out and on her back—because of her problem, her big problem, her husband's bigger problem, their terrific problem.

She said, "No, this is not it," whenever the driver beamed a light on a house.

I said, "It is so dark." Finally, I said angrily, "Is this even the street?"

The driver said, "Yes!" and then I saw LOCUST in block black letters on a white sign on the corner at just that moment when the driver spoke.

She said, "No, this is not it."

When finally it was the house—those relatives, those people up there who came out onto that cement porch, who maybe call themselves friends, were not happy enough to receive their guests. That chirruping woman with her arms around the other woman didn't fool me. Nobody fooled me, but probably somebody was being fooled.

At least I knew where I lived. I could say to the driver, "Straight east now, and then left at the light." I could say it and say it and keep on with it, even with a righteous sense of anger—thank God—with a sense of—*You listen to me! This is how you get somewhere!*

But all this is not about failed love.

Somebody please tell me that this is all about something else entirely which is more important.

Somebody smarter and dearer than I, be the one available for my best, my most tenderest embrace when I have been convinced by you.

I could be a believer.

WHAT IS IT WHEN GOD SPEAKS?

This was the house which once inspired a sister of one of the guests to declare, "People kill for this."

That's where the guests were on the perfect afternoon, not the sister.

It was a shame the afternoon became evening before the guests had to leave, not that anything was less lovely because it was evening.

There was a tender quality to the lack of light on the screened-in porch where they all were sitting, as there was also a tender quality to the small girl too old to be in the highchair, but she was not too large for it. The girl had insisted the highchair be carried out from the kitchen onto the porch. She had insisted on being put up into the highchair. She was ecstatic to be locked in behind the tray.

Her hands tapped and stroked the tray. She was not up there to eat. It was past time for that.

Behind the handsomest man on the porch was the array of green leafy trees and lawn, lit by a yard light, veiled by the black porch screen. The handsomest man smiled. He was serene.

Across from him, his wife, on the chintz flowered sofa, who was the most beautiful woman, smiled serenely at her husband. She said of her husband to the others, "He never wants to leave here. Look at him! He likes it. The food is so good and healthy. He can keep swimming in your pool. Look at him. He is so happy!"

Then the man lifted up his girl, who was smaller than the other girl, who had never ever—his girl—been irritable even once, there at that house, and he put her up onto his shoulders. Her short legs were pressing on his chest, because he had wanted her legs to do that.

Her father felt his daughter on the back of him and on the front of him, on top of him, all at once. She was slightly over his head too, her head was. Her light heels were tapping lightly on his chest. He took her hands in his. She was ready for the dive that would not be possible unless he would fling her from him.

He should.

TO DIE

———

I undressed myself. I wanted sex—I wanted sex—I wanted sex—I wanted sex.

I climbed into bed with my wife.

She wanted sex with me. She always wants sex with me.

When I discharged myself this time into her, I was feeling myself banging as high up into her as I have ever gotten myself up into her.

I had just done the same with another woman who always wants sex with me, too.

There is another woman that I do the same with.

There is another woman.

There is another woman. There are five women who always want sex with me. They are always ready. It does not matter when or what or where, but they are ready.

I have a great deal of money which I have earned. I have physical beauty for a man. I have intelligence. I have work to do which I love to do, but women are what I prefer to anything, to lie down with them, the turning to touch the woman and knowing I will be received for sex as soon as I wish to be welcome.

I have been at it like this, this way for years. It does not matter when I will die. I have had everything I have ever wanted.

I should die now.

There should be a killing at my house.

There should be much, so much more for me, which I am not able to conceive of.

A CONTRIBUTION TO
THE THEORY OF SEX

D anny Ketchem had found himself compelled, or rather, *repelled* by his lack of understanding of what had become her whole life.

It is immaterial who *she* is. She could be his wife, his mother, his daughter, his best woman friend, these, or any combination of these, or add in any other female you can think of that she could be.

What the female's life had become is also immaterial, because Danny, in any event, was bound to get confused.

Her name is Nancy Drew. Real people do have her name.

Then Danny was towering, when Nancy held him, which was her idea, and his penis was sticking itself in between her breasts, as if a button were being pushed.

Remember, Danny could be a small-sized boy standing on

a stool, getting hugged by Nancy, or a tall grown-up, not on a stool, and Nancy could be short.

Some time later, but not much later, Danny was on Nancy's lap. This could happen in all of the conceivable cases.

The object—Nancy's idea—was for her to wipe that grimace off his face.

Nancy cannot, she will not bear an ugly face. She tries not to—poor schmuck. She'll try anything. I know Nancy.

I want to wipe that grin off her face. It's so easy when you're one of us.

MARRIAGE AND THE FAMILY

Every time I go in there I am thinking, This time I will get the sisters straight, which one is which. But each time I go in there I think there is a new sister, one I have never seen before, who gets me mixed up. This new sister will act as though she knows me very well, as though I am quite familiar to her.

What is the same or almost the same about all of the sisters is this: their hair and their clothing, their faces, their jewelry, their ages, their expressions, their attitudes. I do not think they are quintuplets, if there are that many of them, or anything like that, but there is the possibility.

The sisters run a business where there are balloons around. It is a print and office supply shop in my town. It is new, and they behave as if they will be very successful, or as if they already are.

Everything is clean, such as stacks of tangerine and fuchsia paper for writing, and pens to match, which must be too expensive to buy. I wouldn't buy the pens.

Two or three of the sisters may be married. They wear tiny rectangular or round diamonds set into gold bands, and plain gold wedding bands to go with. A couple of the sisters only wear the diamonds.

There is a blond child I saw once, who looks happy and well adjusted. One of the sisters laughed and joked with the child. She hugged him and she kissed him.

A mother of a sister called in once, and she was spoken to sweetly by one of the sisters.

They do wear very tight pants. The pants hug and squeeze their bottoms so that there must be some discomfort for the sisters when they have to sit down to do their work, or even when they just stand—the pants are that tight.

I have never had an argument with one of the sisters. One of these sisters has never ridiculed me, or made me feel unwelcome, as if I were trying to take over in there, or take advantage of any of them, when I shopped there.

Not one of the sisters ever yelled at me, told me to get out of her way, or implied that I came into the shop too often, and that something was suspicious.

I never yelled back at one of the sisters to say I buy a lot in her shop, and that I could just go somewhere else. I never said I have my whole life in my hands when I come in there. I never got myself into a rage. I never looked at a sister and thought, You frighten me more than anyone I could ever look at—take a look at you—and your whole attitude is wrong.

Your attitude is abysmal. Your attitude is as if you have been stung, or are stinging, or are getting ready to be bitten, or to bite.

The last time I was in the shop, this is what happened: a man was in there. I didn't know for what purpose. He looked suspicious. He didn't buy anything. He was darting around, and he was looking at me, and looking at me, until I had to pay attention to him. Then he said, "I saw you out there," meaning out in front of the shop. What he meant was, he had seen the way I had parked my car. I knew that had to be it. I had even surprised myself with the way I had done it. I had never done anything like that parking.

I was proud of myself like a hero should be proud, who risks her life, or who doesn't risk her life, but who saves somebody, *anybody!*

"You could have killed somebody!" was what that man said to me.

OH, MY GOD, THE RAPTURE!

The man was looking at the woman's breasts.

The woman thought, Oh, my God, I've forgotten myself, as she saw the man, another patient, at the end of the hall, looking at her, as she realized her paper robe was open, that she had left her paper robe open like that, while she was going as she had been directed to go into another room for the cardiogram. But since he had already seen her, there was no point, she thought, to closing the robe up.

"Go in there," the nurse had said. "That's right."

Lying down, waiting for the nurse, the woman looked at the tall window that rose at her feet which to her showed a very boring sight—some greenery and sky—and then the woman thought it would be so right to have a man who was not her husband make love to her. She thought it would be the rightest thing imaginable, and she was feeling what was to her the glow of perfect good health.

It was like hand lotion, the woman thought, that the nurse was putting on her breasts in small dabs. The woman didn't look—like white—she didn't look, lotion, and it was gooey and cool, not painful, very relaxing, the whole business.

"Now don't be alarmed," the woman told the nurse, "because my cardiogram is like the cardiogram of a sixty-year-old man who has just had an attack. Did the doctor tell you not to be alarmed?"

"No," the nurse said, "not for you he didn't."

"I'm just too small in there for my heart," the woman said. "It's being squeezed, so it looks funny, and it sounds funny, but I'm all right. It's all right."

There were short black wires that the woman thought the nurse was either untangling or rearranging in the air, and to her the nurse looked happy.

The woman wanted to make the nurse even happier by chatting with her, by making the nurse laugh. But the woman's mind came to a stop on it, on the thought of it, on the thought of wanting to make someone happy.

"Oh, my God," the woman said.

The nurse opened her mouth and smiled as if she might be going to say something. She was operating the machine behind the woman's head which the woman thought was making a small unimportant noise. The whole business was so soothing, the whole cardiogram part. It was the easiest, the most relaxing thing, the woman thought.

When the doctor hung the woman's X rays up in front of her, the woman didn't even want to look.

When the doctor said, "You see, I think it's pancaked," when the doctor said, "I think it's because of your funnel chest," the woman said nothing.

"You know," the doctor said to the woman when the woman was leaving, "you ought to come in here more often."

The woman didn't have to pay the bill just then. The nurse said she did not have to, that it was not necessary, but the woman wanted to do it for the nurse.

So the woman said to the nurse, "I want to pay you now. This was wonderful. This never happens. You hardly kept me waiting at all. You took me—" she said, "you took me just when you said you would."

THE FUTURE OF THE ILLUSION

It was an intimate relation that we had had because hardly anyone else was listening in, except for a new employee who was learning the ropes.

The clerk looked at these beans, and she said, "Those are the ones I always use." And I said, "You do?"

Then she said, "Why don't you use the canned?"

That is the finale for that. That is the end of my retelling of it, because that is the end of what I view as the significant event. Everything else about the event withers away for the retelling except for the sight of the clerk's mouth.

Questions and answers: How did the clerk and I know when enough talking was enough? I don't know. Did we care that we were deadly serious? I was surprised by it.

The clerk's upper lip is neatly scalloped. Together, her lips pout. They are the same to me as my childhood best friend's lips—the friend I had physical relations with, with a blanket over our laps on the sofa in my house.

We were girls side by side touching each other up in there where the form of the flesh is complicated. I do not know if I touched as well as she was touching me. We were about nine or we were ten, or we were eleven, or thirteen. I have no memory of sexual sensation, nor much of anything else.

I see us from the front because I am the person watching us, standing in front. I am the person who was not there at that time, who does not know whose idea it was to try, who does not know if she was the one who was afraid of being caught, if what she was doing was being done wrong.

I am still the odd man out, going backward for my training, for a feeling.

The odd woman, actually.

BOYS!

It was as if I heard a hiss come out of my mother, or she was letting me have it some way with air when I said to her *You look so beautiful.*

But she didn't do that.

What she did do was she looked at me.

Maybe not even that, because I was standing—my mouth was at her ear—when I said *You look so beautiful,* so that no one else sitting at the table would hear. Was I whispering because her face had looked to me manhandled, if that were possible, with dips and curves lying pleasingly on her, pleasingly to me on her face?

So what happened then? Because it was *her* turn. Was I pulled away to say something to someone else?

No, I think I sat back down next to her. There was no

getting away from her. I had been put there with her for the meal.

But I did not look at her. I was looking to see the shine on my plate rim, the sauce shine on my meal, and I was seeing the beauty of the man next to me, which was so careful in his hair, in his wife's hair that matched his hair, in his wife's pink mouth when she spoke. And with all this beauty going on, my knife, I kept it slicing competently through my meal. I kept it slicing, and I kept putting my knife back into the correct station on the rim of my plate after having sliced.

So when my meal was finished, and I felt that it was finished with no trouble, I got up and I left the people at the table. It must have been just for a moment when I got up, which was to go to the commotion why I finally got up, not to leave my mother—because I am a mother, too, and the commotion was my problem, my children, a disorganization.

My children were going around and around the table. I think that they were going so fast that I could not have caught the sleeve of even the youngest, even if I had tried reaching out for it. I think, maybe, I did try reaching out for it. But perhaps I didn't.

They all must have been waiting for me for what I would do, everyone else at the table—all the grown-up people—but I was just looking at my children, my children going on and on, and their noise was like huge spills to me that kept being sudden and kept pouring.

And it was pleasing to me, *then it was*, in a certain way, the motion and the commotion, the children getting away from me, and I was watching it, and it was all my fault until the time when it would be over, and it wasn't as if anything could be ruined, I didn't think.

Then I called *Boys!* which I thought was loud, but when I hardly heard the word, because it was as if I had sent the word away, when the children hardly heard the word—they must not have—then I knew it must have been very faint out of my mouth, or just loud enough to be just another push of air to send them around again, to keep them going.

Then I saw a little girl, little enough that I must have missed her when she was going around with the boys, someone else's little girl, shorter than my littlest boy, that I did not know.

She must have thought she was so cute. The girl looked full of glee to me, and I was standing there, waiting for some other mother, the mother of the girl I did not know, to stand up and *do* something—because it was clear to me then that this little girl was the cause, that it was *all her fault,* and that she was the one in charge.

ULTIMATE OBJECT

She did not know there would be a cupboard full of vases, but she had had a hunch, as when her tongue on someone's skin could give her a hunch of what would happen. Let me repeat—a tongue on someone's skin.

She was with a friend with whom she could share her joy that there was a cupboard full. She said, "We're okay! They've got everything we could ask for!"

She was crouched, flat-footed, her body nearly into a ball, except for her neck and for her head not conforming, so that she could look into the cupboard to let all the joy which was packed inside of the cupboard for her, into her.

One plastic vase with a bulb shape, with a narrow tube protruding from the bulb upward, was light as a feather, and was as warm as plastic is.

One glass vase, the shape of a torso, was covered all over with rough-grained glass, when she took it out.

She did not let her friend take vases away when she held up vases to prove they were unsuitable because she pronounced it was so.

Each time she went down, to look in, the quality of the joy was as good, did as much for her—four times.

It was festivity.

And to her, it was festivity, the cooking or the heating, that the man who had nothing to do with either her or her friend was doing nearby at the stove.

His peaceable plan—to lift and to unfurl, flat, round, yellow, black-speckled cakes—was the only other romantic transformation—not the product of imagination—going on in the place at the same time. And the man had no more right to be in this place—he was on the same shaky ground as she was, and as her friend was, by being there—which she saw him confirm with a smile.

It did not occur to her to get close to the man, to make an advance to taste, to do anything at all consequential vis-à-vis the man.

At the risk of startling readers, there was a dead body hidden not far from the man, which was the body of a woman the man had killed the day before, with a sharp enough knife, then lying—the knife was—in a drawer above the cupboard of vases.

The woman's naked, somewhat hacked body, decapitated

and frozen, was in the institutional-sized freezer, adjacent to the stove. Out of her swollen face, her tongue protruded. The wrong door, for all time, had been opened.

AGAIN

Earlier, when my son was with me against his will, only for a moment, there had been a lot of baying we had heard on the radio. I had called to him, "Come hear the cattle!" but then thought, What a lie! when my son walked back out. Those had not been cattle.

On the radio—on the same program—I heard this woman saying she was better off. I was all by myself then.

She said the animals she ate were better off too. She said, "They're better off and so am I."

She said, "Most people think only of the chops and the steaks. They don't think about the ribs and the flanks and the neck."

She said, "I'll show you." She had some man there asking her questions. She said to him, "Let me show you." Then she was doing all this breathing, this gasping. She said, "God, I hate

97

this. This happens to me every time." Then she said, "Come here, honey. Come here."

She was trying to get a lamb to come to her, I think. It was small, I imagined, like a baby lamb. She said, "Honey." She had to say it again. There was lots of wrestling that I heard.

She was wrestling with an animal which had ivory curls all over it, and gray, red-rimmed eyes, in my mind. She grabbed that baby lamb finally around the neck, her head on top of its head, I was thinking. She was hugging the baby, her pistol pressed into it somewhere, while the baby twisted to get loose, and she said, "Honey," again, and then there was this dull bang that I have heard, and the sound of falling down that I have heard.

It was at breakfast time when I heard the falling down, when I was caught next to the table I had set up for the breakfast. It was time for me to do what I do. I call.

LIFEGUARD

We had tried we had tried my mother and I to get someone to help us stop the flood in the house. We had tried
to get some man. So that when my father and the man who
guards my father returned, but when they were not yet inside
the house, I went out to them.

That man who guards my father was sizing me up like
he was wild. His head was on its side in midair bouncing, his
shoulder all dipped down because I was forcing him to leave
me alone with my father, and I was forcing him to go into the
house to deal with the flood and with my mother, so that I
was the one left guarding my father, who was wearing those
shoes, who was taking those small steps toward the house. I
was saying to my father, "It's not so bad, the flood. You'll see,"
and I was talking as slowly as he was walking in those shoes.

Those shoes on my father were the worst things I saw when I was getting him into the house, not getting him into the house, guarding him while he inched his way toward it.

Those shoes did not look like shoes that could hold a foot. There did not look to be room for a foot of flesh inside them, just a foot of bone, long like a pipe and they were forcing their way to the door of his house which was open, but from which we could not hear yet the rushing of water that I had felt rushing inside of the pipe—the hot rushing that I had seen blur the floor so that the floor was no longer a clear thing to see, so that the ceiling of our house was shedding through its lights the way rain comes down out from under a bright sun.

So that of course we were wet, my mother and I, with water binding like bracelets on our wrists, up and down our arms, like extra hair on our foreheads, on our clothes extra shapes, in our shoes which made my feet feel larger and heavier than they had ever felt.

At the door with my father, it was as if everything was hotter and wetter and louder in the house than I had remembered and was getting more so, just with us about ready to enter—and my mother and the man who guards my father must have been the cause. They had had so much time, I thought they had, and together they had not stopped it.

And then, before we ever entered, my father was telling me what we should do, even though I could not make it out, not the words, but I knew he was telling me how to stop the flood, if we wanted to.

THE NUB

The cantor was slumped in the winged chair on the platform behind the pulpit. For the time being, she was finished with her part.

I felt sorry for her, that we could not have given her applause for the job she had done. Something was definitely wrong when she was done, when we could not give her any applause, because she had sung her heart out.

That's what was wrong. I was thinking about the rabbi too. How could he know it right away that I thought he was boyish and candid, so adorable and appropriate for everything he had said to the thirteen-year-old girl on this great occasion?

He had stood with the girl in front of the open ark with his hands on her. I have never seen this. He was staring into her eyes. She was staring into his eyes for how long? for how long?

A matron with a navy velvet hat on, cocked saucily, began to weep when it was her turn at the pulpit, when she said the girl's name.

Then all of that was behind us.

Then to kick off the snowball dance at the luncheon party afterward, thirteen-year-old girls asked grown men, most of whom they did not know, to dance with them, on the order of the bandleader. Dessert—a sugary baked apple with cream—was served ahead of the main course, and then there was another dessert.

I was saying all of the appropriate things to everyone to get happiness from the happiness, to have a good time at the good time and I was getting it done.

Then, with the band, the thirteen-year-old girl was singing "I'll cry if I want to," and the bandleader told her she had done a good job when she was done, and we all gave her a lot of applause.

Later, at home, on the telephone, talking to my husband, only about this and about that, when I was in the same room with my children, I was pressing the nub of myself for the pleasure of the pleasure of it—my—what I am calling the nub—call it what you like—it was at exactly the point of the corner of my bureau top. I was pressing on this nub to get aware of the possibility of the pleasure, up and down. Then I did these very gentle moves over to the side of my nub on it, while I was talking.

What I was doing to myself, just so, was working for me, but nobody could appreciate what it meant to me, except for me.

A child learns from this. Children can learn all by themselves, if they have to, not to show off.

MYSTERY OF THE UNIVERSE

The five-year-old sitting at the head of the table said, "*Think!* You're not thinking. *Think!*" So I tried to think, because he had said I had to.

"It has something to do with the angel," he said.

We all looked up at the lit-up Christmas tree, to the top, where I saw it pressed into the wooden beam, something golden and bent. The question, the child's question, was "What made the roof cave in?"

"He changes the rules when you start to guess it," his ten-year-old brother said.

It was true. I remembered his first hint—"It has something to do with the train," which was on tracks at the base of the tree.

The size of the child's forehead, of his whole head, is astonishing for anyone of that age, for a child of any age, for any person—the breadth and the depth and the length of it—and then at dinner it was full of the question.

"You're not thinking!" he said again. *"Think!"* when I said that the top of the tree had pushed through the ceiling, had made the ceiling cave in, and I am forty-two.

"No!" he said. *"That's not it!* Who can guess it what it is?"

There were two families together, guessing while we were eating. He wasn't my child with this question, but I wished that he were. He is a child to be proud of, who would force us to think, who would not let up. I didn't mind that he'd stoop to being sneaky. I was proud of him. I am proud of anyone who stands up to everyone, who would say it to everyone in front of everyone—*"You're the kind of person who would pull out a tree out of our front yard and throw it down on the house!"* I was so proud of a person who would think of doing the scariest thing he could think of, and he isn't even Jewish.

EGG

She had never allowed any egg of hers to get into such a condition, looking unlike itself and bulging, which was why the egg had all her attention from where it was in the depth of the sink, and from the depth of where it had been all dark yellow in the bowl, which had not been very far down inside the bowl, for there was no depth of anything inside the bowl, no particular depths of anything in either of her kitchen sinks either.

When she walked off from the sinks, thinking of the egg—"How unlike itself!"—she heard a yell which was noise produced by standing water which was falling suddenly down deeply into the pipes below the sinks.

Variously, this yell was a choke to her, a slap, or the end of a life, so that she stopped when she heard the yell with her back to the sinks. She had the impression of a preamble.

This is the beginning of something.

She went and got another bad egg and gave it to the dog to eat out of the bowl, so that the bowl was scoured and banged about.

The dog, she thinks, gets everything, she was thinking later, walking the dog. He gets it, but pisses it and craps it away—daily—everything, and yet everyone shows the dog all of their love.

Even she loves and she loves and she loves the dog.

The dog goes along down the street and the people say to her, "What a nice dog," and "That's a nice-looking dog you've got there!" The dog takes her farther down the street than she intended to go, where then she is murdered.

The murderer loves and he loves the woman's dog for the rest of the dog's life. The dog loves the murderer in return. The love that they share is perfect. It is not a love that would stoop to being sexual.

WHAT WE WERE THERE FOR

She revealed a sweet temperament over and over again. Her companion kept showing her respect.

I interrupted the two of them once, before they stood to take their turn. "Mrs. Gackenback!" the secretary called.

So that's who she is! The thought expelled itself with such force from me that it startled me.

I had startled Mrs. Gackenback when I interrupted her and her companion. I interrupted Mrs. Gackenback to ask, "Was it the Pointer Sisters?"

Mrs. Gackenback told her companion, not me, that she was not sure if it had been the Pointer Sisters.

I had heard Mrs. Gackenback say to her companion just before I had interrupted them, "It wasn't the Andrew Sisters."

After being startled, Mrs. Gackenback appeared to me uncomfortable, perhaps upset, not ruined.

Mrs. Gackenback had to be helped to stand. She had to be helped to walk. Her companion did that for her.

When it was my turn, when the secretary called me, when the secretary examined me up close, she said, "You should have been a Balinese dancer." Then she said, "You do with your eyes what they can do with their hands."

I paid no attention to the secretary's hands. Her shoes were not white nurse's shoes. Her mint-green nylon dress had buttons up and down the front. Something momentous was being revealed to me which goes up and down over and over again. It was being revealed. I had to put my head down between my legs. There is nothing I can think of that is fair. There is nothing I can think of that is fair. There is nothing I can think of that is fair. There is nothing I can think of that is fair there enough. There is nothing I can think of that is there enough.

SCIENCE AND SIN OR LOVE
AND UNDERSTANDING

I am not going to look it up in a book or do research. There are those of you who probably know why the small switching tail of a small animal makes me remember how I want to copy lewd people.

If the answer to the question is: Animals set an example for people, then I accept the answer. Do I have a choice?

I gave my husband no choice.

The last time I shoved something down my husband's throat was when I cheated on him. Now I say to him, "I didn't want to shove anything down your throat."

"It's because I love you," was the puny thing to say. It was puny compared to the size of the power which had made me say it to him.

The power had made me see things too. The power had

turned him into the shape of a man wearing his clothes so he could leave me in the dark, standing beside his side of it, our bed. I knew I was seeing things.

He said, "I hear you."

I may or I may not cheat on him again. But the last time, I was standing up when I knew I was going to do it. I see myself on the street, deciding. I am holding onto something. Now I cannot see what it is. This is no close-up view. I am a stick figure.

I am the size of a pin.

SOME SEXUAL SUCCESS STORIES PLUS OTHER STORIES IN WHICH GOD MIGHT CHOOSE TO APPEAR

(1992)

Oh, my God!

THE LIMITS OF THE WORLD

My adventures have led me to believe that I possess two powerful powders—genuine powders. The "I command my man" powder is one of my powders. When I put this powder on my body, then I will command my man. He will always be my lover whether he wants to be my lover or not. He will be obedient and satisfied, whether that's what I want him to be or not. Nothing will ever take him away, whether that's what I want or not.

I'm not sure what the purpose is of my other genuine powder.

Now what?

What would you do? Would you go ahead and use either of these powders, if you, as I have done, had gone ahead and paid money for them?

Keep in mind, we are past the age of enlightenment. This is past reason. We are pretty deep into modern history and the decline of religion. This is when Nature itself has been stripped bare of its cozy personality and we all feel homeless in our own natures as well.

To say it another way, I gave away a pure love powder with no conditions on its use, or specifications warranted. (A lusty friend of mine grabbed it out of my hand.)

So now what?

Whosoever reads this, write to me if I am still alive, or please write to my children, or to my children's children, who may yet be even still deeper into the farther reaches of our common history. Give us *your* opinion. Provide please credentials for you yourself, who you are doing the talking.

Are you a superior person? Or, how soon do you think you will be? I can ask because I asked.

MY HIGHEST MENTAL ACHIEVEMENT

Baby, I will miss you with your common sense, and with your blindness to psychology. My prediction for you is that you will have a fascinating life and that you will stay eternally young, and that you will never lack for love. I am interested in all aspects of you.

If I could know what happened the last time you had sexual intercourse with me, and what your opinion of it was, what your experience was with it, I would be so interested to hear. Could you tell me how this time this sin was different?

The last time for me, when I saw my own hair there beneath my swollen belly, the sight of my hair offended me. I would rather see how I pinned your legs. I had opened my legs for you, and with my saying "This is better for me," I had twisted around onto my side for your sexy behavior. The big baby which was inside me took a beating. In any event, I do believe that sex, or even love, is not inappropriate for the very, very immature.

It is so much better for me to be the one who loves rather than to be the one who gets loved! It is so much better for me not to be the one who can take it or leave it—as you take it. Just think!—I actually became radical at the Grand Canyon when I looked around us and just kept my mouth shut there. It was the full scope of my achievement that I wanted to take a running start and then leap in. Don't forget, I like a mess!

CLEAN

This begins where so many others have ended, where the man and his wife are going to live the rest of their entire lives in perfect joy, so they arrive at the train station.

Now we're on our way. I'm dooteedooteedoing as if I'm happy. Went to the mail where I go to get it. Touched it. Washed myself. Meticulously washed out my contraceptive device with Cascade or Joy.

I toasted a piece of toast for myself to eat, buttered it, put cheese on it, drank coffee I had made, orange juice I had squeezed, took care of the other people. Put away food. I washed. I washed. I never thought I'd get the semen off my ring. The speed of my thought was a deep offense to me. It should have taken me a lifetime to find out how not to be happy just to ensure perfect success.

THE GOOD MAN

He called it a triumph that he never controlled her passions. That gadget with propellers, with the pads on
the propellers, that he had used to produce ultra-pleasure
for Darlene—his dream come true—was swell.

He was consoled by this ultra-pleasure briefly. Soon
afterward, he died. He was alone when he died, because his
pleasure-loving daughter had gone off to the theater.

As a dead man, prone upon his bed, this gadgeteer
would be an inspiration either for Darlene or for his
daughter.

One day, when he had been alive, so to speak, he had
killed a hornet by slugging it, and then, before he realized
what he was doing—seizing for himself an opportunity—he

had consumed all of the fresh greens which he had heaped up on his platter, plus the strips of the boiled meat. That should have been the test of his manhood, because he is a darling.

PUSSY

The woman's knowledge gives her vicious pleasure. She could have understood sooner if she had only tried to understand. Now that she understands, she will just not leave the men alone, now that she understands that everything that matters has nothing to do with her expectation of loyalty and devotion from a person she is hoping is nearly perfect. Oh yes, now the woman is full of desire as she climbs the stairs to her room. The stairs glow for her eyes. The woman sees a man heads taller than she is jump out at her and then turn back away. He is subtracting things from himself, because she can see only his trouser leg and his one shoe as he goes into her room.

Upon her entering her room after him, the woman does something significant and full of meaning.

Albeit, the orange orange, the thin, dry, oval slice of gray bread—oh no, there was even something more concealed in some silver foil—the elixir the woman knows emanates from these hors d'oeuvres which are all hers, on her tray, on the table, at the end of her bed—amounts to what the woman is if I say so. She equals anything at all on my say-so. The woman is a little dirty thrill.

This is the haunting story of a young man who married for love and who found himself in the grip of a considerable poonac.

TURNING

We kept on and I did not break into tears. Meanwhile, I am wondering which one of us is the cruelest. I can hear my voice saying all of those things.

A few months later, he reminded me that our misfortunes were almost identical, because, he said, we had become inextricably commingled. When he said what amounted to that, I put my arms around him and I kissed him. However, my suspicion is that he cannot tolerate being confined by a woman.

When daylight came, we made our preparations for the day, by bathing, by dressing, by eating. My own appearance was of concern to me, but there was also my great suspicion about what we had been doing throughout the night. Had we succeeded? Should we have been rejoicing? controlling our anger? openly admitting where the true superiority resides? Or should we have kept on with our spirit of rivalry?

Anyway, I spoke seriously with him about my violent disposition. But just around the corner, I did not know what it was. No sooner had the summer arrived—it was a day like today—with the sea whipped up by the wind, the sky was filled with action—with tumbling clouds, carrying on how they do, erratic, totally unstable, disorderly, maltreating each other's lifeless bodies, fabricating, evaporating ominously. I trust the unknown. I could never be astonished by such painless deaths apart from one episode, wherein I attempted to twist my fate, and to rear a child, among other things.

THE DOG

She had every reason to think that he had had a good time with her when he licked thoroughly with his strong tongue the private parts of her body. She was in bed when he did this. He was her best friend.

When she awoke the next morning, she smelled the sweet lilac and the roses in her garden—she was aware of the thump of his tail—and felt a breeze spring in through the window screen.

She ate a small piece of fish for her breakfast. She hummed a little tune to herself—and when she opened a drawer, she observed an old crumb from some food in there and she thought, This is unbelievable.

Her husband, Frank, came in for his breakfast. Frank is clever, of course.

She said to Frank, *"Sit!"*

Really, she did not understand at that time why Frank didn't.

THE MAN

It was the best week of his life. I wasn't there for much of it. He used to try to copulate with my boyfriends when they'd come to the house and he'd chase around and chase around. He'd come when I called his name, and I would go wild screaming his name until he came running to me faster than I could ever run, so I'd sink to my knees sometimes to get down on his level with him, with his excitement, which was often running rampant. His bed was filthy where he rested and slept. He ate with gusto, made a great noise, and drank what he drank with a power to drink I will not ever forget. He influenced me a lot.

THE CIRCUMCISION

The infant is too young to hear the credo he should live by: *He should marry and do good deeds.*

I want to know what is going to happen—you know—will he end up being one of those people? I am one of those people—leading my life. Almost daily, my life is ideal for a person gifted with power and reason.

That the infant was substantially drugged was a good deed. I left without paying any respect, or without saying anything to the infant, because *who is it?*

Walking to my car, I see the other cars available to other people. I put my key into the lock of my car, but my key doesn't fit the lock. I am going to have to stick my key into another one. This is being repeated and repeated and repeated all over the world with impatience or maturity or dead to the world.

The ease with which my key finally does do the trick puts a knot in my throat. I am a sad woman. My face is hard. My car is enormous. The road is an outrage that I follow with a blood lust to get to my home to my husband.

Whom I uncritically love.

ALL NEW

When I was still a girl, I did this. When I get to you, you have such a stake in warmth and affection and you are drinking up your wine from a golden goblet. You have out the cracked mixing bowl and your steel spoon for you to mix with. The fire is the blue ring of light on your stove and your music is here. Flutes, I think, and entreaties from a gang of women. I suppose I am supposed to live or die without such a brilliant man as you.

First, I have to climb a hill—not a lucky omen. Then it is easy going until the storm bursts out. In the storm, I hear the shouting. The people swearing to God. Wet again! I am heading to somewhere else I cannot stay, having such a good time, not lost, and I like to take breaths. I have been doing this. I did not make this up.

THE REAL DIANE WILLIAMS HAS CAPTURED THE WHOLE OF FREUD

My son Eric Williams told me how he'd jump over or he'd jump on top of a car that was going to run him down, rather than go under the car. We were riding in our car then. I was the driver when he told me.

My errand was to get my new nightgown to fit—the silky, soft, shiny, creamy, slinky nightgown that did not fit me when I bought it, that has more flowers than I'd care to count all over it. I was taking my gown to the woman tailor whose husband invited Eric to his boy's surprise party by calling me up on the telephone to tell me about the party.

The two times I have been to the tailor it was very bad weather. This was one of those times. Sleet slopped on the windshield. Pointing to the windshield, Eric said, "If there was nothing there—if you stopped suddenly—I could go right through it and I wouldn't get hurt!" He meant if there were no glass. I knew what he meant.

"That's the way to think!" I said, "and there's no reason why no windshield would not work except for bad weather," and then I was thinking about my beginnings.

I undressed for the tailor and for Eric, too, so they could both see me naked. I could not figure out why. It wasn't required.

At the tail end of her decadent sofa, I stopped, so I did not have to go into her dressing room. I took off my clothing, throwing it all down on the sofa, and then put on the shimmering gown.

She had me stand up on a pedestal from where I admired in the mirror the gown shimmering and shining on me, and I admired her nimbly squatting to put pins into my hem, and she kept both of her knees up off of the floor, which surely was a feat!

Even Eric was jolly—we all were smiling when her husband emerged out of nowhere. My clothing was all back on then, so all of us were wearing all of our clothing, *the hell with that!*

When her husband held on to his belt with two hands, she crossed in front of him to go to the cash register with my money, which is when I admired her shoes. I was looking down. When I saw her belt, I was looking up, and when I saw her smiling—I was looking up even higher into the middle region which was my warning signal to stop looking.

I determined that her husband is sly on this basis—I've determined this on this basis more times than I can count about so many sly people—that a person is sly if the person seems to insist upon keeping a smile on his or her face. I would not smile—that's not fear!—if I had to say what he had to say about me in front of his wife!—but maybe it will make her happy.

The clear plastic cover for the gown on the hanger that she gave me was far more brilliant than my gown is. It's scintillating. The clear plastic cover was also longer than the gown and it's lethal for a tiny tot whose desire is to put it over his head and with it smother himself, as we all know.

When I piled the gown onto the backseat of my car, I had no opinion of the gown except that it was practically a weightless gown.

When I was with her husband, and when her husband saw me walking toward him, and when he said, "God, look at yourself in the mirror! Will you go look at yourself!" I refused to go look at my white skinlike covering.

In conclusion, human beings—my worrying about them—it's over, it's over, and it's merrier!

THE FLESH

⁂

As a couple, I admit, they had me transfixed. They were so alike in everything, with their skin still intact, side by side, under our dining room table, close enough to each other to reach out to each other if they had not been all encumbered because of what they were in actuality—slices of cucumber. I scooped them up.

What is missing here is what I did then with them.

That's when all our company came in, our friends and our relatives, not all of them all together, but the stream of their entering our house began.

I was hearing myself say *sometimes,* and *I'm afraid I don't know* and *yes, I do hope* and *think of me.* My friend R. exclaimed "Cliff!" Then C. said in a somewhat louder voice than R.'s, "No doubt he will come."

Plenty has been missing here all along, in addition to most of the people's names in their entirety, more of what they were saying, also the overtones and the undertones of their major statements.

Later, when everybody had said their good-byes, I told C. that it had all been like a dream—dinner and so on.

He said, "Tomorrow is another day."

I didn't mean for what I had said to make such a muffish sound, from where there was nowhere further naturally to bounce.

This happens, though, to what gets eaten up. That's all my fault Betty McDonald is a doornail.

PENIEL

The child who became a very great president of the United States of America scolded Dr. Tiffany: "You got me in the eye!" because some of the novocaine Tiffany withdrew with his syringe needle from a vial shot into the child's eye on account of the doctor's clumsiness, and the doctor knew it.

For these purposes, *a very great president* means a president who understands the meaning of the word *good* and who is capable of leading the country, and therefore the world, at least several giant steps toward *Good.*

After the child was shot, Dr. Tiffany commanded the child, "Don't move, that's all you have to do."

The nurse attending both of them, holding the vial, was acting as a nurse for one day only. On all other days the nurse was a fireman at the army base.

There had been another nurse attending also, but she had been jubilant to excuse herself: "You know what to get him!" she volleyed at the fireman; then she had taken off, as if she was flying.

When she did so jubilantly, the child was doing a quick, wild writhe after having been shot. He was lying down. Dr. Tiffany was standing big and tall—the tallest one, with a robin's-egg-blue paper mask, masking half his face, tied behind his head, and the abashed fireman was confronting Dr. Tiffany.

So far the clues are: the word *Tiffany*, probably from *theophany; robin's-egg-blue; fireman*; and *vial*—the same sound as *vile*.

Whoops, before the presentation of clues, more information should have appeared concerning the child—that the child scolded the doctor again.

"Trust me, trust me," Dr. Tiffany said. "It's safe, I know, in your eye—because we put it in eye drops. That's how I know."

The fireman was too abashed to speak.

The fireman never in his life told anyone either the particulars of his masturbatory techniques, and they were manifestly soothing inventions. The fireman knew how to feel as if he was with someone he could love when he was all alone. He should have told at least one other person how.

SPANISH

I wish that everything is enough for Mr. Red who is the husband, who has a heavy Spanish accent. He is a scholar. Mrs. Red speaks English with a heavy Spanish accent also, and she is a full-time scholar, too.

Yesterday, I saw the Reds' bed of scarlet impatiens waving in the wind, which was quite unremarkable. But, that is not all.

Mrs. Red, who is probably responsible for the planting of the flowers, was on her way, carrying her folded-up folding chair and several other things.

She was big enough, even with carrying all of her things, so she could fit comfortably between my thumb and my forefinger from where I sat inside of my house watching her—that was my perspective on my hand.

To me, she is like a cutie-pie! like a little doll!

Society, schools, hospitals, factories, and homes are the other victims of the perpetual movement of philosophical thought, as well as many other organees.

A FIELD THAT CAN NEVER
BE EXHAUSTED

I must let you know how urgent I felt racing down the stairs. We did that—the whole group of us girls. Next winter I am going to be in Florida.

I didn't have any money with me. There was an additional obstacle. Things were probably not that simple. He said, "Follow the good-looking blond!" He was the blond he was referring to, and he was very good-looking, and jaunty, I thought. It was a cute idea to tell us to follow him and to use a line like that. He was having fun I think. Off we trooped. He shouted, "Single file!"

I suppose he had to shout that. I suppose there was no other way to do it.

What do you expect? Don't you expect him to get a little fun out of his job? When he was telling me to pull my pants down, he said, "Pull them down lower."

But how should I tell this? I have been waiting for years to tell this anecdote that any civilization would need to illustrate that there are people, you know, who are perfectly capable of being cheerful.

THEY WERE NAKED AGAIN

In an instant she may not see it as it happens, how light crowds in and around her red hair, and all around her head, before vanishing into some other light, which is likely having nothing more to do with her hair?—but this is wrong, because there is no inkling of science.

So—I'll get her into his bed, looking at his carpet, which is on his floor, rolled up. Together, they look at it, not for any reason they guess might augment them.

He is prepared to get rid of the carpet. It has been causing him to feel bereft of something he probably never had—something which I could give him.

I could.

She says, "Please don't get rid of it. It comforts me."

I would never say that to him. I would never say that to

him in this situation, which is a situation which is a spectacular opportunity for them both, and it is my time they are taking.

You know what happens when they both are thinking so much about the carpet at the same time?

His experience appears to be one of elation, such as finishing. Then she says something obscene, which happens to be clairvoyant. Then I say, "I gave my own carpet away like that, *bitch!*"

But they cannot hear me.

I'll threaten suicide!

You—you think about a carpet.

Me.

THE MEANING OF LIFE

One point must be made and this concerns what we learn from the history of the world. It must be noted that usually men do not possess valuables or huge sums of money. Their sense of their being sorry about this grows and it grows and it grows. A woman may be their only irreplaceable object. That's why I think the meaning of life is so wonderful. It has helped millions of men and women to achieve vastly rich and productive lives.

Recently, this woman appeared on TV. She has a small head, a big head of hair, and she sings solo. She's wonderful, but because of her dread fear of almost all men, she does not want any more than one man at a time in her life, which is reasonable, but she is always at a loss.

THE BIG PARADE

The only beginning to this I can bear is "You weren't wearing any!" which a woman who would not hush herself in a restaurant declared. I am asserting she wanted to set another woman there straight, who, with some shame, I suppose, did not hesitate to put her hands up over her ears and to ask anyone at all, "Where are they?"

All of the above stirs me.

All of the above stirs me no more than does the most urgent matter in my own life. The damage is done.

With some difficulty, I could tell you more. I could name *you*, the unnamed you.

Here I am with what has happened. I am not now going to back up and go around to where this is supposed to end by rule, to where I would have to publicly proclaim my loss, as my husband did yesterday, hunched over, carrying my suitcases, headed with his head down—that attitude. I followed him down the big avenue, through the big parade—we cut right through it, and I followed, and there at the big hotel my husband said, "I want to take these inside for you!" and I followed him to where he delivered me personally, so passionately, to my next husband forthcoming.

I had a strangely tender attitude only toward myself then, not toward either one of them, which I have been told is the motive force behind anyone's pursuit of novelty.

THE HAG WAS
TRANSFORMED BY LOVE

The guys, oh, how you longed for them, round and savory, and just how they get after a few days in their gravy, in the pot, in the refrigerator, and then they are heated up, and then they are eaten up.

I know what Terri Great thought because I remember my thoughts to a tee exactly about my own little new potatoes I just ate, and I am calling myself for the hell of it, *Terri!*

She was sticking her fork—Mrs. Alexander Great—into the little new potato, thinking, I may be the only one who likes this!

For the hell of it, Mrs. Great, you should have stayed there sticking in your fork, tasting and enjoying, and eating up little new potatoes until you had finished all four of your potatoes, *Terri!*

Say it, Terri, from the two and a half little guys that you did eat, you got all the stimulation from the spree you thought was wise, because, if she's going to say, "This is the best it gets from a potato," then Terri Great has stretched her mind beyond the wisecrack fully—stop!

Terri left the house then, and her husband Alexander never saw her again, nor her little guy Raymond, nor her little guy, Guy.

She spent most of her time in the company of people like herself who said they knew what they were thinking. For instance, *she* thinks any penis is ugly.

The enormity of what she had done, leaving her family abruptly, suddenly, and with no warning, gave her lots of other thoughts, too.

She did not upon arrival, speak well the language of the country she had fled to. When she asked a man, for example, on the street, her first day in town, "Where is the train station?" the man told her kindly that there had not been a war in his country for forty years. (He wore a brown, ankle-length, belted trench coat, was about sixty years old.) Miraculously, she thought she could comprehend every word that he had said. It was a miracle, too, that when he flashed it at her, she thought *his* penis was a beauty. Like magic—the colors of it were the colors to her of her own baby's shirt, face, and hat that she had only just left far behind, and the form of it was like a much much much bigger dewdrop.

At home, this rich man had a thin wife. He supposedly

worshipped his old wife until old Terri Great came into the picture. Then just forget it. (Things keep happening so perversely for zealots.)

For Terri, she got her first six orgasms during penetration with this man during the next fifteen weeks of their intercourses together.

In the weeks that followed these events, she renewed her days, and she became intrigued with finance.

JEWISHNESS

When the bird was upside down, going along by bumbling, a small one, hanging from the underside of a branch, it was during the snowfall in our mid-April season here. Bobbling? Jerking? An insect would—mice and rats. A bumblebee would do it underneath the branch like that, before returning to its golden world.

The bird then flew up off back the other way, showing me something or nothing I did not understand, like a mood swing.

The experience of getting one to die for me hangs on. I literally ran into it on my lawn, the mouse. It was upside down, with an open mouth, I remember—for cuteness, I bet—a pink tongue behind the teeth.

So I saw the conclusion. I was grateful to see it dead.

I don't have to say how I knew previously about this

mouse. I knew where the mouse had been. I had introduced myself into the picture with this mouse. I don't have to say what I was doing to the mouse. I deeply dread it was something wrong. I've told the story other times. Some of my stories get told more often than they're worth. This one is one. It signifies not much. It signifies a story I remember. I remember how my forebears ran like rats escaping, stubbornly clinging, because they had never gone along with an idea—an investment in the future. It was just a grand idea, such as *Hope springs eternal*— but they must have got bored.

THE MISTAKE

She is looking at me curiously. The natural thing is to act sympathetic to her, so I go ahead and do that.

Meanwhile, down the hall, a girl is getting angry. I can hear the telltale sounds. This girl comes in to say something.

She is looking at me curiously.

I don't know which horrible thing happens next in my real bedroom. The new carpeting is familiar. I know the bedspread. I know the room well, but I don't remember a clock around here that chimes. I remember mystery, suspense, and adventure.

Even as I blot it out, I was dead wrong to summarize.

CLUNK

Stephen still has had no contact with Miss Klinka's hairy pink crack, and we are—even my brother is—spending a lot of time pacifying the aggrieved Mr. Maurer. Meanwhile, Klinka moves ever so slowly, but surely, because I believe in her, toward an evanescent moment that will be worth everything *anyone* has suffered, in my opinion.

I had the opportunity to feel very sorry that nothing sexual was going on, or would ever go on, between any of these people, because their business happens to be my business, and my business is what I usually think about when I try to summarize my life so far, which has been completely bereft of sex, except for self-abuse.

I self-abuse.

I dropped Klinka off today for her clinic. She needed to

bring a sack lunch because the clinic runs from nine to four o'clock. I saw her standing in the doorway of the hut. People were going in and coming out, and a few of her friends smiled at Klinka when she said hello. It's just as I thought—people of all kinds convening, to be organized by the organizers, by the persons in charge of the clinic. All of their arms and their legs were in motion, often—their heads turn and nod—there is some mobility in their faces, some nobility. I wonder why.

I always wonder why.

CHARACTERIZE

The hostess created them in their image. The cookies are turkeys inscribed with edible names on the butter plates.

There are two cooked, twelve-pound turkeys, no longer in those images, on platters for the entrée, waiting.

The guests are waiting for the entrée, discussing the weather, because winter has not arrived, and one month previous to this time, it should have. (This time, in this place, the winter never does arrive.)

The comments of a husband and a wife about how they feel about the weather prove dramatically to any omniscient thinker that they are dramatically unsuitable, maritally, for one another.

Their infant, who can understand their language better than his own, is listening.

A catastrophic earthquake occurs on another continent in a geographical zone that has never harbored a vicious winter. This is in the country Turkey. There they have certainly had a number of earthquakes in the regions where the winter is mild and only rainy and in those other regions as well.

That's how the cookie crumbles.

No, seriously, my darling, "thou art my bone and my flesh."

ICKY

Her curtains actually do stiffen and then billow into a deformity because of the warm gusts of wind which are periodic. The carnations in her vase tremble when it's their turn, which is poetic. In her beautiful room she is a bit ghoulish even when she is still.

She is also youngish and balding.

She is so lucky because a picture painted by her son in her beautiful room is revolutionary in its scope, scale, and ambition. All of the knowledge her son will ever need to know about ghoulishness is in it.

The son is correct if he chooses to believe that his mother is a ghoul.

He thinks her armchair is as comforting as nobody he has ever known. There are flowers he cannot identify, printed on the upholstery, but their type, he is well aware, is icky. In her beautiful room where he has gotten her riding crop wet, among other things, his mother has stuck his tiny last lost tooth, with glue, onto the frame of her mirror.

A sensational evening is ahead for the boy, even though he is not allowed to bring food or drink into any room outside of the kitchen.

His mother has just asked him to do a couple of odd jobs for money.

ORE

A generally reliable woman was pestering the seed—or is it called a pit?—that she had noticed was blotchy. The reliable woman at work in her kitchen observed privately to herself, for no reason she knew of, that the pit had been discolored by avocado-colored markings. The woman was using her fingers to wrench the pit out from the center of the ripe fruit. The pit was not coming along willingly.

No, this is not about childbirth.

The surprise is that anyone as reliable as she is had not had plenty of experience wrenching pits.

The pear's pit—this is an avocado pear pit—was not of a like mind to hers—like, *What is the matter with you, pit?*

What is the matter with her very reliable husband, who could not extract this woman, his wife, from their home?

The wife had been making her husband miserable for years, being the unbudgeable type.

I'd say time for a change.

In their secret life, the husband and the wife then sought the usual marital excavations—their aim being to meet their troubles with equanimity.

For starters, they agreed. They agreed how excellent their sexual satisfactions together were, how much more reliably attainable these satisfactions were, more now than had ever been the case before, now that every other aspect of their life together, they admitted, was so unsatisfactory in such extreme.

No, no, no, no, no!

This discussion never occurred. The husband and the wife no longer had the means to conduct such a high-level discussion.

These people are annoying. You know how annoying? To me, as annoying as it was to see for myself last night at twilight one bright sparkling spot in the sky that did not move. It did not get bigger, or brighter, or smaller, or dimmer, and for all intents and purposes, it is stuck there.

As I am.

THE CARE OF MYSELF

So why can't everything be perfect? God love him, he appealed to me. He had startled me into feeling an incredible amount of affection for a stranger—him—this inspector who rang my doorbell, who had dressed himself as a fireman.

"Do you have a wound? Is that a bandage on your head?" I asked him.

He tugged on the stretchy cloth which was not supposed to be hidden under his helmet. He said, "We all wear that."

The days and the years pass so swiftly.

Now, what I am doing for *my* wound is this: I stick any old rag or balled-up old sock I can find as close to it as I can get. Belly-down on the floor, with my reading glasses on, I've also got some filler sticking almost into my asshole. With my bawdy book here to comfort me right in front of my nose—we are both, the book and I, products of a great civilization—I take the plunge. I am thrusting mightily, and sometimes I manage to get hurt again.

CRUSH

There was no Weinberg. The server barging into all that with his tray of only a few nuggets on a doily was peevish with his back arched, with his chin up. A deadly serious woman was introducing Mrs. Williams and a Darnell Hyde. The woman showed me where her waist was and her curved legs were visible to me when she marched over to a dressed-up man to say his name.

The rest of this story is about my family's poignant meal in the elegant hotel dining room. Within striking distance, there is a celebrity who thinks she should be eating here. She is exquisite and brainy and delicately made, it appears—or she is fashioned to appear to be delicate. Her lacy necklace sparkles around her neck. Her lacy bracelet on her wrist sparkles. At her throat her skin is deadish white and, elsewhere, her hair is white. The rest of this story is about my wish to be her. Her escort should be ashamed of himself. His back was turned to me the whole time.

My mother loved the food. I loved mine. I was marginally disappointed in it. I escaped when I said I had to go to the bathroom, the same way I forgot with my hand on the handle of the fridge door why I had wanted to look inside. It is a great natural law, I think, but of what?

Diane, I was the first of us to swoon, entering the glass elevator, descending—my only purpose being to resemble a human being going down.

A PROGRESS IN SPIRITUALITY

W e were in our own backyard, with everything that that could mean, portending. This could be important.

To taste his drink, to look into his eyes, to be shocked, to give my opinion, I had been up on my feet.

"I am shocked. It is so sweet," I said. I was.

He said, "It is."

I sat back down.

The wind took his paper cup, almost blew it away. He got it back. He put it down. He picked it up. No-handed, he bit the rim.

"It's no trouble," I said. "I'll take it inside and throw it away."

My guess is, it was my "trouble" or my "no" he heard, when he saw my shapely form as I turned with his paper cup.

Things got all knocked back—I don't have a clue how.

To have seen his face then—what's it called?—turgid with

lust for me?—was a forgotten truth, and tonight I am destined to shoot the rival woman who tried to snatch him. I shoot her by shaking her hand.

When I take her hot hand in mine, we could be the rivals dipped in stone, in the antique story. There should be a story. I don't know the story. There may be a story of them getting a grip on each other forever.

What does that mean? Nobody gets killed. I'm stuck with her. He's stuck with me. All I remember is our kinship, which makes me sick. I have gone so very far to deny death.

It is already only a memory.

THE BAND-AID AND THE PIECE OF GUM

There was the possibility up until five o'clock—then there was no more possibility. I expected to hear from Walter today. When I woke up, I was cheered by the thought that maybe today, *today* would be the most important day of my life. Today I ended up using the Band-Aid Walter had given me on my toe. He had thrust it into my hand. "Take it. You never know when you may need it." The piece of gum he had once given me I chewed finally today also. "Try it. You could learn something," is what he had said. Remember how I told you he grabbed me around the neck the last time I saw him? It was practically impossible to walk, which he was trying to do all at the same time, and trying to get me to walk along with him, too. There was the possibility, perhaps, that we could both have toppled over onto his floor.

That's it. Usually they start where a person was born, then their parents, their parents' parents, where they were born, occupations, so that includes dates, names, locations, character traits of all the parties concerned, chronology, trauma, wishes, dreams, eccentricities, real speech, achievements, including struggle, the obstacles, someone's dementia, another chronic illness, a centrifugal drama, certainly all the deaths, photos, paintings if any—likenesses of many of the parties concerned, plus summary statements made periodically throughout to sum up the situation at any given time.

THIS ONE'S ABOUT (_____)

This is being written to explain my sister's most fundamental, the most important discovery ever made in human history so far by an individual. Her discovery—it is so shocking—stemmed from, as in every other sphere of life—a rude awakening.

My sister, who made the discovery, was doing the driving. My mother was in the backseat with the attorney. I was in the front seat next to my sister—the discoverer!

We had the attorney in the backseat scrunched up. This is now thirteen years later, after our fierce journey that night—it was indeed at night.

My sister at the wheel—I forgot to mention she had a lame right arm and bad vision, which had been allowed to go uncorrected, and that, also, she had forgotten to turn the car headlights on. I forgot to say that it is easy to see how this resolved, but all quite obviously was not quite lost.

At the great speed I turned around whenever I wanted to take a look at the attorney when he made his statements. I did not get a look at my mother. In fact, did she ever speak?

At the great speed what did my sister say about everything that hung in the balance—that is—how we were doing, when the attorney told her to check her speed?

Strange as it sounds, I still do not know how clear the danger was then. Speaking for myself, I felt then, This is an important drama. If I were the driver, I would be questioning what our alternatives were for where exactly we were heading.

When she got out of the car, all that was real to my sister was the answers to the questions. At the beginning of life we are not in perfect harmony with the universe. I am fond of my sister's idea, which is slowly gaining favor, that at the beginning of our life, when observers are observing any one of us, metaphorically speaking, they get sick. Most of the observers refuse to observe that all this all really has to do with is *clothes!*

And finally, a big thank you to Chuck Cohen in Highland Park, Illinois, because he gave my sister her idea!

TORAH

I carry this plate of triumph into the school building with my Saran Wrap all aflutter all over my iced cakes. I have iced my cakes because I think everyone nowadays has an expectation of icing on it from a cupcake, as I am sure I do, too.

The corn candies I pushed into the icing are the tough lumps, my vicious triples, my quadruples, the repetition of an idea an idea an idea an idea an idea. Are you keeping track of this as I did? This situation could be handled.

I took control of the situation when the official in the office did nothing when she saw me create a situation in her office. But I gave up control when this official declared that no man had ever hooked his fingers into her vagina and then keenly observed her face, or pleaded to go down on her, or pushed her against a wall into her own shadow and said, "We call this dry humping when we do it in school!"

As it turned out, for no good reason, I tested the woman sorely.

I was wicked.

Yet perfectly delightful when I was God.

AN IMPERISHABLE ROMANCE

I've been trying to get hold of someone to have some fun with. They both have. Let's pretend nothing is awkward. Three of us abreast, with the ancient and august chapel behind us, and in front of us the alarm was not so great. It was the moon. When he squealed about the moon, what I said was, "You should have seen it this afternoon! It was so big and red!"

I had made a mistake.

The crux of her advice about walking in the cold toward our car, way down the road, was, "You just have to do it." We were not dressed for the cold. As a group, we had looked at her black suede French oxfords because we had wanted to, and she didn't want to get them ruined in the dark. She watched her step. I watched my boots. Yes, they sank into the grass at least an inch, not out of sight. I had told him which of his shoes to be wearing. When we were alone, I had spoken to him while tapping, "I like this and this and this."

Certain things should not be spoken of in front of children. I agree with that. Children should not do certain things, and I agree with that. Thank God, she ran like hell, once out of the car, at her house.

It's a Japanese lantern hanging up there—wildly picturesque—before you get to her front door. Has this person never heard of a *bood*?—my favorite word for it.

NUDE

The parrot's owner gives me information about the parrot that the parrot is molting, or something that is awful—that it hates women. The parrot's owner is also a treasure house of information about libidinous debauches.

The parrot's owner should be a handsome man. He has wrapped himself in a white bath towel. His hair is wet.

His little girl is sort of chirping *She hates me! I just hate her!* about their parrot, as a little girl will. She sort of bounces brightly in her swimsuit with its dots of purplish blue and reddish purple, and purplish pink.

I am wearing my brand-new nude—what the shop owner called the nude. The slip has a crease running down its center, not between my legs, from its having been all folded up inside of a drawer in the shop before I took it to try on.

I bought a robe, too, from that shop, which I could have had in any one of three different colors—which I will not name—the colors. But I could have.

However, when the shop owner spoke to me of underclothes the color of pink ice, I sort of lost hope that I would ever get them, but I have imagined nothing strong or deep or vivid or very dark or bluish in all the pricks I will have.

How could I?

How could I?

How could I?

JEWELING

In the deep dark recesses of her curse, there lay everything she had.

She was an expert diver, but this had nothing to do with that. She opened her purse and she told her friend, "Look in here."

He said, "What?" but he looked inside. He was used to acceding to certain commands.

She was showing him what he had given to her, where she had put his gift—how the thing was situated in the deep dark recesses of her purse.

Someone thought the object he had given her was an object beautiful to look at.

He had just given it to her, and that is where it had ended up being—for the time being.

He needed no special perspicacity to know that she meant, *See how it looks in here, your thing in mine.*

He is a friend in a clandestine, passionate arrangement.

He is mine.

It is my purse.

Now his gift is all mine, with its deep capacity for spectral light. It is as cold and as hard an object as is the love I receive from two men. It is so hard.

I believe in coincidence and providence.

I believe in these two men as I believe in my right hand and in my left hand equally, and in my two eyes, that they are equally mine, and in my ears, and in the two of everything for and on me.

Two created me thereof, in the beginning. Is it precious? It took two to make me what I am.

NAAA

There's the baby who gets the bee sting. In my opinion, there's the baby carrying around a paperweight that, if he had dropped it on his bare foot, would or could have broken his foot.

The mother of the babies has sprained her ankle, and chipped a bone in it, and she is using a cane to help her get around.

Here's where the plot is thickening. Here's the plot: When the baby was stung, at first no one was sure what had happened, but then the mother said, "His arm is getting all pink." Not to go on and on—the sting was discovered on the tip of the baby's thumb. Finally—I was there—at the moment of the discovery, when just then: the baby stopped his crying.

I was the person who took the paperweight away from the baby. He walks. He's old enough to walk, just old enough, which is why I call him a baby. He was disappointed, but did not appear outraged, when I took the paperweight away from him. "You should not be carrying this around," I said.

If this were an issue larger than the worry about human extinction, I could allow myself to think about it.

Secretly, I believe the paperweight is an item which should never have existed, *ever*.

The facts of the matter are complex, but this baby's power is nowhere limited.

This baby's power is his renunciation of all power.

THE FULLNESS OF LIFE
IS FROM SOMETHING

Exploring the front of her blouse herself—she leaned her head down—her nose, her mouth, her eyes became unpleasantly close to the rest of her. She did not feel, however, disgust. Happily, she was imagining a dark rose-red rose on its black bed.

In her present mood, unfolding before her, she saw valleys and shadows upon herself with something else—we'll get back to that—introduced that she did not crave, that had nothing to do with the turmoil of her spirit, nor with her modest capacity as a person.

This was happening not purely by chance. What had happened was that she had said, "The roses are so beautiful."

"Do you want them?" he had said. "You paid for them."

Next thing, he was wrapping the three roses up for her to

take with her. Next thing, she had thought about nipping a bud and wearing a bud. Next thing, she had thought about it again, more nipping—because she had not nipped any bud yet, nor had she put any bud behind her ear, nor fastened with a hairpin a bud into her hair, nor stuck a bud into a buttonhole on the front of her blouse, where a bud would barely make itself famous, because it was not a bud that would glow in the dark.

Next thing, when her sister was putting her face unpleasantly close to hers, she was uncomforted by the nearness of her sister, or by the apparent growing kindness of her sister, as her sister talked, talked, talked to her, as officially as her sister could manage to about the void.

SEX SOLVES PROBLEMS

There is no going back, and no use insisting I have a bath to look forward to. Is four o'clock too late? Dinner, sure.

As I carried the baby off for her bath, I felt I was doing the right thing. It was what I had been asked to do, and I was trying to be helpful. The baby was naked as a baby, and she took up almost all of the sink, and she was slippery when wet, and not at all easy to hold on to, and I don't think I got much of the soap on her, and she kept shutting her head up into the faucet.

"I have an idea," I said. "You better go to bed."

It was the greatest stroke of luck. It was like putting the baby away. I am not a fusser. It was like having any old thing for dinner and not giving a hoot. This is so basic.

The first person who decided a problem could be solved came up with the idea the same way I did.

We are easy lays, too.

SERAPHIM

I suppose that I do have places, a few places, left to wear my
mustache to. I have worn it almost everywhere. Before we
go, I put on my fur coat inside of my house simultaneous with
my putting it on. My mustache is faint and spiky. My coat is
thick and dark.

Going around town tends to be sad, like walking around
behind a dog who won't go. You wear what you wear. Tonight
we are going to the Fontana for pizza. There will be a TV on
in there. There will be plastic chandeliers to simulate glass
chandeliers. There will be simulated oil paintings on the wall
to simulate the idea of things: a woman with a hat on, perhaps
her skirt roughed up by the wind, her hand lifted to keep her
bonnet on her head.

When the pizza comes, I put a fingertip into my plate to get a crumb stuck to it, then to lick the crumb off.

This is my gift to my children—whereas theirs to me is not to be nasty about having a mother with facial hair.

I am telling you, I never wear it anywhere near my perianal or my vaginal-lips locations. If it as much as touches my eyes, I wash them out with a solution. I promise you—*you are an angel!*—I keep it out of the reach of the children!

NO, CUP

G et the family out forever, out from around the table.
Now, at breakfast, the most important objects on the
table are the way-out-of-whack coffee cups for the parents,
twice normal size, and their double-sized saucers, all shiny
black.

The cups are almost as tall as the normal-sized white
pitcher of milk that was there for the children, when the children were there.

The white paper napkin, not nearly as important as the
cups are, partially hidden under the biscuits in the basket, and
getting soiled by biscuit grease, is sticking up. The points at
the corners of the napkin are what stick up the highest, but the
points do not reach as high as the white milk pitcher reaches
with its lips—*pardon*, lip. Even so, allow for the possibility

that both the lip of the pitcher and the napkin points express human aspiration, conceptually.

Already, there is too much to think about on the table. What is the most important thing? One of the cups should be enough to think about.

Cup.

The shine on the cup. Light.

No, *cup*.

The most important thing in any circumstance is what people want to believe is all wrong, you asshole.

Defecation.

MY RADIANT GIRL

I am not so sure there is a reason to tell this except for my wanting to say things about magic, about myth, about legend that might brighten up your day, if you believe in magic, myth, legend. It was Coleridge who said we might brighten up the day this way. Emerson might have said there are real nymphs in your city park, if you look. Oh I'm sure Cocteau and George Eliot had their opinions on nymphs. Let's say Edith Wharton's daughter had the last word. I'm adding, though. My nymph in Central Park I did not know was a nymph right off. I believe thoroughly in her now.

The nymphs don't have to be little. She was. She had removed most of her clothing. Men watched. There she was, oiling herself—an unblemished beauty with her teacup breasts, with boy hips, covered by her sunning suit, which she had had concealed under the other clothes, a necklace rimming her neck, and yellow hair tied back.

She looked at nothing except to do the sunning—to take care of the oil, her skin, and how she should rise up, or she should lie down, or turn—she had to look. Two men next to me, whom I also earnestly watched, watched earnestly.

I'm a woman. You don't take that for granted, I suppose, or that I believe in ghosts just because I say, "See the nymph!"

As Yeats said, "There are no such things as ghosts. Ghosts, no! There are those mortals who are beautifully masquerading, and those of them who are carried off." Okay, as Yeats did not say.

Sometimes girls like her are gotten rid of in a not so gentle way. Socrates said of one, "A northern gust carried her over the neighboring rocks, because I said so." He said, "I was swollen with passion." Nietzsche said the people of the cities have the machine to get rid of them if they are annoying.

It was Captain Stewart who informed me that because I saw the girl, "You will rise to the summit of your power, then you will die a violent death." He said that. His records confirm this fact.

So far, I have told the truth. It was straight from my heart to say we would be killed.

CANNIBAL, THE NATURAL HISTORY

Everything was so bad because of what happened in the spring, but I eat it.

I asked Chuck, "What happened in the spring?"

Something very very bad. I couldn't get to what without Chuck's help. The reason to remember was to keep talking to Chuck for X amount of time.

Chuck said, then I nearly said, the *drought*. He said it first.

"Is there good news?" I asked Chuck. I did not address Chuck as Chuck, who was unaware I knew his name or his secret.

Chuck answered me spitefully. "They are ripening them artificially."

Spiteful Chuck. I knew. The secret about Chuck was that everything was nice about Chuck except that he did not know how—*anything* about being nice. Something else about eating—the train of my thought—in X amount of time, nowhere near Chuck, I got to it—it was mothers who would not knowingly eat a coward before their babies were born. Among these people, the diet restrictions were severe. Strict for a purpose.

I'm a mom like that. Not to brag, today at lunch, Maggie did not smell it on me, what I have been cooking. She guessed wrong. *Chuuuuuuck!*

I know one thing about Maggie. She is a very, very mixed-up person.

BLOOM

The ham, the sweet and the tender cookies, pecans—heavily grooved the way they are—candies wrapped in green foil, in red, or in any foil, are the custom, so is the attitude of the little girl named Sandy.

A man and a woman, not married to each other, who had just returned, they said, from a romantic holiday together in Capri, took turns to speak to each other respectfully of their spouses and I listened in. One attractive man was there. Well, I like him.

I leaped to my feet to go over to the attractive man, and Sandy followed me. Since then, many others have tried to stick to me like glue.

Please believe me that there is no part of me which is sad, angry, or resentful when I remember suddenly leaping up that time, or many other times since this time or before. The cause of my serenity may be that I am not ashamed to just go through the motions of having naked power and ambition, as in fucking.

This burgeoning is gratifying.

MEAT

The prince's house makes me feel respect for his house. The house causes me to stand and look at his house as if his house deserves all of my attention. I will need to be butted out of this drifting off into full respect for his house by something necessary or urgent, and nobody will get me to speak about my mother's new boyfriend instead of the prince who lives in this house.

The first time I met the prince, he was talking to his hired man inside of my neighbor's garage, and he told me to come by sometime and we could have an Ovaltine at his house.

I just don't want to say why we were all in the garage. It is not even as germane as the rumpled prince on the edge of his property today, talking with the three hired men. His hair, his shirt, his trousers were rumpled.

There was a rather smooth aspect to the shirt of one of the hired men, how it stretched itself smoothly down, then down in under and behind his belt, which reminds me of the food galore at my mother's boyfriend's party, which an overweight woman dressed in white with bleached yellow hair prepared and served to us—meat.

I loved Gwen—the woman sitting next to me at the party. She bakes her bread in a machine. It doesn't swirl, but since it is better to be impetuous, she puts into it anyway cinnamon and raisins into the white dough!

I am tempted to not say anything more which could imply anything, because this is not literature. This is espionage.

N.B. If you like, change all the words.

THE STRANGEST AND
MOST POWERFUL

"Look, we've been over this and over this."
I giggled. I began to blush. I stammered, "You—you—
Dicky—I—"

It was all unnecessary because—*blaaruah!*—the doorbell
rang. Behind the window adjacent to the door, I saw a face and
a fist.

Where we all were, at my aunt and uncle's house, was a
particularly lovely spot. A group of people not yet too terribly
tired continued making comments while I sat in a trance. My
uncle opened the door. I heard my uncle say, "No, I won't do
that," then another man's voice, "Why not?" then my uncle, "I
am afraid," then the other one, "Poor girl, she's the kind who
gets taken advantage of." "What on earth do you mean?" my
uncle said.

A certain kind of shock had set in, which protected me. I thought of going home. Of course, I made no attempt to leave. I was puzzled, and as per usual I spoke up. I did not comprehend or enjoy what I said, despite all of my experience talking. Then I laughed, and turned away with embarrassment. The next thing I imagined myself being spoken to. My uncle was handing me a drink, and a big stranger, with a purple orchid in his buttonhole, with his hair combed down flat, stood beside my uncle, gaping at me.

Clinkety-clink! clinked the ice cubes in my drink. I spilled some of my drink, of course, on my sweater, when the apparition began a conversation, which constitutes our culture. It seemed so trivial, our culture.

THE SEDUCTION

You try so hard when they are sick. He's very sick.
When I cooked, I'd cut up a little liver before I left, and
he ate it. Do you think that's good?

He is a significant figure. There's a treatise on him I am
reading now. There is to be a thoughtful conclusion forthcoming, I hope.

It took a long time for historians to develop the notion of
objectivity, because of their compulsiveness, which is a never-
you-mind that overcomes logical thinking.

This calls for an explanation. I'd say it does.

Let me see: Do I remember? I ask myself. Let me see: YOU
ARE TOO BIG! I did not know what to do. I did not know if I was
pushing or if I was just trying to push. I did not know the difference.

Despite the promising start—I was so excited—things went badly, but I haven't spoken ill of him. I've heard others say, "What a bastard!" I've heard his dreadful sobbing. He has clutched at me. He has spoken reasonably.

"Yes," I said.

"Darling," he said, and I got frightened. And then he said, "I was afraid to touch you." I let him hold my hand. I could not tell what he wanted—a theatrical marriage? I'm sympathetic to the most simple human act.

HA

———✦———

"See if you can find a whistle, even a toy whistle, *any* whistle," she implored.

He knew he'd never find one in their town. When you know how it will turn out, you feel tired. So do I.

There ought to be a brilliant portrayal of the home-coming—the boy with what? or with the lack of what? the matriarch to be reckoned with.

An hour later, the boy returned with nothing to say.

After her hesitation, his mother asked, "So?"

He heard her clanking their plates.

But instead of answering his mother, the boy went back out into the backyard.

Because the mother's confusion was even greater than her boy's, she said nothing more either. But oh, how she thought!

Oh, this is hopeless! she thought.

What would her boy's fate be? she wondered. Well, she decided, they need a victim. I need a victim. We all need a victim.

The boy's heart heaved. He thought he was confident of the future. His house had been through fire. Things needed doing.

As for his mother, her voice had positively no timbre. She barely got her words out. In real life, she was barely heard.

About other details—or more about the boy—I don't have any ambition for any more, except to observe that the boy squatted on his haunches in the flowers.

The mother remembered then—that, as a baby, he had looked a trace displeased to be born.

THE REVISION

You should not read this. It is too private. It is the most serious. It is even too serious for me. I should make something of this.

Here is the best part, when he said to me *come here.* That was the very best part of my life so far. In the doorway to his bathroom was where I was. It was where I was when I asked him, "Are you peeing?"

He said, "No, but now I am." He was seated to do the peeing, so it would not be any problem to do it, facing me. I didn't even hear it, the peeing, if he peed.

Well, why?—why can't all of it be dirty parts, every part a dirty part, or quickly leading to another dirty part?—the part when he just put himself into my mouth?—or the part when he said *you looked*—I can't remember how he said I looked to him, with that part of him in my mouth, but he jiggled on my jaw. He said *open up* before he went ahead and he peed. Oh! That's how babies could be made!

THE EARTH IS FULL OF HER GLORY

Mary Lugg had not perceived her fate.

It would seem so cold-blooded, wouldn't it? a planned thing. She stood straighter to see if that would help her back feel better. That helped. Then she put herself into her chair at the table.

Alan Hatt was speaking, "—for years. That's what I think. In my opinion, you deserve it."

"It's witchcraft," said Amanda Hatt.

Rod Rowan had a toothache. Rod Rowan whispered, "I can understand it."

Alan Hatt had a brain tumor he knew nothing about. Nobody knew if it would eventually kill him or if he's to die of boredom.

Mary Lugg said, "She's a good cook. Don't tell, but I can't

eat these." Mary Lugg was referring to the dumplings in the soup. She could not eat them.

"It was a horrible experience," Rod Rowan said. "I told them everything."

"Good Lord, Rod!" cried Alan Hatt. He grabbed the edge of the table for support.

If the truth were audible, the actual world was moaning. It began to dawn on Mary Lugg what was happening. Her thought produced a fine dramatic effect, not unlike what she endured whenever she lied, or when she got what she wanted. It felt good.

THE TIME OF HARMONY,
OR CRUDITÉ

I would say I was half the way through when I thought to myself: Be careful. Anyway, there were twenty of them, to begin with.

I cut every one in half.

There were six.

I cut one to pieces, wedge-shaped. I'd say there were nine wedges. This is the estimate, generally, I get from thinking back on it.

I cut slices from it.

I'd say there were six slices.

I sawed and I sawed back and forth.

I cut stalks. I made chips. There were about fifty more wedges. There were wheels. One wheel which I had produced took off, rolled along, and dropped. I made sticks and I made slivers. I made raggedy bunches, stalks, chunks.

The house was neat and clean as ever. I got a lot of things done. I fully enjoyed sex. It turned out I was very deep into being.

On so many occasions, what goes with what? I do not want to leave behind anything during the accumulation that I will have to grasp at one glance because it is not a piece of crap.

BEYOND PRINCIPLE

It predestined her to become a thinker, to become a woman in a storm center for many years to come, because she did no fornicating with any other. She never left him out of it, *never*; not before she met him or after she had met him.

Into her mind she liked to keep adding what she called "a little curve" or "a little fork" among the pathways. She was ready to change her mind. Original conclusions were not her aim. She preferred to lay claim to the obvious.

One time when her hands were on his naked flesh, he said, "I love it when you draw me in." Squeezing his rump, "Like this?" she said.

Doing her job, she thought, *Who says that men aren't soft?* and the one man became the multitude through the backward path that leads to satisfaction, toward the upshot of all far-fetched speculation and curiosity—which is an example for example of how she first thought her idea of giving herself a little pinch or little pushes, of getting her hand up in between her and him in the very middle of their act. Not seeking to interrupt, to fail shamefully, or to baby herself, she intended to be serious—not to goof up, not to fuck up. "You're going to have fun with it, I know," she said. She thought, *I want to know how this turns out.* She said, "Come in and show me." She wagged her finger.

She cut him out of her life.

Isn't she wonderful, if an assumption is permissible? It looks as if she ended those embarrassing situations at any cost.

Her terrible war gave rise to pathology of this kind, but her terrible war finally put an end to temptation. Now I could throw in something that's so sensual, that's full of an object.

SCRATCHING THE HEAD

We respect her from learning from her. Let us compile the factors of her failure. We could not find hereditary factors. We said, "Tell us about yourself."

At the zenith of her life, in her mid-forties, she changed. She met the man who awakened her oldest erotic feelings.

"What a nightmare!" she said. "Why can't it be over? When I touched his arm, my hand was on fire. When I am nowhere near him, there's a sledgehammering down here."

She gestured, not shyly, toward her genitalia. She inquired, "I have never heard of that. Have you?"

Perhaps we should leave the question as it is.

She asked herself aloud, "Do I have the moral force to finish my life?"

Her *phleglomania* was the *phenomenomenom* that had set

in. Her highest average speed of forty-five miles per hour she achieved in her automobile. Sometimes she briefly closed her eyes, she said, while driving, because, she said, "What could possibly happen?"

She had a regal calmness. That should sound familiar.

Her instincts for victory, her naturally fierce nature, the entire inheritance of her species, the will to seduce and ensnare, all her cruel powers were melted into a cordial, into a very old sweet, smile—but that's what's been said.

Let us endeavor to sum up. How much repetition does it take? A perseveration? Biological investigation is required to explain the impulses and their transformations—the chief traits of a person. It is easy to forget, not that we ever should, that everything in this world is an accident, including the origin of life itself, plus the accumulation of riches. We should show more respect for Nature, not less. An accident isn't necessarily ever over.

IDEA

The sound our feet made when we walked across his floor-boards was a rhythmic accompaniment to physical desire both of us could have thought to put a stop to. It did occur to me, just on principle, to end that noise.

When I took off my coat, he said my coat was gray. I said it was green. He said it was gray.

In the upstairs of his house, when I sat myself down to look around, I decided I liked everything I was looking at. There was nothing I did not approve of, or that I did not admire that I could see.

He said, "You make such fast moves," when he was kissing me. Then he said, "The watch—you have to take off the watch." Into the palm of his hand I put my watch, my four hairpins, my necklace made of silver beads.

He said, "That! Put that in your purse. I don't like that!" when I took off my brassiere. It remained there, though, curled up on his wooden floor, curled awkwardly for a piece of clothing, not awkwardly if it had been something else perhaps, a creature.

He said, "Now," he said, "use both of your hands so that I will feel you are really with me." Or, I was the one who said that to him—that's right, because I knew he could do things he would never want me to do. Add to all of that another distinctive feature, an atmosphere of awe, and something else that could be wet and gleaming which would not ordinarily be symbolic.

IT BECOMES TRUE

Someone said, "See!"

I saw the chimpanzee doing some of its typical twists and it was flourishing its tail par excellence up in a phony tree. We're all here for a party.

If I said I love this, then what would happen to me?

"I love this!"

Nowadays it comes to the surface. This is the zoo. I am at a party which will be of considerable benefit to the zoo.

And fortunately for me, I got myself squeezed up in the arms of a man.

A good ways away from the monkey, we were dancing in a tent. There was not one whiff of the monkey. The man swept me off my feet. It was my privilege. He swung me around. For this, I will always, always be grateful to him. I love this! Also, he surreptitiously slipped his hands along my body, lightly, so I would not notice, out there in front of everyone, while we were dancing. I was so grateful. I loved that.

It was not crude to break away to eat our food, to stick our forks into it by the prevailing standard.

There was nothing crude about my breasts popping up, the tops of them, when I just sat—the corresponding evidence pretty much up for grabs.

When did it happen?

I looked in vain for just one member of my family, or the most prominent person in my world. I was so grateful.

Typically, we are left, so many times. I love that routine— the horns of my dilemma—when they try to drag me forcibly away.

GOING WILD

It is a dirty lie that there were no promises at this event in any shape or form because there was food.

There was also a discussion concerning the intellect of children. There was a child sucking a green lollipop and being admired by an adult for being adorable while he was sucking, lying down.

Based on my intuition, my dead father would not have had fun at this event.

I had some fun while I stuffed myself to the gills with the food until I was uncomfortable and then I was no longer having fun.

I petted the head of a two-and-a-half-year-old boy. I succeeded with him by petting him while he was doing something—anything—and then I was redirecting him gently toward something less appropriate for his age.

We all stopped what we were doing, even I had stopped my chewing, and we had orchestrated ourselves to stare as a group at one child who acted as if he knew he should be center stage. I could have asked myself, What does this child wish for more than anything in the whole world?

Maybe there is one correct answer!

The one person who was giving me the most attention at the event is gone! evaporated right out of my sight! He's off into the pure air of my imagination where I imagine him with me lying down in a bed, where we discuss by what method everything is ordered.

Has there been one grand enough moment of either sex, or serenity, of soothsaying, or of silliness at the tragedy, during which time we paid homage to one object, or to a notion, or to one of us?

Thanks for letting, letting me even address you.

Satisfied is what I am.

CORONATION

A royal person, wearing a royal robe, with something royal on his head—something exciting—there are other smudges, other noble people with him, fine furnishings, and precious objects, and so on. From where I sit on my toilet, the chrome soap holder, built into the wall, is looking great.

This magic makes me wonder. The concaveness is going convexly. It is a grand, miniature, several-storied window to look through, or a glass revolving door.

My *New York Times* I am going through inspires me to think about our Colonel North and about other terrors today which are described.

What is this like? (No answer.) Is this like anything familiar? (No answer.)

Are you familiar with this? (No answer.)

I will answer that it is the burden. It is intellectual work which is as degrading to do as being in the presence of some very great person.

It is so similar to bowing to regard the genitals.

What is it that I would like right now?—to suck a very clean penis? (Yes.)

I am very embarrassed.

HAPPY

The child arrived in the nick of time to eat a pancake. She wasn't trying to escape from sadness, and she wasn't dying for a pancake, but she could handle a pancake standing up, without using a plate or a fork.

The wife wasn't eating yet, but she was cooking and preparing to serve. It meant so much to the wife to do that. Her husband would be served. The wife must have given him an ultimatum. He wore pajamas. The wife wore daytime clothes. The child was dressed for the occasion, and wore these sturdy toddler shoes.

Surely it is a fact of experience, that a young enough child who believes that pancakes are delicious, usually embraces an opportunity to eat one. At the age of two, this child considered her opportunity and made a decision that was plausible to her at the time. However, as an adult who is a happy-go-lucky person for no good reason, she marvels at how jubilant she was, so young, when she missed out on a pancake in a circumstance when nobody preeminent was sneering at her.

THE CASE OF THE COLD MURDERER

G etting the lid off the stuff, Mrs. Lewis knew, might mean she would save her son's life, so she worked at it. You uncap it in extremis.

The doctor had advised her by telephone to give it to her son. "This will work if you say to him it will work."

Louella Stack always said it was a simple death, this kind, although unexpected. One feature in the matter was Glenn Gould's playing piano to accompany the death. To get him calmed down—not Glenn Gould—Mr. Lewis embraced his gasping son. The mother, Mrs. Lewis, tried so hard to uncap the bottle.

The prescribed medicine, in these cases, tastes lousy.

Not long before he died, the son—who is also a suspect, actually—shrieked as best he could at Mrs. Lewis, "You have hurt me so much! I don't want to be your son! I can't breathe!"

Nobody denied any of this.

But perhaps if I speak to him . . .

Regrettably, the parts you will not hear are the parts that sound the best, as I, your host, shrewdly unravel the tangle of motives and human relations. For instance—I'll mow the fucker down—who is this fucking Stack? Was she really worth the mention?

MACHINERY

He moves around in his gloom and then he does something with something. He is calmer about his longings.

He sits for a bit before he hears whatever it is. Hearing it gives him the sensation of holding on to a great instrument which is at work.

He discovers a small square white cardboard box and he opens it. Inside is a disappointment.

His children hold him responsible for everything he does. His house suits him.

For some idea of the full range of tools at his disposal, one would have to know what human longings are all about, a calm voice says calmly.

PERFECT

"You want an insight? I'll give you an insight," said a perfect stranger at the children's ball game. Then he gave me his insight, which proved to be exactly correct.

"People will cheer him when he gets himself up," the man said.

I had thought that the child's ankle was probably shattered—that was *my* insight—that the child would not be able to walk, that he would need to be lifted and carried, that he'd never walk again. I thought, Now he is a cripple for the rest of his life.

"He's fine," the man said. "I know he's fine, because, you see, he's hiding his head. He's hiding his face. He's making such a big deal. I know. Sure, it's very painful."

The man had told me that the hardball had hit the child in the ankle. I didn't know where.

I said, "How do you know? It might be shattered. He's not moving."

"Because he missed the ball—" the man said, "because he wants everyone to forget he missed the ball, that's why he's making such a big deal."

If I could have an insight about this man's insight, I could probably save myself. That's my insight. I could save my children, my marriage, the world, if I could let enough people know—that there's a powerful solution in here somewhere—a breakthrough trying to break through.

The stranger was so angry talking to me. I don't think he believed I was believing him, and I didn't.

Will you please rise and Shame us not, O Father.

THE STUPEFACTION
(1996)

Thank goodness.

AN OPENING CHAT

I am glad he is this man here so that I can do a fuck with someone, but I am regarded as a better cock-sucker. It is one of those lovely times when a crisis does not come as a surprise. That is how I feel. I am glad he is this man here so that I can suck his cock and lick it. This goes on a little longer. I understood everything up to that point. This goes on a little longer. This—this cock is swollen. The throbbing of this cock begins. I felt sorry about what he had to do to me.

After this time, I noticed that I was not the same again as I had once been. I was much more swollen when the doctor arrived.

"We will get you back—we will get you back to where you were when you were feeling strong. Is that what you want?" the doctor asked.

"Yes. I want to feel strong again. I find that giving a blow job takes everything out of me," I said.

"Yes, that's true," the doctor said.

The doctor might believe that with a person of my age he may be blunt.

You would think that it could not last—his wanting to get straight to the point where something ceases to exist.

A SHREWD AND CUNNING
AUTHORITY

Such a day as Dorriet's is a reminder to the hopeful that one cannot be hurt in a devastating way, that life should be as endless as possible.

So I am very happy, thought Dorriet.

She is a poor, sick person who is very lonely.

Dorriet said, "Come on, Dorriet."

She talked softly, aloud, more than she realized—frequently. She did not often wish to keep any of her thoughts to herself— her tendency to try to persuade.

"Daddy! Daddy!" shrieked a little boy who was sitting next to her on the powerful city bus.

The buses are powerful.

"Come on!" said Dorriet. Her fingers tightened into fists. The father's statements to his child, coursing from him as flowing fountains would in such a desert, had the depth, the clarity of vision which proved to Dorriet that he should be the boy's father—that he was hers.

She can stay in the lap of their luxury if she keeps her voice down.

THE EVERLASTING SIPPERS

I sip the coffee almost stealthily while I wait.

Within my purview, the receptionist drinks something.

"Liz, darling!" the receptionist exclaims when she looks up. She says, "Would you like something more to drink while you wait?"

In my mind, there isn't anything in my mind until I know that I want more coffee with milk.

"Do you want more—" the receptionist asks, "coffee?" The receptionist is drinking something.

Mrs. Fox enters, drinking something.

"You want this?" The receptionist is waving a carafe of coffee at both of us. The receptionist's face is small and round. She seems to have a nervous tic in one eye, squints it unexpectedly several times. She is the most faithful picture of tenderness I can call forth.

At length I rise, saying, "I see nothing against that."

That night, after I bathe, I put on my sumptuous robe, brocade. I spoon raspberry sherbert into my mouth with a sherbert spoon. I drink wine from a fine glass. I take a piece of fruit in my hand, not to eat it, to gaze lovingly at it! It is made of stone. There is no problem here with reality. There should be no additional people here at all, doing things, causing problems, that are then solved.

THE POWER OF PERFORMANCE

They are my protectors, you know. This is my brilliant reasoning.

One of them cried out.

Bridget came bustling back in, rubbing her hands together. She tiptoed around. She was not herself.

I got to my feet, thinking of what I might say to her. What I often do is brag about what I have and about what I can do. Sometimes I do not give a reason for asking for what I want.

Some banging, some thumping had begun out in the hall.

Pots and pans were being batted around, or that was a lot of coughing that I was hearing.

I should have already explained that we are people who only live here. I am not even sure how many people are here!

I heard doors slamming after they all ambled out. Everyone went away. They were being quieter out in the hall.

For me, this is no longer only a matter of mere poundings, or vibrations, or cracking noises.

On one occasion, the pounding was so forceful that one of our antique clocks was pitched forward out away from off of the wall. The clock stopped and had to be put to rights again. I bet my boasting will damage the chandelier.

Customary noise can occur in thick clumps, all of which can be turned sideways.

THE BLESSING

I said so in the letter, but virtually anyone could have said so: *You will have everything you want, but I don't want to get your hopes up and then disappoint you.*

He just loves me. I have a very bad temper.

I walk forward with the letter in my hand, wearing my black dress. I wrote the letter for about an hour, with a dull lead pencil. On the envelope, in ink, dutifully, I wrote the name, the address. The stamp is a large black-and-green one.

Life is curious. I drink half a glass of water. In the corner of the room, rather, in the center of the room, nothing any longer attempts to sing a song, or, on the other hand, is listless, actually sick to death, and will not recover. But I don't mean this as an incitement to get you to go tell people that everything can turn out happy, wholesome, just wonderful.

One afternoon, when you are particularly tired, you sit down. You will be sitting down, or maybe it will be late in the evening, and you have missed your dinner, and you have missed your lunch, and you have missed out on your breakfast, too, and the weather is hot, so that you feel hot. It is an unhealthy climate, which is humid and stifling, and the air you breathe is unhealthy for you, and then, you obtain your heart's desire.

Many times a person seems fairly satisfied already but is so unsuspecting.

EERO

Tthe twwo pairrs off iddentical chairrs hadd been chosenn byy tthe ownners off tthe hhouse bbecause off tthe strengthh off theirr ccharacter. Thhe chairrs neverr beckonned tthe litttle girrls forr sitting.

Tthese wwere gennuine Eero Saarinen chaiirs—yyou musst takke mmy worrd forr itt—sttanding behindd thhe litttle girrls innside thhe hhouse, fromm wwhere tthe girrls stood tto watcch rrain beeat dowwn onn little apple trees, whichh treees hadd been plantedd byy thee owwners aas ann orrchard, delliberately, beccause tthey looked sso muchh aalike.

Sso thenn, bbecause itt wwas theirr gamme, onne girrl waas saaying, "Ddo whatt II ddo!" tto the otther, jjust thhe waay thhe trees seemed tto bee doiing.

Uppon thhe *wwhat* worrd off herr command, thhe otther

girrl ssaid thhe *wwhat* alsso. Ttheir *wwhats* coveredd overr tthemselves, hhers and herrs, andd thhen thhe exxact saame thingg wwas happening tto ttheir *II doos,* whhich arrived—nno jokke—withh aa majjestic simmultaneity.

Att ourr housse, itt's ggoing onn—anny gamme off tormment—wee still doo itt.

EEEverywhere!

APPPPOLOGY: Itttt wouldddd hhhhave beeeen entirrrrely tooooo tirrrresome forrrr meeee, tttthe onnnne whhhho wrrrrote tttthis, orrrr ffffor anyyyyone whoooo rrrreads thissss, tttto havvvve hadddd toooo advvvvance thrrrrough thissss, assss thhhhrough ourrrr ollllld agggge, alllll thhhhe waaaay throughhhh thissss, evennnn thoughhhh thatttt's sssso obbbbviously thhhhe waaaay, wiiiith aaaa grimmmm consssssstancy, itttt shouldddd beeee ddddone.

THE IDEALIST

Without much enthusiasm, he led me down the corridor and opened the door and I knew, I assume he has been places where he has seen beauty, has had some joy and adventures.

He stumbled. He fell down. I might have struck him, that's why.

People have to do so many things just to live their lives. He probably suffered from the fall, but he acted oddly lighthearted. I am tempted to guess why that is. I owe him an apology, but not if he is never angry with me.

How do other people who don't know each other very well count their blessings?

While I eat my hamburger, we leave our clothes on because we are very shy. We hardly know each other. We manage to copulate occasionally and to remain ill-qualified.

A MOMENT OF PANIC

I am not ecstatic about the flesh on her not-yet-womanly body, and her other arm is very much like her other one, and so on. However, none of her duties are undone, or need doing, or are duties which will soon need doing, which could be vexing. She has no dilemma evincing a religious principle. And, instead of a gang of people fucking her, or poking fun at her fat cunt lips, she has under her feet a luxuriant carpet. In addition, her laundry has been laundered by her, and now, in spite of itself, this laundry is soft and folded, or hanging languorously. Some of her bedclothes are trimmed with a frothy white trim, because people she has never met made a decision that that trim would be nice.

From her side of it, looking anywhere, everything is sunlit, entrancing.

But beyond this recognition, which is mine, not hers, there is this aroma, unsmelt yet by me, blowing around through the cool air here, coming along, mixed with some sudden large gusts of true love, which all you do—you want it?—is on weekends, you inhale it.

THE REVENGE

She sat in a chair and looked `out a window to think sad thoughts and to weep. Everything she saw out the window was either richly gleaming or glittering, owing to a supernatural effect. But she was not unused to this. She unlocked the front door. An infinitude of catastrophes was, as usual, apace— even as she walked out to the road. The ground was mushy from a recent rain. Her mind was not changing. Her mind had not changed in years. Somebody's headlights were blinding her. Her idea of a pilgrimage or of a promenade excited her. She was stalking, going swiftly down the avenue. She arrives at a plausible solution for at least 8 percent of her woes. I know what she is thinking, and am envious of her. But I am shitting on it.

O ROCK!

I don't wish to be callous or unfeeling. Go out if you like, but don't expect anything, even if we find the packet.

Actually, it is a large padded envelope that the man she follows into the café drops onto the table, then proceeds to undo. He has to break its seal.

She drums her fingers on her chin, watching him.

Her heart beats heavily, for which she is repaid in kind.

A thousand years are accounted for as he turns it upside down, empties out a dime, a penny, a penny, a dime, a dime, a dime. He empties out Time because of her. I am paying attention. Do *you* have to?

I hate it when you're like this.

THE GUIDER OF THE PRICK

She wanted Bill to obey her. She wanted that very much. When Bill came down out of the tree, his mother was a little afraid of him, but she said, "Good"—meaning, she was glad that he was back down.

Boy, she thought, is Bill ever a handsome boy. She put her arms around Bill. Then she tested the skin on her own arm with her fingertips to see if it was still as soft as silk, and it was.

Would Bill's mother ever say to Bill, "You've done enough for me already"?

Bill gets angry now, as a grown man, when some woman guides his prick for its entry into her cunt hole.

But back to when Bill was the pluckiest little boy in the world, sitting on a tree branch, and his mother had thrown a small rock at Bill, and his mother wept and Bill wept, too.

Bill saw apology, sadness, and disbelief in his mother's face. In Bill's face, his mother saw ordinary crying going on.

This is what Bill looks like as of today: He is large and unkempt and his mother is proud of him. He is the keeper of the flame.

EXCITABILITY

It is all my fault that there is romantic activity someplace in the wide world, amidst mysteries, during a day or a deep night, during a year. The clothing I wear is this new dress I wear to attend my life. I think back on my life before I had this plan.

A person said to me, "I know how it feels."

A girl who reminded me of myself when I was a girl got my attention once. For such a trim person, she had the wrong legs. In all her life, she may never be a beautiful woman. She was with her mother, and neither of them had on the right wristwatches. The girl maybe murmured or was silent. She appeared drowsy or dopey or useless. Her mother was making no effort to keep her awake, and the girl apparently did not want to do that for herself.

Even five years ago, when I had just changed my clothes, or it was at night, or I was out alone, I remember glancing, listening, surmising—after which I'd have had plenty. I remember when there was no nostalgia.

SPEECH

Thank goodness I am deeply sincere, so I stopped laughing. He had dragged me along to this refined filth of a hotel, which aroused my truest false feeling. On the way to the hotel, he was staggering and I was. If my wish is at last coming true, he is going to spring on me something that will make me feel as helpless as a human being.

He'll hear about it now.

A joke he told me had interfered with our breathing. Two women, I don't know, across the street were being dragged into the same experience, too—by a joke, or by something such as a joke.

Maybe he has not figured out yet how much I wish to stiffly represent myself at coital functions as stiffly as I do here as I speak.

FOR DIANE

Very early on, I had a vision of excellence and a sense of responsibility of monstrous proportions.

It is best if no one ever sees me again. (You will thank me.)

I will not go to see someone just because he or she is conveniently located.

And, if you do that thing again, evil people will be ruined completely. Good people will feel great. Springtime will span the year because that's my decision. Anyone who would have preferred some other season may feel a not-so-serious mistake has been made.

When the good people begin their lavish new life, they will be especially indebted to Ira, who will provide everyone with a set of easy instructions to follow so everything turns out all right for them. Oh, they will be indebted to Ira.

I used to see a lot of this one woman. Ira will take care of her, because I've had it up to *here.* Now, do you understand?

PLURAL

There is this one where they all put their feet up or slouch, because of the decree.

The worst of this is now over for Irene. She can just relax.

The iridescent ribbon, which might be regarded as pure or perfected, is in her hand. Her knees were drawn up. Her arms were exerting enough of her power.

Maybe she drew her thighs closed. She has soft, thin skin. She is plump because she has been stuffed with pralines, which is the secret of her plumpness. She likes to eat sweets.

She touched her genitals, thinking wistfully that they were flawless.

They are at their succulent best—red and yellow, but still firm—and if the skin is tender, you do not need to peel them. You can have the butcher make a series of fine, shallow cuts on the surface.

GODS OF THE EARTH AT HOME

M r. Moody and I were standing still for the sight, mentioning the sight, leaning slightly, or touching each
other.

The soda was fizzing and the redness and the whiteness of
the soda were dull compared with the redness and the whiteness of a fine radish.

It was Mr. Moody's boy Jim who had danced in with his
bottle of cherry soda, turning the bottle, which was capped,
over and over, and shaking the bottle, and the boy was spin-
ning and hopping.

Mrs. Brute deplored the champagne we were drinking.
She is my invention. She is going to take care of Jim.

Our exceptional meal was served on the golden plates. The
silverware was real silver. Mr. Moody's face flushed when he

drew me to him. He touched my beautiful auburn hair and my rich black velvet jacket. I had removed my deep sable. He could not be restrained from embracing me in the full view of everybody.

I just kept saying yes. When he said what he said, I said yes yes yes yes. I say yes yes. I say my excitement is so great, so huge.

I heard Mr. Moody's respiration. I heard him sort of faintly groan as he does sometimes at the very thought of having to eat my twat.

My imagination tells me that for everything which is not rewarding during a day, a heavy price must be paid.

I hope all of this will turn out all right.

What if it did? It did.

We should all be so pleased that for the time being we must abide with growing up, getting married, having servants, slaves, houses, holidays.

DESPERATELY TRYING TO LIE DOWN

Sometimes you were held, fondled, commented upon, weren't you? Yet I was told that nobody else had ever wanted you or had even asked about you, that I was the first one who had asked about you. When I grasped at you, twisted you, I saw some strands of your hair, the rather imprecise sketch of your eye, the overwhelming importance of your eye, and one of your eyebrows desperately trying to lie down sweetly on your brow, and with this view in mind, your face is as composed as my vulva is. I would like to suggest that the smartest, the strongest, the most perfect person in the universe is my property.

I am the dark one, the short one, the thick one, the coarse one, who is so unsatisfied with all of my suggestions.

You said, "Here, let me help you," and there was such a really happy expression on your face that you must have been happy.

I AM A LEARNED PERSON

My name is Valery Plum. There is something funny in that. I cannot presume how true to life I am. When I see myself combing my hair, I seem true to life. I am so starkly represented. I try to see through somebody else's eyes, which would be a remarkable view. This is the second day in a row I have tried; that's because I—I am really looking forward to it, because, even though I have no devoted friend—my newborn is pretty, my lips brightly colored, and there's plenty more of that where that came from.

Up the spiral staircase I go to get the baby, who is not big. Only on the inside, the walls of this tower are the color of a butter cookie. *Heh heh heh*, he's wailing. Under these conditions, nothing but children is so much better than custard or genius or fame.

This may be true or false, but here I am.

An entire formula for feeling good is fitting for someone like a bat out of hell like me who does not tolerate flying with any aches or pains.

Miss M. Murray quoted some ingredients in her own book, and a Mr. Trevor Furze confirmed the same in his own. One of their key ingredients is yummy, would make dogs bark. I go up and down the stairs with it in my mouth. It dangles.

I can make it leap up again.

CAREFUL

We could hardly bear it when she arrived home unhurt. The situation had grown intolerable. A week or so after that, we saw her again, still no accidents. She's a young woman. Maybe sometime soon she will be destroyed.

As a matter of fact, just now she is in some peril. She is having a conversation.

Among her lady friends, her masters, her heirs, she shouts, "Charming!" Her voice is high, thin, nasal.

Just before this, we had thought of calling out to her to wait, but she was already waiting.

She had heard the sound of her own voice without any assistance or advice.

What if we never see her again?

We have nothing for—we have no plans for—we have no

ideas for your—we have no wish to make you—we are—we—feel no—Let's just say there are other people, other than her, that we could speak to. We need to match up our feelings to our ideas for them.

Yesterday, we found it charming—all that shooting the semen around that they do.

THE FUCK

Mother of God—he actually had a cloth and a spray bottle of something, because he was dusting his truck. His truck was blocking up our street that we live on.

As I ran away from him, I shouted, "I am not trying to run away from you!" Brutally, I kicked what I decided was my own stone, and I found a limp walking stick—a dead tree branch, smooth, just the right height—after it was boring for me to be brutal.

Ferocious, hateful dogs, working as a team, barked at me.

What are the Williamses putting that up for? I wondered, when I turned my corner. Now, he was over there, in their yard, not looking at what he was doing with their swing set, speaking only to me, when I came along.

There was no mention of being ill or an illness mentioned

which was of an extreme or of a debilitating nature. Pleasure was the centerpoint, sexual pleasure, fun, surprise, gamy delight—seldom—well, all right, *once!*—disgust. He did not express desire other than sexual, which he was confident he would gratify soon. He had no concern that any woman, man, girl, or boy would not be a good-enough provider for him, or could somehow disappoint him, or turn up incompetent. Beauty, intelligence, education, gentility, cleanliness, worldly success, a moral attitude—none of these he ever referred back to. No concern over betrayal, no money problem was expressed, and yet, even so, I behaved curtly. I behaved as if he had digressed.

THE GOAL

"I want to use yours."

"Use any bathroom you want to," she said.

He said, "Oh, you are my friend!"

He put his hand between her legs. He said, "Come. Sit up here. Back—*back*—"

He mouthed her; he tongued her; he nosed her between her legs. He murmured, "Let go."

"Oh, that was a treat!" she said.

He said, "I have to go to the bathroom."

"Use the children's," she said.

He twisted to gaze at her while she was not straining to be anything more than what she is. He was free and happy, too.

In her bathroom, she was reaching to turn the little spinner, to twirl the screw propeller which releases some of the water through the bunghole into the remarkable.

MY REACTION TO LIFE

It is hard to describe these animals which are so stiff-necked.

I petted my horse, told it to stand still. I can be indifferent and patient. Although, I am one of those who keeps expecting the dark heart of human desire to be revealed to me.

Others were looking down into the gorge, with their mouths agape.

Chet Henry said, "Now what?" and there is no going back and changing what he said, because that is what he said. He is a man who may have temporarily gotten off of his horse so that he could be loved, or so that he could be hated, or so that he could hate me.

Now what? I am going to answer him the only way I know

how. I said, "We're going back to the ranch." The ranch has real log buildings, cowboys, excellent meals.

Nobody has to tell me how we made it back through the thicket to the Ridn-Hy. The traveler in me is full of hope. She is a splendidly bland and a smug woman.

THE DIRTY NECKLACE

She used the bath mat to dry the wet necklace, and dirt from the necklace showed up on the bath mat. She could wash the necklace again. She put some bar soap on the necklace, not too much, and then she rinsed the necklace. She repeated this. The necklace could be washed again. The necklace could be scrubbed with a scrub brush. The necklace should soak overnight in a basin. She dried the necklace by rubbing it against the bath mat, so that more dirt showed up on the bath mat. She put the necklace on. She fingered the necklace and saw that its parts were cut glass, amber, or plastic. The necklace was meant to be hers. We do not know who else, if anyone, has ever worn the necklace. There are other necklaces which she owns—not exactly the same—but these necklaces are series of misunderstandings—as is everything—your throat.

THE HELPMEET

To my surprise, Diane Williams wants me to hold her fucking ass. I am an annoyance rather than a deep disturbance. In other words, I go to my room when I am told to, shut the door, and I stay there until I am given my permission to come out.

When I come back out, some secrecy is necessary. Nothing could have seemed more essential when I took off my peg-top trousers. I untied my shoes. Stood. I felt so tightly bound to her while we were stiffly rocking.

If I go away someday, I want to know how she will live without me.

I will ask her to go into detail about her sexual needs.

Why do I even care how many of her needs there are?

Just for conversation's sake, let's say there are just two.

THE MASTURBATOR

We are all so much the same—our size, our shapes, and we are perforated. I put my finger on a crack in my skin. I have been searching for one gesture of my own such as this which I can remember—return to, and return to, which could direct and give sense to my life. I had ignored other motions of my heavy body—the lowering and raising up of my hind end, which I often do. My legs are tired, and I feel weak-kneed, and it looks to me that there is a place to sit down to rest near a tree. This tree's trunk is a subtle tawny color. The ground is dark, has speckles. I press on my hand. I am still not uncertain what to think when I gently rub my hand, which seems to me dirt-free and oldfangled. There are much more up-to-date revealers of the truth.

OKEYDOKE

The man lied is the best ingredient in my veal steak deluxe. I am going to vacation in the man lied. I never will the man lied for the third time.

I the man lied that that's wonderful and exciting and I look forward to it. He is telling me how many the man lied he has to have in a day.

I expected to the man lied blood.

The man lied, "I have never seen the man lied like that one."

On the man lied, when some chicken and a potato were roasting in my oven, I would not leave the man lied. I liked to tell the man lied how many orgasms I had in a day.

The man lied was sure I was hearing a waterfall. But what I heard was the grinding of the man lied.

THE FUSS

First of all, I do not want to keep the thing a secret, because they were not doing any harm, I assure you. They ate. They drank heartily. They threw stones which sank into the sea. They jumped into the sea. We followed them. The sea was bright and whirring. I was not used to being cold in the water. I am not used to keeping a secret, either, which I think is the best plan. It was a journey. There was a beautiful sky. We were too cold creeping under it. A little farther on, they marched. I cannot form an idea from this.

THANK YOU

Amargay has heavy black eyebrows, heavy, black, wavy hair. An ocelot is very much the same. No margay has been seen around here, but we were determined to find one if it is in the books. We crouched in a field studded with hares and cows and dogs. We were in extreme agony because we were bewildered and we had been wandering. (I was in a very bad mood.) Several of us have long, gray, matted hair and are extremely ugly. I wear a black skullcap. An odd-looking stranger (but what stranger isn't?) hobbled up to us and told us what to do. She squatted. Her knees bumped into her shoulders. She told me to think about something else for a change.

THE PURPOSE

This is better than what I had last year. People are happy for us. They are happy for both of us. I said that I am content to have very little. I could want more if other people would just tell me what I need.

I cough. I do not like my spaghetti. I ask for another cola drink, could I have one more.

I am told, however, "No!"

Every now and then for me, cola can be cold and abundant, its scent not objectionable. It is not fragile or flat, or well chosen, well placed enough to serve the exact same purpose as she does for me.

She was everything she said she would be.

I am noticing an outcome when even an indescribable force can change a fact.

To herself, she said, "I put too much of this on."

Even if not one interesting idea occurs to me, I also have something I could say which I would like to say about my opinion that my ideas give me something to talk about.

Could I have one more?

I said, "Have one of these."

I was told, however, "Not on your life!"

THE PRIMARY INTUITION

We have conspicuous yet, I think, respectable hair on our heads. Even so, my son and I could scare people. We have. We walk along. I see scarlet-fruited, big-leaf winter creeper, inkberries. At last, we arrive at the village. I knew what we would do, where I would accompany him.

Pierre and Esther, our enemies, entered a shop. I had seen Esther, with her trailing spray, wearing her *sautoir*, open the door. The light spreading rapidly from the shop windows was not warm and inviting.

We had the advantage of staying close to the building.

By the time we left town, I had an invisible ring on my finger, as well as a strong brown cut, which has the appearance of an aeriel rootlet. I had watched my son drink from a swaying glass of juice, which is perfumed, forms in clusters, turns yellow, before it comes into sight.

THE FESTIVAL

I put pillows under her head.

I don't just sit around, either, and why? I am surprised that they didn't tell you about me, that I had a good upbringing!

How much fun I had with my prick up inside of the great Diane Williams. She held the tip of the prick firmly. She is pleased to feel.

I know that whatever I might decide to do, it could be what you might do!

It's just happening sooner! For more than for four years! Go on in, see Diane. I was told that all sorts of people are in her room. She opens her legs this way. You must avoid the decay at her stem's end.

Yet joy is so memorable! And, when this holiday begins, it is twice as rewarding as pain is.

THE BUILDER

I drank dark water, later on, afterward. I urinated, emitted gas. I was pleased, tired, had cramps. I could not stop the monster from causing its destruction. It had left no real damage after the cleanup. Out of devotion? Because of fear? Or pride? I often have an outburst of my free will. I know what I will do if I have sexual intercourse, how I am going to hump and plan. I suspect many others need to plan your sexual intercourse.

THE ANSWER TO THE QUESTION

A coil of green, a part of me, or any additional garnishing, when assembled, can produce sufficient allure anyplace.

The old idea that enticements should be ever more sophisticated is what prevents most seers—plumbers and electricians alike—from being optimistic.

Keep on hand containers which you have filled compactly. Wrap these securely. A stream or a flow is a thing of the past.

THEIR PRIVILEGES

Do not say there is no information about us. He had one leg in the air. My head was down.

Living can provide a sense that everything has already happened.

I have admired as many trees, as much shrubbery, as I could have. I am not lying. I have gone out of my way to say how grateful I am for shrubs, over and over. I know I spent enough time on that.

I never joked around with anyone. I don't think I have been very foolish.

Then it is my turn to sit and to think about what I will get.

THE SUITOR

We are becoming persons who should, of course, be loved and honored. We become people who can do the impossible.

Was anyone surprised to see us take on a different shape and character? In the name of everything which is sacred, I can predict your fate to ensure that you will never worry.

I am your friend, if you do what I tell you to do. Don't worry.

Let's pretend I have made mistakes. Let's pretend that these sorts of mistakes are the ones I never should have made. I have no respect for you, for instance. I think I can just pick up anything of yours and look at it. I hear myself shout, "That's the trouble!"

THE STRONG PETALS OF QUIET

I saw the duster after the duster had bloomed. The duster leads me where I should go, encourages me. The duster advises me to lie down on the lawn to rest, takes me to the sweeper's shop on Gower Street, which is not in an uproar. The duster is my shepherd.

It comes toward me, to guide me on the darkening plane. I could show you how if you could see me on this peninsula.

I will never put the duster away from me.

THE
STUPEFACTION
a novella

ONE PLACE

SAME PLACE

EVERYTHING

FOR

YOU

Is it necessary to state a guarantee of my goodwill?

If they come in, they go right back out again.

—SEVERAL OF MY NEIGHBORS

1

OH, I HOPE YOU LIKE
EVERYTHING I SAY!

Somewhat embarrassed, he would not admit that he wanted to do something with her right away that might surprise her or possibly cause her some pain.

"I came directly here!" he said. His sad expression had vanished. He said, "Let's go!"

They did not take her little dog with them. It is dangerous to show her dog too much affection, she believes. This could cause harm.

She had another one of her own ideas when she saw a pool of some forgotten water, when she saw some of the forsaken hills. She said, "This is the nicest part of the trip!"

More of her own ideas occurred to her when they were up in the hills.

If she is not much different than I am, she was hoping I would like everything she would say.

He said, "We must hurry," and she said, "I will."

By this time, it was twilight. They could barely see the ground or the form of a person doing something carefully and patiently. And this apparition is what she has so often feared. She said, "I think that that looks real."

"Can't you hurry?" he said.

2

THIS HEAVENLY LIFE IS
NOT FORBIDDEN

She felt the need to urinate.

They crossed the bridge on foot and they entered the woods.

This heavenly life is not forbidden.

"It is heavenly!" she said, and she wondered about his bobbing cock.

Something else crawled away and hid under a log. Something else brushed his side. She had had to shoo them off.

He begged her to let him keep on talking.

He likes it when she is acting as if she is nice and friendly, when he is thinking he wants to be with nobody else.

Amazingly, they did not lose their way in the woods. Yet neither of them had the ornament that wards off evil and that could bring either of them good luck.

When she squatted down to urinate behind a tree, she listened to her noise. A trickle of her urine wet one of her shoes. She had a tissue with her so that she could wipe off her shoe that had been wetted.

Once in the course of her entire lifetime, she almost saw where that urine of hers pours out from.

But no, sorry, she never did actually exactly see.

She was summoning more pleasure when she heard the squirrels.

These squirrels are so fidgety. A few of these squirrels were becoming violently ill and would have very little cover when this was the case.

What's more—her dog, in her garden, far away—was chewing on a rosy green pear that he held between his paws, and not at all tenderly. The dog was gnawing, biting on the pear as if it were his own flesh and blood!

In the evening, she put her hand down inside her blouse and there between her breasts there was a little something which she would set free.

3

IT WAS A JOYFUL TIME

She pulled out the honest soul but did not examine it before she tossed it away.

It was a joyful time.

Soon she had a fire going in the fireplace.

They have located this ideal cottage. This cottage has been created to augment, to ease an intimate relation, to provide long-lasting help, to reduce the possibility of sin. She will never be one of those people who is slain.

He's probably happy. He is probably happy.

She'd like to tell him, Stay there where I put you.

He was opening drawers—drawer after drawer.

Clearly the cottage had been prepared for them, or so it seemed to them—firewood in a basket, a packet of matches, common white spring blossoms in a vase, soap, towels, food, clean bedding—everything!—even a freshly laundered blue terry-cloth robe was there! Before long, the cottage had lost its chill.

She followed him into the kitchen and watched him open a cupboard door.

A surprise clattered.

4

CAUTIOUSLY, SHE LOOKED AROUND

Soon enough, there was the fragrance of cream—and she did not remain calm. "Stop your looking!" she said.

She had prepared a full-fledged cocoa bread pudding.

An insect drifted up before her eyes, then flew away. She briefly inspected the ether for the insect. Then she looked for a miracle of beauty high up in the air in the out-of-doors.

He lit beeswax candles—dripless, clean-burning—which produced soft light.

"That's ours!" he said when she found a jar of red jam.

She saw him steadily stride and when he interfered with the fire, orange sparks sprang up the way they often do.

On the hearth was a pair of lady's dancing slippers, of delicate dark velvet, covered by gold embroidery and braid and daisy patterns made of ivory-colored small pearls, as well as a pair of man-sized, wide-topped, funnel-shaped half boots of embroidered leather.

Offering him his pudding, she said, "This is cozy!"

Cautiously, she looked around.

5

DON'T START IMAGINING THINGS

"Don't start imagining things," he said while he was slumped, eating his dessert, in the chair, his trousers lowered to his ankles.

Contents of the drawers were scattered on the floor.

He laughed and she did not ask for an explanation, such as, What amuses you? She never wants to cause him to be cross or to speak harshly to him.

She was attempting to handle another one of her concerns when the telephone rang. She had forgotten about sexual pleasure. The ringing reminded her.

He said, "Uh-oh!"

She grabbed his arm and then she guided him through the cottage. He was using his knees to hold up his flapping trousers. She was behind him, her hands on either side of his waist. "In here," she said powerfully, flinging the door open, pushing him forward.

6

SHE PUT THE LID OF
THE TOILET IN PLACE

"Don't do that," he said.

After all, he had invited her to come with him because he had thought that he might have some fun.

And what if the telephone rings and rings, or if there is a knocking at the door?

The telephone is an obdurate potentiality.

When he was stepping into the bathtub, she fretted, I should do something.

Was she in fact supposed to lightly touch him in this circumstance?—or to grip him otherwise.

She put the lid of the toilet in place, then she watched him from her perch on the toilet lid.

She is just here to make herself happy.

"I want to touch you," she said.

"Fine," he said. "Do it wherever you want."

She put her finger on the tip of his penis and she pushed it down. She bent it.

"Can I kiss you?" she asked.

"Fine," he answered.

Then she petted the top of his head.

"Do you want me to stop?" she asked.

"No," he said.

He said no.

7

SHE STAYED ALERT BUT WAS
ONLY FAINTLY INFORMED

She kissed his waxy pate many times.

"Oh," he said, "where did you learn to do that?"

She was sure she should not answer this question. This is the oldest, the most difficult question.

Meanwhile, the night advanced.

She stayed alert, but was only faintly informed of her total helplessness.

She flinched whenever he spoke and had nothing to offer that might reveal the secret meaning of things—the truest things.

Her interest in teasing him startled her also.

"Oh, yes, I want to," she said.

8

I BET NOBODY HAS EVER
DONE THIS, HE SAID

Earnestly, he kept on having these amorous sensations, although he was still afraid of being scolded.

When he got up out of the tub of water, he predicted some horse sense and some wishful thinking.

And since she knows in general what to do, she did not feel ill-tempered, even though her first efforts to please him usually did not work.

When he gleefully played with her, this might not have been a dream. Although, presumably his life had occasioned a type of slave labor.

"I bet nobody has ever done this!" he said.

"I don't know," she said. "Just stick it in and I will think about it."

9

SHE WAS SOILED—BUT WETTED?

The accounts of how she lost her dignity vary. She does not know that she is vehemently inclined to be made happy at any cost.

Force it on me, she is craving, and please forgive me for anything I could ever do that is wrong or that I have already done that is wrong and forgive me for what I am doing right now!

She is slack-faced and reddened after that. She has a sense of a heartening achievement.

"That's it, my darling," he said. "If I were your mother, I could not be prouder of you."

To her surprise, when she was not asleep, he reached out and insinuated his arm around her!

Late that night, water is running. He must have been getting into that bathtub again. Oh, the nice bathroom.

She was soiled—but wetted?

He said her name sweetly, which caused her to feel fortunate.

Perhaps this should have been brooded over—what her name is.

Her eyes, ears, anus, legs, and other parts of her are wrongly formed.

Her skin is extraworn, extraunfirm. Her character, her intellect and her health are relevant but not known now.

He is gentle, nervy, but this is not all that he is.

10

HIS ROBE MIGHT APPEAR
TO BE ONGOING

He is terrific.

His robe is something I have worn. It is deep dark blue—rude, but not handmade. If someone were to take his robe seriously, his robe might appear to be ongoing, as if this terry-cloth robe could stand up to the test of time, or to the open air.

The question is, What more should this man and this woman do there in that house? All of the usual methods of sexual intercourse can be delightful, especially if done with care.

Behold! The man is going to give the woman something!

It is a ruby ring, which fits her, with a single ruby as shiny as mine is, which he discovered in a cake pan—and he gave it to her.

Imagine! She can hear the splashing of the light inside of the gem.

This ruby once was filled with blood.

11

SHE IS NICE, BUT SHE HAS AGED

She is nice, but she has aged. Now she is pulling her blouse about her. But she is not sad.

And, there is a storm outside—wind and rain.

Dirt is blowing into the cottage from under the window-sills. The amount of dirt, the power of the wind, is a bit of a shock to me.

A lot of age-old dust is turning itself into black water around here.

12

HE SAID, "LOOK OVER HERE!"

He said, "Look over here! Come over here!"

To her, of course.

And they both saw what they should see when I observed that they did not want to look at each other.

There was the scent of a charred lamb chop, but there was no indecency in this fact, either.

It was then that I saw a body with a slender neck, a darting head—when the door blew open.

13

I SAW IT ENTERING

I saw it was dressed.

The man raised his voice—crying out to it, but no answering voice came back to him.

It was necessary now for me to be reassuring. I was curious, too, and intrigued by the suddenness of its entry. But I was certain we were all still safe here.

Within less than an hour, I promise you, this visitor was capable of feelings and was wishing to steal back to its own people.

I could have touched it—the newcomer was so close. Its face was somewhat adorable.

But, for all that, this creature, in my opinion, had barged into a trap.

14

YOU SHOULD HAVE
SEEN WHAT I SAW

Its profile is remarkably like my mother's and you should have seen what I saw.

This thing was not much larger than you could manage to see.

The man went to clutching at it while the dearie was holding its palms together, trying to keep its chin up.

15

IT WAS A GOLDEN STRUCTURE

I knew that I would have to make proper use of this radiance. It was a golden structure—brighter than any of my daydreams.

With my step-by-step intervention, especially that all concerned should keep on breathing in their fashion, I tell you that the woman thought to place in front of it a small dish of condiment.

"I think I'll sample a bit of this," it said.

Oh—but oh, oh, oh.

Choking, having done so, it declared, "I have been killed."

16

HE SAID, "LOOK! HERE'S SOMETHING! THIS MAY BE VALUABLE!"

"A little of that goes a long way," the man said.

He gave it something to drink.

"Have a glass of this," he said.

And eventually this substance proved to be soothing.

Mentioning that it would return again soon, this dream-come-true was able to disappear gracefully back into its origin, but not before the three of them had achieved a certain sense of society with one another.

And while it had seemed that the darling had actually put a toxin into its mouth, in fact, this had not been the case.

And so then the old house seemed snug again to me and the man was whispering—but he was not whispering to me!

He was unbuttoning, unzipping, pushing everything down.

When he throws his arms around the woman, he does not know when to let go of her.

He should never know absolutely.

So far, he has made some correct judgments.

He was taking off the woman's old shoes, even though she was telling him, "I'll take it off." They are the kind with laminated leather inserts and fabric laces.

You know.

17

"DO YOU WANT TO HELP?"
SHE ASKED

She is behaving as if she is a pleasant woman.

She says, "There is a way you can help me."

He said, "Oh, no, not this time!"

Who would have thought he would be braver than he usually is?

He goes back along a corridor into the bathroom, and she follows him. They are just like ordinary people—and it's not funny!

He is emptying his bowel into the toilet in front of us!

This event has gotten her strangely worked up.

Let me say that the scent of this man is fantastic, distinctive! It is nutty and sweet.

The linens—the towels in the bathroom—are not stained, but there is a blot of something awful in the sink.

He asks, "You look sad. Are you sad?"

18

HE SAID, "OH, NO, NOT THIS TIME!"

She is not sad.

She is nice.

At some point soon, she will be down on her back, with her knees up against her tits.

The man tries to remember what to do next.

"Don't forget whose idea this was! It was my idea!" he says.

Nothing too fancy. That's the beauty of it! And the murmur of peaceful waters starts up somewhere else, while thick foliage is being crushed underfoot.

She fingers the hair on her head, which to her is stiff and dry—and she is right, it is, it is.

This sparse, messed-up hair on her head, her legs, that most unsightly site between her legs would soon be prodded and disturbed.

Where's peace?

The greatest feeling of satisfaction, the way to deepen the experience for her, would be not to let her legs move very far apart, or, in fact, to go ahead and let her legs do that.

But for now, his twitching—his very best flesh—is in her fist.

19

HE DID NOT KNOW IF HE
SHOULD BE THINKING

In a moment, out beyond, in a not so thickly wooded place, a flying thing is buzzing around an ultrasexy flower. Here, too, is the sloping wall of a cavernous pit, with a post at its center—many feet long—which has been sharpened at the exposed pole for one of us.

This is the way of things, as the man glances at their food. He checks to remember a skillet peach dumpling, a folded rug, or folded food.

20

WHAT IS THIS?

Neither of them is bored with either of them.

She wanted to keep on seeing his helike face.

So do I.

"What is this?" he says, indicating.

21

AT FIRST, SHE SAW
NOTHING UNUSUAL

"Is it a door to a secret room?" he asks her.

She shuts the door to the broom closet and puts on those brand-new slippers that are not characterized by a rear opening and have an almost complete lack of a heel.

She says, "You are my favorite person. How do you like that?"

She is warning him with such confidence.

At first, she saw nothing unusual.

A few shoots of dark hair on her belly can be seen on her belly.

The door to the kitchen stands open, where fragile porcelain, of various cherished colors, is streaked with a fricassee and a small figure from another world needs my permission for a taste of something. I signal—to show that this will be okay.

"Don't forget whose idea this was!" the man is saying to the woman. "Mine, you thief!"

"We can speculate," she answers.

Nearly naked, she is being pulled by her arm and I can hardly stand up or even keep sitting here any longer—and then the man's trousers fell down around his ankles again.

And she feels weaker, weaker, weaker, weaker.

Perhaps the secret concerning sexual intercourse, which she does not know, has made her secretive.

22

IMAGINE!

"Were you here?" the man was asking of somebody.

What if he was asking me?

"I just have to know!" he was saying. "Were you here this time?"

I do not know what more to say—so I could have stopped myself from speaking.

Why don't they just live and live here? He doesn't even have to answer the phone!

He told her, "Sit down."

I think it was for sex.

She pretended to sit.

He was afraid. He drank some cold beef tea. Everything about the tea was unbeatable. It was the best tea.

Why could she not leave well enough alone?

I wanted to believe that she has an elegant mind. But she just doesn't.

She watched him watch her. This is what is keeping her aroused—her pigeon-blood, cushion-shaped gemstone.

I just love that knickknack.

The man tries to do what he should do next.

The telephone is ringing.

And, even though I do adore almost any racket, I always think that this kind is tiresome.

I was hankering for my own home a thousand times.

Both of the woman's hands were on one of her knees. They had torn the blankets and the pillow from the bed.

Then themselves.

23

SHE WILL TAKE A BIG BREATH

I found out what she was supposed to do next: enjoy the experience.

She says, "Thank you."

I'd never say some of the things she brings herself to say.

"But—I don't believe it," he said. He said, "I don't believe it."

Neither one of these people is the one who gives me a reason to live on when there is no other reason. It is somebody else!

Any day this woman will be down on her back, with her knees up. She will take a big breath. She will be encouraged when he plugs up her awry anus with his straight penis.

24

DID HE STAND UP JUST
TO LOOK AROUND?

Yes, I could see that there had been a willingness in her to feel herself split in half and there is a part of a walnut clinging to its smashed shell in the waste bin.

"What are you doing?" she asks him. He is on the toilet with his elbows on his knees. Then he leaps up.

It is just terrible to see him this way, yet I do have a fondness for this place because of the stuff strewn all over it.

25

IT IS JUST SUCH AN
UNPOPULAR THING TO DO

Even in this bathroom there is a skinning knife!

Will she miss it here as much as I do when I go away?

Did the man stand up just to take a look about and to let his thing be seen?

She says, "Wash it."

They really haven't had much privacy. But they have so much time on their hands!

And I do, too!

"You take your time," a kind gent said once so sincerely as he labored to provoke me with his caresses, for heaven's sake.

A big brute stood by us to keep up our morale.

I did not think I knew either one of them. But nearly everyone I know resembles someone I have known or someone that I know.

The men, the woman, the children are just unfamiliar enough to me so that I do not mind telling any one of them to take as long as is necessary—even if it is just such an unpopular thing to do—to take forever to come.

26

I COULD DO THAT

When you are inside of me, this is not unlike my reaching down into a barrel or a big pail for something which I want, which is out of my reach, but the barrel needs to be knocked over onto its side.

I could do that.

I graze the back of her hand with the tail end of his penis.

This time at least, I am not waiting for matters to be made clear.

27

I BEND DOWN

But everything was what I hoped it could be, when I sat down on top of him, having put his impressively distinct member up inside of her.

And I told him that nobody could fill her shoes.

I would have sat up late, by the fire, every night, so horribly worried about this fact. But that was in the old days.

So, in the afternoons, if the weather is acceptable for this work, we will think more about you.

Did I already tell you about the bugleweed that climbed up over the log?

Now the weed heads for the mossy bank, for shade that is too shady for any grass. It is twisting itself up beside a brownish material, climbing up over the log, all because I intend to bend down.

I bend down. I am hearing the rain. I am expecting the best for you because there is more to come.

28

YOU WILL SEE ME

You will see me not stop being a visitor who could cause a difficulty to such an extent that we would have to handle the ensuing catastrophe, which is ticklish—get some other people to try to get me to pay attention to us.

For example, my mother is a woman who believes my father is more powerful than I am.

My usual rule about building a life or a vase is that it must be slightly tapered.

Most objects require form, don't they?

Small rarities, which are strongly made, well braced, pasty, jellylike, soupy enough, or that are the right distance apart, will increase in size.

One day, when I walked along the street, I saw my brother carrying a chair.

One of the ears of the chair and the top of rail of it, of the chair, were scratched. A stile was scratched. The apron of the chair was scratched. One of the finials of the chair had broken loose, was wavering. A joining looked well joined.

My brother had the chair hoisted over his head.

I am not saying there was anything more to this since there was no weather, no water, no barren plain, no rill, no cleft, nor any hillock for as far as my eye could see, and the central peak is so far off.

My brother is somebody I am shy with, who is my idea of a friend, although I hate the nature of everything he is.

If I say that he is really my brother, then I could say nothing is wrong with me except for the aches and pains.

He put the chair on the sidewalk.

"That's a very nice necktie," I said. "Do you always wear that necktie? You always have on a nice necktie. Is it the same necktie?"

"No, this is a different one," he said.

"You look wonderful," I said. "I can't remember you looking as good as you look."

"Fuck you," he said.

His little girl tugged on the back of his shirt. She was chattering. She—she wants to tell me everything she can think of which is more interesting than anything that you or I could ever think of.

There is a cure for everything.

29

I SHOULD BE CARRIED OFF

Considering my increasing interest in, and my knowledge of, the most distant future, I should be carried off for a rendezvous to a place that has an undulating surface, which is inconceivably swampy along the coast—to a life I might not ever think of, where there can be some volcanic activity, some full understanding of human health and disease.

The largest city there, which is located in a cultural and medical center, has a great deal of quarried pink quartzite, which I know I like. There is a lake there, too, far above water level, in a sunken volcanic crater. Camellias bloom at the lakeside among live oaks, and azaleas. This is where the temperatures and the humidity have combined to produce the newest conditions.

I still intend to meet up often with you. You listen through thick and thin. You urge me on. I thank you. I thank you. It is high time to give you a complicated sentence.

If you think I will never see you, you are wrong.

30

BUT IT ISN'T URGENT

I will see you!

At this time, I am staying with friends and it is difficult to get into the bathroom. My sister never says, Don't run the washing machine at all hours.

My sister, my husband, they should offer me a drink.

"Let's have a drink," my sister says.

If it had been urgent, I would have told you that it was urgent. But it wasn't urgent.

My sister asked my husband if he would go to the market to get us something to consume.

He said, "Eat this."

She did not say, Could you go now?

He never went off.

No major detriment to life or to property otherwise occurred. But I learned a lesson I will never forget.

31

AS IT TURNS OUT

I will encourage myself to lead a more up-to-date way of life, in a rarer atmosphere, where something in the world is really wanted or needed.

People either like me or they don't. Nobody is ever completely persuaded or enthusiastic, though.

Many of those who have thought that they enjoyed my company have not, in fact, been charmed, as it turns out.

I think that they pretend to be in dreamland, which is rather romantic.

Heaven all around us, I am fond of saying.

My husband gave me something which demands something. He said, "See?"

I put it on.

He said he had paid for it.

I wear it, paying for it, too.

32

AND NOW

This is the happiest day of my life, even when I remember this day.

I start for home.

I say to myself, "Never for as long as I live will I forget this happiness!"

Am I not an important person on my way to do something very important for evermore?

And it seems too strange a coincidence that I should get so distracted by you on this day. Did I carefully plan it that you would show up?

I confess I have always prayed that you would be my friend, even though you are a fucking dirty Jew sort of person.

We are as friendly as I have ever been with anyone.

I can talk to you solemnly. You seem to listen, calmly, as I offer you my home, my protection, my love for the rest of my life.

I would like to let go of your arm.

33

JUST AS A JOKE

I put my lemonade on a table.

I try to run past you, just as a joke, but you catch me up in your arms.

After a while, you say hoarsely, "I wish I lived here."

"But you do!" I tell you. "We have a lot to be thankful for."

I haven't been complaining. After all, something seems to have happened.

Did you think you would not be invited back?

34

I AM IN LOVE

You should know, if you want to come with, that what I am going to do now is go to the bathroom down the hall.

My feet on this floor should be in my own shoes.

I have not gotten to the bathroom yet. I will—because I want to finish this up so I can get on with your life.

I do not want to have anything more to do with most of the other people.

You could be the one who is all so certain about what somebody wants to do next, about what we should do next, if we should appear to be going to the bathroom next—at the same time, of course.

We should be certain. We should have no doubt.

Everything should feel natural, normal, and as if we were being swept off our feet.

Or at least mine.

Isn't this what you want?

35

IF WE ARE NOT CAREFUL

Why do you think this is?

Say something!

If we are not careful, this could go on and on. We could stay in the bathroom whenever we get there—for a while.

This is not a good time to take a shit.

Now I am beginning to get worried.

I am worried.

I want your assurance.

I want your reassurance.

Perhaps I do not know what to do next, but everyone else does.

But do you know how to do anything under these circumstances? You don't speak to me.

I close the bathroom door behind us. I appreciate the

greatness of most of the articles in this room, whether we like it or not. Some of them were your idea.

The seventeenth-century pikeman is on loan from a relation.

I could tell you what I know about your possessions, because sometimes this ignites a tender feeling in both of us, I think.

Yes, there is tenderness here, and occasionally I forget why this is. Sorry.

36

ONCE I HAD TO DO WHAT I HAD TO DO

Of all of your favorites, I used to be the prettiest one. That's the kind of person I am. I have had some difficulty conning everybody, you first of all.

You are sauntering toward me.

Are you going to express an opinion?

I am the witness when you are silent or tedious.

I am a little worried. I am getting tired. I am getting sleepy. Hurry, hurry. You have to hurry. Can you hurry?

"Here, take these, too," I say, removing a few items from the hiding place.

You ask me, "Are you quite certain?"

Would you know how to find out?

"You are inspiring," you say, politely, I suppose.

Those are my instructions.

Pretty soon, one of us will leave the bathroom.

I think you will disapprove. You will think less of me. You will not like me. You won't like me anymore. You will stop liking me, which might impair the summer.

37

PLEASE

Don't hate me when this is really all over. Do not go around saying crappy things about me.

Walking around outside, when the sunlight is bright, we might enjoy this, don't you think?

Suddenly, a breeze will arrive, a lively breeze.

Please, this is not such a hardship to be such winsome people, because we are not in any trouble.

Returning now, to your inquiries, to your concerns, returning to anything that concerns you, you can take care of it, or just briefly consider how you could take care of it.

But briefly, it's always, I expect, too long.

38

THE EVENTS OF THE MORNING
WERE FAIRLY INTERESTING

We could talk about it. Yes, your situation is certainly more of a monstrosity than mine is. Don't you have many more reasons to die than I do?

I admit everything gets easier and easier for me—as time goes by.

I get what I want when I want it. I have been, am, will be, well served.

We did get the celery soup. It's what I'd like, you know.

The events of the morning were fairly interesting. This is my news. We were on the toilet, you realize.

39

EVERYTHING OCCURS AS PLANNED

Everything occurs as planned. I am thrilled. I do not consider it poor taste to be this proud of a pair of shoes.

The shoes I am wearing are a recollection from your childhood.

"Don't you like them?" I say.

"They're so strange," you say.

40

ANYTIME OF THE DAY OR EVENING

You have been taking advantage of some enjoyable moments. But you might be mistaken. Finally, you have come to believe that you should savor life. All of this adventure of ours has used up only about thirty-five minutes.

Time for our copulation.

I feel so sentimental, but only a colossal effort has entitled me to feel this way.

"Please don't. Please," you beg me.

You have more than one deep, oozing starting point, it looks like. How did this happen?

You give me a playful kick. My foot is on you.

Why don't you let me stand on you even fleetingly?

Should I remember this?

Is there any reason to remember this?

To remember you? Oh—

41

HASN'T SOMEONE DONE THIS
THINKING FOR US?

Hasn't someone done this thinking for us?

Look out!

"Sorry."

Will you get away from these discomforts? The smell of mice? The plain ordinary dirtiness of my wanting to push yours or my filthy hair around, without my having to have one tremor of sensation?

I am ardent in the afternoon.

Perhaps I am a smaller, darker person than what you had in mind.

So sorry if you are not completely happy.

Be assured this repulsive moment is coming.

It is not safely past.

Nor passed.

42

THIS TIME YOU SAY NO

You just want to be here with me.

The temperature of the room is cool. I want to pet you, but not your private part. I would not touch it with a fork.

You would think if I could tolerate the bedside clock that I could bind up your parcel with the cord!

They did not know why I felt this way.

You saw my nakedness. You had a great deal to worry about, even if I had made much of bathing daily. Yet you treated me courteously. You told me that you wanted me to remain in good cheer.

I was given a washing, which nearly fortified me. I was fed the right food. Let me tell you it will take much more strength to stop my pleasure in the nick of time than what I now have.

I forget—where did you say came from?

No, come.

Why don't you answer me?

Here is my solution that could help you anytime anywhere. Here is my advice, even though many of you consider me to be unclean.

Sweetness! Something wonderful will happen to you, which will make me happy!

They can keep remembering this—even if we do not.

43

WE COULD FIX AN EGG

I could do something so that you and I would not be invited back.

You are better-looking than I am, better prepared, better behaved.

I do not like these men as much as I know I am supposed to.

I am so glad there are no little girls here. I would loathe it if there were little girls here. Older women give me that sense that I have value, but little girls make me feel like shit.

We could fix an egg.

Don't keep saying that! I don't agree. Don't tell me what to do!

44

A NECESSITY ARISES

I am the one who tells you what to think.

We are very similar to people who stay together who do not really love each other but who want to love each other so much.

A necessity arises which has caused both of us to tremble all over. We—nobody could say why this is.

We could give this necessity the wretched synopsis it deserves: The Story of Our Lives.

One never knows, not for a thousand years, the way to speak to a woman such as I am, one who wears such footwear, who goes into the courtyard, who reposes at the fire, who undertakes the tasks—the tufts, the hollows—it is indescribable.

What if she even knew what she was doing when she

cooked almost every vegetable available? Fruit is what she claims she likes. The liar.

The sounds on the roof could be scuffling, if it is a good night. We hear its goodness.

Some human beings do not hurt people or damage property. They do not intensely glow, or become indivisible by merely looking at you.

To learn more about them, people should use you.

ROMANCER ERECTOR

(2001)

I must eat my dinner.

—WILLIAM SHAKESPEARE

NANCY WEAK

1

She stepped over a stone, a stone, not exactly. And, at the very least, what began as loitering in the green yard, was not calming for her.

She wore the sundress which was not dull enough and with every stride she took, her hair was bumped by her hat.

2

She entered an old-fashioned shop on a famous street where more than several damaged objects are kept.

"Can I help you?" an old-fashioned woman said.

"Oh, you have this!" Nancy said. "It isn't comfortable. It hurts. It's heavy."

"Yes. It picks up all of the lights in the evening."

And then as a household fly might do rudely, Nancy left the shop in a rush.

3

In this same year Aborn stumped toward Nancy.

He was intending to be useful to her, not to appear to be ill-timed or unreasonable. If he gave her hand a friendly shake, he might startle her.

Even so, she was roughly grasped from behind.

Unaware who held her, she tried to pull free.

She thought, I may be in distress!

She worked to free herself, did not turn, did not speak, but presently, she was let go.

"Mr. Aborn!" Nancy said.

"Nancy!" he said, "I wish I could think of your last name."

4

"My name is Nancy! You saw me."

No, no, no doubt, Aborn saw all of her displeasure, and how unsafe she was.

"My dear!" he said, "I like your hat!"

"Thanks," she said. "I got right into bed and went to sleep after you left."

"Then you must have felt fine."

Past the terrified shrubs, they bothered to go, and then

they went along toward an old-fashioned shop where Nancy pressed the bell. When the bell signalled its habitual reaction, they went on in.

5

"That's what I want," said Nancy.

"Did you look at everything they have?" Aborn said. "Let us look at everything."

"This is eighteen years old," she said. "That's old-fashioned. Is it old-fashioned enough for you?"

"Which one do you want?" Aborn said.

"Is that old enough? This one," Nancy said.

6

Well, well, next they sat side by side in a taxicab sedan and the world was crammed high, large, and long.

At the restaurant things are not too bad.

There's a pancake for dessert.

The server's face—her hopeful fur-lined eyes—please Nancy and Nancy wants to charm this girl. She is unable to resist that, so the server says slyly, "I will never forget you," when the moment for parting is clear.

7

It was a breezy lightness they ambled into and many things were being put upon. A huge flowery bush had no self-command and Nancy's petals bulged a bit. She had bought herself some roses and the dream flowers, the unpretentious hovels, and the places all about were particularly dreamy, she thought.

8

Aborn, quite brightly, went on ahead, all by himself, in search of some dandy souls he'd never known before.

But where are you now? Nancy had to think inside of her house, as she unwrapped her buds and trimmed their stems with the boning knife.

The roses were just too weary and they fell all over themselves.

Still, she did encourage them so that they did not lose heart inside of their tankard, nor did they ever much resemble the living things.

9

Her immature new brooch she skewered onto herself, and she hung her hat on the genitalia of a chair.

The roses were okay. They were scented with Beconase.

10

Those Floradora roses.

"Hi," said the girl to her old mother who was dressed in quilted slippers and bunchy clothes.

"Good afternoon," the woman said, "dear."

11

Nancy's father would need to have his coitus with the old woman when he got home, so the old guy did.

Hush!—they went up the stairs to do this in a room pale as this is where among other things the tables are surmounted by lamps and the decorations are bronze-tinted.

Welcome to the afternoon.

With slight astonishment, the old man said, "I will, of course, I will, if you want me to, do it again."

"Now you rest," his old wife said.

12

Nancy's old mother is so old—such an outmoded thing, even the finger ring she wears is a mess.

It should be kept on her body for the best results.

13

Nancy's father is ordinarily weak.

"Can you remember?" his wife says to him, "something good about me? Would you remind me?"

"Sit by me," this mother of a few incongruous people says.

One of her feet is curled on its side, all floaty on the floor.

Her mouth aches. Her irradiated eyes are fine.

She is regarded in certain circles as a slacker.

14

"The floors look bad," the old man says. "Next time bleach them or use a more powerful cleaner."

15

"I'll bleach them."

16

Then the mother says, "Tell me again how did Len die?"

17

"He was an independent boy," his father said.

"How did he die?" the mother asked.

"He was killed," said Nancy.

"He was not killed," the old woman said.

The father said, "As I said before, his head, his head was lopped off with a clasp-knife." Whatever that is.

18

Father, oh father of people!

"I hurt my head," he said, rubbing a knob on his face near his ear.

And his old wife is not as well-liked any more.

19

For an instant the old man appears highly intellectual.

20

He could see the sharp small hairs above his old wife's mouth and on her arm.

21

During the intermission, Aborn arrives.

"Just point the way," said Nancy. "Thank you."

22

And the old woman butchers bread to a fare-thee-well.

Upstairs the topsheets won't overstrain themselves when Nancy does not wear her loose outer garment or her overshoes.

She is lying down on those linens with Aborn and the original extent of her relief points upward undoubtably.

VERY, VERY RED

1

I have too much of a sense of myself as a man to be reckless. I tell myself, "Get it done!" Robert and Buster have volunteered to help me, but I am not an invalid, Mary.

I have asked myself this question: "What does she need?"

Mary, I am not ashamed she is naked in the bed, waiting for me. I told her I knew how to behave. This time, however, when I became bored, I had a very, very, very, very long conversation with Diane, Mary.

She says, "Remember who you are. Remember what you do." She promises me that I will be pleasantly surprised. She promises. Sometimes, afterward, I hate her. She pities me.

2

You poor thing is what she says.

I will yawn significantly after dinner. "Diane," I will say, "isn't it time that we went up to bed?" Mary, you say to ask Diane to give me one of her fancy handjobs. Will you be home on Saturday?

I thanked Diane for petting me.

These days Diane's skin is waxy, cold. She fell off of the chesterfield. She was weary from swimming. I did not try to help her. I was afraid, so this is sad. I unfastened her belt. My hand was strong enough, capable enough. I remember. I remember my enjoyment of our happy home.

We went into the dining room, and Gretch came over to us and Gretch said, "You can have whatever you want!"

Gretch is another one. I am going to sleep with Diane and I am going to sleep with Bill's wife.

Buster said he didn't like Diane as much as he liked our other girlfriend.

"Better eat up those peaches," Buster said.

I said, "Buster, right."

Buster, Buster, Buster.

3

Perhaps, Mary, I just want to see what will happen to Buster.

One would not know why any of this is, if this is a drama or if this is a pageant.

Mary?—could you be with me here, Mary? This would not

make things easier for me. I just wanted somebody like you to change her mind.

I don't have to say everything I could say about Diane.

The doctor asked Buster to carry Diane in. Her skirt was short. She had bobbed her hair.

She accepted a cigarette from Buster once she was back up on the chesterfield. She also accepted an ashtray from Buster, and she did a lot of throat-clearing. The doctor treated her like a friend. "Do you have a sore throat?" the doctor asked her.

She'd be perfectly capable of that. I think Diane did have a sore throat! Diane is lifelike.

"I'll have a cup of tea!" Diane said.

They all agreed with her about that.

"She can always make me laugh," Mother said. "She is the smartest person I know!"

I will tell you this—I had the shivers and my neck hurt from sitting in my chair. "I love you with all of my heart," I told Diane. I think it is thrilling to hear people say that.

Diane said she would not mind if I told you how she and I do it—I am on top of her, then a little on the side of her.

What a night! I thought I saw you and somebody else, high up on our wall, tiny-sized, getting ready to fuck each other, or you were just finishing up. Together, we had here great rivals in a house.

There are many imitations of Diane here, made of horn and rubber and plastic.

I merely tapped Harriet and she broke.

4

I wonder what this is. Diane was wearing crazy clothes. Her hat fell off of the chesterfield where she had set it.

She had sprung back into a curled position. We washed the girl carefully.

You think to yourself, I slept with that thing.

What Diane still needs is what I need.

I gave a little tap tap to the vagina of Diane—where there was a sizable stain on it—ink—still wet.

When I took Diane to the bed it was so easy. "Isn't this a nice ruffle?" I said.

For your information I said, "What did they do to you Diane? Did they sew you up? Look how little you have made it!"

Aren't I a lucky boy?

Diane gave me something which looks like Honorene. Diane fixed it so that I could wear it on my little finger. It's a little chipped. It's tight on me.

She said, "I think I got that in Burma!" and when she asked me for it, I threw it across the room. Just joking.

I woke up sexy and frightened, thinking about the girls in the window stacked up on top of each other, and thinking about you, you frightening person.

5

I have been expecting a nice compliment from you.

Then they threw Buster across the room, when Buster tried to protect Diane.

They pointed at Diane, and Buster tried to protect Diane. They threw Buster across the room.

Diane had her hat on and Diane said, "Where are we going?" and I said, "What do you mean where are we going?" and Diane said, "I am going with you."

I said, "Oh, Diane! Diane, oh, no!"

One day she just left town and she went out West. She called me, she said, "I won the lottery."

Diane—the girl—she was not running away from me! I did a dumb thing! I did such a dumb thing! My hair is sticking out of my head because I did such a dumb thing!

Buster returned here with Diane, saying that he had not had much fun with her. He carried Diane back to the hiding place after we had eaten our dinner with Betty.

Diane's vulva is a bit better now. She wears lip rouge. She wears a necklace of pearls. She wiped her hands.

She can climb in, she can climb out of an auto. She can drive it up onto, up on top of a roadway. She will do the cutest little trick. We are going to have to touch her vulva.

We were not wrong in believing that she had been a full-fledged girl at one point, and we thought of touching the vulva.

6

We have pried her apart, divided her again, discarded the center portion, given her a good soaking. We behave, for what it is worth, with our dicks protruding, as if we were gentlemen.

I have worked pretty hard at this. This has taken me a long

time. I expected this to be scratched or chipped by now and it isn't.

Diane touched the collar bar you gave me.

She said, "What is this?"

I said, "I found it. Somebody gave it to me. I found it."

She said, "Which? Did you find it? Or did somebody give it to you?"

I said, "Both!"

Mary, I spoke to Diane as frankly as I speak to you. I thought she was doing fine. There was a fluttering. I felt a tickling. I was stung.

7

I said, "I was stung." I said, "Would you look, Diane?" I said, "Diane, dear, Olga wouldn't mind it if you fished around inside of my trousers."

"Diane, you have been here forever," Olga said, "haven't you?"

"No," Diane said, "just for two years."

A woman asked us if we had seen Diane. The woman said, "That one wasn't Diane."

I said, "It wasn't?"

"No," the woman said.

We were so surprised. Janet said, "That wasn't Big Gretch."

"It wasn't?" I said.

Janet said, "No, no, that wasn't Big Gretch."

I said, "Where in the world does Big Gretch go?"

"Up and around," Buster said, "that way."

I have a terrible tale I could tell you about that. That that is.

Oh, my Mary!—I can tell you anything!

I behave myself.

I use simple words that you can understand—*the vagina of Diane, the children of Mary.* There isn't any puzzle. I could have caught sight of you I realize now.

I felt as if they were doing your fucking for you when I saw some people fucking.

Can you remember my exact words out here in the blue?

You should receive my instructions today.

I apologize, Mary, for hurting your vagina. I apologize, Mary, for being so clumsy with your vagina. My worry is, is Buster fine now? Uh, the doctor spoke to Buster. The doctor said, "Good job, Buster."

Buster hasn't been that careful and I have had to say to Buster, "Please be careful!"

8

What will Buster do for me? is what I ask myself. What do you think that Buster will do for me?

Will Buster help out? Buster can be so clever. Mother is clever. It is no surprise, I suppose, that we are clever.

I spoke to Buster as frankly as I speak to you, honey.

I don't think I will ever speak so frankly again. Buster can do anything within reason with Diane and Diane agrees with me about this.

I cannot tell you how wonderful I feel when Diane tells anyone, "You are right."

Mary, I wonder what you would have done. One day you will tell me.

We have another hard week next week. It will be one thing after another.

To put it another way, it is not too difficult for us to get up into an asshole, and yet it makes some of us say our knees hurt to just think of going up there.

In driblets, we execute our duties toward Diane.

We have promised to carry her, to collect her, to distribute her, to fully dispose of her and her name. Daughter of William, second daughter of William. Born 1946. Helpful, tactful, genial—hasn't she often tried to bring herself back to the table?

Listen, she had gone off into the kitchen to get the dessert, to bring it back to us. We were waiting for her. No one was with her in the kitchen.

We might feel a dessert is too scratched up or too cheap, that it is cheap. We could think it is thick.

9

Diane has to throw herself into bringing us some dessert.

"What happened to her?" we said. "Is she coming back?" Boy! She should take every opportunity to come back.

That was her in the window. We could tell by how she was hunched.

At last she peeped in.

Diane said, "Fuck me. Touch my breasts."

She comes forward. She greets you. She does not go backward. She says hello. Isn't it strange she does not go backward when we walk forward?

We make an effort to avoid getting angry with her. We try not to talk to her in a loud tone. We try not to interrupt her. We try to understand a girl when she speaks to us. We say, "Would you mind going over that again? Will you be kind enough?"

Diane doesn't have your confidence or your courage, but Mary, she is a good person.

10

Now Mary, Thelma is designed as my new friend.

Mr. Cohen said that I should never bring Thelma to London because they beat up people who bring Thelma to London. If she is in it, they will even burn a store to the ground in London. I can bring Thelma to Paris. Paris is fine. Mr. Cohen does not know anything about Prague. Vienna is fine.

I said I have been so careful of Thelma. I said I have never taken her anywhere. I have not fully enjoyed Thelma for all these years. I said I really wanted to take Thelma to Europe. Mr. Cohen said, "Not in the snow! because the skin cracks!"

I am aware of the risks.

I do not want people to gossip about me. You said, "I understand they question you."

We are not the only ones here.

Mary, some of us found a sexual one, but we do not have

enough wisdom to take care of so many full-fledged girls and their vulvas. That we still love those girls gives us some reassurance.

11

A girl should be entertaining and instructive in life. Will it ever be different? Marjorie said she didn't think so.

We can celebrate in the old style. Ahead of time, we prepare.

We push our tongues, some do, into some of them, into their anuses.

"You are pretty, too!" they said.

They were the biggest, the most beautiful batch of people we have ever seen!

The eldest of our girls was the fiercest. We don't care. We hope she does come over. Something better comes along.

She was pure gold, Ma'am. We have always said she should have lived in a fairy kingdom, fitted snugly into the fairy kingdom.

It takes us so long to believe what we are saying.

UPRIGHT PEARL

How about the deity responsible for me?—why should it not move me through the realm, escort me to the other side of the predicament?

"Come now," I said, "I admire you. Can I ask you for another favor? Please, please. I am a friend of yours."

I heard singing, high and happy.

There is another oddity over the last years. I admire my darling husband. I gave him my little paw. I said to him, "Are you lonely?"

"Yes, I am," he said.

He took me by my sleeve which is wrapped in very delicate skin, so you treat it in a special way. He treats all the skin that way. We go into Illinois.

Now come the other ones who stand like peaks, who wear the brown coat, the ochre jacket—very short.

One arrived who ate savory goldfish. She stopped. A surprise now would be best now, a nice one. The trees would not be melancholic. The lightning would be decreasing. An old woman who does not look well would show me her reliability.

The wind would roll us over a ledge and when the rain starts we would go home.

I am ashamed to say I am unhappy and we poured out liquor into our glasses and we drank it.

The disorder in my left knee has returned, and this time for a different reason than the last time, I have pallor, debilitating pain, possibly fever, a noticeable tumor involving a tendon, and persistent tingling in my affected good try and first haunting.

ECSTASY OR PASSION

While I am alive, I have raptures. I have troubles with my nose. When I fell, I broke both of my arms. I didn't know I had broken my arms. I sat down after I fell. There was semen on my penis. My hands were together on my belly, the way Bob's were, as if somebody had tampered with my body. Somebody else—I did not do it!—must have killed me.

HER HAIR IS RED

I would not have seen the tiny indiscreet comet. I am weak. But what I think is I saw stars, stairs, stars. I have been permitted to stick these last together.

There is anything I should see.

I should stand. I comb.

Laws of nature can neglect a human. Herb helped me and my mother helped me.

I did not know she liked those grails at the house. Saw her with the sack I gave her. I should ask for a sack back for more repose of my soul.

In jam jars, she puts sundrops around and she buys small things such as toothpaste.

What I think of she provides. In fact, sure she does.

"How is Thursday," she said, "or anything else?"

There is all of this to say.

They were proud of me. There is all of that to say at the time. I was made into a more womanish girl. I tell myself not to run away, whatever that means. Thick folds of my skin prevent me, whatever that means. Rather, it is from the blather, rather, I am made.

I parade around plenty, which means I do have the globular breasts. Yet, I am watched.

MADDER LAKE

"Well, yes," says Jack, "but there are Frenches!"

Uh, that's very specific this time that here is Marcel French and George French and Steve. It's Steve. It's Mike. Mike's companion's name is George. He's a French. They have their obligations. That's Colleen and Marcel French and that's Sherwood French.

I'm the wriggle upright who is wearing women's slipper-type shoes.

I speak to Jack.

"In a way," I say, "I like it here." It is not difficult to understand why.

I do have the summary of quarrels. Yet, Jack and I, we are boxed in with painless prickings. We chew our morals. Our clothes are good.

Uh, that's very specific this time that it's the stuck-down Frenches—Steve and Mike French. All else is undulation and the inlaid outline.

Frenches say—"I was there." "It is my belief." "Try wide in the last four years."

Colleen French is featured with tapering legs, with a raised back. She wears her woman's head, her padded arms. I dare not to speak a word to her, in front of her, at the end of March, near her. I spoke to Jack. My feeling is I should have.

Tell Jack, Jack, tell Jack! Jack! Jack! My apron, it doesn't feel too bad. My decorated hand, my pierced-together stretcher, my displayed mount, the hanging space on every side—sliding. They do not terminate! I left lunch cooking on the stove and I made coffee!

Get myself endeared I should, endorsed with a day in mind. This day is Wednesday.

All Frenches are not dispersed. They'll lunch. A French says, "You don't usually wish?"

"Yes," Jack told Mike, "I do wish, despite my mind."

I do wish too despite my mind. I feel quite sincere and Jack is wise. I take his arm. Uh, the day—if you want one of these days I will save it for you. Jack puts his hand out for my hand, puts an arm around the waist of my madder lake crepe dress. He is one of our ablest and most crafty.

Now, for goodness' sake, here is a girl who is formal and exceedingly general.

The girl—a friend of Colleen French—says, "Are you all right? I think you're over it."

I notice the shade of the sky. This shade of sky is "orange glow," a visual effect usually created by lower skies, not often by this sort of sky which is so very high. This sort of sky's highness manages to preserve the charm of direct sunlight.

The girl says, *"Pourquoi êtes-vous si triste?"* There you are. *"Il ne faut pas être triste."*

Our sky's so high. It's at the gravel stop of a tall building.

THEY WERE NOW AT THE TOP

With his wife and his child he had been summoned to come forward to this moment inside of the shop.

The husband said, "Take that one."

The wife put a pair of glass frames on. She waited for her love of the glass frames to reveal itself.

The child dropped its toy. The wife began to feel hatred for her child.

"Please help me out," the wife said.

The husband said, "Take off that one."

The optician said, "Aah."

Someone else's child left the optician's shop.

"Is there a bathroom here I can use?" the wife asked.

The optician smiled. He said, "No."

Inside the bathroom a dish and a piece of soap skip like rams.

The child fell to the floor.

It spent much of its time for any reason.

"You! You ought to pick it up," the wife said to the husband, referring to the child.

"He fell!" the husband said.

"You couldn't reach it if you tried," the wife said.

D. BEECH AND J. BEECH

Some layering is required and some combination of these people.

Maybe I did not make it refreshing enough.

Her robe has the usual fringe of snakes. She wears a wristwatch and a cheap hairclip which was a hairclip over one hundred years ago!

The whole idea is that there is the pattern. The patternwork in the woman's head is her attitude, now worn, the upper edge of which breaks through, which meanders, which makes conversational gestures.

She could well belong to a mythological landscape against a deep pinkish orange background—or if she belongs to you—I hope you can restore her beauty.

The man or boy, he used to sit there in the morning. She

would put a coverlet on him and she would pet him and she would kiss him.

Both of these people have ears which are just wrong.

It occurred during this phase yesterday that their rough tongues seemed to be merely pegged on.

It seems they live in a lush era.

He has already had his best day, the man has. The woman, she has not yet.

Now then, her hand—flat—she must do as others do.

If the two of them have really ever been tender with one another, these people, this morning, will be so mythological as if not to be yet beyond belief.

ACTUAL PEOPLE WHOSE BEHAVIOR
I WAS ABLE TO OBSERVE

I want to act as if I love them and then I want to hurt at least those two during the next period of my life. For years I will do no other difficult work. I am so pleased to ruin them, you know. I said to Gor, "It will be as if they have never run around or as if they have never twisted upon their beds."

They both need affection, constant coaxing, intimacies. If I talk to them sufficiently or if somebody wiser than I am speaks to them concerning me, they will have sympathy for me, I think. I will kill you if you tell anybody I have no anal intercourse, no art treasures. I have an ideal companion I treat tactfully. I poke my hand into the air ceaselessly, as far as I am concerned.

I wipe pollen from the stamens as I was taught to do with paper towel and put the towelling into my bowl. The water jug with the goldband lilies inside of it is like a person with a rag in her mouth. If you can believe it, the sample of cake is on a plate with a sheet of paper towelling covering it.

I said to Gor, nobody would believe it. I wear such a short skirt. I appear to be tied down by my appearance. I should look like someone I would want to see. Someone must have told me to wear this. The fur of it is like feathers. The feathers are like hair, or the feathers are hair. The fur, furry hair swishes. In the day, in the night, I am not impulsive, yet I have to urinate frequently. It was warm enough not to dress warmly. This is what is in the wardrobe—blue, black, blue, light double seams, energetic curves, slipped strokes. There is slim chance that anything is unable to be unmoved.

THE IDEA OF COUNTING

It is five gems. It is eight gems. It is ten gems.
It is three gems.

It is eighteen gems.

It is five gems. It is four gems. It is five gems. It is three gems. It is three gems.

It is five gems.

It is eighteen gems!

It is three gems.

It is more than one gem.

THE DULLER LEGEND

For the duration of my speculation, the girl felt as if she had been in a world.

There is no item so common to us all as she is.

I would eat the girl's food as if it were my food. I would like to have all of her money. She has so much of it.

I try to speak the way she speaks. I wish I could wish for what she wishes for.

"Scoot the dishes off the table," said the girl. "Molly?"

The girl's urn was sobbing. The great hall—healthy and unclean—is so noisy.

The girl—though not at her worst, is not at her best—she is midway between these. A few of her live limbs flare like sprigs. Her young teeth are notorious.

A girl's guests are richly made. Unh!—a thing was perceptive.

Piercing the day is the sun with its flaws.

But that's not all. Here they have a set of sixteen greedy butter knives. Somebody is influenced by what the butter knives do.

Needing a refreshment for myself, I went into the little hills. I sought a hill, but I did not stop. In the glen, I saw three girls. My view passed from the body of one girl into the brain of another. This girl leapt toward me, yelling, dragging itself on two legs, and I went toward her, and I said, "I came looking for you to be my friend." And now I have her.

So I take this opportunity to express my deep appreciation for this most sacred object without which I do not believe my troubles would be over.

It will be interesting to see how my feelings about the girl change. In the best battle I ever fought I was supposed to meet a princess. Within days I received a handwritten letter with the warning which predicted the onslaught. She appeared in gorgeous clothing and dashed toward me, pushing ahead of the collection of pewter plates and mugs, the Turkish cooking pot, strainer and stirrer, the sparkles of hope. In the white bedroom she clung to the curve of my faith and then she sat herself down on the repetitive pattern.

A superb rider, the princess might have seen anyone or done anything. She was famous. One did not often see something so opulent. And yet, next, she threw herself round the room. We all know how hard that is if you are chunky. She is not.

That I made this last effort is not surprising. About five miles away a troop of four girls I saw was looking down into the glen. Now they are dead. They were alive. In another battle I killed five. I was married at nineteen. I have ordered my men to attack and to kill my enemies.

My career—this so-called war—one always knows how these things are going to turn out.

What else could there have been besides a battle? The baby.

The midwife had come along nicely. I heard myself say that I felt fine. A long explanation was embarked upon about flagrant kicking. No attempt was made to conceal the baby which was soon known to all as cool, intellectual, and young— the sort who moves on easily from one person to the next—is handed all around, because the thug is thoroughly emancipated.

We have banded together, the strong ones. I have engaged in sixty-five battles. Small fires are lit in the houses. The children are bathed. This is the first time I have had an infection in my mouth and it pains me to chew a juicy piece of meat. I have not been able to notice any other pain of mine.

What is this made of? I love this! See the tartan rug sits on an old chair—sits, and sits, and sits.

THE SOURCE OF AUTHORITY

A sad story I heard is that I have to have someone take care of all of the bothersome aspects of my life. Tooth, leg, wrist, vein.

It feels so unsexual to complain, but when the weather is bad I go walking. I wander about, but I go to the lake because I believe the lake is better than I am and I want to be in good company. Its beauty, its success, its remote aspect, its inability to speak, hints at intelligence and virtue more pure than mine, better.

The lake means something. I rub the lake and my veins wriggle. I try to make a few things real.

There is so much silver.

Occasionally the lake looks at me coldly which gives me the creeps.

I have had no subsequent conversations with it. We speak about nothing, I tell myself.

On the shore, to myself I say, "Do you really need all of this? It's so crowded. Do you really need all this?"

I am trying to be independent. Is that wrong?

THERE ARE SO MANY SMART
PEOPLE WALKING AROUND

I would be manageable if I am encouraged to eat during these days. I should not have neglected to eat more at a grand party where loquat pie had also been served and crayfish soup had been served and we ate that.

When she started to eat me, I asked her if she was tired. She said yes. I told her to sleep. Then she cried. I brought her back to my beard to eat me. She started to cry. I told her to sleep. She started to cry. I asked her if she was tired. She said yes. I told her to sleep, except that I ate her until she started to cry again and she yelled.

Our beards thrown together caused her to yell at me also.

You said it was ugly. It is not ugly. What if the young person is as hungry as she is tired, how can I help out? Do I keep trying to feed it, and then do I keep trying to encourage the unreasonable thing to sleep? I am only mentioning this because I thought I was supposed to. You ought to go out there and mention this question of mine as well. Mention it some-where in an awfully nice locale I am trying to think of. I would if I were you. Is there another purpose you could go there for?

IT CAN TAKE YEARS TO REMAIN

A t the Fort the mister ate fat. He is made to stay inside. He has a plan, otherwise he'll just be ill.

The missus at the foot of my chair reclines and she opens her legs so I will pet her. She is shareable. Every few hours I take her outside because it's necessary. She thinks her property will keep her from getting up in arms. If she sees her property, she thinks it keeps her from getting up into someone's arms.

At the Fort, the houses are made of Portland stone, very formal.

A steady program of repair on the heavily tree'd land leading from the Fort to the Lake is now in progress. The community has transferred the Fort to the Preservation Trust.

Several people who come through here act so bored. It's nothing surprising they prefer to emphasize the human ideal.

RULING

This is right, more pious, they said. They leave notes in the mailbox telling me to come upstairs and they are naked. They offer me food, whatever I want. They offer me whatever I want.

In the evenings we celebrate. Other people live happily also.

I said, "I wonder if I should become beautiful again." I held the hat. I held the hat. I said, "I always want a hat, but I never wear a hat."

I put salve on my hands.

My hair is not red. My hair is yellow. My hair is brown. My hair is plaited, too. I haven't waited to walk around with a certain somebody. I said, "I like my money better than I like you. Do you need me to take care of you?"

Most said not entirely.

I put ten dollars into an envelope and I wrote on it, *For Elizabeth. Thank you. Diane Williams.* On another envelope, I wrote, *For Henry. Thank you. Diane Williams.* I put ten dollars into that envelope.

A maiden washed the twat of mine with the tan spots. The soap is red. The soap is yellow. The soap is a little bit of soap.

"How much happier do you want to be?" I was asked.

"Not much happier," I said. "A little bit happier."

I said, "Don't do that! Would you please not do that. I don't think you should do that. Are you really thinking of doing that? Is that something you would do? Have you ever done that before? I never thought you would do that. Don't do that!"

SPOON

The person has no sanction for sucking. We had surprised her while she was in the act of sucking. She was a sucker who could make a variety of noises. She was spoony—we had thought she was easy to describe. I had thought she was a wallydraigle. She might not have been. Her hair was a moderate brown and it was aimed at her head. She was suffering from vulvovaginitis.

She was too big. We had climbed into a dominion to conceive of her. She had rushed to separate the covering on her meat and on her fat. She had veins. She had turquoise eyes and her belly is a knob.

Her wan skin was her best female element.

We could have put a tumpline on her.

I have to put the worst of her into her.

A CAUTIONARY TALE

The water is rubbed into my hair and the black hair is moistened and twirled unprettily. I hope I am not too dry for anyone.

In fact, last night in Britain, a woman came to me. We talked quite a bit about what she was—a cruel fighter. She lives in England. She has vanity, old age, ignorance, and all the rest! If I suffer, I think I please her. We drank bonnyclabber. It was this that gave—We kept talking about what we used to know, when in came another human being in a dress who dusted an inner form and the faience washstand. Did not see the babe leave, although she's all gone.

My mother said she herself would stay longer if not for my certain coolness, my unspecified dimness, my slowing down, my not-looking, my over-heard meekness in this phrase which portrays me and betrays me and portrays me and portrays me. I have fewer goings-on, even cried at times, went on lying on part of my face on the bed, fell asleep! My first few nights in sight are such rubbish. She does not want to love such a lack-luster person.

The worst jolt about being loved is when it will have to start.

IT IS POSSIBLE TO IMAGINE A
MORE PERFECT THING

———

Now my father is better than my hat is. My hat is better than my mother's shoes, yet her shoes are better than these socks. My hands are better than her wristwatch. My nose is much better than her hair. My teeth are a far cry.

My carpet is inferior to her breasts, but my carpet is better than either one of my legs. My large-sized saucepot—I acted as if it is a failure compared to her personal hygiene.

I go scrub yams and put yams into the oven so that dinner can be served.

"Is this spinach?" my son said. We got a good look at it— this is clear, very active, bland, soft, runny, a fluid, a drink to drink to improve oneself with by becoming familiar with it. I acted as if I could do that.

PRICKER

Everything here is bleak this, bleak that. We will see what your conclusion is. It's as if, it's as if you called to me and I did not answer you. It's as if your call to me is sufficient, but your allure is such a weakling. I am unimpressed by your allure. Or, it's as if I took my foot and squashed it inside of the squashed towel to dry it.

All over the place, after all, do you remember how I try to listen? There is a tale told about you in which you tell a better tale than this one is, one that inspires both of us—a story about something not as vague as a wet foot, veined with gray.

There it is this afternoon available from your prehistory to my present—a new reasonableness in you when you tell a person's story from various angles seen here. Really!—men love it.

Yes, true, true, you're grand to look at. You look like a nice tweed coat. You have such a kindly chirp too. We experience what is known as love, sexual intercourse, and friendship!

It is true it is difficult to talk to you in natural life conditions as a trusted friend.

What a day! Got up at 6:45. A few bashed heads. Your story is still the best story because you said you were chased by a bear, run over by a car—rather, banged into by one—and bitten by a snake. You say nothing about food even though you own a restaurant. You note the weather, what time you arrive at the restaurant, that the patio is all wet.

What a day! One is supposed to be like this and get ideas one needs!

DEAR EARS, MOUTH, EYES,
AND HINDQUARTERS

She crossed the main street which is enlarged by sexual stimulation. Then that's settled and I want to use the word sexy. I go for the rather goddamned bitch with my beloved arms and hands.

I have a job and I have that large now ripe sea beside us with its operation of forces.

Now she is climbing, now running, I say, trotting, typically swelling so that she can be seen. It is called profane. It is not such a time-consuming process. Imagine spending part of every day after her. She may be completely different with Mr. Reinisch who conducts her through the isolation and the cool. What is there that is good about her? Something important—this is in the land of your bitch. I had hoped to get those boners.

I want Mr. Reinisch to tell this who has the true interest to tell this.

I don't get money out of it. That is my sky and my favorable opinion of a leaf over there. That is my mother, not your mother. You would like to stop this. I would, too, but not just temporarily. You have your own mother and terraced land with vine bowers. A street runs along by many hotels, but don't bother to remember that.

It is all so multicolored. I like the stick part and what's underneath it. I just don't like the decoration on top.

I miss you!—and I want to see you! That is not such a good feeling to have at the end of the valley, at the last spur of the ridge.

FIFTY YEARS OF QUALITY

All the little problems of life do require solutions I need to say here, although nobody has ever come back from the north to tell me this.

"You are the only one," said Jack, "who has ever said that that hurts. You probably don't even know what your hand is supposed to feel like."

His flirtatiousness with me is not unpleasant.

I had that frothy feeling.

I saw Jack grip his hand. I thought, What did he do to his hand? Did he put his hand on the spine of a soft animal? His head and his rump were raised.

"Were you hurt?" I said, "Jack?"

He said, "No."

Together we ate a plate of almonds beforehand. I have

heard the vague terms. The details of this story will become clearer—the satisfiers, the expectations, the lusters.

When I heard Jack locking doors, it is a full account of this structure because a luster can last us for fifty years.

THE DESCRIPTION OF THE WORLDS

I am the same as another person. There are certain circumstances I find myself in. My friends think so too. Frank or anyone does.

I have been going into another room. Coves and console brackets on the bed of the ceiling remind us many monarchs lived here.

There is not too much, fortunately, to describe. They said I found domestic life, that I eat food. I know the outcome. I am the beloved of Frank. Eventually this became a curious change Frank and I regarded highly, even if the log jumped out of the fireplace and burnt the rug in the daytime, I mean really.

Something else happened which created strong force,

I have been given the task of sweeping away my neighborhood.

I asked them to remove those little pieces of something so I could live somewhere. I like to be there, have big gardens, smaller gardens, a small unknotted garden. On Grain Street, I should ask them to remove those little pieces of something so I could live there. My description of the world is similar to Ed's. I have thought so. I know this idea I have is true, not false.

When I was asked to make a terrible mistake, I said I would not.

BILL

Of course, the ideal way to have enjoyed Bill is to have done it long ago, thoroughly. Bill was sexually mature even then. At one time Bill could be enjoyed regularly, but now sadly, no more.

Other people I know should be more like Bill. Oh, good, oh good. I can be more Bill-like than I have been. Let me tell you, don't you know I am in a position to try to understand Bill. I think he should not be wrong! Bill should be right!

I saw him!

Naturally I asked myself to remember remarks of dear Bill which seem unusual.

There are some who know what is true because they have only Bill's opinions. They settle down easily to new work, to new surroundings. These are very sensual people, extremely so!—they eat, drink, sleep.

Between ten and two I was between Bill's bookcase and his table.

"Sure. Sure. Yes, well, then, good-bye," Bill said. Before I get all upset, let me find out if Bill has really become a person who would go for a stroll.

RED ROSE

Her fur neck seemed to me to be on top of her head, its color ordinary. She must have seen my neck.

Let me see what I said.

I'll have to get out, get my astonishment, and get back in here with my goggles on.

I think I do not like her genitals any more. I see hers. Under the water, it did not occur to me what she might have thought of mine. This will not be an isolated incident.

Here, again, animals, vegetables, and minerals are under or over—wedged. My body I show as a striking sword and people scold me for this.

"No! No! Don't!" she said.

She was permitted to correct me.

"If you want to, you can," I had said.

I think she should have her head and she should be authorized to wear a necklace.

MY COAT

As I did before, instead of only just trying to, I tied my coat sleeves together around my waist so I was buoyed. It is less tricky not to be buoyed. I am not worried now or then, overly concerned now, troubled, bothered by my effort.

My feet are where I put them when it was too late. Bernie apologized because it was his fault. I was not supposed to show up until eleven o'clock or much earlier. I have apparently excessively walked in before I finished.

TONY

Tony's children are pretty fancy, good for everybody. These are cleverly pointy offspring I wished Tony could have because I want what's best for Tony.

They all like that word *for.*

I spent the weekend with Sally. I don't want to smooth out the edges of life by telling you how I feel about Sally.

I am not going to tell all of my enemies. I am not going to tell you—my maker, or repeatedly pester you.

May I please have a bronze flower vessel, a vase with tiger handles, edged weapons, a fine goblet and cover, a blue and white underglaze painted dish. May I please rape you?

AN INVENTORY

She was a tree like that, a pot like that, a pan like that. I was wearing a hat like that, a wig like that.

She was becoming more earthly as I turned. I have never had any complaints about her. Do you want her?

"No," you say?

Take her, I say.

"No," you still say?

Certain other people think you must. You are making the biggest mistake of your life. She is Norwegian enough, more of an inhabitant than I thought she was. When they were holding her, she looked fatigued in the field of thought. It is an impression I have of her that is not flexible enough to be spread completely out.

I FRESHLY FLESHLY

—◦—

His block is washed clean and covered with new paper because he says one area of the block has the scent of a fish market. Because his shop window is open I have left his shop door open even wider.

Freshness and quality are just as important in people. He has a long neck and mouth, a neat fillet between foot and body, flat shoulders, and a stepped foot.

I tug on myself and cry out as if making quite an effort.

He is the only one I did that with.

"They can see us!" He leans.

"They can't see us," I say.

"They can see us!" he says.

A number of people asked him for German bologna—an item he seldom will sell. We were rushed to the point when a woman requested half a ham. In general the customers are not too concerned. She took what she ordered and she vowed she would never return.

A man came in and after that I went home. I came home at 3:00 P.M. When I started seven years ago I was a very shy person. I don't think anyone would guess it now. The ability to meet people and to talk to anyone will be an asset all of my life. I have learned a lot about people and I have made some great friends.

GREAT DEED

Far off he saw his peril—that is, a friend—and she waved. So he went to her and he took her and you know it is dark. The last lantern had been put out. Have you ever?—hold this.

She intercedeth. She was lying down you know the way a woman would. Do you see what I see? She was slipping from one side to the other side. I think of her.

Finally, he said, "I can't stand this any more." He got very sick from that. He had to go to the hospital for a long time. Everybody prayed. Everybody was shaking and crying.

Every night for twenty years thereafter, stones slipped down over the rooftops and that's noisy. Finally he said, "I can't stand this any more."

Everybody was shaking. He said, "Everybody pray!" Everybody prayed. The stones stopped slipping down over rooftops.

He got very sick from that. Oh, he was very sick. A lot of them had to go to the hospital. He had to go to the hospital again for a long time.

They did not have—the heat was more horrid heat than our heat. The sleep, dear guest, was sleep. Dear guest, your request not to be disturbed has been acknowledged.

TUREEN

This is for me to say since the old times.

We can come in out from our history to lie down. I keep rolling their limbs between my hands, tap these gently against a hard surface, tap you against my arm, roll you lightly between my hands, break you the desired number of times. Right? Right? Right? Wrong.

On the basis of your outward appearance I may wish to vary you, to adapt you to my preferences.

You cannot be blamed, although at the end of March you spent time with my enemy.

You are not going to say any of this. Good. I am glad you are not, that I am. How long will it rain? Okay. How long will I live? Okay. Don't have any difficulties, okay?

No, I won't tell them anything about you. I won't. You don't tell them anything about me.

I am sorry I am dangerous, that I usually do and I say the wrong thing and grow old. I should not. That's what I wanted to tell you. Peter said, "It is better to make this move quickly."

Go up the stairs and you have gone quite beyond me. My room's on the first floor. This is one of the oldest human crafts—dashing on through it, being pushed through into a thing.

WRONG HELL

"Take my plate!" I said.

"No!" he said, "Not yet! Do you want these? Have you any interest in these?" he said.

They were dished up, compressed, difficult to crumble, much like any child.

"Did I do wrong?" I said.

"You did wrong," he said. "Don't cry," he said. "Don't put that there," said he. "Is it asking too much?"

"Sorry, take my plate! I am so sorry," I said.

"Don't cry," he said. "Do you want these? Have you any interest in these?" he said. The melon and the figs.

I rubbed a napkin over my hands. That is to say it's the finish of a meal even if only just a little more bleating is required. In my private act, I depend on the ending for my simpler, better, and richer act. It's not good enough, toying with figs, even if they're indispensable to enthusiasts.

"Is the salad good enough?" who says.

"Yes, yes. Ye-es. You remember? That's amazing, that last time it wasn't."

"Ye-es."

"That's remarkable that you remember."

"I remember."

"That was so long ago. She remembers!"

THE UNDERWEAR

That will be prim of you if you wear something if you have to not be home.

I tell my friends who could be similar to you—wiry arms, nipples which are not similar to mine—I am hankering to see you and I will sort of die if you do not come on over here. Hi, how are you? We need to take care of next week.

It is a trick to speak as if you would hear me. I am silken nowhere, here, by the water, by the sea, by the fleshy, thin, almost leathery bump.

THE PENIS HAD BEEN
PLENTY DECENT

The food broker, the housepainter, the swimmer and the husband's friend had liked the husband's penis very much.

The husband's penis had been plenty decent.

The wife would have walked around with the penis inside of her if that had been possible.

The husband was dead, the husband who had not been dead for very long.

The grieving wife goes to bed too late and she awakens too early and she eats a girls' party salad in the morning. She speaks about people who should receive money.

She tells people, "We have a lot to discuss."

She mourns the husband. She ties a mortifying scarf

around her waist which had been the husband's own. She wears his unmerciful nightshirt. She wears the frown which had once belonged to her husband's mother.

Then she clumsily prepares a miracle.

THE BRILLIANTS

The sky might not have been too disorganized for them. The clouds were innately ornate. There were too many clouds.

The man was elated by the abundance of decorative clouds, by their prominence.

The man picked up off of the ground scraps of anything from trees. On that particular day, the woman had forgotten her purpose.

Yet on another day, the woman had been the one to clean up. She vacuumed. She washed. She sponged the surface of a bottle of mineral water. She rinsed the nail parings down the drain. The sink was wetted with greasy water, leftover water, yellow water, white watery water, water which is not transparent water. This is water.

The water has only been appreciated since the beginning of last week, after the discovery of the patches of iridescence in it.

The water is somewhat rare, has a slight turbidity. The value of water is fairly low, has a very low value, the lowest.

The woman and the man are of modest value.

One method is used to determine their value—mine.

Pairs of people have a relatively unimportant vitreous luster. They command sympathy, have heart attacks, weeping spells. They grow suspicious.

A man alone in the natural world is tidy.

YELLOWER

The house looks younger and yellower and yellower. The dog appears larger and proud. The house is much skinnier.

The dweller looked smaller and humble and smaller. Her husband looks fatter.

Everything is fine, but not much greener. On Friday her husband will do anything if its characteristics are not insisted upon.

LARGE ORGANIZATION

Malus held a dog who tongued her hand as Caladium told her what she should not do. If she did that, Caladium said, he would not think she was a special person any more.

The dog wore a condom.

"That is not to say," Caladium had said, "that every time you give a tour it's a poor idea, or that your tours are harmful. I am saying that when you think, Let me give a tour, let me introduce myself so I can talk to you—don't do that. Don't. It would be better for you if someone came up from behind you and pushed you into an automobile or truth."

They didn't like my listening—so I walked along the sweep and I heard a boom crane.

In the sweep, another dog grew bold. This dog played beautifully with a boy.

The dog dragged down its haunches and produced an object about the same size and shape as the boy's phallus.

Now I can understand the difference between "systems." I can understand the normal sequence of events—even simplified information I can understand, and which hairstyle I get. The question always becomes for me—who becomes my friend?

CAKE

I am four feet long. I am no bigger than a dust mop. I won't bite you. That is something Tom would say. Tom would want to blurt it out.

When I got here, I said to myself, "I hope he's here."

He fed me cake which is particularly bulky, medium to large, covered with rigmarole, quality good, pleasant, striped with carmine.

He is medium, pleasant.

He cleans stains from the two quart aluminum saucepan. He does not show undue concern.

He is as beautifully browned as the beautiful girls in fancy bakeries.

So many times he was heard to say, "I wouldn't mind being here if I only knew I was supposed to."

I am comfortable at a table or desk, eating.

The table is by the window. This is not a nightmare view of life.

I was filled up. I was bubbling one day. I am changing. I am changing. I am different!

I want to gratify my little cock, but I do not want to be thick. I do not want to thicken up the way Diane Williams did. I talked to her. She said the services are not as good. Well, she said, they are still as good, but you have to ask for them. It used to be you didn't have to ask.

Actually, he stood by me while I was bathed. The flattened hollow of my back is where there is a spot to brush the edge of.

I eat cheese on toast most mornings. What would Diane Williams think about me? What?

I'll find out all about it at dinner and then I may change my mind about my life.

What a triumph to have food placed before me for me, so long as you and I meet.

ARM

My favorites among my limbs and my many patches of skin—anything he asks for that belongs to him—I want to keep those. A nice bright unsealed box of his he did not, in fact, give me, I want.

I could not relieve myself of an entire region, please! I want to keep those.

There is a nice naturalness of his I'll keep. His seriousness of purpose which he advances, I want.

I am so tired, though, of a nice bright sensation.

Back it goes to him!

My patience is his.

ROW OF US SURROUNDED BY
SEVEN SLIGHTLY SMALLER ONES

Her future will have been brought to a sad end if it is not incessantly, daily decorated.

The Williams woman opened the gift from me. The immoral wrapping paper lay on her leg.

"Oh, please and thank you!" she said.

"You are loved," I say. "Would you like to play a game of checkers or of chess?"

"Oh! I am very tired. I am just too tired. I am waiting for my boys and then I am going upstairs."

She wears several small jewels and lesser chains, a waist buckle, shoe buckles, and an arrow brooch.

When a big jewel was handed over to the woman, I said, "Do you really like it? Do you really like it? No, I really mean it. Do you really like it? Tell me how much you like it."

She said, "I cannot remember."

So said, so seen. I will tell you I was an elder clothed and fed.

I would like to go to that store to get gemstones for her to wear with that gemstone, something with a crystal! When was the last time I knew what was best for someone?

Most nights I never knew if I was going to give her a thrum or a finger ring.

A WOMAN'S FATE

This suggests that exposure to her may have been difficult, that an animal became sluggish instantly in her vicinity and dragged its tail along the paving. I am terribly sorry because this was a creature destined for a habit of vigorous walking, who is restrained from too much activity. I do not want to make a joke of this. Every animal I know is extremely sad or a little sad.

On her fence sat an animal with its face turned away from her. Its penis was at an upturn, and she called authorities to inquire about that one. There is something in her inquiry which is a shriek.

In swollen volume, animals dawdle beneath her auto and they surround her auto. She notifies authorities. Come here. I want you to feel what this is like.

An animal on her roof—its silhouette revealing a narrow waist—spit—spat its acorn at her.

Certain animals have intentions to awe, to comfort, to guide, to be gossipy—to be observant, to be sly, to be thoughtful, and more. To be witty, to come to light, to be worth waiting for.

ROMANCER
ERECTOR

a novella

1

How keen I have been with my thinning mind, with my large feet in new shoes, to have a life story.

I feel unsteady and am afraid of my boyfriend.

I unbutton my vest and I say, "What a marvelous, adorable boy!

And for now, there's a slight bulge in my acumen.

2

Soon I laugh and am willing to stay the night here.

There is old pottery and a gilt chair, and an unold mouth about to kiss me.

I'll wind up in this position with the boy's father, our host, Don Musgrave.

I regard the boy's boyishness in the morning.

I show him part of my breast and he puts crayon marks on paper.

"May I have a drink of water?" the boy asks, for he is not aggressive, as if in romantic trouble.

A dark pink river is visible beyond the window. This is the dark pink River Urine.

You'll see.

3

As a woman of my own devising I have had an actual undoing—a fairly smooth, horizontal, waist-high undoing—at this residence.

I took my bedding downstairs for washing in a big heap that was teetering. It isn't peaceful here and there is gray in the child's hair.

He digs a hole in his mother Cora—or something—and she groans and then the child's charm briefly reappears.

The Burgundys—two other guests—keep speaking coarsely. And the dirty Burgundys are the first guests to go home.

That Musgrave boy with the gray, black-tipped hair is now bathing and there may be some similarity between Don Musgrave and me—a slight fullness of the throat, deep creases about the cheeks.

4

Can we do any more with this—with this encampment? It is on The River, on the corner diagonally across from the other corner on which stands the Church of Transfiguration. This encampment is very small and is slightly under the overlapping folds of its surroundings.

Not surprisingly, the settlement narrows into a cashew shape that conveys a frowning expression.

5

It's as if the Musgraves work harder than I do.

They talk to me. They give me money. I don't have much money, but I love to be with young kids.

The boy's eyelid area is rounded. He has a triangular face. His lower lids swell. Everybody loves this boy.

One night his dad Don told me to sit down or to lie down on the mat.

"What is it?" I say.

He isn't lucky with his wife Cora and I come here all the time and he gives me clothes.

"Harder, even harder," he says.

He says, "You don't have to do that unless it gets you excited." He says, "I'm going to the bathroom."

6

While he uses the facilities, I loll, because I have been running around all weekend, sort of like a crazed man.

I have small breasts and a sharp-edged collarbone and hard flesh. My nose is long and my eyes are slits.

It is difficult to explain the true details of my head.

I am two-thirds life-size.

My costume ties behind my neck and fits over my trousers. I have chains and strings around my neck.

At this residence I am a guest and I am with the rest of them, in a gown, eating.

7

I see the sofa I am sodomized on often enough and although I qualify for a big romance, most nights I am in bed by myself because the child who might be at my side has gastroenteritis.

So let me start again to be sweeter. I will someday cook them all a meal.

8

To two medium pieces of bread I add a pulpy center.

The process of letting my spirit rise in a warm place until it's double its size used to occur to me more often than it does now as I sit at my desk.

I make notes, drink up, and try to forgo indifference. I take a brief nap in my chair.

9

Later I'll explore the stylish rear of the house.

For nothing is so hopeful or so merry as rooms in which there are garlands and bow-knots and a great deal of plaster paneling.

But my neck doesn't look that good any more and Don says that's because that's where people have tried to strangle me.

10

I go out to The River and stare at some of the forces of life.

There is another one of them every time I turn around.

The orchard within my reach has a complex past and the trees are fragile.

I am angry toward the end of the day, but you won't have to find out much about that.

11

If you're still here, you'll have some food, which is very tasty—whole wheat bread!—no-meat croquettes, and creamed green beans!

The real story begins on Wednesday—although I have storyish ideas, but no story in me.

And, admittedly, if you speak to me, I cannot hear it.

12

This is my friend Kim Burgundy, my friends Steve, Cora, and Don.

Should we change the furnishings? Are they nice enough for you?

My acquaintances—propping themselves up among their pals—are pretty much as you might expect.

And an examining hand may soon be proceeding along you smoothly—even bringing about that old bugbear pain.

13

You can still have a cup of coffee—plus you will need to produce at least bits of rugged individualism because this is America!

14

A group is yapping away.

15

And if there is any great USA supper it might be braised beef balls and creamed potatoes.

16

Although, if any of this needs to be any different—it can't be—
this is the end.

IT WAS LIKE MY TRYING TO HAVE A TENDER-HEARTED NATURE

(2007)

Again, you decide what appeals to you.

—JO IPPOLITO CHRISTENSEN

ON SEXUAL STRENGTH

a novella

THE WIFE WOULD COME TO US

Mr. Bird was sexually strong. That sounds good. Three—four times a night—he'd wake his wife up and thereby pass himself off as a man who encourages one to get certain ideas.

The wife would come to us and cry! That sounds harsh.

They're all dead now and perhaps I am.

"She is not a slut," Bird had said, when he introduced me to his wife.

From his wife we heard she spent her life obtaining troubles.

Mrs. Bird's name was Blanche. I am the neighbor.

My eyes are brown with a dash of green, with a dash of gray.

2

"STAY FOR LUNCH!"

One late morning when Mrs. Bird came over, I said, "Stay for lunch. Why won't you stay for lunch? Do you want to stay for lunch?"

"No," she said.

I did not manage to exit the room. It may have been that I opened my trousers and I regarded my long penis.

Blanche smoothed out her blouse. Her blouse was very lavish. Lavish? I mean that her blouse was very large and very clean!

The noise of an airplane engine rubbed at our heads.

Her hair she kept off of her forehead with a headband.

My semen dropped onto Blanche's beige slacks.

3

REDDISH SKIN AND THIS RED FLESH

Hell, I had been putting things into myself and things were coming out of me and I couldn't close enough up.

Blanche had reddish skin and this red flesh.

I was very worried about sex, because, you know, I'd never had any formal training.

I offered her a molasses nog.

She wept and scrubbed at her slacks with a dishtowel.

Blanche, who is a big-busted woman, neatened herself. I do not know why, but in my big kitchen back then, almost from the start of her visit, I was thirsty for embarrassing moments.

We sat in the room and I tried to attract her. It's fully air-conditioned for summer.

She wiped her cheek with a blue sponge from the sink. Her short pigtail was tied with a red ribbon hanging down her back.

4

OH, IF YOU WANT, YES

I live in the domicile I did back then and at the upper end of my property is Voight Street.

I've still got the damask curtains and the mahogany cabinet, the flowering currants and winged euonymus, the inkweed, and my downy serviceberry.

I am an American fur sales manager.

My mishap with Blanche Bird could have been shrugged off. Oh, if you want, yes, I did shrug it off.

At any rate, Blanche even returned and she said she appreciated many of the things I had done for her.

My wife was sick and she stayed in her room.

I brought out my silver sedan and asked Blanche to take a ride. After questioning her, it appeared we'd go.

The state trooper found us and returned us to my home.

5

BOTH WERE BUSY WITH THEIR PENISES

I heard myself called by name. My wife was in the vestibule acting uplifted by daily wear and tear.

The pets we own, I noticed then—one with a tan muzzle, the other with a dark brown muzzle—both were busy with their penises.

"Do you want to be petted?" I said. "Then come here." They have pointed small snouts and erect ears.

Neither of—neither, none of us, we did not, nor did the Birds have children.

They're like little snails without their shields.

6

I KNEW I LIKED SEX

I went outside to toss the slugs off the lettuce and Blanche excused herself.

Try as I may, I was going over my morning stuff.

I knew I liked sex. I just couldn't get enough practice.

I wouldn't be surprised if many, many people know the whys and the wherefores of the modern methods for sex—up-to-the-minute, well-balanced information.

Well, my wife has a customary sympathetic manner and she enjoys breast play. Her mother told me.

Somebody said if you bury a bottle of beer, all of the slugs will leave your lettuce alone and they will drink your beer! Now there were so many slugs it was just crazy!

7

A VERY PERSONAL MATTER

The afternoon at the factory was quiet. Athena brought a big pie and made coffee.

I am a perfect bore. That sounds harsh.

For the hundredth time, my factory is in the rear, past the showroom.

I was happy to get home as early as I planned.

My wife was seated, maybe, with her hands at her crotch. "If my life is ruined," she said, "it was the right thing to do." She smiled over it.

This—you can see—is a very personal matter.

I am Enrique Woytus and nothing remained for me except to figure and to doodle into a space between a few hours earlier and the next moment.

At this moment my wife offered that she did not feel influential.

8

FRUITS AND FLOWERS

The Birds, on the other hand, went out a lot. And they even traveled to cities in the north and stayed at hotels.

Sight seen! At the back of the house, between clipped hedges, there are fallen fruits and flowers. Let it remain so.

In point of fact, this is a story dominated by activities going smoothly before the interruption.

To this day I think I hear a bird's wings flapping or a dog shaking his body in the showroom.

9

"DON'T YOU THINK
THAT WILL BE NICER?"

Mr. and Mrs. Bird were visiting us. Mr. Bird said to me, "I think you're excrement."

I had just kissed his wife Blanche, either on, down inside, or near her collar. On my mouth, her flesh felt much to my liking. She had a tiny amount of hair dragging around her neck and one or two small, dull dinner rings on her hands.

When the Birds arrived we had opened windows, saying "Don't you think that will be nicer?"

Those were the days when the troubles were gradually beginning to fit the occasion.

Before throwing open the door, I had cooked a tropical supper, and I had been looking forward to a vacation.

Mr. Bird made a comment about the smell of mold in the house, about which I am very sensitive.

I thought to suck my pipe and I invited all of them to have a drink.

10

GUIDE MY HEART!

I pulled myself back from politeness.

"We are not your guests," Mr. Bird said.

Guide my heart! I had labored over my wife and I had labored over his wife, using my back rim circular spreading.

This is a mercy how I defended myself in the combat. I did not get really wet. It might have been only a few drops.

11

BOTTOM TO TOP

I got down and went to the bathroom to clean up. I changed my garments, bottom to top.

The first part of my body hit was my head—next my happiness, my thoughts, my fears. I suffered a concussion. Was knocked out for a quarter of an hour.

I ate a lot of fruit as a remedy. I had pain in the spleen.

12

MY WIFE SAID

The house behind you—where you see craft items and the specialty products on the lawn—is where the Birds used to have their activities and their intercourse.

The street is arched over with trees.

My wife—my wife is resigned to a life somewhere between laughter and tears. "We'd all be blamed," my wife said, "if we were never misunderstood."

To my credit, at the factory, the in-rack was filled.

13

I HAD TOSSED IT ASIDE

The morning when the Birds made another entry had brought cooling seas and high altitude winds.

I wonder if the head of the penis has the most nerve endings. I had tossed it aside, moistened.

Rudy, the Birds' large pet with rough fur came in. The door to the patio was open. Mr. Bird moved the table. Sure enough, there I was, but nothing appeared more firmly rooted than did Rudy with his caramel face.

I lowered my head while my neighbors advanced.

"You go back home!" Mrs. Bird told her husband.

14

COLDLY IGNORED

A letter from Blanche arrived which highlighted what I felt had been coldly ignored.

> *Dear Enrique,*
>
> *Your skin was not broken, but you call your doctor!* (The rest of the letter from Blanche was chatty.) *We are in the North and the coffee shops are better than those we have at home. Constipation is another reason the travel is not so simple. Nothing to do is another reason for the same problem, in one sense.*
>
> *Blanche*

I read the letter twice. I had the letter from Blanche and I was busy all day and enthusiastic.

15

DEAR BLANCHE

Dear Blanche,

I am doing and planning heartfelt, helpful things for myself.

What suits me is a moment for something to enjoy.

Enrique

I really felt ill. I wiped out the back of my throat with my finger.

16

GOOD BEHAVIOR CAN COME ON

Dear Blanche,

You are not fortunately at home. Listen, good behavior can come on slowly in certain types. Do you know the reason for this letter? This is a roundabout way to talk to you, to be calm and to be reassuring.

Enrique

I did not open Blanche's next letter to me at once because one of the worst days of my life was over.

17

BLOOD-BLACKENED CORDS

Things get my attention and I horse around into them!

My job includes giving moral support and I also need to make an impression on the customers.

I thought I should leave on vacation.

That night, at home, my meal with my wife would begin slowly and routinely as usual.

When Mr. Bird arrived, he was off-color.

He wore blood-blackened cords and requested the whereabouts of Blanche. I said I could conclude that I had not ascertained her location.

Which of us is wise in the solemn hour?

18

A YOUNG GIRL WHO MARRIES

The next letter from Blanche:

Dear Enrique,

    Can I be honest? Truthfully, take today for instance. I am ashamed of it. This is what I want and nothing else, to feel like a young girl again who marries. I know you are close to the edge and I am up North and I cannot get your answers.

Blanche

19

"SILVER BACON," "SCRUB"

I was unaware the envelopes addressed to me did not interest my wife. My wife wrote, at this time, two new songs that have since become hits: "Silver Bacon" and "Scrub."

She fills our home with the sound of triumphs we must endure.

I wrote Blanche a discouraging letter that like the others she'd receive when she returned. I always imagine I am able to explain what I mean by my words.

> *Dear Blanche,*
>
> > *I was just kidding around.*
>
> > > *All yours,*
> > > *Enrique*

20

COLD CUT

After that, like a beauty, Blanche Bird passed close to my house. I followed her to the post office. She was eating what looked like a cold cut sandwich.

She didn't see me. Nobody thinks of a ghost of a chance as a real chance.

In advance of their deaths, the following communication arrived.

Woytus,

    Two o'clock, Saturday, you are expected.

                              B. Bird

21

THE *Bs*

The handwriting was large and cordial-like. The signature matched the script of the text except for the *Bs*, which went over, round about, and hooked and pinned each other up, like they were sexually stimulated!

It seemed wrong-headed to miss an interesting event. There's an old saying: The back foot does not leave the ground until the front foot is planted.

I took Treat along on the leash. I went there posing as a threat, in a series of actions, passing small grave-fields, mainly mounds.

22

THE ODOR OF FAT

I tried to console myself, but I was not the one doing the praying.

"God forgive you!" Bird said. His lips were puffed and his eyebrows close by his hairline.

The weather made it possible to go indoors. It had started to rain. I followed them past the goutweed and the flame honeysuckle at their front door into the house where there was the odor of fat.

There were drop doughnuts in the kitchen on a tray, draining. There were stools, low tables, high furniture, a multi-colored woolen carpet with an allover pattern of cup-and-saucer vine.

Bird said, "My wife wants to marry you!"

Was I duty bound to her? For there is no pot so crooked that it cannot be fitted with a crooked lid.

Fret langsam und du ahnst nieht was du bepacken kannst.[1]

---

1. Eat slowly, and you'll be surprised what you can pack in.

23

THE HOUSE RULES

Blanche went into the dining room to get a breather perhaps. The house rules were posted there. There were loop back and fan back chairs.

Although Mr. Bird looked somber, I could see he had just put food to chew into his mouth.

The Birds' rules were detailed in adult handwriting and were posted inside a frame.

The minimum I need for the zest for life consists of nothing less. I took a stick from the collection inside their front door.

24

"I'LL KILL YOU!"

"I'll kill you," Bird said. "I'll kill your dog."

It didn't feel like such a hard blow.

I was eager to get to the garage after checking for my keys and my wallet.

My dog at some distance stayed with them.

I had opened my big mouth. I had briefly explained the marital duty and falling in love in a speech—one to one-and-a-half minutes in duration.

This is like the lure for the Japanese beetles. They fly toward it and once they are there, they fall into the bag and they don't get themselves out.

I have, in other words, I have spent the whole of my life

permitted to love with plenty of variety, like a camel who whizzed along in the desert.

They were neighbors one should and one does love. There is that old saying.

25

I WAS ACTUALLY
HORRIBLY WEAKENED

I had been given a push. There were demands on my skill and on my ability in the garage. Below my knees, I was actually horribly weakened.

Why, how did I get back into the Birds' house? I ask myself, What is the source of all blessings?

Inside their house Blanche was breaking new ground. She was hard up against her value as a human being and she could not last much longer. She wore a middy and fashionable Bermuda shorts. The buttoned breast pockets of her husband's shirt were packed with things.

Mr. Bird is a civil engineer and there was a thick unclean blueprint on their kitchen chopping block. He said, "I screw back!"

26

I HAD RUN UP THEM

At every change of direction at the upper part of the stairs—I had run up them—I saw the balustrade and fine flock paper.

One wall had a pastel portrait bust of Blanche in profile. Her facial skin was pink and white and her bare chest, pale yellowish brown. To this day it remains a moot point how it was I felt so at home in their house. She had this metal in her character, you know, which made her point of view stand firm or made it altogether too unusual for her to manage.

27

MY HEAD, MY SPINE

My assessment of grip pressure and other factors led me to believe my head of humerus might have been broken or my spine of scapula, but I was mistaken.

28

FIFTY-TWO OR FIFTY-THREE

Blanche is either fifty-two or fifty-three years of age when she dies. Mr. Bird was sixty years when he died instantly.

Meanwhile, Stella is dead and Rose is dead. Ruth and Hy are dead. Willie is dead. Harold is dead. Al is dead. Yale is dead. Jon is dead. Harvey is dead. And Patricia and Bob are dead recently.

29

"OUR POSITION IS HOPEFUL"

I keep a diary of events. In my pocket diary I just read, "Our position is hopeful."

The cliffs were probably green with plants, huge deer, trees, and fish lizards are up there.

I saw the same cliffs and lights close by. There was pressure putting me back. I was sitting in McDonald's because I needed to get off of my feet because my ankle was badly twisted. My calf was bruised. Something out there was green and left hanging alongside the paved lot. It is not clear how people disregard all of the indications of danger.

30

AFTER DOING SOME
HARMFUL THINGS

After doing some harmful things, I made a pencil mark to begin the vacation plan. Later, I added headings.

Against this backdrop, my wife and I, we took up two tiles in the hearth. Don't look at me like that! The body had been kept out of all air and light.

The dead body was not Blanche Bird.

This event took up many months of our time.

Certainly nobody may be hidden from my wife Bernadette. Even so, Bernadette nearly died of it that time. It didn't occur to her to stop trying for the name of the deceased. She couldn't speak it without brimming over because she wanted to spill the beans.

The house was so full of tramping, and splashing, pretty chintzes, and the motor sound.

31

I SAW A HAWK

Bernadette was sitting by her rock crystal sphere in front of the roll-up blind.

I saw a hawk through the window lose its footing and fly.

"Go ahead of me on the stairway," Bernadette said.

We have a half-tester bed and jugs and bowls on the side table.

A claw caught her knee and both Tammy and Treat jumped up on her and I sweated. It was like my trying to have a tender-hearted nature.

This is how love can be featured.

32

I ALSO SAW THE DEUTZIA!

Over the centuries people live happily and make pictures of it. I thought I might be witnessing some of this.

I saw trees I didn't recognize from the window, but I also saw the deutzia!

My trouser was stained and some of the color was on my carpus.

We are pleased to get all over this on a regular basis.

I found myself with pain, exactly like a burn, chair-bound and with a slightly twisted trunk, my thigh to the flank of my wife. Both the physical and the emotional elements almost forced me to have moderate satisfaction.

I lifted my testicles. Maybe this will put balance into the story.

33

THIS MAY PUT BALANCE
INTO THE STORY

A red, long-haired dog—who didn't belong to the Birds—may put balance into the story. He belonged to the other neighbors down the hill. He was—I can't get the breed. Irish setter is what he was, named Flame. He was very often around the house. These neighbors never took care of him and he loved to be around the house and my wife would feed him and then one day we had a barbecue and we prepared steaks and put the herbs on, ready to go to the grill, and, then, when the crucial time came—the steaks and Flame were gone! I suddenly flashed on Flame.

34

I WAS UNDRESSED AND LISTENING

I was undressed and listening to soft music. My wife was pleasant and smiling. She has pin veins in her legs that I especially like. My reason for loving her has been brought under control.

I did some upward pulling with the pulp of my fingertip beneath the opening at the end and dampened myself.

With a rug over her knees, she had held out her arms to me. But you ask yourself: Where does one end begin and the other end end?

35

DAT IS SCHENE

I have swollen fingernails and toenails, dry mouth. *Einer allene, dat is nich schene. Aber einer und eine und dann allene, dat is schene.*[1]

I had lost the feelings of being swept and/or of being pushed—which I often look forward to for more of. There was a cold front and the seeping around of moisture and lowland rain. It was sort of a night. Bernadette used her clear stone for gazing.

An interesting point about crystal-gazing is that the image usually is not where you'd expect it to be—inside of your head! It is inside of the ball. Our ball could show us any of our experiences.

---

1 One man alone, that is not pleasing. But one man and one woman and then alone, that is pleasing.

We could see ourselves in the short dry yellow grass in our own yard. And we saw a cougar, a barn owl with yellow eyes, an ape. We were stared at by an ape. Two unknown persons came through the yard, too. One was lightly crying, the other one was alarmed, I think.

36

A SIGN THAT SAYS WELCOME

I was staking out the area. I was figuring how they were in relation to the sun. When I saw them I said, "I'll never get them out of here." I think it took me two days. But the feeling after— I am extremely proud of myself.

THE GLAM BIRD

That's the way to eat lunch. We shared the macaroni and cheese. We both had the pestilential drink. The forest beyond is green. The table is brown. There is more than one coyote, it's a dog.

We walked barefoot on the pebbles. We looked at the bleeding hearts. My mother cooks bacon. My father makes foreign foods, pies, preserves, croquettes, and all the equivalents.

A car pulled into our driveway and the tires' contact with the pebbles sounds like lucky me counting out my paper money.

I think I'm modern. I've got to where I am today by going around being pretty. Aren't the houses all around us like blankets of glittering buttons? The sky is like a nose that's been pierced as a mark of prestige. I am like a woman who wears a hat medallion!

Three of us deeply believe in me.

WHAT A GREAT MAN LEARNED
ABOUT REFLECTION AND EMOTION

There is a little money for him and a deficiency of sex.

A tad unwisely he supervises his little infant and he fumbles with its little foot.

Now let us suppose, no matter how right, he has a mush of understanding which is a false alarm because on their way to him are a little more wealth and a little health.

SWEET

It was so sweet of you to come. I am glad you are here because otherwise I'd be so lonely.

To get me here they had to pick me up off of the sidewalk and put me into the limousine and I tried to stop them from doing that.

One assumes there is an end to this initial phase.

I saw Lesley and asked to talk to her because she is usually nice. She just wants to be finished with this and to become a doctor. For some time now she's been considering that employment.

The man remember I told you about?—who calls me?— called me and he wanted to come over and I told him that now really wasn't a good time for me to have sexual relations, but he came over and what we did was peculiar, not very good, very odd, not right.

He said, "I always tell them hot! hot! hot! Otherwise it's cold. What is the matter with you?"

(I can't believe I told you that.)

There is in his face a dingy hopefulness. As the afternoon increases itself, of course, he is hopeful.

At Bloomingdale's, he put tinsel down the neck of my jacket in the back so that he wouldn't lose me.

He is tall. He has red hair and a goatee. That's what he looks like. I met with him this morning and at length we discussed that things have not been going swimmingly.

He is standing right here. In level flight he is faster. He is probably flying out of here on Friday. He's a pilot.

I have more of the story of my life and not much of his. He barely does a thing, and then he goes ahead and does it.

He is plenty sore when weather keeps him from traveling with the wind. He hit the ground to avoid hitting another biplane. He burnt his hands. He had a fracture of the skull—I mean scalp wounds—and then what adds to the confusion is the dreamlike crack that developed on his head which some call a gash, others say it is the invisible damage.

I think it will be hard to give you an accurate report—a gross report, yes.

I sleep for a few hours, turn around and drive all the way to Baltimore without stopping and run into Chester. We are sitting at a front table and I feel comfortable that my attention is on incredibly important matters. Equally important to me is my deepening and developing interest in national and global politics.

This is the next day and I go buy expensive silk pajamas and two very heavy books.

Even though I'm broke I take several people with me to a restaurant. Across the street at the bank I take three hundred dollars from my account.

I get into bed when I become displeased. My brother and his wife stop by and I tell them we will eat a late dinner. I have had a bad case of food poisoning. All in all it is a fine Christmas. It's efficient and polite. Although, in the same manner a bowel movement is held back—a feeling dawns in me—which is not hiding, and which seems quite separate from my other feelings: I feel good that circumstances are well in hand, that I have returned from being alive.

THE RING STUCK ON

I drank a warm soup solution after. I felt mental symptoms. I threw up. After all, many who have dined with me have done so.

Significantly, I have a picture-perfect headache and hard stool in the rectum.

Into the telephone I said, "What did I tell you?" I said, "Leave me alone!"

I ignored the bedclothes or I just endured them.

I wanted to hear his voice again. I telephoned him, but said nothing, and the spirits of the dead must have hit the roof.

A moth toiled in the pointy peaks of flowers in the tureen before I killed the moth.

I felt strengthless the next day, although I kept speaking to you!—much of it to my mind too thoroughly personal.

Perhaps it is only in a story that a woman or a man can be amusingly betrayed.

Paving a way to the entrance of this house of brick and of stone, there are woodland trails. The exterior decoration of the house (I did not build it) is in a grayish, brownish stone and there are many ways to overstep the influence of this torsade band, awkwardly.

At breakfast, "Eat," I told myself. "Talk." I served myself salt mackerel and a little stalk with the leaf still attached to it, which I had paid for with hard cash.

The end of the line is massive. There is laurel all over the garden, as well as my dog Cyril, and the fowl who walk without the benefit of their arms and hands to swing. And, there is a live oak—squarish, nude, and badly executed—carved from one solid piece of pearwood.

I WAS VERY HUNGRY!

How often do trees move with such quick light steps? In
fact, the place is pierced through with pear trees that
approach the house. The efforts of Elizabeth Hodson have produced a young orchard.

I don't think you'll like it, but I like gaudy things.

The fruits of the climate and of the surface surround us
and it is all very gaudy.

I have to get back inside of this house by 7:30 at the latest
for human relations. I do not have time enough for my endeav-
ors with the Hodson woman. She has a sad face now—at the
mise-en-scène—that signals much pleasure, good fortune, and
longevity for me.

And, this is the type of flesh I just ate—I ate a steak and I drank a big glass of wine. Elizabeth ate a double-bone. Then again, she takes so many pills for her kidney.

She wore her black sweater with the black buttons that buttons tightly and she wore a red flannel jacket with the rare green velvet collar.

Hot water was prepared for tea and Dark Pfeffernusse were served.

Looking up the cantilevered staircase, with its dopey newel animals, I think, Aren't some animals so cute!

Upstairs, I straddle Hodson and keep her lying down and warm. Then I get her into a warm bath and encourage her to try to void. I get her out of the tub and put a hot water bottle on the pain area.

In this position I reach over her and bring my top arm over her shoulder and then place my hand over her breast head. My other hand grasps for her hip. I hunch and I hunch and I hunch. It is hard to lie here and struggle with something I had thought was finished.

There's such a thing as recalling some of our confidential fretting or exultation. I've required myself to preserve some of that in a greater number.

A DRAMATIC CLASSIC LEAP

Most of my romances are like this, so that I must conclude my behavior produces the poor result.

I present my problem to nearly everyone I know well and there is no solution to my problem. They ask me, "How did that happen?" or they say, "This is not right." They want to talk to me about sex, what I should know about fortune-telling, how to think logically, how to improve my conversation.

I took to fluffing my speech with the details of the day, with some unrelated subjects about my health, my salary, with absolutely worthwhile questions on poetry and art.

I learnt that being partially helpful and light feels as if I am a dear, and, that whatever else I do I expel this.

A THOUSAND GROANS

To get back to my success, I am easily upset. They think I am afraid of this kind of thing.

This shows especially in a few details. Later I give assurances or I am not brooding.

I see a roundabout young man with relatively wide, entire segments and I embrace him. He is brisk and undecided. He embraces me. But I have the discovery of my success in the morning. To get back to my success, I am frantic and romantic.

To get back to my success I warn the man when he unties— I warn the man when he makes the soup because he has not slept well. He does the work of four men. He permits happiness to raise him up and to revive him and he thinks he is the greatest enjoyer of all time. His desire to eat peelings and his desire to boil peelings and new vegetables—it is an act!—it is an action!—it is a seizure!

I HOPE YOU WILL BE MORE TIP-TOP

Soon after we can have this feeling. Thanks so much for joining us. The room is a short, humid room. We have not told anybody not to go in. As far as exactly what happened when this broke out, I can tell you everything. This evening the room smells like high heaven, but this is not as coast-to-coast as it might be. At this point what I'd like to do is tell you who's here. Two men are in the room. Unfortunately, as I've said over the years, we can spend a lot of time playing cards and yet everybody enjoys that. We want people to come forth and to show their colors particularly. Don't be worried about me. I am worried about you. You're the one who's really in trouble. You need help. I can help you on all problems of life. Why don't you get my help? One visit solves your big problem. Don't be worried about me. I am worried about you. You're the one who's hospitable.

WELL, WELL, WELL, WELL, WELL

She took the bellows from me and she told me if they didn't work, she had bought them to have a practical function, but they didn't have one.

She said she wants to be around someone who isn't unhappy and gnashing his teeth.

"I am too late," I said. And she said she liked the way I remembered details of her life—the other end of the expanse she'd lost track of.

I trusted her rectally, but she did not trust me.

This was clearly December. I had some sense of being excluded, given that everything around me was not mine. She inquired if I liked cheese.

Sometime in January the meeting between us went well. She said she never discussed true or untrue sex with men, yet she consented. She said the charms of sensation depended upon so many things going well and the stakes were too high, that she is sexually unfit. I talk the way I walk, eager as I am to make sexual advances with my friends. I do not mean to suggest social life. (Another ineffective stimulant.)

She said, "You can call my friend S., but she doesn't speak English or you can call my friend A., but she isn't nice."

Let me tell you about our organization. We have our mishaps. It's a large team, but a necessary team—families and individuals.

I came out into the street and searched for my connection to the easy future. I mean to suggest that anything else will ever happen, will introduce fresh air, will rise to the surface. She followed me in near racing condition. She caught up to me. An effervescent cab came by.

Another sort of exquisite situation was drawing a crowd out and among the theories in town while we were busy.

EVERYBODY'S SYRUP

"She's even prettier than you are," the host says.

"You really like this one?" Mr. German says.

"Have an Anjou pear," says the host. "Yes, I do."

"You didn't like Marie?" Mr. German says.

"Nope."

"Remember," Mr. German says, "you said she will slip onto your plate like syrup?"

"Like syrup. Now the question before the house . . ." the host always says.

"What are you doing?" says Mr. German.

"I'm trying to get the food out of my teeth with my tongue and I can't."

From the storyteller, an endnote: That's a Butter Nuttie in the host's mouth and his Irish water spaniel is licking grains from a pan, and, finally, squared cooled buildings, in the square, fresh and moist, intrigue townsfolk. Serves 1.

THE EASIEST WAY OF HAVING

They are not like you.

This is what occurs. Fancy work.

Under no circumstances is sexual contact permissible.

They use smooth knitted bath towels at home, smooth knitted hand towels, washcloths. They move their bowels twice daily if they can. The husband eats very slowly. Although, I thought last night he did very well with the sandwich!

These two work alongside one another the way the pharmacist and his wife do—day in and day out—and the way Stella and Harvey did, day in and day out. It is judicious to defer intercourse with persistence.

From a card table on the sidewalk they sell necklaces, earrings, brooches for the throat, or for near the face, for on the chest—bracelets and sometimes a bibelot. Everybody's got about eight. They are all wrapped up in tissue paper, although everybody didn't figure on being so tired out, so hungry, and so sad, and so lonely.

You see the wife has permitted a sensible and complete entrance of air into the vagina.

She has a large bosom and otherwise is a small, narrow person.

This is what shall occur—a complete new set of prohibitions—because there is pretty much wrong with practically everything that they have ever put onto their table for their enemies, come to think of it.

THE LIFE OF ANY COOK

The cook verges on spooning food into a bowl as the evening flows into a glass. The cook holds out the glass.

This really thrills her. She cries, "It's the prettiest; it's the best-looking one, Mom!"

There's something else to tell and I will coordinate it.

Now in the bowl, the contents where she put them are copulative—I mean it's the finish for a raw meal—salt and vanilla, the egg yolks, and hot milk.

She baked, dressed, ate one tiny Snickers and an Almond Kiss that she had had to fish out of the trash. Made supper and now it's ten o'clock. Think she slept for an hour and a half.

A cup, a dog, a knife, a cook, a cat, a very earnest cook can get into trouble for slipping. Then there is just one more, just a moment, a sigh of relief as the light of dawn almost pours itself back into a six-cup, paper-lined ring mold.

RICE

"That doesn't matter to me if you do not trust me," she said. "That doesn't matter. Is that okay with you?"

"Of course you know now that I will never trust anything you say ever again about anything," he said.

Her voice got baby-small, so faint that it was no longer the most beautiful sample in existence. He could not have heard her. She had to have a baby, she said. Had to.

He put his open hand on her breast. His parents had been childhood sweethearts.

The woman had the chops arranged neatly in the pan and there's a small television on the counter. She had been cooking long slender grains of roughleg when he arrived, so he hadn't smelt the perfume of the paper whites in the clay pot on the sill of the window which was a lookout onto the little bog and accumulated plant sphagnum.

She had put on her red skirt for his arrival and possibly a brassiere and there's definitely the motley ring of troubles and the deafening ring of troubles in the air because someone once said, "I have so appreciated serving you. I look forward to many years of giving you the highest standard of excellent service."

STRONGER THAN A MAN,
SIMPLER THAN A WOMAN

"Take it easy, Diane," Jacques said. "What do you want to fight with me for?"

I was embarrassed. It was like appearing in broad daylight. Even in those days I worried myself for nothing. Marie-Rose ate a few pieces of the corned beef with her fingers, not showing warmth or enthusiasm. She took a dish and emptied the contents into the sink. "Do you have any sour pickles?" she said.

"No," I said.

Jacques was vexed. I will describe Marie-Rose to you. She is tough. Tough getting tougher. Very tough. Hard. I'd say hard.

I had never met Marie before this. Fran had interviewed her.

Marie-Rose put her hand on her chin, then on her neck. Jacques was embarrassed by our women's breasts, I think. Jacques stood to one side. His nipples were ignorantly abused.

He threw me off balance. I had to catch my fall. I braced myself against the plate of beef, which tipped. Then I saw a rib of bread, picked it up and it was in my left hand, the knife in my right. I licked my lips, scared of what might happen next.

To give a time limit, six weeks have passed since. It's not unusual to see older people get aggravated. But this happens among every age group.

Am taking this in steps—as I was telling you—Jacques (thirty-two) and Marie-Rose (thirty-six) came over in the morning and brought corned beef. I got Marie-Rose a fork and the knife. I motioned for them to sit down. Then Jacques had Marie by the wrists. Hurry up! As you mature you ought to have control of your emotions (all yummy and delicious—satisfactions). A thrill. I go through the material balance in my rational capacity.

Oh, is it Wednesday?

Marie squeezed my arm. Her eyes blinked as if I didn't have a chance. The side of my right leg felt a kick. Her hair is long. She has a small thin bumpy face and thin lips. Hitting, kicking, hitting and pushing. She scratched me.

I noticed blood on me. My groin hurt.

Those are the quarrels with Jacques and Marie. I told you about them because you interest yourself in what happens when men form part of the goods exchanged between strangers. I mean the weird, old-timey men, under all sorts of disguises, who've not been heinously altered.

THESE BLENCHES GAVE MY HEART

L ife is fair I must confess. I am indebted to Erika Amor for
the years 1946 and 1947 which were marked by the full
flowering of the fairness. It can be expressed thus—that she
did not imagine me a shy person, determined not to disobey. I
had an idea she liked me and I chose her.

Her father said, "Stay with my daughter."

I agreed to, not impolitely. Lots of times it was a pleasure
to be with her and I was frightened. (Some days they tell you
what you said and that makes the blood flow out of your face
so that all of the color goes out of your face.)

She accepted a glass of liquid and I took her to the window
where she talked.

"Bring me the towel," I said. "You can lie down here instead
of there."

Arms folded up over her torso—being thoroughly stretched through the torso—her hips are stuck. Her hips roll finally. From the excitement I rub her under-lip. I spank the girl flat. She is near now.

The green chair under the phone?—that was hers and the dark wood chair under the window?—that was hers— untouched by the sex, the ax.

Across the way is a cozy Hungarian restaurant with its Kugelhopfs and sausages and The Roving Finger Barber Shop which has been there since 1930. Much of the shop is going to be demolished to make way for Malaysian Crafts.

I feel that my only big problem over the past year has been to trim myself with enough devils, beautiful women, owls, and hooded figures that will be of more interest than anything else I can make clear. Blank.

THE LESSER PASSAGE ROOM

The voices, as if we rubbed them with our palms, reassured me. I don't formally know the place of origin for our voices.

A container for holding liquids stood on a marquetry table by the bed. The room had darkened some. The curtains were closed. My Pearl Spar collaborated and lustered.

I got up and turned off the faucet and released the water from the basin into the drain. It's all set.

The room we are in runs ultramarine underneath the main block. In the main block a girl crosses the brook. Two seated humans embrace. A child offers fruit to a woman. Many vessels sail. The laurel is obtained. I've heard all about it here.

Here as elsewhere one is refreshed.

THE FACTS ABOUT
TELLING CHARACTER

Against the wall opposite, she sat with her bread and her soup, which were both of them grained, strong flavored, and the best or better than there is. The effect was cosmopolitan.

Oh, he loves her so much. He loves her so much. He loves her. He loves her so much. He unlocks the door and pads into the back garden in his silk body.

By the time he is neither too ashamed nor too peculiar to answer her question, she has finished her daily intercourse and she is—this much must be conceded—that she is forward moving with—I don't think I have ever seen such vigorous smirks.

Here we come to the horrible part. It is pretty horrible for Steve throughout last night and into tomorrow. It doesn't look as if he paid much attention to this book, to its advice, and to its instructions. You have got to have boots on the ground for this. I know he sleeps a lot and he eats a lot. That's probably very healthy.

I think he will pad back and have grapefruit. He is hungry. Have grapefruit. It's the size of a clock radio. Do you mean it's the size of a shoebox? You can't be certain without precision measurement.

One needs a more professional atmosphere. The information minister and the people are very much against that, so that didn't happen. Everything went smoothly as silky.

FLOWER

"He is the only one you will sleep with and you two will consult with each other about everything!" her father said. "Go live with him. He will welcome you. I am certain. Do you want to be rich?" her father said.

"Yes," she said, "I am sure."

"Susan," said the father.

"Yes?"

He said, "To get that nipple to stand up, squeeze it."

DOODIA

By day I see the fine future—the ordinariness of festivals, the house, gulping wine.

By day I dream of a real and good dog.

This is not the unknown and neither is a pregnancy, a miscarriage, durableness.

It has been raining and the houses are up on stilts.

There are a lot of stray dogs and there is a sweet one we call Bride and we fed him and he went to the bathroom and I rushed to get some paper. "He's all dirty. Clean him!" I said.

My mother laughed and she said, "They clean themselves on the grass!" I wanted her to clean him up the way she cleans me. It would have been hopeful enough for me.

I do not know what to do. I do not know who to trust.

HANDY-DANDY

"I feel fine today, actually."

"When you grow up are you going to marry some nice girl and have children? Of course you are, and are you going to make your children eat food that's good for them? Of course you are! I know that you are! Just put on the coat and go outside."

"Even if the coat will get dirty?"

"Yeh-es."

Mom and Buzz—both of whom have gossiped this week—had been sitting down to their lunch. After what seemed a long wait, Buzz, holding his side, complained of an ache.

Mom examined with her fingers, smoothing the phenomenon away. The boy set off for some good fortune along the parched pathway which led away from the pathway.

Surrounded by shrubs which had stuck their thorns into him, he had climbed into them. Couldn't I get out? he thought.

He thought, breathless with the reversal of fortune, How can I be so clever? What was it my mother said? He contemplated brambles with monoecious flowers and globose fruit of woody carpels.

To him, this midday felt like his first midday, of his not being soothingly cut.

AGGRESSIVE GLASS AND MIRRORS

"I didn't know he was famous," my husband said.

I said, "He said all he knew is that he wanted to be famous." I had praised Yves.

Later that night I glared at my husband. The time limit was a few seconds. I think when you're younger the first idea you have is that adults want to talk.

My brother Joe—I was at ease with him—arrived shortly. My chin hit something.

"Do you have something in your eye?" my brother said.

"Yes."

"Go rinse your eye."

"What's the matter?" my husband said.

"She has something in her eye. Go rinse your eye."

"I should clean it."

"Yes, you should do so."

And agitate slightly. Rinse with water and wipe dry. If laden with dirt, apply cleaner with brush. Don't vomit. Flood with water. Continued use is approved.

Accomplished a feat. The sky turns a different shade. It looks like it usually looks for weeks now. The glass roof of the sky is tilted up. Peeping underneath, I see the world the same as this one.

TIME-CONSUMING
STRIKING COMBINATIONS

———◆———

The future has not yet produced anything to be happy about.

Yes, yes, they saw the bunching up that forms chewed-up gum, an assortment of pretzels, mustachios, and puzzling sex.

They are prepared for frosted coffee rings and something terribly wrong and they have just bumped into each other which signifies their marriage.

There is lip smacking even if their infant comes up and goes down covered with hair, face, shoulders, and arms.

The man wears his fawn needlecord coat under the evening dress tailcoat and the pecan brown corded cotton jacket with button-attached sleeve extensions under the white coat and the melton woolen black overcoat when their promenade begins to flood.

Suitcases have been packed and crucial packages and cartons are labeled sacred.

They can fly and love to shock. Rain clouds are secret, hidden, hidden, secret, secret, secret, hidden, double and pleasant-faced.

The rainy afternoon is not hot, not peaceful, and is perfumed.

Pastry is fancy rolls, sponge-type cakes, egg yolk cakes with creamy chocolate frosting served with unusual, very strong, formerly filled sandwiches that open with a bang and leap toward a breathtaking eater.

The nourishment, flapping, crammed its heavy-scented stuff.

BOTH MY WIFE AND I
WERE VERY WELL SATISFIED

—————

It felt unfortunately like a bite of a good meal. He likes his wife so well. The smell of beets was not easy to shake. He put his glass on the table. He said, "Most people who come in here, they're weak. They want you to drink um three or four of those a day. I had to drink ninety ounces. First, it's a ball. I will tell you how it goes. They're really good with these kids. They're real witty, every one of them. I know for a fact. Who, oh, there are so many more! There are women in the world!"

"My wife never threw away any piece of toast!"

"Mine did."

"My wife is a good scraper. She isn't a good scraper, she just scrapes a lot. I'm a good scraper."

"I know you are. That's not that bad. Oh, I could. I'm going to give credit where credit is due. I lay no claim. She said um she said if there's a conflict where we live at, she'll handle it. Giant. I mean giant."

"Yes, and fun. And dishes of nuts and dishes of chocolates and dishes of cigarettes and light real water."

SHE BEGAN

She is slow-footed and her underparts are clean. She crosses the garden and sees dust which has fallen neatly into the basin. She could want to make this crossing every day.

There is a mound in the garden three to five feet or more across. She crosses over that mound. She steps on a succulent with salverform flowers and oblong leaves. She steps on an inflorescence or on an efflorescence. She crushes a dense rosette. She spares some racemes and plantlets and not because of special circumstances.

An American couple does recognize her because she is famous for her great success on the earth and please don't add silence into this because it is making me weepy—so they extend a sincere invitation to her for her to stay with them in

Philadelphia and she thanks them again for the drinks and for the conversations and for their delightful, spreading, nodding, insignificant flesh, and for the palpability of the big strides they take with their mouths somewhat open.

BABY FLOURISHES

The baby spent time on a pitiful romance. She felt herself
to be in the arms—somehow gathered, forcibly invited,
incapable of enjoying herself, and very much in love.

OPENING THE CLOSING
MOUTH OF THE WOMAN

A penis leans on walls inside her. Faustine—that is her name—is dedicated to the rammers after she has been loaded with their meaning. A corner of her is being slightly shaped.

THE KING EMPEROR

They say they sat on the moldy border near a Kousa dog-wood, under a different low-growing tree, which is the oldest tree in the story. It has arching branches, red berries, and fine-textured, robust bark.

Both were commenting that there is always something each wishes for that comes true.

He took his neckerchief off and the gauntlets, and his soiled coat—touched it willingly on the sleeve—and fawned over the woman whose name is Beth Schwenk and I am not just blowing smoke up your ass. He said, "Oh, you have been everywhere!"

People—and I do too—present stories and stories about him just to destabilize.

He had the clamber to hump Schwenk and to enjoy what he frogged or was able to wring off as a prisoner of the love scene.

There is much impertinence in trying to make more of this public.

He's sure got a weak spot for her, but it's getting harder all of the time at the dirty end of his stick when his chances come to pass in reality.

Just to have a name like his name must be such a pleasure. He's had two chances. Now they hear him promising.

It sounds as if he's right around the corner now in all of June, even if he had to stand in the no-hope-for-you corridor.

He knows the collections of laws.

He has relief in The House decorated by Blue China Furs and semi-evergreen shrubs with poorly-stemmed flowers planted in well-drained soil. The House is equipped with tiles and portraits of people who see right through me. It's heart-breaking pretending to be sympathetic to him. He taught his horse to jump. Yes, he's voluptuous and kind and the eldest son of the first gentleman. Some of the most momentous daughters and sons come from that guy.

He is popular with the people, unplain in face, and one of the great men with his plump heart so animadverted upon.

He wasn't as great as this before this rain. He will be hardly much different after the rain.

He took the candle and the blankets and is noisy and

difficult because he's the fellow who lives with Beth Schwenk and what shoots forth from him he pledges is the light in his eyes. Schwenk waits for me.

I see what this is. I've screwed my head off in the middle of my neck for the royalty.

PLEASE LET ME OUT AGAIN OF
THE SMALL PLUGGED HOLE

Her face was as useless to her as hot stew. Her breasts were tight, unripe. She wore a that's very funny expression.

Another thing, her old clothes were tight.

In a frame on a wall was a picture of an old baby. Furthermore, a tailor measured her for tunics, for a decent striped skirt, for a sash, for underwear to cover her buttocks.

She didn't dare to say what she was getting at.

Her socks were twisted. She climbed back up towards the benefits of better function and pleasure, although she was developing a head cold.

And, the woman had trouble with her socks, but no trouble with sex she could sneeze at.

Step this way. Another thing, they were awfully tight, her tight clothes.

But, uh, her hips spread as she jumped through where all the candles were lit, where people entered, and where there was a rose tree, at any rate.

THE PHILADELPHIA STORY

1

For several years now I have been a girl who is not married and I like to get married while I am still charming.

We open the house and gardens regularly for my weddings, although at some point I have to get reassurance in serge clothes and with my fingernail varnish on.

For as long as I can remember I think pleasantly about the town's library. So now, how about a trip to the library?

2

Jimmy Stewart wrote a book I'm reading here that puts me in mind of a November in which the whole world has a familiar large lamp—gold—that flaunts its gleam on the nineteen hundreds. His hero looks in my direction so that I'd like to go over to him and beg him to help me. I'd give him more beers so he'd talk to me about me. He really wants to be looked at and to be questioned. He says, "I am perplexing."

On a more cheerful note, while lying in bed with Jimmy Stewart, I got very excited. He's a good friend of mine, although the next thing to be concerned about is that this is being written.

3

I should give myself the name Lord. I am haughty enough.

My father was Uncle Willie. The treasures at home with everything else elegant on display include a rare William and Mary silver-gilt traveling spoon with a detachable handle, just for me and mine; an elaborate eight-piece sterling silver tea and coffee service; my gingham ruffled skirt; the silver cigarette box. Bins are filled with eyeglass cases, shoelaces, and Tru-Touch vinyl gloves for the manor. The pleasures are the family atmosphere.

C. K. Dexter Haven, the man I love, he's been able to get his popularity numbers up there. I need to move on this very quickly, although I petted other men, not meant for me, nearly all day, and nearly all night long. Ruth Hussey puts up with so much from me. Ruth Hussey should not put up with so much. Nobody could know how much Ruth Hussey put up with.

In the morning, for a few minutes, I sit between the wall and my bed, on the floor, ungowned.

Let's have one last drink!

4

Mother Lord, I see, drinks two capfuls. I drink one capful.

I look—look, I look like a white woman and there are people among us having terrible emotions.

I describe myself on foot en route to the north parlor. I admire the plate on the wall and the dish hung above it, and the long guns.

I say, "Sex-see-ool!"

And there's the bowl of avocadoes.

"Answer me!" says George Kittredge. "Where have you been?"

This was to be our real-enough wedding day, but not now.

C. K. Dexter Haven says, "You worry yourself for nothing."

Jimmy Stewart says, "She has not lain with me."

"Come, Daughter," says Pap-pah. "Hold me. Encourage me. Be strong."

EAT THE DEEP TOO!

Some of us are very good and some aren't. You know, some did their homework and got good grades. Likely they'd get a blank stare from you.

"I have to put in the medicine," the girl said. "I have to brush my teeth."

"I told them you do everything better than I do," the other girl said.

"Who did you tell?"

"Bett!"

"Bett! Bett!"

Bett started to cross her mind. Bett hung there waiting to be helpful and then Bett groaned.

In any event, people show you there is a way to have pleasure.

CUTTING AND DRESSING

The doctor said to me, "Then you have a wonderful night."
The term *wonderful night* is used to refer to the inner
sanctum that has sex feeling in it.

There is a widespread misconception about the look, feel,
and texture of a doctor's waiting room. The doctor asked me
did I want to give him my co-pay now.

For the handover, I wore toreador pants and bone leather
shoes with little heels—backless and strapless. I did not bend
my knees, but instead stiff-walked to my sitdown in a chair.
My feet I kept up parallel to the floor and I crossed my legs at
the ankles.

Back at home for a cold lunch in my house with a red-tile
roof, I sat in my own chair for sitting stiffly.

People are lovely things. People must have seen that my

hair was in flat-knuckled curls and really inconsiderately fixed. My walls are papered with a moiré pattern. My floor is covered by split brick pavers. I've got a tea cart set out with plastic cups, lime green drink, and a plate of dry baked products.

My tot Silvanus—with bad habits and suddenly—we had set the boy free!—pulled himself up onto our lyre back side chair. Completely frenzied, the chair fell—and, because this child has never been significantly maltreated, he was stunned by the fall and he's dead.

DANGERESQUE

M rs. White at the Red Shop showed me the beady-eyed garment, but I can't pay for it. I'm broke! I already own a gold ring and a gold-filled wristwatch and I am very uncomfortable with these. My eyes sweep the garment and its charms.

I am tempted to say this is how love works, burying everyone in the same style.

Through a fault of my own I set off as if I'm on a horse and just point and go to the next village.

This village is where flowers are painted on the sides of my house—big red dots, big yellow balls.

At home, stuck over a clock's pretty face, is a note from my husband to whom I do not show affection. With a swallow of tap water, I take a geltab.

By this time I had not yet apologized for my actions. Last

night my husband told me to get up out of the bed and to go into another room.

My husband's a kind man, a clever man, a patient man, an honest man, a hard-working man.

Many people have the notion we live in an age where more people who behave just like he does lurk.

See, I may have a childlike attitude, but a woman I once read about attempted a brand new direction with a straight face.

JEWISH FOLKTALE

Around here, I see plenty of Haddock, an overall figure with his meaning growing, with a friendly frown, flanked on each side by a dog. I wonder how his bowel movements are.

I saw Mr. Haddock at the bay, perhaps picking up his spirits. It's peaceful at the bay and Haddock says he does not have an ailment. He has no eye problems and perfect ears.

You know—fluid-filled space!—a bay, the bay!

Fancy cushion clouds at the bay are the same shapes and sizes as I saw when I had an exact understanding of conditions greater than my emotions.

Mr. Haddock's laugh—yeah, it is similar, but that's not what it sounds like. I remembered what it sounds like—then when you did that—I forgot.

There are a lot of young, forgetful people taking one up these days. At least I can make my claims.

Fifteen years ago there was a cloud I saw which moved around, traveled, came by, fled into the woods, exerted a strong influence, spent more than half an hour there, was free to roam, before returning to the village, where the cloud added up to a source of pride.

TO SQUEEZE WATER

"You need to," the woman said. "People should be made to say. People should be forced to say I am not a bad person," the woman said. "Can you talk about that?"

"That's very private," the man said.

JESSAMINE, EWING,
ERASTUS, AND KEANE

I mention to Happy the honor of knowing Earl. I have loved Earl for months and for months and now get relief from not loving Earl.

I try to be most agreeable about this—I tell Marquis Abraham. It could have been the Marquis, but the Marquis's hair would not bunch up like that.

"Happy! Happy!" I say.

"Eat this," Happy says, "it will help you."

A loaf with a sauce.

They fired Happy, then Megdalia was fired and Sandra, not Marvin. Percy can't help me anymore.

Percy once helped me. He made a hole and took my blood. He said, "I just want to cut through the fat!" He said, "Everybody who comes in here has the same color blood!"

"Take the food with you, your underpants, and the directions," one woman who created and arranged me said.

And sad to say, I don't find that very interesting.

HER LEG

"I would do anything for my son," she said. "But how little we know of what he really wants."

Meanwhile, her arm would release me. She told me what she serves for meals.

"It's all going to all work out," my husband said. "She will love you as much as she loves me."

His mother had a way of being strong, but not nasty. It was so sensuous. She and I both are short, short-haired women without eyeglasses. My husband has big eyes and he is large and muscular. I am very shy. His mother put her arm plus her leg around me— just live with it for a while. I, myself, how gladly I do.

Before long, legend has it that when a partnership works, it is no accident. More accurately, more importantly, this illustrates this: I learn more about the arts and skills.

INSPIRING ONE

I am living in a lively way with slight sobs now and then. My face squeaked under the pressure. I came to as many conclusions as possible, which puffed out loudly along with sobs. In this I was much helped by Fred. I took a look at what looked eerie—Fred. I am excited. He appears to have just had very good news. He can be receiving it every day.

If I don't refer to anything sexual, I'll be a much more likeable person, for lack of a better idea.

I am a weak woman of thirty-two in a metropolitan area. Life might be gaily spoken of.

What Fred said: "I only hope and pray. I should so much like to help you. I hope you are keeping well. I hope you will have peace of mind. Do not bother to answer me. Of course, don't reply. Please accept my sympathy. Sorry for this intrusion. I would love to see you again some day. Please never think of answering. I am horrified."

Some months later I was about to go on a dangerous expedition to see Tiny. I can tell you about Tiny. She gave me her stationery. She's the messiest writer of bills. She used to have crinkling paper, but this time it had Tiny Boynton written on it in big letters. And she's been together with Marcel all these years and it's a very poor relationship, but then he had an affair, of course. They must have seen one another enough to have twins. I don't know how she does it. I used to chat with her. She spends all day long and she takes all the dogs on this big loop. I was wondering, not knowing what her schedule was. She walks around in jodhpurs and a riding crop and totes the dogs along, and so I was desperate and I was running after her and I introduced myself and I am at the end of the world!

THE WIDOW AND THE HAMBURGER

I can't be expected to remember his privates—a pink head or yellow head. She wipes cream off of his face and I thought, I like his haircut now. She needs to take out whiskers. I don't see why any opportunity can't be taken to do something beautifully. I look for people to admire and she is one person.

I have on Billy's robe. The robe is filthy.

I saw his penis.

She wiped shaving cream off of his face. Those two never helped the poor because they were too poor.

Sometimes he sat near her, but tried to get away if she tried to greatly entertain him.

People say the dog lay on its back, some blood near its tail.

Their house has plain bricks painted red and a shaded

porch. They set their table with a cloth and the dishes and the cups—they kept them dashing off through the empty space.

If she had worried about money all the time, she'll have much more money.

For instance, your wishes are fulfilled and the dream comes true.

It is a great pleasure to be in a fascinating group.

SATISFYING, EXCITING, SUPERB

It may even be her real name. Lucky I called out to Swan-hilda. I was in the bedroom concocting rocket fuel. I had a fold-down bed and it was in the fold-up position. It had like a long shelf and the bed was tucked in underneath and the shelf was fairly high and when it ignited it was just one bright white yellow flare—the rocket fuel! I used the shelf of the bed for the laboratory. I went into the hallway where there was a full-length mirror. I looked at myself, at the little scraps of thrushbeard peeling off of my hands and my face.

We should all attempt to send rockets into space. Maybe it would be a good idea to ask someone how to do it.

There was a wooden shelf. There was a wooden shelf and there was a curtain over the bed, so that the curtain caught fire and the wood caught fire but I was able to put it out. I didn't feel this was serious.

I was the one who got blown up.

I tried it a number of times and sent off a number of rockets. I tried to improve on the fuel mixture.

I may have put too much magnesium in my mix.

Well, the whole thing was like my mother used to say.

So we attached fins at the bottom and made it heavier so it didn't tumble.

I say it too!—our mother used to tell us—"A burnt child smells bad."

But after that incident I gave up my career as a rocket builder. How far did it go in the air? I try to figure that out.

Magnesium—it is not controlled, nor is sulphur and today you can buy it. Okay, and then I'm going to blow myself up.

AFFECTION

She did so very slowly and needless to say she had to go get something in the dark room. She stepped into cold liquid. There was the crap in the dark and she hadn't reached any stream! She cried!

Like her father she had an ordinary way with walking, paying no attention to daylight or to artificial light. Sometimes she would pass on her philosophies to her son. Her husband also encouraged her. His job was mainly looking for nests and getting into mischief and he made quite a name for himself. Their house sits beside a dried-up tree. All the gaiety and the color she finds in sex.

OTHER RASH

Peter pets her. He says, "I said I've been experiencing a little rash on my wrists and just under my eyebrows from exposure to epoxy resins which I have been working in to complete the sanitary project. I have to get some medicine to treat it."

She says, "Good luck."

You hear the snap—it really pulls the two halves together!

There were dark red dots—they were small—and Peter said they were a nuisance all over the place on the second floor verandah. The tree had three or four branches. They were growing and he was thinking he should get rid of them. So, he showed her this—this which—he picked up one of them—well what do they look like? They look like little, little, li—very small olives, so he dug his nail into it and he peeled off a little of the meat, little more than a skin, that's it, and the pit is big, is big, and the color is—he is tasting the meat and it was dry and sweet and a little bit leathery—an intense flavor of cherry—so Peter said they shouldn't cut the tree.

It's a very nice tree. He said they were very lucky to have this very nice tree. He had no intention of using the fruit. This is a black cherry tree, so now, so what else do you want to know about Peter's cherry tree? It grew out of a cluster.

I bet you that tree was about sixty or eighty years old. The problem is it shades his whole backyard, but then after he tasted the cherries and they were good, maybe he reconsidered. His house doesn't have a cellar and the first floor is really—the tree branches are all around you, really quite beautiful, if you need this vapor.

VICKY SWANKY
IS A BEAUTY
(2012)

Perfectly safe; go ahead.

—DIANE WILLIAMS

MY DEFECTS

I'm happy at least to do without a sexual relation and I have this fabulous reputation and how did I get that in the first place? I am proud enough of this reputation and it stands to reason there's a lot that's secret that I don't tell anyone.

I want to end this at the flabber, although I am flabbergasted.

I opened the cupboard, where the treats are stored, and helped myself and made a big mess, by the lakeshore, of the food, of the rest of my life, eventually.

Michelle, the doctor's nurse, showed me a photograph of her cats. The smart cat opens the cupboard, Michelle says, where the treats are stored, and she can help herself, and she makes a big mess!

I crossed the street to survey the lake and I heard

crepitations—three little girls bouncing their ball. I used to see them in perspective—my children—young people, one clearly unsuitable. She can't help herself—she makes a big mess.

With my insight and my skill—what do I search for at the shore?—the repose of the lake. But sadly, although it does have a dreamy look, it is so prone to covering familiar ground.

IF TOLD CORRECTLY
IT WILL CENTER ON ME

Jack Lam sat me on the bed. He didn't sit me—first he had to park the car.

Then Jack Lam sat briefly himself, put his chin down, frowned. I acted as if I was biting the top of his head—setting my teeth on, not into him—not to mention the fact that I was also swallowing darker areas.

Over the next seven years that I kept this project close in mind, I came to understand that my devices belonged to a lost age.

I took measures.

Jack had lost his vigor. I was unwell.

My luggage was packed. I'd be solitary when I arrived in Tarrytown. Stella Arpiarian still had The Curio Shop. Nikos had gone back to Greece.

I like Jimmy here. I have to face Marlene.

I heard the dog next door making a good imitation of what my asthma attacks sound like. Everyone is sounding like me!

Don't forget me!

PEDESTAL

H e had chafing and I'm not having luck with anything I'm using. We had agreed to meet where they know me. The server put drinks down.

"Hey!" he said. "I happen to have a chicken. Why don't you come over?"

I would say that to a friend, and it would be true!

My anus is now irritated. My vagina's very delicate. My stomach hurts.

His sconces were shaded in a red tartan plaid and there were side-views of sailing boats in frames.

I was getting to see the hair cracks in his skin that suggest stone or concrete as it hardens.

Back out on Ninety-first Street, a man and a woman were walking their dog. The woman had turnip-colored hair. The man wore a felt hat and he motioned to me. They could have both been exhausted and penniless. No! As it turned out they were assembled there to talk me out of that. Let me think about this further. At a stand, I bought a few strands of daisies. Every bone in one of these blossoms is mended.

DEATH BED

"Now, say good-bye to your mother," Ruth Price says, "before you die."

I've got that confident feeling.

Then we hear the toilet bowl water.

"Go away!" I said to Mother.

Everybody in the original cast appears at my door—my father who was the President of the United States; Mother, who was also a President of the United States. I was a President of the United States. My two children are here who have been Presidents of the United States. My neighbor Gary Dossey who was in my high-school graduating class was a President of the United States.

GLEE

We have a drink of coffee and a Danish and it has this, what we call—grandmother cough-up—a bright yellow filling. The project is to resurrect glee. This is the explicit reason I get on a bus and go to an area where I do this and have a black coffee.

I emphasize, I confess, as well, that last night I came into a room, smiled a while and my laughter was like a hand on my own shoulder. As I opened up the volume of the television set, I saw a television beauty and a man wants to marry her and she says, "I don't do that sort of thing."

While in their company, the woman changes her clothing and puts down an article of clothing and folds it. How finely she shows us her efforts. Even as we have that behind us, the man speaks. His side-locks are worn next to his chin and his hair is marred by bright lights. The woman's head is set against a dark-purple shield of drapery. But when something momentous occurs, I am glad to say there is a sense of crisis.

And for Vera and me—we are no exception. I've lived for years. In Chicago our sunsets are red creases and purple bulges and we can amuse ourselves with them.

MY FIRST REAL HOME

In there, there was this man who developed a habit of sharpening knives. You know he had a house and a yard, so he had a lawnmower and several axes and he had a hedge shears and, of course, he had kitchen knives and scissors, and he and his wife lived in comfort.

Within a relatively short time he had spent half of his fortune on sharpening equipment and they were gracing his basement on every available table and bench and he added special stands for the equipment.

He would end up with knives or shears that were so sharp they just had to come near something and it would cut itself.

It's the kind of sharpening that goes beyond comprehension. You just lean the knife against a piece of paper.

Tommy used to use him. Ernie'd do his chain saws.

So, I take my knives under my arm and I drive off to Ernie's and he and I became friends and we'd talk about everything.

"I don't sharpen things right away. You leave it—and see that white box over there?" he'd said. That was his office. It was a little white box attached to the house with a lid you could open and inside there were a couple of ballpoint pens. There was a glass jar with change. There were tags with rubber bands and there was an order form that you filled out in case he wasn't there.

He wasn't there the first time I came back, at least I didn't see him.

I went up to the box and those knives were transformed.

As I was closing the lid, he came up through the basement door that was right there and we started to chat and he has to show me something in the garden, so he takes me to where he has his plantings. It's as if the dirt was all sorted and arranged, and then, when I said he had cut his lawn so nice, he was shining like a plug bayonet.

All the little straws and grass were pointing in one direction.

"I don't mow like my neighbor," he said.

Oh, and then he also had a nice touch—for every packet he had completed there was a Band-Aid included. Just a man after my own heart. He died.

I was sad because whenever I got there I was very happy.

ON THE JOB

He looked like a man whose leader has failed him time after time, as he asked the seller awkward questions—not hostile. He was looking for a better belt buckle.

The seller said, You ought to buy yourself something beautiful! Why not this?

He paid for the buckle, which he felt was brighter and stronger than he was. His sense of sight and smell were diminishing.

He could only crudely draw something on his life and just fill it in—say a horse.

"Can I see that?" he said. "What is that?"

It was a baby porringer.

At the close of the day, the seller counted her money, went to the bank—the next step. She hates to push items she doesn't approve of, especially in this small town, five days a week, where everything she says contains the mystery of health and salvation that preserves her customers from hurt or peril.

That much was settled, as the customer entered his home, approached his wife, and considered his chances. Hadn't his wife been daily smacked across the mouth with lipstick and cut above the eyes with mascara?

She had an enormous bosom that anyone could feel leaping forward to afford pleasure. She was gabbing and her husband— the customer—was like a whole horse who'd fallen out of its stall—a horse that could not ever get out of its neck-high stall on its own, but then his front legs—their whole length—went over the top edge of the gate, and the customer made a suitable adjustment to get his equilibrium well outside of the stall.

"It's so cute," he said to his wife, "when you saw me, how excited you got."

His wife liked him so much and she had a sweet face and the customer thought he was being perfectly insincere.

He went on talking—it was a mixed type of thing—he was lonely and he was trying to get his sheer delight out of the way.

THE USE OF FETISHES

"I was a lucky person. I was a very successful person," said the woman. She was not entirely busy with her work. She took cups and tumblers from her cupboard to prepare a coffee or a tea. She thought, We have some smaller or even smaller.

Her Uncle Bill said, "Have you been able to have sexual intercourse?"

She said, "Yes! And I had a climax too!"

This idea is compact and stained and strained to the limit.

WOMAN IN ROSE DRESS

Her sex worries will be discussed when people worry what happened to her at the end of her life when her chin droops and when her eyes are hooded. Not yet.

Her fervor and her youth irritate her for they provide a sort of permanent entry into a shop. She lifts a bouquet of broccoli rabe. Oh, how awful it is!

"I don't know how to cook these. Do you cook the leaves?"

The man says, "You chop off the ends and chop them up—look!"

She's got some pent-up gem on her finger. (Those colored stones, they're all cooked, you know.)

Didn't she used to appreciate its rays of light? And she used to appreciate the man.

Ask yourself sincerely at odd moments, "Am I prone to

deep feeling?" for it is less than necessary—that very small, bright, enlarging thing. The passions do not knock one out, but they may permit you to have carnal complaints before proceeding further. Let's visit another woman—Deirdre—and then Donna. What's more—Doris grew up exhausted by shock and word of mouth. She hadn't been married long, it was a spring day, and she was uninterested still in her own love story.

WEIGHT, HAIR, LENGTH

They had admired a bronze sphinx with an upraised paw
and an elegant and extremely fine clock on skinny legs.
The husband tried to buy a jug, enameled and gilded.
A number of his parts are modern and wide. He looks well
made for sustained and undemanding and justified indulgence.

COCKEYED

She was cockeyed on her settee—her face considerably close to the cushioned seat. She righted herself, but she dropped the book.

She was sick and her mother had died of typhoid, her sister of parasitic worms.

This had been one of the few occasions when she had been charming and tactful.

There were bruises on the lady's face and indications of other injuries upon her delicate structure.

Her library table desk is made of sycamore, painted in the classic manner—the type of thing that seems peculiar.

HIGHLIGHTS OF THE TWILIGHT

The clerk reminded me of my dead husband who used to say he was always going around all the time with his penis sticking out and that he didn't know what to do.

"Lady!" the clerk said.

A little old lady jerked herself toward that clerk.

A motley group of us was looking at a wristwatch and inwardly I prayed I'd see a glow of dancing matter to lead me. I am another little old lady.

"Mrs. Cook," a clerk said, "are you here to have some fun?"

This is a shop with a bird on a branch in diamonds and pearls, a ruby-eyed dog, a ram's head, a griffin, a cupid in gold.

"It'll be entirely discounted if I understand you correctly—" my clerk said, "this is all that you want!"

"I can't afford it and I'll have that one!"

"You've broken it! You've ruined it!" the clerk said.

I said, "Don't look so awful," but he had already so imprudently advanced into my hell-hole.

THE NEWLY MADE SUPPER

The guest's only wish is to see anyone who looks like Betsy, to put his hands around this Betsy's waist, on her breasts. He's just lost a Betsy. He followed Betsy.

In front of Betsy, who supports on her knees her dinner dish, you can see the guest approach.

"You got your supper?" he says, "Betsy?"

And Betsy says, "Who's that in the purple shirt?"

"That's not purple. You say purple?" says the guest.

"What color would you say that is?" says Betsy.

"That's magenta."

"I have to look that up. Magenta!" says Betsy.

"That's magenta," says the guest.

"That's lavender," says another woman who's a better Betsy.

PONYTAIL

The woman secured her hairs together in a string. The child ate a donut. The woman suggested someone throw a ball. The woman fetched the ball, and then the woman fetched the child, and she bunched up a section of the child's T-shirt, as she bunched up a section of the child's neck, and she secured the child.

CHICKEN WINCHELL

The waitress who is badly nourished or just naturally unhealthy has a theory about why the daughter never returned.

The daughter did return, for only a little stay, to ask which chicken dish her father had ordered for her.

The mother experiences her losses with positivity. She even frames the notion of her own charm as she heads into her normal amount of it.

Yes, she confides in the waitress, both her daughter and her husband have disappeared, and yes, her daughter is a darling, but hasn't she made it clear to her there isn't a boy her age to admire her within a hundred miles?

The mother roams home, wearing the fine check jacket and her black calf heels, alone.

She sees the pair of doors of a little shop where they are selling magic and all kinds of things. Inside, the clerks with elf-locks are dressed for the cold. There is a bakery the mother thinks would be nice and warm. It is okay, and after that, she goes to the gift shop, and gets those sole inserts.

Normally, the family's frugal. They eat at home, buy groceries.

The mother's legs are trembling, yet she has a good conscience and a long life.

She used to weigh one hundred and thirty-five pounds. Now she weighs one hundred and fourteen pounds, but it's been very hectic.

As she sleeps, the telephone rings, wakes her, and she thirsts for a glass of water. She finds that one thing neatly, reasonably, takes her away from yet another.

THE EMPORIUM

I had stretched my body into a dart, inhaled deeply, and passed through the aisles at top speed and then a man with a red-nailed woman and a girl came up to me, and the man said, "You don't remember me! I'm Kevin! I was married to Cynthia. We're not together any more."

They had been the Crossticks!

What he wanted now, Kevin said, was peace, prosperity, and freedom.

And I more or less respected Cynthia Crosstick. I didn't like her at first. She is not very nice. She's odd, but that's the whole point.

I didn't like my fly brooch at first either. It's fake. You can't get it wet. It's very rare and the colors are not nice and I get lots of enjoyment from that.

I picked up Glad Steaming Bags and Rocket Cheese.

"It's very cold. Do you want some lemonade?—" said a child at a little stand, "we give twenty percent to charity."

"No!" I said loudly, as I exited the emporium, although there might have been something to enjoy in swallowing that color.

"Why is she crying?" the child had asked an adult.

Why was I crying?

I had tried to hear the answer, but could not have heard the answer, without squatting—without my getting around down in front of the pair, bending at the knee, so that the proverbial snake no longer crawls on its belly.

I should have first stooped over.

The lemonade girl hadn't mentioned the gumdrop cookies they had hoisted for sale.

Just the mention of cookies brings back memories of Spritz and Springerle and Cinnamon Stars—party favors—attractive, deliciously rich, beautiful colors, very well liked, extra special that I made a struggle to run from.

PROTECTION, PREVENTION,
GAZING, GRATIFIED, DESIRE

Vera Quilt knows the princes she says. There was some big
event—a horse with plumes, and soldiers with ruby buttons, shiny helmets, and swords—when she met them.

If there had been any doubt about my feelings for Vera,
now there was not. I looked at her warmly.

The air was cold and I mention this because this is a miniature world with levels of experience where people may starve
to death.

At some distance from us there was a mob of people—
they're wonderful people—and broad-leaved evergreens, and
a flock of birds behaving normally.

"Hoo!—hoo!" Vera began again.

"Now, what do you want, Vera?" I said. Vera and I—we
resolve everything in under an hour. She said, "I talked to my

husband. It is too hard for me. I come home and it's late and I am tired and he is tired."

And, truly, it's as if people put big branches out on the ground so that Vera can practice climbing on them. You should know that her mind bubbles up in her brain, showing movement, lift! It comes about this way—her confidence, all of it that goes to make a woman.

A large vein showing on her hand curves around her knuckle. She had a cuticle nippers in her hand. Her breath smelt of nothing. Her skull was quite large, but her coat and her skirt were short and there was, pinned to her lapel, a generously sized gemstone flower basket that most people are assuming is a gift from the crown.

"I'd rather not go any farther with you," she said. "I am very tired."

"Exactly," I said.

However, Vera and I had resolved everything in order to push on. She's the best living woman. It was six o'clock, end of the day, as we smoothed farther into the unknown, which is sometimes described as a plot of evil—cliffs and or swamps overshadowing one another, hideous plateaus, and phosphorescent glimmers. Vera protected, pocketed her nippers, and there are the conquests of happiness to be considered that must be produced in the future, and in a series.

At the level of the street, we looked through the plate glass of the department store, a department store erected on the foundation of a princely court.

Vera is young and she still has her woman's flow and we take a glance at something to watch out for in Macy's window that has bulk. This is no drop in the bucket. You must have heard of the expression—*the apple of my eye?*—And we know how to cry—*Help!*

VICKY SWANKY WAS A BEAUTY

You'd have thought her burden was worthy of her, although she shouldn't keep trying to prove she has common sense.

She's Vicky Swanky. She addressed an envelope and wrote her name and address on it also. She is my ideal, my old friend.

The letters of her script are medium sized with slim loops. Her ovals are clear. There were nicely turned heads.

She is still going through a divorce and her children were running around there.

"I forgot to take a shower," she said. "Do you want to take one with me?"

Since I didn't want to do it, I said no, because I'd get confused, and this is too important.

To repeat—I met up with Vicky Swanky whom I hadn't seen in years—who said, "Why don't you come over? I've had systemic lupus erythematosus and when you get through that—"

In connection with sex, we lightened up a little then and we dumped some of it off the edge at a minimum. We could be put through a few strokes like everyone else amid the overall circulation of water.

Human bodies are just not good enough!—and in this way we represented two weak powers.

She has adult-sized fist-sized hands with smooth joints. She has smaller than normal hands. Her hands are not smaller than my hands.

I brought Lee over in the late afternoon, the dog. He has the disposition to avoid conflict, is good-natured, and sets a fine example.

It was getting busy concerning the basic meaning, the degree, and the quality. And by late afternoon, the snow was staying on the surface. No one knows that any better.

Cruelly, I've seen nothing in the book I am reading—about me. I need to see specifically my life with pointers in the book.

May I suddenly drop in on Vicky Swanky and ask for favors?

Years ago Vicky Swanky was a beauty.

Now, here, there were vases of blanket flowers, pancakes. I am so confused here.

She served us pancakes and syrup and coffee and milk and butter. Her breasts were flat. Her hips were flat. She looked older than her forty years and she plays with all of us.

She has a strange way of showing it. There was a skirmish.

The plumber arrived and he said he'd have to remove everything from the nipple in the wall to the toilet. Vicky Swanky said, "Is it true? One would think perhaps you might. I thought so. You were right to tell me. I won't enjoy it very much. Naturally enough I can find that out for myself," she said.

CARNEGIE NAIL

Doubtless, early on, in the ultra-fine beginning of the day, others were spectators as I withdrew into Carnegie Nail and I showed the coarseness of my nature in a new sense, for I kept my hands forever forward until at Mrs. Oh's behest, Dee took them.

As a courtesy, to some extent, Mrs. Oh kept her cell phone conversation brief and her voice low.

Mr. Oh sat unspeaking in an aimless, I mean, armless chair. He was less husky than I would have expected—composed, nonetheless, of curving segments. Then, as if by the flip of a lever, he fell from his chair.

Others jumped around.

Strangest of all, whoever enters Carnegie Nail is exempted from the bitterness of experience.

Oh, Mr. Oh found his way back up to good effect while Mimi supported the shop's potted, toppled plant.

The damp day got me as I left, but I did not publicly condemn it.

At home Wanda appeared with our infant and the infant's father—my husband—was seated in a chair that's sufficient to defend itself.

My next step surely was clear, for life presents the flowers of life. We'd been viewing the infant as if it'd been wrenched off a tree branch or a weedy stem.

But the question is much more complex. A child needs to be cut down to its lowest point compatible with survival.

STAND

My friend said, "I fell in love with the neighbor."

I said, "Your husband fell in love with the neighbor?"

My friend said, "No!" She said, "*I* fell in love with the neighbor!"

She was counting her fingers. She said she couldn't get the neighbor's penis to do anything.

As a matter of fact, I couldn't get his penis to do anything either. It hung like a mop or it had a life of its own. How it came up in the first place, I don't know. He couldn't get my vagina—I wanted to say—to utter a word.

But since one should always make room for fun, we all ate food and we laughed.

The last time I saw my friend was when she was finishing her drink, gulping. Was it like the sound of the sea perhaps?—how the sea very slowly and with great effort laps but does not go down—I want to say—in one gulp.

The last time I saw my friend's crêpe de chine skin, her frizzy hair—her dark breasts that wriggle raw, I said to myself, "You had enough?"

COMMON BODY

So, I've got good news, but I also felt so bad I was crying. She's so wrongly old and I'm her daughter, but can she still have children?

HUMAN BEING

Now I have a baby boy and a five-year-old girl.
Being married, I thought I'd always be married to
Wayne because he tried to be perfect. What more could he
ask for?

RUDE

There's a cloth to wipe clear her muscular organ with the foam or the scum on it. People were talking too loudly. "You can't tell grown up people what to do," someone said. One person had fever, pain in the abdomen that develops normally like a sixth sense, and he wasn't careful choosing a marriage partner. He is noted for his humor and his favorite color is dark purple.

The physician covering him called him to report: "I find myself shocked and deeply hurt by your condition."

MRS. KEABLE'S BROTHERS

Her fate was being rigged for the rough surface. Nothing was omitted from her desirable world insofar as she likes Mr. Keable and other men in suits with short hair; patient service staff who smile; all the people with large, accurate vocabularies; big blossoms; logical arguments.

If a poached egg, open and bleeding, could give us the color palette, let us color her home in with that.

In the evening, Mrs. Keable's brothers, arriving in a black Volkswagen, often visited. She had in the past been scared to death of them.

As the sun comes up, it's as if, for Mrs. Keable, there's a slice of lime on any serving of her food.

ARM UNDER THE SOIL

It might seem to me that Chuck and I have a very happy marriage, which I cannot, I cannot believe I believe that.

I had gone out to look at what Chuck calls the dot plants—things out of proportion with the ground for which they are intended.

They're a focal feature to form the centerpiece among the many plants that are not valued. In the house, he has his cascade bonsai tree on a high stand.

I could not get between him and what he was in front of and I found myself waiting on some joyous occasion.

By the close of the day, I had no idea how to be practical. I'd lost control of my life.

Chuck tapped me, saying, "Who is that woman? What did she want?"

It had been our neighbor. I wish she had been thinking highly of me, while her husband looked on, forlorn in the car. "Your quack grass!" she had cried. "Why don't you just let me kill it for you?"

They have a rock garden, steppingstones, a perennial border, and then I could see that our weeds were menacing those.

The suspense in that moment had drawn me in and I was fascinated to hear my answer to her that was delivered in a weepy form.

In addition to the quack grass, we also have plantain, chickweed, thyme-leaved speedwell—curiously green and brown.

I understand. Hunks and slabs of weeds are not enjoyable to view.

Pressing the heel of my hand against my trowel, with a quick motion of the wrist and forearm, I repeat the motion. I am jabbing side to side. The tissues attached to the stem are softened enough for the root to be slipped out, so that I may remove my muscle section.

BEING STARED AT

I was ready during the reunion back at his house in April and I had a feeling he was present.

Most curiously he had asked us to call him Uncle Chew and I'd been fond of him.

The elderberry lemonade reminded me of when we were young inductees to the religious world and we sat around here. I was very impressed by the box lunch.

They handed out sheets with the lyrics to the song we'd written as a farewell for Uncle Chew. A part was missing.

When we arrived at this reunion it was chilly. The next day warmer. The next day chilly. The day after, I had a speech to make. We had hiked a certain distance past the church doorway, the hearth, the courtyard, along the village lane, the rough brick wall. I saw the same backdrop more than once so that I got my bearings. I was a woman in a fur collar and false hair, reminiscing.

They handed out lunch-box sandwiches as I came slowly down the length of my time, which I have become very attached to, and my memories and my remarks—hurt my pride.

EXPECTANT MOTHERHOOD

I don't like them or my brother. My children don't like me.
I count the affronts, mindful not to give up all my views.
I'd rather contort my guts. Conditions are somewhat unfavorable, despite strengths. I'd feel so much better if Brucie influenced me.

There is a side to me they have not been exposed to. I mention this. They take up their tasks. In short, my daughter told me to wait a minute, that she'd join me.

I said, "No!"

She put her head back and closed her coat at the neck. "I wonder if you realize . . ." she said. It took me a moment to.

Everyone else was hurrying. We stood. She was leaning against the mantelpiece. "Why are you so unpleasant?"

I answered, "I don't wish you well."

I threw my gloves on the floor and my hat. I had been wearing my dark blue coat. Drops of moisture were on our windows, and fog. We are a family. There's a point to it and to the dimmer switch in the foyer. The next thing—my daughter was stepping along the corridor and out the door. I seriously did not think I was in the state I describe as reserved for me.

COMFORT

She made assurances that satisfied her ambitions—saw the body interred, spent the rest of the week asking questions, suggesting action. She visited with her family and reminisced.

Getting routine matters out of the way, she headed home after buying a grounding plug and ankle wrist weights.

She fed the dog and put the boys to bed. Allen didn't go to work.

She received a call from a woman whose sister had died.

She made some of those unequaled assurances, was escorted with the family to the grave. People seem to respond to her. She talked with them, gave a woman a played-out peck on the cheek.

Getting routine matters out of the way, she attained

riches, social position, power, studied for an hour or so, cleaned up, took the family to a movie, after which she fore-casted her own death with a lively narration that gave her gooseflesh.

She felt raw, pink and so fresh!

THE STRENGTH

—◦—

"I am going to cough," I said. "Cough, cough."
I left Mary, my mother, to experience that by herself and
went to get the dish—a lion couchant—with a slew of nuts in
it, and I served us wine, and I coughed.

Mary put her hand on the top of her head, as if she could
not rightly rest it there.

"Mary, how are you, Mary?" I said. "Now, Mary."

"Not so good," she replied. "I've just been lying around."

Then she changed into the shape she pleased—an upright,
independent person.

My father, her husband—we were surprised—walked in,
buttoning himself to depart. I had thought he was dead. His
bad foot had killed him.

My mother and my dead father provide strength for me.
They recklessly challenge their competency.

It is senseless to prevent them.

THIS HAS TO BE THE BEST

It isn't until a Bengal cat comes by—the Sheepshanks' cat Andy—that I can see my way in the dark so to speak.

This flame design decorates almost all of his body and the brilliancy demonstrates exceptional technique.

When I pet the cat, I rough up too much of the detail, and the cat is yelling at me.

I went to the sex shop after. I know the saleswoman there very well.

And yet Brenda said, "I have never seen you before in my whole life!"

This must be on account of the harsh light.

A MAN, AN ANIMAL

At the cinema I watched closely the camels, the horses, the young actor taking his stance for the sexual act.

He started up with a pretty girl we had a general view of.

I felt the girl's pallor stick into me.

Another girl, in pink swirls alternating with yellow swirls, intruded.

The girls were like the women who will one day have to have round-the-clock duty at weddings, at birthdays, at days for the feasts.

Unaccountably, I hesitated on the last step of the cinema's escalator when we were on our way out, and several persons bumped into me.

An ugly day today—I didn't mention that, with fifty mile per hour winds.

But here is one of the more fortunate facts: We were Mr. and Mrs. Gray heading home.

It has been said—the doors of a house should always swing into a room. They should open easily to give the impression to those entering that everything experienced inside will be just as easy.

A servant girl was whipping something up when we arrived, and she carried around the bowl with her head bowed.

We've been told not to grab at breasts.

Before leaving for Indiana in the morning—where I had to clean up arrangements for a convention—I stood near my wife to hear her speak. So, who is she and what can I expect further from her?

What she did, what she said in the next days, weeks and years, addresses the questions Americans are insistently, even obsessively asking—but what sorts of pains in the neck have I got?

Please forgive our confusion and our failures. We make our petitions—say our prayers. It's like our falling against a wall, in a sense.

On a recent day, my wife gave me a new scarf to wear as a present. It's chrome green. Her mother Della, on that same day, had helped her to adjust to her hatred of me.

I'd have to say, I've given my wife a few very pleasant shocks, too.

SHELTER

D erek is somebody everybody loves because everybody
loves what Derek loves and he is handsome. I've left
Derek behind on the veranda, in the vestibule, in the passage.
He is fifty-two years old and behaving properly. Every day he
thinks of what to do and wonderfully he tries to do it. I can
make out his force, his shape. He sits at a shrewd distance from
the dining parlor, now.

I poured myself a cup of coffee (none for Derek), bad tasting, that satisfies my hunger.

Oh fine—pretty rooms, opening out on either side. I am
refreshed, filled with sweet feelings, enjoying a revival, long
and looping, and I pull a door shut and take slower steps, as if
walking to my bus stop.

I'll be unmanageable at the back stair's spiral.

Not a correct use of this residence.

But how odd it is—I recorked a bottle and stowed a jar of mayonnaise and Derek came in here for a particular reason.

Derek's task is to provide continuity room to room—thoughtfully—consistent with ensuring that no violent breaks occur and shouldn't I appreciate this?

Also, the recent calming wave of walls and ceilings has helped me very much.

However, the shovel and tongs, upright against the mantelpiece, you could argue that they just don't belong!

I make every effort not to crack or to split and to fit in, albeit, fitfully.

ENORMOUSLY PLEASED

Like this—leaning forward—she spit into a tulip bed within a block of Capital One—with her head like this.

Passing Rudi's, she saw the barbers in their barber chairs—four, five of them—in royal blue smocks—they had fallen asleep.

There are so many more things like that. She had spent the morning with the problem of sex.

Now she was making her progress into town. The sun was low. In any case, the weather—there are so many more things like that.

The woman made her progress as if she were an ordinary woman who was not aware of all her good fortune. The pear trees in bloom looked to her like clusters or fluff. She saw more things like that, that were complete successes.

She had spit into the tulip bed, as so often happens in life, with verve, and that was fun. Neither was the sun too low or too cold.

The documents she signed at Capital One glittered like certain leaves, like some flowers. That bending, that signing had hurt her back. She had more money as of today in her everyday life and she was tucking her hair and bending her hair as she had so often planned.

When she awakened that morning, she had smoothed her hair—when semi-alert—but she was still capable of adventures and their central thrust and with some encouragement, the penis of her husband had been leaning its head forward and plucking at her.

The barbers in their smocks, in the town, had awakened and were busy with their customers. And, she's a doctor!—or a lawyer!—with only a few griefs to her name. She's great!

If we trace the early years of her life, the intricacies, the dark years, the large middle zone, the wide-spacing between the fluctuations, as between her progress and her verve—the balanced tension—we see that the woman turns everyday life into daydreams, trusts in the future, is gullible and has some emotional immaturity.

HELLO! HI! HELLO!

M y association with Moffat was the luxury of my life or a decorative keynote—a postage stamp.

On Moffat's recommendation I took a meal alone at Cheiro's Café. I drank ginger ale with my black cherry linzer. I ate one fried egg and that felt as if I was eating a postage stamp— with its flat ridges.

I had begged Moffat, to be completely fair, to keep on with having what he called fun with me. Although, I have a respectful attitude toward the public status of the person addressed, he had become, he said, disentranced.

There is a reasonable code of conduct concerning Moffat.

I found I was a bit cold-pigged—drained, not dried entirely.

I came to rest in front of the elegant Blue Tree.

I had on a gather skirt—steeped in red—a blouse with

a series of buttons, hair combed. I noted my showy, stylish approach in the shop window glass with relieved surprise.

Once inside, I bought a simulated coral and onyx necklace, colorless beads, another necklace with swiftly flowing floral decorations, with ruby and gold glints that gives me a liberally watered shine.

When exiting, I studied trifling clouds stacked deliberately.

By and by, Moffat came along, popping out his fingers bouquet-style and calling my name.

He made a simultaneous outward swipe, with both his hands, with his fingers spread.

What a darling! No bad side. He has a strong activity level and a good sense of presentation and he's tentatively changed his mind—about me!

He's added, throughout his life, quite a rare group of us to his collection.

Penelope, for one, has a coiffure with a small, japanned bun and she's very neatly sweet.

My intention, with my own flourishes, is to create an impression of frankness and ambition.

I am prepared to be examined again.

I should be observed strongly and for a long time, so they can see the changes of my colors during the goings-on.

AS THE WORLD TURNED OUT

There's usually a side table in the story—a place to put a vase of flowers—or a potted plant—a clock, a book. A late-blooming flower may show up in the story—a swimming pool, a carefully groomed garden, pheasants touring the grounds (I mean peasants), Bella Donnelly, the Fraser family, one-on-one meetings with people enthusiastic about work, laughter and companionship, the great tragedy inflicted when people go under, the notion that even a woman can thrust herself forward and up and so-to-speak out from under on the first step down.

LORD OF THE FACE

The fact that she's backlit makes her look ambitious and she tickles my funny bone.

First I thought that her blue eyes on a pink and yellow background looked a bit purblind, but then their general dimension intrigued me. They have a nice design—glare—and they're not generous.

It's hard to slot him in. He seemed novicelike, uncertain of himself, but he was efficient.

She said, "I am Diane Williams."

They went out to the terrace for a cigarette.

Italy itself is very lovely, but as the brightness of the sun hit the terrace, the figure of a six-legged star—a sign for sure—was produced on the bluestone.

All six legs of the star were fairly straight. One leg of the star was not exactly the same length as the others. One leg was perfectly straight.

Their housekeeper grabbed at her own leg and at the top side of her foot.

Their cat was yanked up off of the terrace by a bird of prey and then dropped!

For the cat's recovery there were five thousand dollars worth of veterinarian bills and for the housekeeper—a premonition she'd be hit by a car.

The star! The cross! The square!

A single sign shows the tendency. Can people avoid disaster? Yes. I leave my readers to draw their own conclusions.

Some years ago, I was satisfied.

Stop!

Diane! So many things are clear. Diane was blushing. Her yellow fuzz shows in the sun. She no longer has words of her own and so chooses grunting. Diane! Open! Contribute! Inform! The place!—her brown fuzz, a yellow fuzz over it. The curtains are original. A room contains medical equipment. Diane's an early type who before arriving in Siena had a day planned for her departure. She had made the arrangements so she'd stay during the spring in Italy as an imaginary character with hope.

FINE,
FINE, FINE, FINE,
FINE
(2016)

How long will Harry Doe live? . . . Who will win the war? . . .
Will Mary Jane Brown ultimately find a husband . . . ?

—LEO MARKUN

BEAUTY, LOVE, AND VANITY ITSELF

As usual I'd hung myself with snappy necklaces, but otherwise had given my appearance no further thought, even though I anticipated the love of a dark person who will be my source of prosperity and emotional pleasure.

Mr. Morton arrived about 7 P.M. and I said, "I owe you an explanation."

"Excellent," he replied. But when my little explanation was completed, he refused the meal I offered, saying, "You probably don't like the way I drink my soda or how I eat my olives with my fingers."

He exited at a good clip and nothing further developed from that affiliation.

The real thing did come along. Bob—Tom spent several

days in June with me and I keep up with books and magazines and go forward on the funny path pursuing my vocation.

I also went outside to enjoy the fragrant odor in an Illinois town and kept to the thoroughfare that swerved near the fence where yellow roses on a tawny background are always faded out at the end of the season.

I never thought a big cloud hanging in the air would be crooked, but it was up there—gray and deranged.

Happily, in the near distance, the fence was making the most of its colonial post caps.

And isn't looking into the near distance sometimes so quaint?—as if I am re-embarking on a large number of relations or recurrent jealousies.

Poolside at the Marriott Courtyard, I was wearing what others may laugh at—the knee-length black swimsuit and the black canvas shoes—but I don't have actual belly fat, that's just my stomach muscles gone slack.

I saw three women go into the pool and when they got to the rope, they kept on walking. One woman disappeared. The other two flapped their hands.

"They don't know what the rope is," the lifeguard said. "I mean everybody knows what a rope means."

I said, "Why didn't you tell them?" and he said, "I don't speak Chinese."

I said, "They are drowning," and the lifeguard said, "You know, I think you're right."

Our eyes were on the surface of the water—the wobbling patterns of diagonals. It was a hash—nothing to look at— much like my situation—if you're not going to do anything about it.

A GRAY POTTERY HEAD

How tenderly she had arranged the gray pottery head of a woman on her mantel—the subtly revealed head of an archaic woman. It exhibits some bumps and some splits.

This was a gift from the Danish gentleman who had also given her a Georg Jensen necklace in the original box.

She had been lucky in love as she understood it.

And that night—some progress to report. Something exciting afoot. She has a quarter hour more to live.

Even if she only gets to the lower roadway, she'll have to manage somehow.

Her boiled woolen cloak was wrapped around her tilting body and she was driving her car as if it were being blown away by the wind.

She had gone down this particular road to go home for

years. This time she also arrived close by the familiar place, dying.

A tulip tree, tucked into a right angle formed by two planes, was brought into her view.

The police officer who inspected her dead body saw one area of damage and the pretty mother-of-pearl, gold and enamel Jensen ornament that was around her neck.

She has been associated with sex and with childbirth. No less interesting, she was a traveler on this unsophisticated country road.

Her facial features are remarkably symmetrical, expressing vigor and vulnerability.

GULLS

The gulls in the wind looked to her like fruit flies or gnats. Two gulls flying suffered an in-air collision. One fell. The other briefly stood there—appearing to do next to nothing.

The woman didn't think she was supposed to see that.

So how far did the injured gull fall?—for it did not show itself again.

From the ninth floor, the adults in the street looked to her like children. But who were the children that she saw meant to be?

"We'll have to knock ourselves into shape, won't we?" the woman told her husband. She had once intended to evaluate their options for the improvement of their understanding.

She was fingering her glass that held water—the water that,

of course, slides downhill when she drinks it—the water that one could say stumbles.

Now, in the back of their building beyond the river, there is a hollow—the unfilled cavity—although nobody can escape that way.

The woman went to bed that night with nothing much accomplished vis-à-vis the mysteries of daily life.

Her husband, next to her, squats carefully. Then he is on his knees above her.

He keeps his chin down, giving proper shape to what he is trying to express—his romantic attitude toward life.

TO REVIVE A PERSON
IS NO SLIGHT THING

People often wait a long time and then, like me, suddenly, they're back in the news with a changed appearance.

Now I have fuzzy gray hair. I am pointing at it. It's like baby hair I am told.

Two people once said I had pretty feet.

I ripped off some leaves and clipped stem ends, with my new spouse, from a spray of fluorescent daisies he'd bought for me, and I asserted something unpleasant just then.

Yes, the flowers were cheerful with aggressive petals, but in a few days I'd hate them when they were spent.

The wrapping paper and a weedy mess had to be discarded, but first off thrust together. My job.

Who knows why the dog thought to follow me up the stairs.

Tufts of the dog's fur, all around his head, serve to

distinguish him. It's as if he wears a military cap. He is dour sometimes and I have been deeply moved by what I take to be the dog's deep concerns.

Often I pick him up—stop him mid-swagger. He didn't like it today and he pitched himself out of my arms.

Drawers were open in the bedroom.

Many times I feel the prickle of a nearby, unseen force I ought to pay attention to.

I turned and saw my husband standing naked, with his clothes folded in his hands.

Unbudgeable—but finally springing into massive bright-ness—is how I prefer to think of him.

Actually, he said in these exact words: "I don't like you very much and I don't think you're fascinating." He put his clothes on, stepped out of the room.

I walked out, too, out onto the rim of our neighborhood—into the park where I saw a lifeless rabbit—ears askew. As if prompted, it became a small waste bag with its tied-up loose ends in the air.

A girl made a spectacle of herself, also, by stabbing at her front teeth with the tines of a plastic fork. Perhaps she was prod-ding dental wires and brackets, while an emaciated man at her side fed rice into his mouth from a white-foam square container, at top speed, crouched—swallowing at infrequent intervals.

In came my husband to say, "Diane?" when I went home.

"I am trying," I said, "to think of you in a new way. I'm not sure what—how that is."

A fire had been lighted, drinks had been set out. Raw fish had been dipped into egg and bread crumbs and then sautéed. A small can of shoe polish was still out on the kitchen counter. We both like to keep our shoes shiny.

How unlikely it was that our home was alight and that the dinner meal was served. I served it—our desideratum. The bread was dehydrated.

I planned my future—that is, what to eat first—but not yet next and last—tap, tapping.

My fork struck again lightly at several mounds of yellow vegetables.

The dog was upright, slowly turning in place, and then he settled down into the shape of a wreath—something, of course, he'd thought of himself, but the decision was never extraordinary.

And there is never any telling how long it will take my husband, if he will not hurry, to complete his dinner fare or to smooth out left-behind layers of it on the plate.

"Are you all right?" he asked me—"Finished?"

He loves spicy food, not this. My legs were stiff and my knees ached.

I gave him a nod, made no apologies. Where were his?

I didn't cry some.

I must say that our behavior is continually under review and any one error alters our prestige, but there'll be none of that *lifting up mine eyes unto the hills.*

HEAD OF A NAKED GIRL

O ne got an erection while driving in his car to get to her.
Another got his while buying his snowblower, with her
along. He's the one who taught her how to blow him and that's
the one she had reassured, "You're the last person I want to
antagonize!"

The men suspect her of no ill will and they've stuck by her.

She's enjoyed their examinations of her backside in her bed.

And although there's no danger, one of the men had a
somewhat bluff interest in her. He was handsome with dim-lit
eyes. She liked to joke with him.

While she bent forward to her comfort level, at her sink,
without holding her breath, she kept her mouth open. He
applied himself against her and she allowed his solution to
gently drain from her.

The paper she'd gathered together, and added to several times—to dry herself—was unfairly harsh—so often, such a number of times, regularly, usually.

But something more. Another man, when he stopped by, noted that things had become almost too satisfactory. He saw copies of old masters on the wall, not obvious to him on his previous visits.

"Is something wrong?" the girl asked.

As a rule, she blamed herself—for yet another perfect day.

RHAPSODY BREEZE

Her salesman had hair like a fountain on top of his head, and then it came down around at the sides of his head to just above his shoulders. He had a boy's physicalness, yet his mustache was gray and he never thanked her for the big sale.

No one would ever say of him—He has such a nice face or that he looks like such a nice man, but he had not intended to misuse her.

After all, hadn't he tried to stop her from buying one of the heaviest mattresses that she surely will regret purchasing.

That poor decision of hers is well past her now as she presses her paint roller from here to there and back while she is uttering little grunts that sound reasonable as she shifts her ladder.

The ceiling turns terra-cotta—the walls will be red, the

door cerulean blue, the sills and window sashes kelly green. There'll be a turquoise mantel—and, for her dinner—more pleasure and change. She'll cook a strong-juiced vegetable, prepare a medley salad with many previously protected and selected things in it.

The salesman, at his home, empties a pitcher of water into a potted plant that has produced several furred buds that he's been studying and waiting on—courting, really—but it's as if these future flowers intentionally thwart him. He assumes responsibility for their behavior.

Also, he thinks he doesn't know how to get people to do things.

He takes a cloth and wipes the greasy face of his computer. He checks his mustache in the mirror to see if it is trimmed properly.

He asks himself, What do you want to ask me? Will you look at that?

To begin with he thinks he's had enough of chewing on his mustache. The next thought after that is—What a lot of wild sprouts there are above his mouth—and he assumes responsibility for their behavior. The step after that is to get his hairbrush and the scissors and to approach the real challenge, which is to steady his oscillating hand so he can aim it at the appropriate section of his face where the offensive hairs are. Then he brushes the mustache to see how unevenly he's cut it, and then it depends on how much time he has, not enough. Should he adjust the one side to match the other side?—because there is a limit. He may end up cutting off his entire mustache.

He presses his face closer to the mirror. He could not make it out, could not recognize the opportunity for bewitching himself.

LAVATORY

There had been the guest's lavatory visit—to summarize. She did so want to be comfortable then and for the rest of her life. She had been hiking her skirt and pulling down her undergarment, just trying not to fall apart.

Once back in the foyer, she brought out a gift for her host. "I tried to find something old for you to put on your mantel, but I just couldn't. I tried to find something similar to what you already have, to be on the safe side, but I couldn't."

It was difficult for the guest to comprehend easily what the other invitees were saying, because she wasn't listening carefully. One man happened to have a son who knew her son. He had learned something of importance about her son—about his prospects. Something.

But the guest interrupted him, "I don't agree that there

is a comfortable space for each of us out there and we have to find it. I think this is so wrong. It assumes there is a little environment that you can slip into and be perfectly happy. My notion is you try to do all the things you're comfortable with and eventually you will find your comfortable environment."

A man they called Mike smoked a maduro and he had a urine stain on his trouser fly. He was very attentive to the host and to his wife Melissa.

"Stop!" his wife cried, but he'd done it already—tipped the ashtray he'd used—the dimpled copper bowl—into the grate behind the fire screen. The ashes fell down nicely, sparsely. There was still some dark, sticky stuff leftover in the bowl.

The host called, "Kids! Mike! Dad and Mom!" He called these copulators to come in to dinner. In fact, this group represented a predictable array of vocations—including hard workers, worriers, travelers, and liars—defecators, of course, urinators and music makers.

THE ROMANTIC LIFE

"Gunther should show up and act as if he's learned something," Rohana said. "But he has a very good situation where he is—I am sure. I don't know why he'd want to come back here."

Gunther had died young and she thought he visited the house whenever she traveled. This was her explanation for why a five-hundred-pound mirror had fallen off of the wall when she was in Cannes. Gunther was to blame. And his pet dog Spark—long dead too—had trotted out of the boxwood to greet her upon her return. However, unlike Gunther, the ancient Airedale had chosen to stay on.

Aunt Rohana offered me my favorite—her red porridge specialty—a compote made from berries and served with heavy cream. "You can always cheer me up!" she said.

And, really—wasn't this a lavish new world with new and possibly better rules?—so that I would no longer be sitting along the curbing. And, I thought Rohana loved me, whereas my own mother, her sister, did not.

I tried not to pry my thoughts away from my new surroundings, because I had been left alone for a few hours—and I was almost successful.

As I was a young woman without a sexual partner—awareness of the deprivation was not half the battle—I was thinking about sex and at the same time I was moving my attention to the furniture, the fireplace—the walls and all of the doors that bore oak carvings in art nouveau.

Then I saw Gunther!—or he could have been a replica of the lost original. A small bent male figure was on the threshold of my room, close by a tripod table.

He slouched toward me and there was something that was not eager in his eyes. But nevertheless, he looked determined.

"Why don't you speak?" he said.

He was zipped into a fur-trimmed anorak—and not at all dressed properly for the hot summer season.

He kicked the table.

"Where have you been?" I asked.

"Dead," he said. He made his way into the kitchen and the dog Spark and I followed him.

He put two hands on the sink rim to begin the maneuver

and next he pivoted on his heels. He pushed in the upper dish-washer tray that had been left out and was overhanging.

The dog gasped behind me. I turned—and when I turned back around Gunther was gone.

My memory is that Rohana had run an errand that day to get a chicken to roast, a box of soap, and a ball of twine.

"Oh, God! What do you want me to say?" she said, when I told her.

I stayed at Rohana's another day or two before I went home with a new backbone for my plodding along.

Sudden sounds didn't frighten me and I didn't mind the sense of being stared at when I was alone.

Rohana has a nerve condition now, such that if she sits still and doesn't move her left foot, she is fine. Otherwise she needs to take a lot of pain medication.

And as Gunther has done—I have shown up in certain places with a bang. And when I come into rooms, it's surely a relief to one and all that I am helpful.

I feel there is so much yet to explore about how people experience a "pull" toward anyone.

THE GREAT PASSION
AND ITS CONTEXT

She bears the problems inherent in her circumstance that are not suddenly in short supply and she sways while guessing who really looks at her impatiently while she faces all of the faces—the multiple rows of the pairs of persons—the prime examples in the train aisle.

She has her shoes back on, because she had to get up to dispose of her lunchtime detritus. But fortunately she did not fall onto the passenger next to her, that man, when she returned.

They are passing through a city center with turn-of-the-century-style lanterns and ice skaters who put their feet down, somewhat decisively, all over a rink!

Some of their legs are bowed and there are the curvilinear, stylized profiles of their legs exemplifying natural organic forms, but they're none of them hobbling.

This woman's foot was recently injured and many weeks' rest were required before she had the rapture of standing on it—in strict accordance with the doctor's instructions.

Oh, cover my mouth!—she thinks, as her wet nose, while she coughs, finds her forearm. And although she is usually an irate parent, she has her share of lovesick feelings, especially during intervals of freedom from her toddlers, such as this one.

She feels the onset of arousal, of genital swelling that is triggered by no one in particular and she has the inability to think normally.

What's still to come?—a warm flat landscape?—a shallow swimming pool?—the complete ruin of her health?—her absolute devotion to anyone?

The top of the woman's foot is still puffy and she has had quarrels at home every day this week and she goes to sleep distraught.

With dexterity, she had managed the bundling of her lunchtime cardboard tray, some cellophane and the napkin and a waxy cup.

Children, who belong to another woman three rows up ahead, are singing a duet—two boys—in unison, and then in contrary motion. They offer their share of resistance to you name it!—in a remote and difficult key, and in poor taste artistically.

SPECIALIST

"For a blue sky, that blue's a bit dark, don't you think? And the sea's a bit too choppy," I said, "for that dog to be dashing into it."

"You mean the man threw something into the water?" my son said. "That's why the dog jumped in?"

An hour passed. Why not say twenty years?

In the Green Room, I had fortunately ordered Frenched Chicken Breast—Chocolate Napoleon.

And at a great height—up on a balcony, as I readied to depart—a pianist began his version of Cole Porter's "Katie Went to Haiti." I waved to him.

He nodded, likely pleased by the attention, but it was hard to tell—for only his radiant pate was made visible by a tiny ceiling light.

To my surprise, the air in the street was too hot to give pleasure and a cyclist was mistakenly on the sidewalk.

The cyclist hit me, and it's vile after my life ends in the afterlife. Lots of incense, resin, apes, and giraffe-tails—all acquired tastes. I don't like that kind of thing.

THE POET

S he carves with a sharply scalloped steel blade, makes slices
across the top of a long, broad loaf of yeasted bread for the
dog who begs and there's a cat there, too.

She holds the loaf against her breast and presses it up
under her chin. But this is no violin! Won't she sever her head?

AT A PERIOD OF
EXCEPTIONAL DULLNESS

The influence of the early evening's sunset was much less bloody inside of the salon, spreading itself like red smoke or like a slowly moving red fog, unbounded.

Yet, Mrs. Farquhar's hair was nearly bloodred, and it behaved like dry hair.

The hairdresser lifted a clump of it, dropped it. To soften it, she reached for her leave-in detangler.

She looked for more signs of neglect, the thread connections that could come to light. She said, "It's all broken. It's much worse."

The haircut trickled along, and it would take a long time.

But how terribly unhappy Mrs. Farquhar was. She must not have been adaptable to something else much more serious in particular.

However, the tea she had been served had the tang of the dirty lake of her childhood that she remembered swallowing large amounts of while swimming, and she wore the shop's black Betty Dain easy-to-wear client wrap robe.

The full view of Mrs. Farquhar's face and of her hair in the mirror was a trial for both of them.

Nonetheless, the hairdresser preened. She wore an elite Betty Dain gown, too.

Later she tidied up and by breakfast time, at home, the next morning—the hairdresser was alone, wedged between her chair and the table. There was a plastic plate in front of her and a ceramic mug. These both had glossy surfaces—impenetrable, opaque.

She removed her solitaire pearl finger ring, put it onto the plate.

Through the window she saw her pruned shrubbery, a narrow green lawn, no trees.

She believed it was her duty to size these things up.

What was it that she did or did not admire? It was a question of her upsetting something.

HEAD OF THE BIG MAN

The family was blessed with more self-confidence than most of us have and with a great lawn, with arbors and beds of flowers, and with a fountain in the shape of a sun at the south end. It is not our purpose to say anything imprecise about their scheme, how they had gotten on with tufted and fringed furniture, with their little tables, a parquet floor, a bean pot.

The walls inside of this country house were amber-colored where they entertained quite formally—until the old mansion was destroyed.

It was a shapely shingle-style house, with bulbous posts.

But what kind of confident people behave poorly by not being confident enough?

Let us examine the case.

Eldrida Cupit had given birth to four children. Three of these and their father drowned trying to cross the Quesnel River in a boat. She later married Mr. Cupit and had many more children. "Imp," as she was known, was famous for her fresh peach sour cream pie, her steak shortcake, and more significantly for her élan.

People often saw her husband Blade on the street and he not only was polite, but he invited many personally to his home to hear about his rough riding days and his numerous good works.

In her later years, Mrs. Cupit dressed slowly for dinner and did not intend nor want to see anyone, except for her husband at dinner.

Frequently her husband left the table before she arrived and then edged himself up the back stairs.

He began to drink and lost all of his money after his wife died.

Often, as in this tale, a downpour with thunder and lightning is sufficiently full-bodied to get somebody's whole attention. In one such storm Mr. Cupit had a vision of his wife. Her clothing was not exactly cut to fit and she showed no sign of affection. "Well, act like you're not going up a hill," his wife said, "but you're still going to go up it!"

For a while, after their deaths, their residence was open to tourists who were apt to get exhausted touring it.

The diamond-shaped hall, placed in the center—its dimensions and spaciousness were rooted, were grounded as if the hall was growing as an ample area. It was finished in mahogany. The dominant message here being: "Looks like one of you splurged!"

None of this would have been possible without the involvement of morally strong, intelligent people who were then spent.

Young farmers and rural characters, obstetrical nurses, scholars, clergy—all the rest!—will have their great hopes realized more often than not—unless I decide to tell their stories.

LIVING DELUXE

True! Yes! Mother always gave me a tribute with a sigh. I was her favorite, and that was another reason I took money from her that rightfully belonged to my sister and my brother.

My mother knew I needed to be a person with flair and I can be.

It may require a little time.

No lack of courage could have caused me to turn away from a day laborer on the foot pavement who sneezed a larger-than-life-size sneeze with an open mouth. Then he crossed himself multiple times, as I went by him.

It pained me to hold my breath while outdistancing him, and I wondered how far I'd need to go to keep free of any noxious air. I thought briefly I might count out the accurate, necessary number of cubic feet or yards.

But I was restful during a letup in the late afternoon, when my sister visited me. Her metal necklace caught at my shawl collar and it pulled loose a thread as I embraced her.

Her appearance needed some repair, too.

She is Liz Munson. She is a judge! She decides whether people live or die!

She declined a drink but ate a few of the hemp seeds I'd left out in my hors d'oeuvre dish.

"How is Maurice?" I said. "Did that one end?"

"He's with the boys," she said, and then took a pause to round out her lungs to their capacity.

Henry the cat put his paws up on me and called out a critical remark. Then he made his other noise that is tinged with bitterness. He is sand color in the style of the day with cement accents.

Liz's Henry is black chestnut.

I'll make no attempt to explain a cat's problems that are basic to all cats—schemes that are unrealistic.

I held tightly, for an instant, on to Henry's tail, when he moved to go far afield, for his suffering and his sacrifice—although the cat's tail is a branch that refuses to break.

Henry had charm once upon a time. Now he wastes it stalking. "Stay and eat with me, Liz."

"Oh, dear," she said.

What had she come for?

My sister picked up a piece of bric-a-brac that was on the console and put it into the unimpressive realm of her handbag.

What I call a toy—what she took—was mine, never Mother's: a leaden mammal of some sort, with horns.

Oddly, Liz has never noticed here her ten-pounder da Vinci omnibus with its gravure illustrations, its spine sensationally exhibited on a shelf, that bears this inscription on the frontispiece: *To Liz and Neville, with best wishes for a happy life in a world of friendship and guz.* (That last was illegible.) *Signed Stephen and Lil Cole.*

Leonardo may not have founded science, but I learned from him that genius does not bog down.

I lit the stove top and put water on to boil and next poured in baby peas. I made parallel straight rules—incisions in the chunk of Gruyere. The water foamed in the pot and I filled a rare antique potato basket with New York rye.

"You are a wonder," my sister said. "I am not after your food. I want to bring you bad luck."

"No harm done!" I said.

The peas had cooked and cooled. I prepared a pea and cheese stuffed-tomato salad. Enough for two.

My visitor was nagging at me, which was hurtful to the pride I intend to take along with me into my future.

And just where am I now?

I live near a dip in the suburbs. Some would call this a ravine—which I make visible at night with floodlights.

I believe it demands cunning enterprise on my part to

reveal the fancywork of bare winter poplar and oak, maple and ash. I saw a sycamore tree bent at more than fifteen degrees from vertical!

My dining table is only nominally illuminated, so that our hands and our arms and Liz's face became quickly—sickly. Unaccountably, she had sat herself right across from me.

My sister sneezed and put her hand to her mouth in time.

"God bless you," I said.

She sneezed again rather more sloppily and that reminded me of a joke. She underwent yet another sudden, spasmodic action—and this time she did not try to keep her bacteria back.

My harrier removed two handmade beeswax candles from their brass serpent candleholders on her way out.

She yelled my name—"Ola!"—and I turned away for relief—aiming to sit in my wingback rather than the lounge chair.

I saw the downed sycamore through the pane, the suggestion of a sky far away, and some of the sharply peaked trees straining to bend or to unbend, or at least to shed their shapes, or to be somewhat more neatly executed.

Very well. I took from my family one hundred thousand dollars—say fifty thousand. Say it was three million. It was thirty-five thousand!—forty. It was two hundred dollars.

There was aggravated tapping near the tall wraparound window.

By way of conclusion—I need to say I had divided a pack

of gems between Liz and myself. In doing this, I'd forgotten my brother. The nonpareils, I wear in my ears.

There was that tapping again—a repeated and demonic phrase—and the repellent sight of animals through the glass.

They are my very own public property.

Such bollixed and blank expressions.

These flocks and herds and creeping things! Don't you think they all go to work so wretchedly for what then never amounts to *a feast for the soul?*

How to live: there are two factors to consider—my husband says there are five!—and one of them puts me into a rage.

My fingers are graceful when I lay the table. My voice is clear when I speak. For God's sake! For the Lord's got such style, such originality and boldness.

PERSONAL DETAILS

On the avenue, I was unavoidably stuck inside of an uproar when the wind locked itself in front of my face.

Nevertheless, I had a smeary view of a child in the whirlwind who was walking backward. He was carrying his jacket instead of wearing it. And he kicked up his feet with such aptitude.

In a luncheonette that I took cover in, I overheard, "Yes, I do mind . . ."—this, while I was raising and rearranging memories of many people's personal details, tryst locales, endearments—faces, genitalia, like Jimmy T's, or Lee's, which I pine for.

This is regular work with regular work hours that I do.

Through the windowpane of the coffee shop, I could see clearly into a hair salon across the street where two men—both with hairbrushes and small, handheld dryers—together—downstroked the mane of a cloaked woman.

The men were performing feats of legerdemain. Streamers sprang up around her head, as if snakes or dragons were busy eating their own tails.

And then, weighing down her shoulders, there was the golden hoard—for future use—of bullshit.

HOW BLOWN UP

A server making noisy cascades was busy refilling their glasses with ice water from a tall pitcher.

That's what it was like in there—all peppy! Wouldn't you know it? It had not been a period of decline.

Having made up her mind, "Why—excuse me," the woman said peremptorily. She left the café and stepped out into the rain. She was not scaled down or reversed in her views.

There was a car just outside that she stepped into. No daylight any longer.

She rode in the taxicab toward a higher order on account of the movement of her thought.

Here's the spot!

We shall see!

Do you know how the animals got their tails? How the lesser gods came into the world?

The longer this goddess lives, the more she shakes her tail—or pulls on it with all her strength.

SIGH

Why would anyone be fearful that the man might become distressed or that he might lose his temper in their bedroom?

He is a calm man by nature and not liable to break anything really nice by accident.

He had decided to disrobe in there—where they keep their Polish woman statuette and the fish dish they use for loose coins.

To be civilized, this man had asked to meet with his wife's new husband.

The three drank tea together, impromptu, from souvenir mugs and paid mind to one another's questions and the uninformative replies. Next, the man had stepped into their bedroom, towing his roller board, after inquiring if he could change into more comfortable clothes in preparation for his travel.

He said he'd be leaving soon enough—flying into the northeast corridor that he'd heard was an absolute quagmire.

Hard rain had been falling freely and for several days. In addition, now they were suffering occasional sleet. The pressure, the moisture, and the black clouds were progressing.

This is a humid, continental climate in turmoil.

"You're wearing that?" the wife said, when the man reemerged in Spandex fitness apparel.

"We found it in Two Dot! You don't remember?" he said—fondly patting lightly his own chest. "It's breathable. It's stretchable."

"I thought it was in Geraldine," the wife said.

"But look here, maybe you should stay the night," the new husband said. He offered seed cake and coffee—the mild and friendly kind—this time, to drink.

"What are you doing?" said the wife—for her husband's hands were filled with the sugar bowl and the creamer and several cups were swinging from his fingers by their ears.

All so beautifully turned out, the dishes found the table's surface safely. These were specimens of the most romantic china service. The gilding was very good—the glaze finely crazed. There were hand-painted sprays on an apple-green ground.

"I hope you are a comfort to her," the man said, "and that you show good sense. Because this is what it is—doesn't everybody have to take care of Tasha?" He did not refer to her sex behavior and instead spoke generally about the dell they had once lived in and lunged silently at his disappointment that he could no longer touch his former wife. He extolled the mountain town where the wife had often reflected that looking up and out, say, over at an elevated ridge—was to her advantage.

Now she resided in this flatter state in an apartment on the third floor across from the church—from where she could see its spire.

Her glance often ran recklessly toward it, as if spurting over a rim, or through a spout.

The chancel and the sanctuary had lately been under ugly scaffolding. A few years back, one of the two aisle rose windows had been carried away for restoration and had not been returned yet.

Fortunately, the inner-draw draperies of the couple's window facing the church were made of cheerful chintz.

"It wouldn't surprise me if I stayed," the man said. "Well, sure, yes, absolutely, you bet!" he said. "I'm a little nervous."

He prepared to eat by sitting down and stressing his jaws with a big smile.

His cheeks are elongated and hollow—his brow highly peaked. His face is not difficult to explain—it's cathedral-like.

The new husband's whole head has an unfinished look that promises to work out well. Whereas the wife's furrowed face—some have said—shows heavy evidence of deception and is cause for alarm.

Right then, in front of them, the woman uncapped a tube of gel ointment and applied a dab of it under a long fingernail. Next she opened a cellophane packet from which she withdrew a cracker that produced plenty of crumbs.

The husband told the man, "Surely you'd be welcome to stay!"

As the wife mopped up her particles and the traces, she spoke somewhat rudely to the man and also to her husband.

"I went somewhere . . ." the man said, expanding on a point. Hadn't he been molded to better express himself?

A small object's overall smallness on a shelf caught his eye—a round-bodied jar of free-blown glass whose neck was straight, that had flat shoulders—a flask he would not get to smash! It was streaked with permanent crimson and cold black. It had about it the real suggestion of the softness of human flesh.

"Did you imagine me the way I am?" the man asked the new husband, who answered no.

"What do you mean?"

"But I am not against you," the husband said.

"Say a little more."

Sirens in the street produced a brief, headstrong fugue.

"Say a little more," said the man.

The husband got up from his chair. Why should anyone be fearful of his certain combinations of words, narrowly spaced?

The husband gave himself ample time to speak.

No gross vices were explored. His is not the voice of a man in the pulpit. No personal impulses were defined or analyzed.

He did deliver a slovenly interrogatory.

He went uphill, downhill with—"Wah-aaaaaaaat waaahz it ligh-ike, with herrrrrrrrr-rah, for you-ooooooo—?"

That's all that he was saying.

Nothing seemed to want to end it.

THERE IS ALWAYS A HESITATION
BEFORE TURNING IN A FINISHED JOB

B eneath his coat, when I first met him, his shirt had seemed to have broken out into an inflammation—into a lavish plaid or a strong enough checkered pattern.

There was the stretch of time when my future materialized on account of Dan.

We fried things on the stove top and made coffee. Formerly, I had been disabled and chilled, the usual story—so then the hamburgers had become fun.

Dan was doing the job of keeping us together and he was creating a little garden at the back of the house and the garden was extending onto the beach and the garden didn't have any grass to speak of, but we had this vision of growing things there. There was a daisy we were trying to grow. There was another flower that looked like an artichoke, but it was not only to be a garden of landscape plantings. It was supposed to be equal to our worth.

One day when we were out in the garden, a dog that had been chasing a rabbit came up to us. Dan said hello and we kept that dog. It was a tan dog and it was a mix of the best available species and the dog was trembling. He had that look in his eyes. He had the heart to do any work that was necessary, but we had nothing for him to do. And I was struck by how the dog was featuring so prominently. For instance, we might think to go someplace, but would the dog like it?

The dog had his leisure hours and Dan and I had been together longer than I expected and I was all tired out because we had indulged ourselves in every desire.

Although, occasionally, we still had a lustrous sunny day with lots of time in it, more than usual.

These days, when we tie up the dog in the yard we can barely bend to weed.

The weeds and the dead flowers—clumps—are like the stacks of our used dishes with the dribs of jelly and bite-marked bread crusts that are hardly ever put away.

So how much more describing is necessary to assess if we're done expecting something even more fortunate to turn up?

I was stepping into a corridor. It was empty except for Dan. He moved backward awkwardly, but then his face rose toward me like a steel magnet and it landed on my face with a bump. He has an enormous head and pale-pigmented skin.

I ran into him again later.

And then there was a long, long time without my seeing another human being.

And after the last years were over, we were dead.

THE MERMAID POSE

The mother had fought a small cause to prevent the little girl from sticking her hand into the pond to try to catch a fish, but the child fell in and went under. Which of them did the wrong thing?

The father wrapped his hands around the crying child's neck as he lifted her up and out and the mother shook droplets from the wetted front of her own skirt.

A rose of Sharon—like an old Chinese, hand-painted lacquer screen—obscured the sight of anything more of them, as the group left. But the mother, I could hear her saying—"The what? I will not!"

But to get back to the pond!—we were at the Burnett Fountain in the Conservatory Garden where a bronze boy toots on a flute at the feet of a bronze girl who holds her overflowing bowl high.

Legs together—the boy reclines in a mermaid pose—and people in other mermaid poses had been taking turns being photographed on the stone pavers at the edge of the reflecting pool that was filled with the blue lilies and the fish.

I also lowered myself so that I was elongated and bent at the waist.

I watched a creamy madcap one ploughing among the others that were, most of them, too good to be true.

I felt an unimaginable touch. Oh, to be sweetly signaled.

A hand pressed against my back. "Come along, Kitty. We're late. You wanted a bath."

He kissed his fingers in tribute to me as I turned. And I got up with slow progress, trying for a look of extreme gladness, brushing off the back of my clothing.

A dead or disabled raccoon on the sidewalk, near the hospital, en route home, was attracting several lookers-on—partially on its side—with its legs opened up like scissor blades.

We've heard these animals in the trees and guessed what they were doing up there that always sounds so beyond the pale.

This was just going to be a sponge bath, God willing.

"You're clean enough already," my husband said.

So that was dear of him and the lineaments of his face are stamped with his best intentions whether he has any of those or not.

I am teal and gray and added colors. I've done nothing to hide the ugliness of my elderly body. And let others regret that my character has no allure, because I am worn-out with that also.

We have a roll-top bathtub I had stepped into. I tried to sit. I was angled painfully and wedged on top of one foot—as if I am intent to prove the impossible—that I don't fit in.

GREED

Each child had a claim to a pile of jewelry when my paternal grandmother died—and how did they determine who was to have which pile?

The heirs were sent into an adjacent room and a trustee called out loudly enough to be heard by all of them—"Who will have this pile?"

My father said he shouted—"August Wilhelm will have this pile!"

Thus, my mother eventually received two gem-set rings that she wore as a pair until she achieved an advanced age and then she amalgamated the two of them into one—so that the diamonds and the sapphires were impressively bulked together.

I had to have it. It was a phantasmagoria. I selected it after my mother's death, not because I liked it, but because it offers the memory of my mother and of the awkward, temporarily placed cold comfort that she gave me.

It's hard to believe that our affair was so long ago.

THE SKOL

In the ocean, Mrs. Clavey decided to advance on foot at shoulder-high depth. A tiny swallow of the water coincided with her deliberation. It tasted like a cold, salted variety of her favorite payang congou tea. She didn't intend to drink more, but she did drink—more.

THE THICKENING WISH

Typically, he walks far enough north so that he sees the bridge and he appears to be so casual as he passes objects, the people, rusticated arcades, and heavy keystones.

Here's how it is—he had just gotten as far as Childs & Son Excavation Company, which has a colonnaded façade.

His wife, back at home, sat in front of their hole-in-the-wall fireplace.

If her husband is delayed, she'll prepare for herself a nice shirred egg.

Has he anything in mind when he nears Mitchell's Sheet Metal and the Nelson Fuel Company?

You have got a lot of nerve! comes to mind. Somebody in his childhood said that frequently, but who was it who said it?

His wife is thinking, *I am usually in a rush, but I am not in a rush today.*

She stows a spool of thread and a needle threaded with the thread. And didn't she put away her ring? It had been prized and placid on the bureau top, with its many little rough points—the prongs—that in the course of time had never gone and worn themselves down smoothly.

This is how her husband's feet move his body—it's a spring-like action.

His wife hunts for more objects to put away. Many are made of cheap metal—boat-shaped or cube-shaped.

She enjoys their real fireplace, sitting by it, studying the in-and-out curve of it and the projecting stub of its mantel.

She tells herself, "Take all the time to clean up that you need."

By chance, her husband has not yet come up against the bridge he seeks—but he has seen many towers and domes, porches and arches and doors, and he always enjoys the step-gabled buildings in the old town.

Then at last, he sees the bridge that seems to him to be sinking. The bridge has become a boob, or a drunk, or a bum.

His wife puts an egg into a greased custard cup, dots it with butter, salt and pepper, and a drop of milk. She slides the egg—which had spent nearly the entirety of its life stone-cold and refrigerated—into the hot oven.

Her husband is now uncomprehending. The road he'd been on was pointing toward the bridge, so now how did the road suddenly take a sharp turn away from the bridge and head over toward this warehouse?

His wife begins to eat, but she cannot swallow.

You blockhead, you ass!

And her husband is back at the business of piling up the sights that have been left lying around.

Typically, her husband has had an air of daring while he attempts—at each important stage of the trek—to take everything in.

LAMB CHOPS, COD

She had stopped insisting that they have heart-to-heart conversations, but for stranded people, they had these nice moments together, and he had his professional enjoyment at the newspaper. He approved the issues there with a scientific mind and he made quite a contribution. He was a consultant in the field of efficiency.

She should have appreciated that, I guess. I don't know—she felt lonely.

After dinner, he would go into his room and sometimes read or do his engraving or follow up on his stamp collection or solve math problems from that year's baccalaureate examination. Once he told me that once a year he reread *Our Man in Havana*. It had something to do with Havana. You know—petty things—I guess my mother wanted full attention, not for him to have private time by himself. I don't know what my mother did when she was in her room. She was working. She was working a lot. She devoted herself to family matters, making trouble. But I am convinced that she did love him extremely and after he died she said that that was the fact.

Then they had golf together and they did trips. There was a French newspaper that would invite him to solve a technical problem. He was amazing that way.

They would playact around the occasion of having dinner. I'm not sure, but I'm afraid that they did it for every dinner. She would put on her best gown and wear the diamond ornament, which she felt free to pin anywhere on her garment if it was necessary for the brooch to cover up a soiled spot.

He wore black lacquer pumps, silk stockings that went up under the knees. His breeches were tied under the knees and he would have tails and white tie on. My mother would provide the basic meal—cod or lamb chops. He would provide—he loved to go to the store that was similar to Fortnum and Mason and buy smoked salmon, cheese, fruit in season, asparagus. They had cocktails at five o'clock. They would listen to the news and then they'd sit down to the table, light the candles. They would have their little feast together. Then after the meal, he'd sit down and do work in his room. His French was very good, so sometimes he translated manuals from French or the other way around. And before bedtime, they'd have a cup of tea together with a cookie.

He loved an existence of this kind and to eat food.

He died while he was still glossy and smooth at the dinner table between the fish with dill—a great favorite—outstanding with butter—and the boiled blue plum dumplings.

OF THE TRUE AND FINAL GOOD

The gimcracks were set out on a jutting surface and the woman listened to the indoor crowd that made the sound of a storm in a dry forest.

Upon entering the mansion—referred to as "the castle" by the locals at that time—she saw the carvings in wood and in stone—and among them a white wolf with an open mouth, made from white limestone.

There was a broad blown cry from the woman that expressed her satisfaction.

By contrast, a man and a boy found the air inside difficult to breathe and they did not view the staircase or the urns in the niches as among the finest in the world. Nor had they walked in there with the notion that *this will do*.

But other people arrived who could be benefited by

observing the luxury—so that the big place didn't rub them the wrong way.

The woman eyed swords and sabers hung on the wall, all exceptional. Next to these was an oil painting in a bulky frame featuring a copper pot and eucalyptus leaves.

The woman stayed briefly in a location close by it.

The true state of things inside of the painting was unclear. The painting needed cleaning. The woman could not sufficiently experience either the fragrance of the leaves or the copper pot's heavenly glow.

"Oh, sorry!" the man with his boy said to the woman.

Something had startled him also. He was a thin little man who held his face in his hands. "I don't like this place do you?" he said.

He didn't approach too closely. But the woman reached out and laid a hand on his arm and she gripped it.

Then both of her hands were pulling at his sleeve.

People who saw her putting a lot of effort into it wondered why.

She was carefully fashioned, vivid and polished, but should her desired result fail to be obtained—she'll fade.

GIRL WITH A PENCIL

The girl's predilection is to trace her hand with a pencil on a piece of paper.

The mother made a rule that her daughter was responsible for something. And what could that be?—to be sulky and disappointed?—to be heavy and club-like? To be backward?

When the child finished her early education, she drew a picture of her future that consisted of a pair of legs, column-shaped, and just above them, the hem of a skirt in bright orange. The legs were decorated—as if wrapped in wallpaper—in pastel blue with red posies and their green leaves. The shoes were clumpy, earthy.

But about the child's later life, how did she fare?

The child showed her picture to her mother.

"And where is her head?" her mother said. "I see legs!" she pointed. "Shoes."

It was just a few words, but more than the child needed to consider.

The child was handed more paper.

And so was invented a kind of brute—a brunette with longish hair, who must love her enemies—who acts responsibly.

PERFORM SMALL TASKS

"One second!" I said—for everything can go cold in a day or hot. For a man like me, there's an on-and-off bulb that does the deciding.

I had to find a red, little glowing button—that I was able to find—that was on a timer switch, to get more light on. The furniture—like worn-out stumps sticking up—had turned into shadows.

I could then see her better—the woman I had settled upon to have intermittent leisure with—Evangeline. How clean she was and how calm. I saw clearly the receptacle for logs by the fireplace filled with firewood that I knew to be far too fine for a fire.

It takes some ability to get close to the extraordinary in life, and I was at the peak of my ability back then.

Back then, Evangeline had informed me that her eldest son, having survived into adulthood, had returned to the States.

I heard the click upon his entry and saw the jump of the flat door.

The boy's girlish mother—who could look secretive with plans wherever you put her—withdrew and then she reappeared.

She glanced affectionately at the boy.

Why was I afraid? Earlier she had informed me he was one of the kindest and one of the most thoughtful boys in all the world.

She carried an appliance in from the kitchen that I did not recognize, and she put it on the credenza.

Such an omen. I have asked myself what darker purpose is being served when a magician pulls his rabbit out of the hat.

I felt a tap on my back, in the middle of my back, as I hurried away, past the woman and her son, with apologies.

I had the long, uneven road to drive.

Evangeline showed up in her sporty car, where I live, on the morning of the following day.

There was something wonderful in this—it's the whole point of the story.

And we had become good friends, occasionally, for normally about an hour and a half at a time.

She said, "I am not blaming you."

My father came down the stairs, my mother, too.

Evangeline was addressing me lovingly.

Mother said, "She was married to Jerry! She's talking nonsense."

Dad said, "I didn't think you wanted us to see her."

My kitchen, where I went off to, has an island range and the beauty of this island is difficult to convey, but pesty problems can seem irrelevant when I am in the vicinity of my Viking.

I was thinking Evangeline had had her say, that she could depart now with a light heart.

When I returned to the foyer, my father was holding the newel-post, my mother—in her short, striped robe with her bare legs—was going back up the stairs.

Evangeline—and I was very moved by this—was still waiting for me and I wondered if I would rise to my own occasion.

Then my mother shouted, "They're going to clean the air conditioners first!" The Best Air van had arrived.

Eventually, Evangeline gave up with some hostility and she drove herself home.

In the meantime, I got a few payments recorded, made out bank deposits, and checked cash accounts. I think I'll be an ideal ally for somebody someday. This belief is borne in magic.

Am I not like the vanishing bead? Presto!

Place me inside of any paper cup. In due course I am in my own pocket, when I cap—carry through, or when I conclude.

REMOVAL MEN

You have people nowadays—the men in general, who were helping the woman—and that which they should not disturb, she had put into a crate.

She put a yellow-flowered plant into the crate.

The men's names were embroidered on their shirt pockets, but truly, there was no need to address one or another of them. A question could just be asked of one—without use of a name.

The pockets of their garments were needleworks with thread in bright white. But for Marwood, somebody had devised an orange and mustard-yellow embroidery.

The woman was standing a step aside and didn't have much to contribute, but she looked at a man—at what he was making ready to take—and she held her hands with her palms turned away from her body with her fingers spread, as if she had dirtied herself.

At the curb, the woman's car was an Opel, and the hood was up, and the door to the car was out, and what was its color? It was a butterscotch and a man, up to his elbows, was under the hood. Now and again he'd go back into the car and try the starter engine. Ted—that was that one.

It could be lovely, the woman was thinking. It was already lonely and there were mountains and mosses and grasses and violent deaths nowadays, and injuries and punishments, and the woman finds the merest suggestion of cheerful companionship and carousal—a bit too dramatic.

A MERE FLASK POURED OUT

———

The heavily colored area—it became a shade dingier—after I knocked over her decanter and there was the sourish smell of the wine.

I saw Mother reaching toward the spill, but the time that was left to her was so scant as to be immaterial.

The little incident of the accidental spill had the fast pace of a race, hitherto neglected or unknown.

"Go home!" Mother said. And I didn't look so good to her she said. "How dare you tell me what to do—when you threw me away! You threw your brother away, too!"

Within a month, Mother was dead.

I inherited her glass carafe with its hand-cut, diamond-and-fan design, which we now use on special occasions.

We do well and we've accomplished many excellent things.

"Don't do it that way!" I had cried. My daughter had tried to uncork a bottle of wine, but since I thought it was my turn, I took it from her.

Here are other methods I use to apply heavy pressure: I ask her where she is going, what does she want, how does she know and why. She should increase her affectionate nature, be successful and happy. Mentally, she must show me she has that certain ability to try.

BANG BANG ON THE STAIR

I said, "Would you like a rope? You know that haul you have is not secured properly."

"No," he said, "but I see you have string!"

"If this comes into motion—" I said, "you should use a rope."

"Any poison ivy on that?" he asked me, and I told him my rope had been in the barn peacefully for years.

He took a length of it to the bedside table. He had no concept for what wood could endure.

"Table must have broken when I lashed it onto the truck," he said.

And, when he was moving the sewing machine, he let the cast iron wheels—bang, bang on the stair.

I had settled down to pack up the flamingo cookie jar, the

cutlery, and the cookware, but stopped briefly, for how many times do you catch sudden sight of something heartfelt?

I saw our milk cows in their slow parade in the pasture and then the calf broke through with a leap from behind—its head was up, its forelegs spread.

"Don't leave!" Mother screamed at me, and she had not arrived to help me.

She tripped and fell over a floor lamp's coiled electrical cord.

There's just a basic rule of conduct that applies here—also known as a maxim—so I held out my hand.

She gripped and re-gripped my palm hard and all of my fingers before hoisting herself by pulling on me.

She kept tugging on my hand on her deathbed also for a long stretch, until she died. For don't little strokes fell great oaks?

A girl from the neighborhood rang the bell today to ask if I had a balloon. I didn't have any and I hadn't seen one in years.

"That's all you need?" I asked her. "How about some string?"

I noticed that the girl's eyes were bright and intelligent and that she was delighted, possibly with me.

I went to search where I keep a liquid-glue pen, specialty tape, and twine. I kept on talking while I pawed around for some reason in the drawer.

A LITTLE BOTTLE OF TEARS

It should have been nicer—our friendships, our travel, our romances secretly lived—if we weren't so old. But still it was an interesting situation to be in.

We all but ignored the wife's tears—which could have filled a small bottle.

And the wife was petite and well groomed and I knew why she was crying. She thought her trials were all about adultery at that time.

As the evening proceeded, the wife cheered up for some of it and her conversation was drawing us in with topics she knew we would feel comfortable talking about, because potentially our relationship could be adversarial and her husband was tending to pontificate, showing off his legal wings with paragraphs upon paragraphs.

You find yourself in a situation where you have agreed, agreed, agreed, agreed and you realize this is not such a good agreement.

How did all this end? Oh, fine, fine, fine, fine, fine—although our process of digestion—they'd served us *kartoffelpuffer* and *sauerbraten*—was not yet complete—when the husband said finally about his wife, "Bettie's tired."

To my mind—she's hysterical, sincere, easily distracted, and not adaptable. I remember when I wanted to know even more about her.

They lived only on the ground floor—the rest was rented out. A trestle table, where you could put your gloves, stood in the long hall that had stone floor tiles set on the diagonal.

Bettie's thumbs were as I remembered—heavy and clubbed—and she wore the eye-catching turquoise ring, circa 1890, with three pearls, that I knew she was proud of because I had given it to her.

"Bettie's tired," the husband repeated.

"I am tired," Bettie said.

And there was no polite way for him to tell us, "Fuck off now."

There'd be no more condescending talk, no fresh subjects, never likely an opportunity to privately reminisce with Bettie about the times when we were side by side, experiencing that alternating rhythm forward and back.

"Can we give you a lift home?"

"No, that's not necessary, we drove," we said.

I went into their bathroom to urinate before we left. I am a man, if that wasn't clear before this, and not a drunken one, not cruel—and I was holding myself then, gently—somewhat lovingly, to relieve myself.

I washed my hands and face and looked into the mirror. My face has changed so much recently. The lines of age were drawn everywhere like the marks made by a claw, and they looked to me freshly made. Then there are those growing fleshy abutments around my jaw and under my chin.

It was rainy outside and we were significantly dampened by the time we reached our car. And, in addition, a smelly ailanthus tree tossed a pitcherful of storm water—as if from a sacred fount—all over my head. There were continuing showers—it was dripping, gushy.

Still it was all so charming and heartening—that is—the summer storm, and the trees and our sky, alongside those several memories of Bettie and me.

My wife said to me en route, "Well, I suppose I'm on the wrong track, too."

Of course, it took a long time for her to go downhill, all the way down it.

Meanwhile, we became very friendly with the DePauls—Clifford and Daisy.

They lived in an apartment crammed with blue-and-white china, for one thing. I thought Daisy usually looked pensive and sad and my wife thought that her scowl meant that she detested us.

A large oil painting of a female nude—hands together as if prayerful—had been suspended over their mantel. Their apartment was in disarray.

But, there's always a moment before it all becomes okay.

WHEN I WAS OLD AND UGLY

The creature had come absurdly close to our window. It had lifted its chin—face—specifically toward mine while we were at breakfast in the country.

I'd say the animal looked and looked at me and looked, ardently.

I was reminded how to fall in love by meeting its eyes and by how long the rendezvous lasted—until doomsday, say.

I am unhappily married. Today I was dressed up in red-fox orange—orangutan orange—apricot orange, candlelight orange. I had on a wool plaid coat and had been racketing around my city precinct doing errands.

Returning home, while in the elevator of our building, facing the closed door, I combed nearly every hair—all that thinning hair along the sides of my skull.

That massive man that I didn't know at all, who had a stiffness of manner at the back of the elevator, he acknowledged me. And the doorman Bill had not averted his eyes.

No, not the sort of thing that I usually report. No, that I had withdrawn the tortoiseshell comb from my purse to do the smoothing with and then re-stowed it on the way to 3A, our apartment.

The comb I keep in the quilted sack, where I also conceal a tiny toothpaste, the easy-to-carry traveler's toothbrush, and my eyeglass-lens polishing cloth.

The carpet was unmarked by dirt, but one important thing in our foyer was missing—the color with the green leaves in a vase. The old floor gets better with age, but boy it needed to be cleaned up—then it will shine.

I also have affectionate and friendly wishes for the brass, crystal, silver dishes, vases and pitchers.

My conversation with my husband was as follows: "Are you all right? What do you want? You're looking at me."

In the park I had wanted to talk today to a bird who wasn't interested in talking to me.

Lust and temptation are sometimes personified. I heard the bird cry—*Chew! Chew!* I took pains to say *Chew! Chew!*—loudly, too.

PALM AGAINST PALM

It is a pity there is also the nature of the surface of the skin—combined with the error of her eyes and the divots at the centers of her breasts.

Her tiny skirt is much like a figure skater's skirt that may—as she lets her legs fling forward to walk—flap.

Clap. Clap.

The girl—to get here—goes in the direction of the vanishing point, on up the steep grade.

These living quarters with the man, that she has entered, are bordered in the front by bluet and merrybells and by the myrtle and foam flowers at the back.

Her exit requires her to go through a door that shuts, ta-ta!—with those two little beats of sound.

Come along!—for wonderful it may seem that those hills

are presenting themselves not just as technical details or as small regions near the tollway.

Did she see those birds that were falling like leaves?—the leaves that were flying like birds?

The girl will extend herself to travel and to sway beyond the sweepgate into somebody else's household and she will hurry to meet up with somebody.

So when she arrives at the northern suburb, she finds a high house with a heavy gate. There is a seat near the door.

Whose house is this?

There is a tent bed, a hearth, and a sectional bookcase.

"At least I don't keep people waiting. Am I doing everything?" the girl asks.

"Hey!"

"Now look at you."

Then she was pulling her blouse together and she went to get a glass of water, a pot of coffee.

The brightly scaled moon was rising, but this girl never became a well-liked businesswoman with a growing family in the community.

Neither is she endowed with any remarkable qualities. We never spoke of her specialized skills or of her inclination to be otherwise. My fault. Go fuck herself.

Apology accepted.

NEW STORIES

THE BEAUTY AND THE BAT

"Please don't say that about me, Diane," Rae said.

"Well then," I said, "you have always worked like a dog."

"Babka," said a lady who joined us. We were at Rae's.

And the lady had a piece of cake on a plate and she sat down behind a slant-top desk that appeared to cut off her head at the neck.

But her face was a vivid face I would have been proud of, had it belonged to me, and it was fully in sight until she ducked down to fork up the cake.

Who was she? Should I have known?

As I mulled this, Rae's daughter—came in to ask—"How do you murder (she meant, how do you *pound thin*) chicken breasts?"

The lady chased her back out—as the pricking of my wig clips against my scalp grew worse.

So, then I was left alone and irritable with Rae, who was saying, "A rolling pin."

And who is *Rae*?

She is my cousin who lives with her paradisiac vistas of Central Park, delphinium with peonies in a vase, and there's the herringbone floor.

In her kitchen, I saw the pink lobes of the chicken breasts beneath plastic wrap.

"Did you wash it first?"—the lady, who was waving a heavy discolored utensil—was asking Maud—that is, Rae's daughter.

And then the lady turned to ask me, *"What are you doing here?"*

"Tea would be nice," I said.

I saw nearly an entire babka tucked beneath a glass dome.

"And, may I have some cake, please?"

Maud had left the room and the lady did not turn back to answer me and with her tool she began again slapping at the meat.

Then the door opened and a young man—my son—stood there who was not invited in.

"What are *you* doing here?" the lady asked.

"Be nice to me!" he said.

"Close the door! Go away!"

With both her arms briefly stretched above her head, she looked like a woman whose identity I knew I should have known.

Surrounding her, on the surfaces, were peas in their pods in a vine leaf, green bowl and some drops of blood.

I stepped farther forward over the checkered black and white linoleum to where there is a charming view of a sphered copper church roof that draws to a point, with a golden cross atop it.

A pair of pigeons were busy mating on a parapet and this looked so hazardous. I could feel talons—Do pigeons even have them?—digging painfully into my back. And then I was distracted by a large, proud aqua mix-master.

Not immediately, but I turned just in time to see the beauty put down her bat.

Speaking of beauty, she was standing in the awful fluorescent light—her heaving and her lifting well over by then.

Would now be the time to take the cake?—I thought.

I admired the color of her shoes, how her hair was coiled and braided. I knew who she was well enough, by then—a competent woman in earnest who didn't like me.

So, she did get excited when I just shoved the bowl of peas aside to make more room for the cake's cover.

While I ate my first mouthful, I saw her mouth open and close as I opened and closed mine.

What she did do—she posed quietly.

All that she said was, "You are Diane Williams? Do you even know what most of your friends say about you?"

WITCHCRAFT TODAY

ther cars with their slit eyes were coming toward us and passing us, as my sister discussed with me her experiments that can save the world.

We were aiming for Vladmir's Vacuum Cleaner Service and Repair, so I drove us down the hill to where a dog was leashed to a parking meter—barking out constructively, his words to the wise.

I put on the brakes in front of Vladmir's for my sister and for her broken down machine. So then, I was feeling tired to death and I cupped my hands and blew into them.

Two women appeared embracing two of a kind—that is each woman held onto a globular lamp base that had luster.

Fused with their lamps—this matching set—the pair went

northward alongside New and Used Firearms, and Massage by Jan and then they reversed their direction and came back at us.

Of course, nobody was there to greet me when I reentered my house.

The exterior of the house is deep bloodred and usually I am alone in it. The day's mail was in the mailbox and a letter had arrived from my son, posted from a distant land. Here in darkish-blue ink was my reminder.

I closed my eyes in order to come round to, to pick up on, to further nose out something like Fresh Flowers For All Occasions—nothing gamey, raw, but true—rather this is a doctrine geared to help me to sleep or to drive, or to again park my car.

THE FORGOTTEN STORY

Please let me speak—I used to want to, but I was still unready at the banquet to air my views, nor was I going to provide any explanation in an area of significance.

Although, I told myself that I would, and then I scheduled something else. I ate the food—pulpous and semisolid and I still have some level of pride. I was wearing my new Swiss vintage wristwatch with its good sword hands.

Now more than ever—I got not much further than at the point of arrival, when I said, "Where is the restroom? Is elevator service available?" and "Could I use the bathroom now?"

I had taken the tiny single-serve butter packs that were provided and the tiny half-and-half tubs and made of them a colonnade that then tipped and leaned itself intact against my water goblet.

One should be able, in conversation to recall, just so, an attitude or an impressive deed in one's life, slot it in, watch it climb.

"Do you know this lady?"—a woman I didn't know pointed at me.

"Yes, ma'am. She's my wife," the man across from me said.

"Why aren't we listening to this nice woman?" the interlocutor continued. "For instance, what does she think about Trey Gowdy?"

My little tower fell down. There was laughter and then a shadow the size and shape of an unclad foot, whose toes were wagging, showed up behind the head of the man, so that I was not left with a positive feeling.

I looked at my empty restaurant plate. It had a green-stripe around its border and a logo with an eagle and the date nearby it.

Oh, listen, I didn't say a word. A waiter brought bread that I took between my hands, broke into bits, and scattered about on the plate. I regained my senses and made a small province with the crumbs, or country.

DON'T TALK TO HIM
FOR SUCH A LONG TIME

In due course, Arthur Churl took some of my ideas, but he had his own angle—he was effecting a sort of spiritual awakening. He had produced an outdoor living room—lounge chairs, a dining set, an umbrella.

He said, "Sure you don't want that yellow bush?" It was a peculiar bush with yellow leaves—not as if the leaves were wilting.

"Do we want a yellow bush?" I asked my wife who was waiting for me in the car. "It's a light yellow color—"

"I don't like those kinds of bushes," she said. "And, don't talk to him for such a long time. We have other things to do today."

I found Churl looking hopeful. He had that row of—not a row, a couple of bushes with yellow leaves.

He raised his arms upward into a V position—while I took some pleasure in the wider view from the inviting grass path of his garden.

As for my wife—no fatal clash with her or disgrace yet and we did continue on to make our stops on schedule, including the one at the picnic grove where I thought that the light of day might send out its messenger with guidance for us.

At the top of a hackberry, I saw a bird that then pounced, landing near our chips with his big mouth open, only sitting and then rising—no beating of his wings. It arose, cheeping something I'd heard many times before, the barest basics, *bare basics.*

OH, DARLING I'M IN THE GARDEN

———◆———

"Tell them all to leave. I won't look!" her husband had said.

He'd just returned from a visit to town when he said, "Tell your boyfriends to leave!"

"Oh, darling," his wife said, "I'm in the garden," and she went back outside to stand a moment near the flowering vine—the trained pillar form by the doorway.

Not today—none of the boyfriends were with her today and she felt poorly on account of it.

Nonetheless, in the salad garden, she could contemplate the bib and oak leaf and the Tom Thumb and she watered a potted plant. Then she knelt to snap off its finished blossoms and she littered the lawn with them.

On the sidewalk opposite, she saw her neighbor Mr. Timmings embracing his Affenpinscher. She left her yard, well-prepared to charm either one of them.

Inside of the Timmings abode, the two forgot about the dog and worked hard to put a positive emphasis on one another. Within minutes—she found herself in the correct position, as if for sleeping—making the minor adjustments of her arms and legs as necessary.

This posture has been her salvation—and Mr. Timmings, on his knees, conjoined soon with her overhead.

Mercifully, she is free of any diseases—is intelligent, outgoing, confident—and also she tolerates hot weather reasonably well.

People who live with her admire her sympathetic nature. Although, she is not recommended for households with toddlers or small children and once she's alert, it takes her a while to settle down.

HAPPY PRESENCE,
TIMELESS INSPIRATION

Perhaps the wife is well enough acquainted with her husband's finer qualities and with his practical knowledge, his contributions to their welfare. Now, if only she would ever smile at him.

Yet, anybody watching guests entering into their home could see that the husband bows slightly. He is courtly and he is constantly like this.

In the aftermath, he remembers the compliment—or was it an insult that he received?—"Oh, how you look like who you are!"

And, while his wife sleeps, he leaves the bed to go to a sofa he likes that is covered in old shawls—first putting on his thick robe. Just a few steps bring him closer to the cushions and to some clutter on a sideboard, including dahlias in a mug.

Surely there is something good enough here, or possibly classic.

The telephone rings. It is too late for a call. He doesn't answer it.

"Who was it?" His wife appears.

"I don't know."

"You don't know?"

"I didn't answer it."

"You didn't answer it?"

He places his hands together—not entirely, only the fingertips, pulls them back apart.

"Why are you smiling?" his wife says.

"It's a sneer."

THE SURE CURE

I did brace her with one hand, but my daughter is remarkably agile and well-balanced.

What I had done in the first place, in the park, was to pull down her trousers and put her up there on the low wire fence post. Anyone—and there were many on the pathway—could pay her mind while she obediently squatted to urinate.

In future, this cynosure will stand her in good stead. In the present, she hardly needs my help.

THE PERVERTED MESSAGE

The sky was roseate at the end of the day, in the east rather than in the west—all wrong—when I encountered a mother and her small child who behaved as if they believed in each other.

The mother had irregular features and a rough complexion. The girl wore a pretty cap—blueberry blue—and they both had consumed only a few bites of their food.

They tapped instead at an activity book page. "The clock doesn't have a face!" the mother said. "Stay with Bunny, while Mommy pays."

I'm afraid the child's toy rabbit had once been fat or puffed up and now it was just skin and bone and unsmiling.

Except that this was such a tender spectacle—perhaps because I am in love these days and, I have recently gotten a better hold of Mr. Rottblatt, and he me—elderly though we may be.

A café employee was sweeping near the girl who had dropped her toy. He lifted up her pal by its arm and he laughed. The child bawled.

We heard a blusterous reprimand from across the room and the mother rushed back to pry the toy's arm loose from the man.

The rabbit was coarsened through use, thoroughly soiled, although evidently suitable to carry around and to really chew on.

I slept well that night. The sky was white when we awoke and showed no significant departure in color from the norm.

It was a Spot the Difference puzzle that the mother and the daughter had been fixed upon, displaying two pictures that at first glance appeared to be the same.

Alas, there was no end to the girl's obtuseness. She was unamazed by the missing pot of geraniums, by merely one button, only one eyeball, and no ice cream.

But how faithfully the mother urged her lamb to see.

GRACE GOD

Scraps of foliage that smelt of urine or of some animal and soil blew into the foyer through the open door as she went out quickly and she didn't close the door. The rain came through it, too. My wife Grace carried no suitcase—because this was just her preliminary, showy act of leaving, which left its trail.

Everything in the world I still owe to Grace. I owe her something, perhaps—oh, god. But what do I owe Grace, God?

Grace came back to me once after she'd left for good. And, in the little room that overlooks the orchard we ate a meal. It was simple. It was nothing.

She was dressed up in all of her fallas and sitting right here unamused, as if there was nothing that had ever happened to her that had been laughable.

But she was so much like an independent woman at that time because she busily, as far as I knew, pursued her philosophy of life.

And didn't she often imply that she knew valuable things about pleasure and about money that might interest me?—with hints such as this: *If reason is the source of desire, then it can do no harm.*

"And aren't you proud of yourself?" she said.

How true. I had formed the Alfalfa Process Company and built the U-shaped house, with its tower that is hidden from the street by many trees.

"I do have a lot of money," I said. "I can certainly give you more."

She drove away happily that day, down the drive, once again, past the pink cherry toward the bottom of the garden.

And Grace did return one more time. Why?

Well, it pains me to make it clear that I asked her to.

"For nearly everything that was faulty between us," she said, "I don't mind if I take the blame."

That day in the garden I held on to her shoulder and kissed her hand, which she kept fisted.

There was a pretty perfume in the air because I'd stocked the rose beds with First Love and Summer Song. All heavy feeders.

"You're too close," Grace told a wren. "Do you remember?" she asked me, "—those birds at The Eldorado. I don't want him to hop up near the food."

An inchworm inched along the table's glass surface. Squirrels made their chuckling noises.

What should I have done next?

"I have everything I ever wanted," Grace said. "I could have
you, too, again—but I don't want that."

I coaxed the inchworm up onto the point of a paper napkin
and offered it to a fern. The insect situated itself on the leaf's
underside—passively and I suspect angrily. I took it personally.

THE FUCKING LAKE

S he was reclining on the shore of the lake when I made my own appearance naked—and I get sentimental remembering my young manhood and the young woman who became my wife.

And as I remember, she did nothing to stop me—no *stop!*— *stop!*

A story is told about this very same lake—something about a man who was swimming in it and displeasing the gods and they did everything to stop him.

But when I swam across it, I had the sensation that I would never get tired.

And that day of the swim I picked up a stone that is likely an ancient whetstone or chisel—and I can summon up a dour primitive person making good use of it.

Somebody lost his whetstone or died beside his whetstone. He was slain! Or in a rage, he lobbed the thing away.

Or let's just say he is modern and he doesn't need it.

At present, I am an old man—guessing that the major events of my life are done with, except, of course, for my final downfall.

I heard shouting and a loud *a-hah!—a-heh!—a-hah—a-heh-heh!* in the street, and Yvette is still here with me and she moved with short, jerky movements toward the sofa to lie down and she's not one to be laughing with me, but she still loves conversation, parties and good food. And, the lake—rather—*the lack* of affection that she now has for me is something for which no person can be blamed.

For are we not surrounded by objects we defer to—for only a certain stretch of our choosing? And, isn't there an august mountain visible from my balcony that I have no need to look at anymore?

Well, the front door lock clacked and opened, and our son Ben came in and he's nearly elderly himself.

Yvette said, "You need to be here some of the time."

Ben wore a T-shirt that had these words all over it—ROCKS THAT LOOK LIKE TREES. His face was flaccid. The street sounds had ceased.

He bent over his mother, his hands on her hands and although she's old, she's beautiful and she was so very docile.

She reminds me of a Greek relic I once saw inside of a

glass case that I have never forgotten—a terracotta siren with a dove's body and a most affable female face.

Yvette said, "Play the piano, Ben!"

And then there was that demoralizing outgush—the piano is so responsive—smiling, crying, just trying for now.

A POT OVER A VERY LOW HEAT

"I am not a bad person, I promise you," the husband said. "But what would *you* do if you were me?"

"If I were you?" the wife answered—"I'd *never* have had such a good time with Della Lou."

Regardless, by that time, the wife had been perpetually thinking about Della Lou.

These days, more typically, her mind is elsewhere paying homage to her seasoned husband or to their loot—to the silver vessels, the Meissen—the prized pair of porcelain magpies, with tongues out, who turn on their perches.

Her rare brass table clock is currently in somebody else's private collection and now the husband is too. He is living with

Della Lou because he could not stop the story of his life from flopping around or from twisting, for which one of us can? Exactly.

Guests come through the wife's home, not always respectful of her habit of orderliness, and they often opine—*You've got quite another country here!*—while she is liable to be emptying a bowl into a pot over a very low heat.

And left to her own devices, she does host creditable house parties and there's her new wall–to-wall French gray wool carpeting covering many of the floors, and on her face, a growing display of maculation. These are the free-form brown marks that attest to her long service.

She often conjures her husband who is stiff looking— backlit by her mind's proprietary light—not aged and dedicated to her.

"You'll be staying," the woman tells her guest, who is giddy when the doorbell rings, and the telephone, and a buzzer for a timer—all in synchrony.

Some of us are subtly drawn out by these elementary wake-up calls that clang.

Some of us have proper brisk responses.

What has been solicited, in this particular case, are the grinning faces of a set of formally attired antique women with crimson traces on their lips, pinked fingertips. They are quite perfect with deeper color in the folds of their clothing.

THE HOURS OF COINCIDENCE

I got help hoisting my saddlebag's cross strap over my head and some cooperation so I could get out of my heavy pelerine and then up onto their sofa with my thoughts for achieving a purpose.

"Please, if you don't mind," Earlene said. "I need to talk to you!" She had crossed the room to ask me questions that I knew all the answers to, but somebody sighing, who also listened to me, begged to differ.

And they had put the food out, so I got up to follow Sol, who was carrying his shot glass, and we passed a mahogany stand with cloth-covered books on it. I picked up *Florence Nightingale.*

"The buffet!"—Sol called to me—for I hadn't moved ahead with him and had lingered alongside the long mirrors—or those are the windows through which you can see the world or honeysuckles or whatever it is that they call it.

An edge of the carpet may have been bent up which was why my Sol fell. Of a sudden, his head was down, face first—way over there at the corner of the floor.

He was breathing, but nothing else.

"Talk to me!" the old lady at the hospital said to him. I was the old lady.

I didn't want to spoil anything, so I gave him no assistance with the questions—with what was his name, our address or, with "Where are you now?"

He said, "Who are you?" and "What?"—inquiries that I answered. But a nurse named Cliantha kindly corrected me because I was supposed to make my replies much more interesting.

I had never realized that before.

THE STANDARD

They looked to me worthy enough or at least quite standard—Mrs. Ryan and her lathy twin, adult daughters—who asked if they could join me.

The threesome is frequently at The Sweetgrass when I am.

I don't know them—but I was, in fact, sitting solo at a table for four.

And it was an eye-catching article near Mrs. Ryan's neck that exerted its charm at first—an impressive brass brooch—floral—whose tendrils curled at the tips.

A daughter held her mother's hand and tapped at her mother's big glassy ring. Then the mother took the end of her daughter's nose between her fingers and lightly pinched it.

"Iris, please!" she asked that daughter, "do me a favor."

And my name is also Iris. *No, really.*

I thought for a moment that I should rise too, while the daughter did as she was bidden, and then she dropped it on the table—the full goblet of water her mother had asked for— and she made a spill that wetted several of us when the goblet bucked and rolled.

"I do not understand!" her mother said, and to the other daughter, she said, *"Please!"*

"She's very cranky," the daughters told me.

The girl called Iris went after her—because her mother was leaving, using a walker that caused the early stage of her departure to be wobbly.

"Don't touch me!" the mother screamed. *"Don't ever speak to me!"*

As her daughters left the premises, the old lady was unbudgeable in that cradle—her walker that braced her for a minute more.

Then she drooped and her collapse looked effortless, but she wasn't dead and I didn't stay to wait for any crew who must have taken her away.

I had a good talk recently with *my own daughter,* who is still very daughterlike, it's true. Although, she's aged now and cine-real.

She has been undergoing her life—and it's not gone too badly—blow by blow.

I climbed the front steps to my town house by pulling myself up them, by the wrought iron railing.

My daughter was there and she waved to me and she had about her an uncharacteristic—unofficial-sort-of-person aspect.

So then I wasn't immediately cast down, by what I most prefer her to be—and that's my lamblike lady's maid.

THE IMPORTANT TRANSPORT

Otto told me that our opportunity had been squandered and that I should have felt compelled to contribute something. He said, "It is too bad you don't understand what is happening here."

And, I saw that it was true—that I had failed to do my best.

This was to be our short interregnum. How to proceed next?

That morning the wake-up radio music alarm had been set, but the volume knob had been wrenched *by somebody*, counterclockwise, full-on. My first thought was that the window must be open and that the wind had caught at the blinds and that it was blowing across the fins—the slats, rather—and that they were vibrating and causing this tremendous sound before it dawned on me that *this* blast was something other and it made me afraid.

And, where did Otto go? He was missing and the window was indeed open and a small breeze lightly batted the venetian blind's liftcord tassel against the wall.

In an hour he was back again and the look on his face was one of gratitude, and to add to this comforting effect, he smiled.

"Where did you go?" I asked.

"Kay," he said. That's my name.

"You're all I have. Where did you go?"

"Do you like it here?" he said.

"No, I don't like it here. Why should I?"

"I know. I know," he said. "Some water?" He had to walk and to walk, to go such a short way, it seemed, to get that for me.

We had another such dialogue the next day.

"Do I have to say?" he said.

"Yes."

"Suzette."

"Oh, Suzette," I said.

Later on he married the young girl.

I have had to wait for my own happiness. I married Eric Throssel, who is a good companion—and I thought I was very happy when we had finished supper one night. But the more important transport occurred en route to Long Grove while I was driving.

Eric spoke, and his words I don't remember them, but thank God they served to release the cramping in my neck, and in my shoulders and my back and they provided for an unexpected increased intake of oxygen and can we leave it at that?

DAY OF AWE

I gave the beggar a dollar for his sorrows and my friend and neighbor David Yip gave him all the cash that he had.

And David said, "*Look! I think the sky is lower!* Well, look at it!"

And yes, a pretty mist, much like confetti descended, so that the day felt so friendly, even profitable. Although my gloves had become shabbier from icy water and dirt because I'd dropped them.

They were solidly on my hands when I found the Campho-Phenique that I needed at the Drug Loft.

The gloves are peach leather—quilted, with fur cuffs—and they have a lining that can become rather too effective.

The cashier was blushing or was that a saintly radiance?

I fear I lack deep feelings, have flighty ideas, and am often irritable over trifles.

The beggar was still there when my neighbor and I exited the shop and he said, again, *"Change today, Miss?"*

He was an ornate figure in a knitted cap—fastened by a long, wrinkly ribbon under his chin and I thought, No, no more. *How much mercy is necessary?*

And then my gloves unaccountably tumbled again.

The beggar returned one of them and my pal Dave knelt to retrieve the other.

At home, I stowed these along with my coat and then I went crazy in the hall mirror, as I sometimes do, over the glow from the heirloom I wear around my neck.

This rope of freshwater pearls was a gift from my husband when our son—now he is a man—was born.

Of course, I had dominion over our baby and I recently tended to my son's new son, my infant grandchild, and was maintaining my grasp of him, and then I tripped, and there might have been an extreme penalty to pay for this.

But the baby made it through the crash well, has satin-slick legs for me to clutch at, and chubby arms that I can fit into my nice vise-grip.

This is an apt outcome for the story of the blest woman and the mendicant—yes, an apt outcome for the story about a woman better known as "Pearlneck."

THE WILDER PEOPLE
HAVE WILDER GODS

I *would like to see you soon in case you have the freedom* was the note I sent to him while in an altered state. No reply came.

Mind you, I had not spoken to him for the last thirty years. But then on the first Sunday of this November—it was at Hart House, no!—it was at The Publick House where I saw the two of them sitting at a free-standing table near the open hearth.

The woman shouted out loudly (that's why I looked over), "Listen, Bob! They jump nine feet into the air!—as high as our ceiling—"

Bob wore a bib—as did she. And, mind you, he is a noteworthy character.

I was on the point of asking Dorothy the server why they had bibs on, but Dorothy was nearly always bent over her heavy tray, and it would have been very unkind to distract Dorothy unnecessarily.

Their plates were not in view and I had bored through the menu, with no luck, looking for lobster.

This synchronicity—the two of them turning up at the historic roadhouse at the same time we did—was surely meant to be—for Ike and I had nearly missed ever finding the inn. We had roamed well past the playing field—well past the little traffic island several times and had signaled to a fellow on foot at the side of the road, who was eating an apple, who agreed to ride along as our guide.

Ike knew nothing about the note I had sent to Bob and less about my state of longing for the "Show time!" Bob had liked to promise us.

I went right up to them—saw no plates of food—and when I touched the woman's ready shoulder, her mouth opened.

"You drunk?" Bob said to me, and the pair surely took in the full panorama of my chagrin as I turned and walked away. Thankfully they could not also see my headache, indigestion or nerve tensions.

And I missed out on ever setting eyes on *them* in toto, because when they left the inn, I'd been disturbed by the outcries of a tiny, timeworn woman whose chin was level with her table's top. She extolled lengthily a man she called Masserman, but said it was a nuisance to have to keep going to him.

Eventually a reply from Bob arrived in the form of a letter. "From Bob," was all there was to it.

I daily wear the bangle—a gift he gave me years ago that bears a finely etched design—berries plus their stems?—balloons attached to their strings?—spermatozoa?

I try to go back in time. Please don't go back in time!

Try to go forward.

How to develop a yen for the future?—not just a yen—find a hankering—or even a stomach for from here on in.